Advance Praise for *North Bay Road*

"In my one hundred years, I've read my fair share of books and I can tell you Richard Kirshenbaum's *North Bay Road* was among the most enjoyable of reads."

—Norman Lear

"If you loved *The White Lotus* you are sure to love *North Bay Road*. Once you start you won't be able to put it down. Did anyone say TV series?"

—Bill Gerber,
Academy Award-nominated Producer, *A Star Is Born*

"*North Bay Road* is not only the ultimate beach read, but the ultimate Miami Beach Read."

—Ernest Lupinacci,
Co-Producer, *The Offer* and Author of *The Godfather Gang*

"A lush, descriptive, evocative look at inheritances of all kinds, even the most unexpected, with Richard Kirshenbaum's keen insider eye at work yet again. An immersive triumph!"

—Zibby Owens,
Author of *Bookends: A Memoir of Love, Loss, and Literature*, Host of
Moms Don't Have Time to Read Books

"Richard Kirshenbaum is a magnificent storyteller. Liz Galin's life is not turning out as she had hoped. When she is bequeathed a palazzo in Miami in need of repair, she sets out to fix her own life as she solves the mystery of her inheritance. *North Bay Road* will find its way on to every beach chair in America and will have readers turning pages long after the sun has gone down. Houses hold secrets, but in Richard Kirshenbaum's hands, not for long."

—Adriana Trigiani,
Author of *The Good Left Undone*

North Bay Road

A Novel

Richard Kirshenbaum

POST Hill
PRESS

A POST HILL PRESS BOOK
ISBN: 978-1-63758-862-8
ISBN (eBook): 978-1-63758-863-5

North Bay Road
© 2023 by Richard Kirshenbaum
All Rights Reserved

Cover design by Tiffani Shea

Post Hill Press
New York • Nashville
posthillpress.com

Published in the United States of America
1 2 3 4 5 6 7 8 9 10

To my muse Dana,

I always love you…just a little bit more!

XO Richard

"Amantes, ut apes vita (m) melitta (m) exigent. Velle"
"Lovers like bees pass a sweet life like honey. I wish it were so"
Latin inscription, behind entrance
House of Lovers, Pompeii

Prologue

Miami, 2020

The vast estate seemed invisible, despite its grandeur, due to the overgrowth of dark jade palms, gnarled bougainvillea, and centenarian crape myrtle. The growth was so dense that despite the Miami sun, the villa lay in cool repose, immune to the resting, prickly heat. The overgrown confederate jasmine seemed to overwhelm the villa in its tense grip; the edifice succumbed as the vines wrestled the chipping stucco to the ground. Unlike its newer, shiny, celebrity neighbors, the villa's imposing gates were swirled and rusted. The ornate ironwork lent an air of bygone glory and obscurity, as did the few disintegrating slabs of pink-tinged coral stone on the exterior columns. If one took the time to stop and notice, the villa could have been taken for a faded, regal estate in Capri on the Via Tragara or in the *colini Fiorentini*, the hills of Florence. The vast estate was a symbol of another era entirely with its formal sentry gate, the center fountain that had long stopped bubbling, and the circular rotunda pitched against the aquamarine skyline, which seemed impervious to the stray overhead planes ferrying vacationers to the southern tip. Occasionally, Argentine black and white tegus roamed the shoreline, oblivious to any other unlikely tenants.

Built in 1927 in the Mediterranean revival style, the estate had wowed its neighbors and was the envy of its lesser rivals, boasting a large folly, a greenhouse, a bayside pool, and an enclosed tennis pavilion. Even neighbor Carl Fisher, the acknowledged founder, and unofficial king, of Miami Beach who had built his palace at 5020 North Bay, had been suitably impressed. Eighteenth-century Neapolitan tiles and lusty veined marble statutes had been stripped from impoverished estates in Amalfi and Tuscany and hastily installed in the new world's Riviera. During one particularly frothy day in the heady '20s market, the owner had approved an ancient mosaic floor to be ripped from a villa unearthed in Pompeii and reassembled in the entry gallery. The arrival of the famous black market mosaic caused havoc in Port Miami; there was even a small mention in *The Herald*, which officially dubbed the new mansion "Villa Pompeii." The name stuck, and the architect eventually implanted a discreet, ceramic tile in the pink, columned archway he had commissioned in Vietri. No one had even considered that christening the villa with such an ominous name might portend impending disaster. When one stepped into the foyer, the ancient, black-and-white mosaic floor, which featured an octopus engulfing and defeating a spiny lobster, added an eerie feel to the great house.

Throughout the decades, the grand mansion had not only seen the booms and busts of the Florida peninsula, but also the waves of differing nationals all adjusting and peeling under the ribald sun. It had also been exposed to larger themes; love and loss, obsession, and, despite the sunshine, dark passion.

It was said that a hint of a woman occasionally appeared on the dock in silk scarves and dark glasses facing a balustrade, leaning on a cane, or sitting in a wicker wheelchair. She was known to take in Biscayne Bay at dusk, the shimmering diamonds of downtown Miami flickered to life as the orange globe bowed to the new skyline. Perhaps the distant, gleaming sprawl unsettled her, *if* she was actually there. Few people entered and exited the property. Real estate brokers could never find a way to contact the owner and eventually gave up trying despite the heat of the market.

"Madame is not at home or is indisposed," was all the remaining leery staff were able to utter. In her later years, her nurse and housekeeper didn't even speak English, only Polish. Shrouded in secrecy, Villa Pompeii eventually became an oversight. The parties, tennis lessons, and tea dances had ended so many years earlier that even the ghosts didn't remember them. The gardeners had been dismissed decades ago, encouraging the overgrown tropical jungle to flourish and strangle the estate's remaining, dimming lifeblood.

Zosia, the Polish housekeeper, would arrive in her rusted Honda before the neighbors awoke and exited the drive at dusk after locking the iron gate. A familiar sight to early morning runners, she appeared thick, pallid, and of no consequence. It was as if the house had taken on the air of a locked government building closed to the public.

Despite its reticence and dereliction, North Bay Road preened and bustled and was dubbed the "Fifth Avenue of Miami." Celebrities found the wide bay, glittering sunset views of the downtown skyline, and easy proximity to the beach a boon, and, best of all, one could get a larger yacht onto North Bay Road unlike neighboring Pine Tree Drive or Indian Creek with their thinner canals. In recent years, North Bay Road had become a haven for celebrities. They waxed and waned like the Florida hurricanes, arriving in a great storm and departing in the jet stream when they were low after a drug high or an expensive divorce wiped out a new fortune.

The great lady didn't know or care about her neighbors; they came and went like tropical gusts which was fine with her. Therefore, it wasn't given much thought when a new neighbor's security team, in an operation that was as choreographed as the Russian ballet, arrived one overheated summer morning to take possession of the house. The team disembarked from sinister-looking, blacked-out Mercedes-Benz buses and began surveying the property, setting the bayside protocol, and activating the new codes on the front gatehouse. They were mostly lean, muscled, humorless men with walkie-talkies wearing discreet noir polo shirts, navy trousers, and opaque wire Ray-Bans. As they surveyed the perimeter of the property, everything appeared as it should; the massive glass box was clean, fresh, and spanking new after the Venezuelan designer's custom gray chalk paint and 30 percent fees. As security walked the property, they found the neighbor to the left, an aging Cuban American liquor magnate with highly secure, but too bright, lemon stucco walls, benign enough. As they approached the hidden property to the right, they were somewhat dumbstruck by the looming verdant jungle, what nearly a century of unpruned growth did to a place.

Bemused, puffed up security walked up and down and poked through the tangled web of mammoth ancient palms and overgrown Japanese boxwoods to see if there was a security risk, as she knew they would. A crumbling concrete wall divided the two properties and what they saw from the crisp, clean, striking, modern mansion seemed like another world entirely. The minions poked, prodded, and viewed the formidable estate and shoreline from their speedboats before finally deeming it of no consequence. She was sure of this as well.

The new owner's Wheels Up Gulfstream was expected to land at Miami-Opa Locka Executive Airport that Thursday evening. Playing stadiums of thousands looked glamorous but proved exhausting, and with the Covid shutdown, he had retreated to his farm, trying his hand at writing new songs for his next album, riding horses, milking cows, and swimming in the lake. Now, he was ready for a bit of civilization again. At 8:30 p.m. on a particularly humid evening, the head of security, a chiseled Israeli named Eliad Shiraz, received a call from the Miami police that a paparazzo was seen trying to enter the property by climbing over the gate of the neighboring, crumbling mansion. Within the hour, the intruder was cuffed and booked for trespassing. That evening, security gathered their information, held meetings, and spoke with the authorities. The lower part of the neighbor's gate posed a security threat, but it was not theirs to reinforce. One consideration was buying adjacent or additional properties, as many of the celebrities on North Bay Road had done, for a larger guardhouse, extra parking or building higher, unsightly walls.

"Create an estate like Barry Gibb," the local security team advised in such matters, by adding an additional lot; many millions more for true peace of mind! However, the next few days proved vexing to the tireless Mr. Shiraz; there was no way to contact the owner. Ringing the gate, sending letters, and poking around at city hall had only revealed the neighboring estate, once called Villa Pompeii, belonged to an ancient and dusty socialite who was never seen, had no family to speak of, and no forwarding address, just the elegant name of Elsa Sloan Barrett.

The housekeeper spoke no English and wouldn't respond to her native tongue when they found someone to speak it. She appeared to be the only resident of the property, living over the garage on the weekends, and seemed either mute or not mentally engaged. There was no way around it. They would have to talk the security issues over with the new owner when he finally arrived.

G Alvarez hadn't become a household name until he'd been asked to perform at the Super Bowl halftime show and strutted his stuff. Reggaeton wasn't rock 'n' roll, but when he took the stage, he wowed the audience, endorsed by the talents, sex appeal, and enduring popularity of J.Lo. He often joked he was the most famous non-famous person in America with forty-five million Instagram followers. As a singer, producer, and composer, he had racked up multiple Latin Grammy awards, and his reggaeton version of "Baby I Love Your Way," the classic Peter Frampton hit mixed with Dominican bachata star Juan Luis Guerra's "Estrellitas y Duendes," won Latin song and then album of the year. It didn't hurt that he had asked Frampton to play the guitar and Juan Luis to sing a duet on the remix. Like Shakira, he was already a huge star in Latin America, and while he could walk down Michigan Avenue in Chicago without attention, he needed top security in Buenos Aires or Brasilia. His concerts were packed with adoring fans, and he made millions in stadiums from his native Colombia to Argentina. Fame meant bodyguards and bling, and huge purses meant expensive toys.

The gleaming, modern mansion on North Bay Road had been hastily disposed of by a film star during a tumultuous divorce where the wife walked in on her husband having a drug-fueled ménage à trois. Upset that she was not even asked to join in, she immediately filed for divorce, and the property was soon put on the market as a whisper listing. Hailed as a modern architectural masterpiece, it was well-known to real estate doyenne Esther Percal, who had sold it twice before. She herself had been born in Cuba and was often referred to as the Queen of Miami real estate. She was tight-lipped and discreet, which the rich and famous appreciated and why her celebrity clientele was extensive. The moment she heard there was trouble in paradise, she went into overdrive, subtly of course. The modern mansion was exactly what her client, G Alvarez, was looking for. It was reduced to $25 million and, under Esther's tutelage and artful bargaining, G stole it for $18.5 million. It had a grandfathered dock for his yacht, 150 feet of pure, unadulterated Miami waterfront, and, as she mentioned to G on the phone in Colombia, it was only twenty minutes to Joe's Stone Crab!

Before arriving at his new manse, G dismissed most of his staff and posse, giving them time off for a long weekend. He wanted to recuperate and experience his new home alone. Before his final concert had been canceled due to Covid, the five-country-ten-city tour had physically and emotionally drained him, and he felt he was scraping the bottom of the barrel—not to mention a nasty case of laryngitis. He longed for sleep and solitude. The farm had provided that, but it didn't provide much fun or alfresco restaurants with beautiful people. That was what Miami was for, and hopefully inspiration for new songs as well—fresh hits currently eluding him.

The stark white architecture blinded him at first as his Mercedes-Benz sedan entered the front gate: skyscraper sheets of glass with lustrous mahogany details. He had only seen photos and a well-produced video of the estate, but he was a child of poverty and such excess seemed otherworldly even now. The first night he crashed, but the following morning, he awoke early and spent hours roaming the rooms, touching the gleaming surfaces, and spent the afternoon tanning at the infinity pool. He called his assistant Karolina in Atlanta and asked her to order in Mexican since he did not know how to do it himself. Once the food arrived, it was promptly given to the security guard at the gatehouse, who gave it to the bodyguard, who silently placed it in the kitchen. Maria, his housekeeper and chef, knew to plate his lunch as usual, since she assumed G would not know where anything was. The day flew as he soaked up the bountiful sun on his $2,500 lounge chair. His skin turned a golden brown, and with his Afro-Latino genes, he only needed one day for a tanning reset.

August had turned to September. The sun burned late seeping into a Bloody Mary sky which contrasted the bay turning dark blue. G smiled when he finally saw the hint of dolphins. With less boating activity during the Covid lockdown, the bay had seen an influx of natural wonders. He rode the newly installed, high-speed, burl-wood-and-chrome elevator to the tower balcony to take in the vista and the apparent sea life before the sun went under. He walked the length of the terrace and saw languorous dolphins jumping and a manatee gliding near the surface. Then he turned to the dense property and tower next door. The old estate was seemingly deserted, so he was shocked to see a nurse with an ancient, ailing woman on the bayfront, concrete dock. From afar, he could see the sobering image of an intravenous bag affixed to the wheelchair, set against the more whimsical candy cane striped, decaying poles implanted in the bay, like he had seen when he was on tour in Italy. In Venice, they were called *pali da casada*, and his tour guide revealed that they distinguished each Palazzo and "beckoned guests and their gondolas." He had been told the neighboring property was vacant, yet here they were, two inhabitants venturing out to see the late Miami sunset.

So, there is someone living next door after all! G thought to himself.

He remembered an elderly woman in Bogota with a lone stray hair sprouting from her chin who made him rice and peas when he was an orphan. Older women and the Sisters in the orphanage had always loved G and cooked for him when he was young. He knew, even as a child, his slightly crooked, smile melted hearts. Did the old woman still cook? Perhaps she was too ill. He saw the unlikely pair silently looking out towards the arts district to the right and downtown to the left. Suddenly, a plane overhead took their gaze towards G standing outside on his balcony. The nurse shielded her eyes with her hands, and the woman in the wheelchair adjusted her dark sunglasses as she looked up at the plane and then directly at him. It was G's natural instinct to wave, and as he did, she immediately looked away.

Not an exactly friendly neighborhood, he thought.

She motioned for her nurse to wheel her promptly inside.

It was just as well. Like many of the women in his life, Elsa Sloan Barrett disappeared in an instant, never to be seen again.

Chapter 1

December 2020
New York City

The call came so early and so unexpectedly that Liz dismissed it out of hand. The voice mail message left afterwards sounded too much like another annoying direct marketing call. She deleted the message and then twirled her caramel-streaked hair into a messy French knot and wrapped an antique, silken, kimono-style robe lined with cashmere around her elegant, ivory shoulders. She had splurged on the robe at her favorite thrift store on Melrose Avenue in Los Angeles. She marveled at the skillful bird of paradise design set beyond a glorious dragon whose teeth were bared; the raised Japanese needlepoint against the silk and fringes was '20s flapper chic. The store owner had insisted that Gloria Swanson once owned it and charged Liz fifty dollars more for the silent film star's provenance. She almost didn't spring for it but as she dug through her vintage YSL bag and scrounged for change, she came across three old, crumpled twenty-dollar bills she didn't know she had. Serendipity! It was meant to be. The backstory was worth the extra money, and she dined out on it whenever she had guests over who complimented her find. "You know, it belonged to Gloria Swanson in her *Queen Kelly* phase," she would say with a smile and shrug in an offhand way knowing it reinforced her reputation for elevated taste.

The cold permeated the wrap as she walked over to the small floor radiator and tried to unscrew the paint-flaking heat knob, despite knowing it would do nothing but hoped the attempt might actually help. Magical thinking.

"Fuck December in the city," she cursed under her breath.

She had never spent the entire winter in her small walk-up off Avenue A on the Lower East Side of Manhattan. Pre-Covid, she was always flying out to balmy LA for a shoot during the winter months and adding vacation days to extend her time there. An A-list stylist in demand for her eclectic, creative curation, and innate fashion sense, Liz Galin had earned a reputation as the go-to stylist for Indie actresses who needed a cooler red carpet look than what top couture houses and more conservative, mainstream stylists could provide. She would scour vintage and thrift stores in LA and Palm Springs for the unusual: a one-of-a-kind, jeweled, Judith Leiber minaudiére in the shape of an ice cream cone or a dachshund, or a smoky, vintage Hollywood mink fur stole that belonged to Jayne Mansfield. She would then pair it with an up-and-coming designer. These unlikely pairings became her signature and, before long, her career was on fire. She was so busy, in fact, she would often go from one shoot to another and had an assistant, Lily, in Venice Beach. It had been an exciting and fairly indulgent schedule; after she completed her styling jobs, she would take a few days and fly down to Cabo with Lucy, her married best friend, or Roy, her makeup artist of choice and other BFF, and they would spend hours on the beach—sipping margaritas, people-watching, rating the bad bathing suit choices, and taking in the occasional whale sighting from the shore. This worked well as her boyfriend Cary, "the nice doctor" from Canada, was always working. His residency always took a front seat, but Liz didn't mind. Her mother Linda would often wag a manicured finger and remind her, "What's hard in the beginning is easier in the end and vice versa. You've gone out with too many schmucks and bad boys; this one's a keeper. Trust me." Sadly, Covid made mincemeat of Liz's career and her travel schedule, not to mention her bank account. As for Cary, she was now in social isolation, not able to see her boyfriend during her mother's cancer treatments until they were all able to get the vaccine.

"Thank G-d for ramen! Forty-nine cents a meal!" she clucked to herself as she brought out the small, wrapped, plastic pack and started boiling water on the stove. She bought packages of the noodles by the armful when she ventured out, fully masked. Ramen was cost efficient and wasn't putting any weight on her, and when she added an egg after stirring in the flavor mix packet, she felt like she was splurging with the extravagance. Little treats were a small consolation after canceling her gym membership since she was no longer able to afford the monthly fee or brave the germs without the vaccine.

"Is shivering exercise?" she asked herself as she turned on CNN, then turned off the sound as she couldn't bear any more election news. Liz longed for the days when the scandal of the day was Clinton getting a blowie, not the divisiveness of two parties on the verge of civil war. A feeling of dread overtook her, and she flipped the channel to a *Friends* episode.

Ah, the good ole days. She wrapped her robe tighter, delaying getting dressed. She eventually forced herself to shower and quickly layer up due to the cold, opening her tiny closet door and pulling on her decidedly utilitarian North Face parka. She topped it off with a navy, Carolyn Rowan, cashmere hat dotted with Swarovski crystals and the matching glove set—she wasn't going to go *that* far down the rabbit hole without any panache. Then she forced herself to walk down the sloping staircase into the frigid cold to the corner bodega to stock up on crackers, mac and cheese, Tic Tacs, and more eggs.

How exciting my life has become! Liz was saddened that the highlight of her day was scanning the food shelves for a sale bargain, Chinese take-out where she could stretch three meals out of one order, or a salad dinner with her savior Netflix. Then she'd call Lucy in LA and spend hours on the phone complaining about her dead-end life or Roy who was living at his ex-boyfriend's house up in Hudson and they'd laugh well into the evening talking about the latest celebrity gossip: who was a sex cannibal, who was gay, and who was dating which Kardashian. Cary would call her around midnight that he loved and missed her, but that was about it. She knew he was reticent about talking too much after an exhausting day and only wanted light diversion. Regardless, she knew he was a Covid hero in the emergency room, and she was proud of his sacrifice and service. She would blow him a kiss over Zoom, then head to bed where she would crawl under three childhood quilts and put on a knit hat to try and banish the chill. And then all over again!

The next morning, Liz was awakened by the sound of a ping on her cellphone and felt an odd, metallic taste in her mouth. She remembered she hadn't brushed her teeth when she got into bed the night before because she was too tired and too cold. She looked down and heard the ping again. She blinked as a text popped up on her iPhone.

"I hope this is the cell phone of Liz Galin. I have been trying to reach you regarding an important legal matter. Please call me back." Information about an office on Biscayne Boulevard, including a phone number, followed. The text ended with, "Sincerely, Ira Reznick."

Sounds like someone's Uncle Ira, Liz joked to herself. *Ira Reznick with a Z. Uncle Ira. The Ira.* She sat up and yawned, then peered out the bedroom room window onto the skeletal, icy branches of Tompkins Square Park. She deleted the text.

The last thing I need is a lawsuit or owing some tax money from an old photo shoot. She yawned again, remembering a shoot she had done in Miami the previous year before putting the text firmly out of her mind.

Walking gingerly into the kitchen, she belted her long, '40s, pink *Laverne & Shirley*–style bathrobe into a loose knot as she inserted a metallic pod in the Nespresso machine—her one, expensive luxury. She saw the long, empty sleeve and realized she was running low.

It's my version of crack. Would I be an espresso pod–whore and give the cute guy at Nespresso a blow job if I had no money? I might, she joked to herself, knowing she never would. The *NY Post* had been delivered to her front door, despite her having canceled her subscription. She scanned an article on Jeffrey Epstein's alleged madam, Ghislaine Maxwell, and her plight in jail. She claimed her hair was falling out due to stress and solitary confinement. The thought made Liz shudder. Solitary confinement was the worst, but then again, did she have it that much better trapped in a 650-square foot studio in the East Village with marginal heat and rattling pipes during Covid and only able to see her mother?

I'm in jail too. She pursed her plump lips. *I can't see my boyfriend because he's a doctor, and my mother is going through chemo and needs me.*

Not exactly an optimal situation. Coupled with the fact that Liz Galin—*the* fabulous, socially connected, and super cool stylist Liz Galin—was currently 100 percent unemployed except for a lone, lifesaving shoot for *Harper's Magazine* with Kaia Gerber in Westchester. Covid had closed down her bread and butter. Movie premieres and advertising shoots were now all done by Zoom, and there were no more red-carpet events. Liz's career had been going to new heights with a prime assignment for the newest Bond movie premiere in Monaco, which was to be hosted by the Princess Grace Foundation, before the premiere had to be unceremoniously shuttered with no rescheduled date to look forward to. Her bank account had dwindled, causing her to eat into most of her paltry savings with seemingly no end in sight. Like many singles her age and background, Liz had always lived for the moment and never given much thought to the future or the possibility of little work and impending catastrophes. Luckily, her mother, Linda, received a generous insurance policy when her father Joe had passed, and she was able to supplement Liz's meager savings. Much of that money was being spent on medical care not covered by insurance, but she was able to send Liz money each month for rent and food.

"You have enough clothes, Liz!" Her formidable mother would both scold and caution her.

With her bank account on its last fumes, Liz sold a prized, vintage, Hermés Kelly bag on the RealReal for her mother's last birthday. This provided her with enough money to not only pay her mother back for rent and a few stray parking tickets that had accumulated, but to buy her a new cashmere zip-up with matching sweats that she could wear to chemo. Linda was thrilled and touched; she told Liz that she wished her daughter hadn't but was secretly glad she had something super comfortable and stylish to wear during her sessions. Liz was happy too as she knew her mother would have never bought something like that for herself.

"You see, Mom. I'll just live off my bags. But each time I sell one, it's like selling a child." Liz shrugged.

"You think that now…until you actually have children, then you'll know what real love is." Linda smiled sadly.

Liz looked away when she saw her mother's sorrowful gaze and the pain in her eyes. Turning thirty, she knew she was disappointing her mother's grand-maternal clock, and with the chemo underway, Liz was unsure if she would ever be able to let her mother see the grandchild she always yearned for. It was hard, that look. Liz was sure Cary would eventually propose; he had probed her on marriage and family on their first date and casually dropped that Park Avenue Synagogue had an amazing preschool. Liz was impressed; a doctor who attended Friday night services at the top prestigious Manhattan shul was hard to find, and when she told Linda, she nearly swooned. Everything was going swimmingly with weekly dates, heavy petting, and then, as the relationship progressed, living together two nights a week. However, once Covid hit, he had other, more pressing concerns than his girlfriend. Liz also made the decision to put off seeing Cary during her mother's chemo treatments and broke the monotony each week by driving out to Great Neck to care for her. Every time Liz resettled into her old bedroom on Long Island, it seemed like her life was a total failure. She was comforted by the pink-and-white flowered wallpaper, quilted bedspread, and old pink phone, yet once her eyes scanned the gold tennis trophies from her Great Neck South High School and UCLA days, it reinforced her sense of failure. She had been well on her way to go pro, but she stopped having the drive to practice every day. She now wished she had been more serious about it during college as she glanced at the faded, black-and-white newspaper clippings of her tournaments and her unfulfilled promise stared back at her. She had been more interested in clothes, boys, and her sorority events rather than practice and that was that.

I coulda been someone! She shook her head at her internal Rocky voice. Now that she was turning thirty, she started thinking about her biological clock. *Just clothes and some old press clippings to talk about. Nada!*

They would order in Chinese takeout from a good place on Northern Boulevard for dinner, and the next morning, Liz would take her mother, all bundled up, to the hospital in Linda's old, yellow Lincoln Continental. Leaving the house by 9:45 a.m., they fell into a routine for Linda's chemo. Mother and daughter double-masked and Purell-ed before they went up to the hospital entry desk. They checked in and sat waiting for the appointment to begin since Liz would not be allowed entry into the inner recesses due to the pandemic. Liz looked down over her medical mask as her phone buzzed.

"Always that phone! Is it Cary?" Linda looked up brightly. Despite the chemo, she was still a formidable, blonde beauty.

"No, but we have a Zoom tonight. How romantic!" Liz sighed wistfully.

"Don't get down; he loves you. I see the way he looks at you. Once you get the vaccine, you can get back to your life again," Linda said, trying to be upbeat.

Liz frowned when she saw the phone screen.

"What? Who is it?" Linda prodded.

"Oh, nothing…" Liz paused, not knowing whether she should say something or not about the mysterious texts she was receiving.

"Liz?" Her mother's strong gaze meant business.

"Okay, this lawyer from Florida I've never heard of keeps calling and texting me. It's weird." She shrugged and showed her mother the phone screen text.

"Well, call him back. He's a lawyer!" Linda admonished. She thought anyone who was a lawyer must be important.

"No way. If someone is suing me for back taxes, they'll win, and I'll have to pay them in Birkins." Liz's expression reflected this possible, impending catastrophe.

"Liz, you've always avoided things. I'm sure it's not that," Linda opined.

"Then why is a lawyer named Ira Reznick calling me from Miami? I'm telling you it's back taxes. I did a shoot in Miami, you know!" Liz groaned at the thought.

"Here." Linda waved her own phone. She made a face like she was tasting something spoiled. "Text me the number. I'll call him. How can you not call the man back? No one will mess with Linda Galin, I can assure you. I've known these Ira-types my whole life…."

"Fine." Liz texted her mom the name and number.

"But Liz, you have to call people back. It's not right," Linda lectured.

"Okay Mom, whatever. Just relax." Liz sighed. She knew her mother had a point and was proud that her fiery personality wasn't being affected from the chemo, but her mother always managed to make Liz feel like she wasn't doing enough despite everything she *was* doing. She was thrilled, though, that her mother only had two more chemo sessions left and was scheduled for the Covid vaccine, a light at the end of the tunnel.

The next morning, after propping her up in her bed and bringing her a brunch tray, Liz air-kissed her mother goodbye and drove her broken-down Subaru back towards the city. She always despised the drive back to Manhattan—the long line of cars idling in traffic infuriated her. What was she driving back to? What did she have to look forward to? Would she find a well-located parking spot when she finally got there? These thoughts always coincided as she passed the huge and depressing cemetery off the highway that seemed to go on and on forever.

Who were all those faceless people buried there? Liz wondered. *Did they manage to have any fun when they were alive?* She pondered endlessly. As the bumper-to-bumper traffic let up, Liz looked out the window at the uninspired Queens architecture and spied a billboard for Jamaican tourism featuring a romantic, tanned couple in bikinis, which made her miss her former life even more.

I'm drying up! She thought. After grueling traffic, the Midtown Tunnel beckoned like an oversized vacuum cleaner. Liz suddenly felt her phone vibrating; it was her mother. Of course. Always her mother. She loved her mother, but Linda reminded Liz of her friend Marisa Acocella Marchetto, the cartoonist who coined the phrase "smother" in her *New*

Yorker cartoons. The two often laughed about how their hovering mothers were so similar.

"Please call me, it's very important," the text read.

Yeah, it's important that I owe tax money, she moaned to herself. She heard her phone vibrating again.

She wasn't in the mood to answer, and soon a voicemail popped up.

"Call me. It's important. Why aren't you picking up? I'm worried." Liz heard her mother's throaty voice. She groaned and immediately called her mother on speaker as she idled behind a row of cars.

"Mom, you want me texting and driving?" Liz complained.

"Put me on speaker."

"I have. What's so important?" Liz rolled her eyes.

"I called that lawyer, Ira Reznick, once you left." She paused. "From Florida!" The gravity of inflection of the words "from Florida" were akin to her making a long-distance phone call to Asia.

"And?"

"And, you'll never believe this Liz," her mother said in a tremulous voice.

"Believe what? Be quick, I don't want to lose you in the tunnel. Am I in trouble?" Liz shook her tawny head.

"Trouble? No, but I'm not convinced that this isn't a scam." She could hear her mother pacing.

"What scam? Please fill me in?"

"You're not going to believe this, but…" Linda's voice went up an octave.

"But what, Mom? You're stringing this out like cheese," Liz admonished.

"But apparently, some old kook I've never heard of, in Florida…" She paused dramatically.

"Yes?" Liz pressed.

"Left you her house in her will!"

Chapter 2

"This is a joke, right?" Cary Simon tried in vain to wipe the creases from his hazelnut eyes and ran his fingers through his short, cropped, tousled, brown hair. It had a touch of auburn in the sunlight, but his locks hadn't seen the sun's rays in months, and his hair was usually damp from sweat. His cheekbones were marked with blotchy rashes from the N95 masks he constantly wore in the ER. When he took the Hippocratic Oath, Cary never anticipated that he would be on the front lines of the worst public health crisis in recent history. It was Cary's childhood dream to become a doctor like his father and grandfather, but he had never imagined it would start off like this. As a young boy, Cary had seen firsthand the trust friends, neighbors, and patients put in his grandfather and father, country doctors in Calgary the western province of Alberta, Canada. Descended from immigrants from the Pale of Settlement, the Simons had started as peddlers. When Cary's great-grandfather Abraham Simon realized that there were multiple peddlers selling linens, pots, pans, and bedding but virtually no doctors in the vicinity, he advised his son Samuel to go into the profession that was much needed, despite how much or how little money anyone had. It was a good lesson in supply and demand, and Cary grew up with dreams of eventually having his own rural or suburban practice with a possible son or daughter to take it over. No one, however, had cautioned Cary on the nature and frequency of pandemics, and lessons of supply and demand took on new meaning with a dearth of doctors, harried nurses, and a limited supply of PPE.

Today had been a particular nightmare for Cary. An older Italian couple, a husband and wife, died within minutes of each other, holding hands in the ICU. He was usually not prone to sentimentality, but it was the little things that broke through. The image of the man's blue-veined hand, the tape around his wedding band intertwined with his wife of fifty-six years, would haunt him. Cary sighed and then went back to the myriad of patients who desperately needed oxygen and respirators. His natural tough-shell and intense energy allowed him to push through, wade through the misery, and swim with the tide. Afterwards, when he finally got home to his modern one bedroom overlooking Central Park on 102nd Street and Fifth Avenue, he stripped off his hospital gear in the foyer, as he usually did, and left it in a wicker basket he had placed next to the umbrella stand for his housekeeper Carmen. Each day, she would wash and iron his street clothes before he donned his scrubs at the hospital. He immediately headed to shower, washing every crevice with precision, and then, still dripping wet, headed for the small kitchen where he scarfed down a quick frozen dinner Carmen had heated and left out on the stove wrapped in tin foil.

Turkey meatballs and a beer. Just what the doctor ordered. He shrugged to himself. *Shit! I totally forgot to get her cash, and tomorrow is Friday.* He hated paying Carmen late, knowing she was braving the subway and the virus to come and do his dirty work. He would go to the ATM first thing in the morning, double back to his apartment, and leave it with the doorman in an envelope. He wrote it down on a list next to his bedside table where he kept a small notebook and a pen. Cary thrived on order, punctuality, and cleanliness and held messy people in mild contempt. It was an issue he had with Liz, his girlfriend, whenever she used to stay over pre-Covid. He gritted his teeth remembering her overflowing bags, stray towels, cotton balls, hairbands, and thongs which seemed to grow daily and spill out onto the floor in piles. He ate his meal standing up in the kitchen, then washed, cleaned, and dried his dishes. He took his frosted glass out of the freezer, poured his beer, sauntered into his spartan living room, turned on CNN, and then switched to ESPN before his nightly call to Liz. Despite her messy gene, these late-night Zoom calls always calmed him and helped him fall asleep. When they FaceTimed or Zoomed, she would talk his ear off before he fell into bed and got some much-needed rest. About what, he often didn't remember, but their conversations were easy, fun, and, at the end of a miserable day, he needed the light diversion. Tonight, though, he was unusually talkative at her seemingly unbelievable news.

"Wait, I don't understand! Some woman you have never heard of or met before left you her house in a will?" He shook his head in total disbelief.

"I still can't believe it myself; I'm in shock." She spooned some Van Leeuwen salted caramel ice cream from the container and onto her tongue.

"Do you think she just picked your name out of a phone book? There must be some connection, or maybe it's a total scam!" he cautioned. He was skeptical, and his prickly side was kicking in.

"Not that we can think of. Her name is, was, get this…Elsa Sloan Barrett. Nobody in my world is called Elsa Sloan Barrett." Liz yawned. "Not much is known about her except she was some sort of socialite from Boston who moved to Miami in the '30s and lived to 104. Mom is as shocked as I am. We Zoomed with the lawyer today, Ira Reznick. I checked him out through Richie Steinberg who lives down there, and he said the guy's a totally major, legit, high-end lawyer," Liz explained, excited but was as baffled as Cary was.

"Well, that's a good sign." Cary was trying to process the information. He was totally a right-brain kind of guy, and this made absolutely no sense to him. He was convinced it had to be some kind of scam or joke.

"And he looked exactly like an Ira Reznick would, right out of central casting…so lawyerly and all," Liz explained. "When we asked him, he said that he worked for Missus Barrett for over twenty years. But get this," she paused, "he never met her!"

"Okay. Normal." Cary raised a bushy eyebrow. It seemed to be getting worse with more facts.

"He said that they spoke on the phone for years and she always paid her bills on time, but he never met her. Not even once! She would just call him and her maid—this woman, Zosia, who still works there—would drive to the office with any papers. The only time she ever left the house, that he knows about, was to have her documents notarized. He said he gave her the name of a notary near Lincoln Road. He wanted to meet her there, but she insisted he not come. He called the notary afterwards, and he said she showed up in an ancient Cadillac from the 1960s. The notary confirmed she was very lovely, refined, and sent him an orchid with a handwritten note. Can you imagine?" Liz scraped the sides of the container with her spoon trying to get every last drop of ice cream.

"Wait, so this Ira must know why she left you the house?" Cary scratched his testicles over his boxers, hidden from view on the Zoom call. Or so he thought.

"Actually, villa. He called it a villa," she said with new authority.

"Fine, villa." He rolled his eyes at the slight pretension.

"We asked a million times, but he has no idea either. He said she was extremely polite but very evasive and that she left it to me in trust," Liz went on.

"Wait what did you say the address was?" Cary probed.

"North Bay Road."

"What number?" He pushed.

"I think it's…" She looked down at her phone. "Oh, 4345. 4345 North Bay Road."

"Wait. I'm Googling it on my phone, and it's not coming up." He Googled again on his iPhone. "The other houses all have photos on Zillow."

"That's because the woman was a recluse," Liz surmised.

"That is just plain weird." He frowned again.

"So is this!" she paused. "The only stipulations in the will are that I have to live in the house for six months and one day out of the year to become a Florida resident. I can only sell it after I have lived there five years. If I don't want it after five years I can sell it, and I can rent it when I am not there," she explained.

"Liz, do you know how crazy this all sounds?" Cary shook his head in disbelief.

"I know."

He breathed deeply. "I'm looking online, and the houses on the water on North Bay Road are like twenty or thirty million dollars. Did you say it's on the water?" He was finally getting excited.

"I didn't ask." Liz shrugged.

"How could you not ask?" he said in a somewhat condescending tone.

"Why would I think it's on the water?" She continued to scrape the bottom of the ice cream container with her spoon even though nothing was left.

"Because it's in Miami?" he questioned.

"So what?" Liz countered and sighed. Cary was very right-brain and could be difficult if one didn't follow his line of thinking.

"Well, it seems that the houses across the street on the dry side are still a few million dollars, but the bayside houses are where the money is. You'll have to call this Ira and ask if it's bayfront." Cary seemed a tad exasperated.

"Okay, real estate broker! That's a good question. I did ask him if he's ever been to the villa, and he said he has driven past it but never been inside. But he's getting the keys now, and Zosia, the maid, is going to open the house for us when I get there."

"Wait, this sounds like a total trick someone is playing on you...or a horror movie," he said firmly.

"Cary, don't rain on my parade. I just inherited a multi-million-dollar villa from some dead socialite who sends handwritten notes and orchids. Let me enjoy it before getting all rational on me." She grimaced at the now-empty ice cream container.

"How do you know she's even dead?" he pondered.

"You don't think I'm that stupid? He knows she's dead since he saw the death certificate and went to the funeral. She was also one hundred and four, not exactly running marathons!"

"Any relatives ready to pop out of the woodwork?" he asked.

"He said no, and no one else is mentioned in the will. It's all left to me, baby, so you better watch out because I am now a woman of means." She teased.

"Don't let it turn your head!"

"You're the one who is going to have to sign the prenup if it's… *bayside*." She smirked. "That is, if we ever get married."

"Clearly." He nodded, thinking about the asset at hand.

She laughed. "So, are you going to come with me?"

"What do you mean, come with you?" he asked in a baffled tone.

"Well, I don't want to go to Miami alone, and Mom can't travel. Maybe you can take a vacation? Please, pretty please?" she begged slightly.

"They don't give vacations for first-year residents, Liz, you know that, especially in the middle of a pandemic."

"Well, maybe you can spend some time at the Mount Sinai down there. It is literally in walking distance from the house. Uncle Ira told me," she said in a more conciliatory tone.

"Uncle Ira? Now he's *Uncle* Ira?" Cary shook his head vigorously. This was classic Liz but at a higher level of insanity.

"Well, I have to call him something. The man just showed up with a very generous present," she said in a deadpan tone.

"Sorry. The two Mount Sinais have the same name but are not affiliated," he explained.

"Well, maybe over a holiday then?" she offered.

"I think I might be able to swing that." He paused.

"I hope so. I'll need to spend at least six months a year there…. It can't be worse than my freezing apartment on Avenue A living on ramen," she lamented.

"What's crazy about all this is that it's starting to sound plausible." He paused. "I'm going to miss you all the way in Miami."

"What's the difference between NY and Miami? We can't see each other anyway until I get the vaccine." She pursed her lips.

"Can your mother go with you?" Cary asked.

"She's finishing her chemo, but when she's vaccinated, she's going to come for a few days. Cary, isn't this crazy? I mean, really crazy? Some old wackadoodle left me a villa in Miami. I still can't get over it."

"Only you Liz, only you." He nodded.

"And did I tell you I get spending money too?" She laughed.

"What?" He perked up, not able to get over what he was hearing.

"Uncle Ira said I can spend money as long as it's for upkeep on the property and that I should just send him the bills. It's kind of great, no?"

"It sounds like you won the loony lottery. Did Linda or your father ever know this woman? They must have. Was she a client of his?" he asked.

"No, Mom never heard of her." Liz shrugged.

"How much did she leave? I mean for the upkeep?" Cary probed.

"I'll find out all that when I get to Miami. She didn't want me to know before I accepted. If I don't accept the terms of her will, the house will be sold and donated to some preservation society of Miami and all her effects will go to a charity," she explained.

"What charity?"

"I don't know. It's part of the will Uncle Ira will read to me when he takes me to Joe's Stone Crab."

"You can't be serious…like, a date?" Cary said in a not-too-thrilled tone.

"Aunt Sheila is coming to meet me too!"

"Who the hell is Aunt Sheila?" He laughed out loud. Liz always had a flighty sense of humor, but this was really next level.

"Stop! The Reznicks have been married forever. She's the head of Hadassah!"

"So that makes it all legit?" He laughed.

"We'll figure out a travel schedule once we can actually see each other." She paused. "I just wish I was sharing this crazy adventure with you, that's all."

"Me too. Liz, I always knew great things were bound to happen for you, and I do hear that Miami real estate is going through the roof. What did Linda say?"

"At first she thought it was a scam, but Uncle Ira assured us both that the will is valid and rich people are eccentric," she explained.

"I'm sure Linda is kvelling." Cary often peppered his conversation with old-school Yiddish words he learned from his grandfather.

"She is. She was so tired from the chemo that she was drifting off, but she did say something weird before she dozed off to sleep, that maybe it has something to do with—"

"With what?" he interrupted.

"'With the photographers when you were born.' That's what she said."

"Photographers?"

"I was literally yelling into the phone, and she dozed off. She said she would 'talk about it with me tomorrow.' Can you believe it?" Liz sighed.

"What could that mean?" Cary pondered.

"I have no idea, but it's all very *Miami Vice*!"

Chapter 3

Yellow. White. Blood orange. Eye-blinding shades of light bounced off the cathedral-high impact windows that refracted the heat, offering a reflection of the confident high-speed Rivas, Wallys, and Donzis cutting through the turquoise bay and strutting their mahogany and fiberglass allure.

G leapt up in one sinewy, athletic movement onto the recently varnished dock and elbow-bumped and thanked his toned yoga instructor, Crystal, as they wrapped up his hour-long session. He ran his hands through his freshly dyed, red, crew cut, and the sun reflected off the tiny diamond stud in his nose. His sleeve of Indian tattoos rippled with glistening sweat; the images undulated as he moved his body in a feline motion. He immediately checked his cell phone and walked back to the house slowly, avoiding tripping by keeping one eye on his phone screen and the other on the creamy, Jerusalem stone pathway. Crystal inhaled serenely, taking in the view she knew she could never afford, before rolling up the two thin yoga mats. She walked across the stone patio to store them in the pool house. G's house manager and his childhood friend from Bogota, Santiago—or Sant as he was known by—met Crystal at the pool house with a cash envelope and escorted her around the perimeter of the house to the newly constructed carport. Sant didn't walk as much as waddle, his overweight frame sweating profusely through his black T-shirt in the searing Miami sun.

Only Sant, G's security team, and G's cook Maria were allowed in the house because of Covid. G's intense, swarthy, head of security Eliad approached; his cut, muscular physique was imposing in the standard, black polo shirt. He tossed G an '80s Blondie concert T-shirt.

"G, you gotta put some clothes on. We paid a lot of money, or I should say you paid a lot of money, to get that photographer's camera. There were naked photos of you that could have shown up on the internet," he griped.

"So, you don't want to see my *pinga*?" G crudely grabbed his crotch through his Versace micro-speedo and smirked. "Did you get off?"

"Everyone wants to see your *pinga*; that's the problem." Eliad shook his head indicating he thought G was acting like a child.

"Well, I was wearing this bathing suit for yoga." He shrugged.

"Your butt crack was exposed during the tree pose," he said with his gruffly tinged accent.

"I spent close to twenty million dollars on this place, and I still don't have any privacy." G frowned.

"You have *some* privacy. But there are boats going by and helicopters flying overhead, and they all want a shot of you naked. It's worth money to the rags," Eliad explained.

G led the way, and Eliad followed into the huge chef's kitchen. Maria had poured a blueberry-chia seed-almond milk smoothie into a tall glass, garnished it with a tropical flower, and placed the glass on a starched, linen napkin on top of the white, Caesarstone island.

"Gracias, *mami*!" G said as he entered the flawless, white kitchen. Maria smiled and revealed a shiny gold tooth. She and her husband Carlos, who doubled as the caretaker and the driver, lived in the small guest house above the garage. She didn't talk much, but she made Colombian food, which G often craved, and seemed to know exactly what G wanted before he wanted it. Today, he inhaled the familiar aroma of *empanadas* and *Ajiaco Colombiano*; the hearty, shredded chicken, corn, and potato soup simmering in a giant pot on the stove. He would have stolen a car or robbed a bank for such food when he was a kid living in the orphanage.

"Listen, Eliad, the security team down here said the best thing to do is buy the property next door for privacy and safety. Where are we on that?"

"We're working on it."

"Work harder." He sipped his smoothie. "Make the old lady an offer she can't refuse." G looked up at the rock-solid Israeli; his six foot six frame cast a dark shadow on the kitchen island.

"Old lady? There's no one living there except the housekeeper on weekends." Eliad seemed annoyed at the question.

"Why am I paying you all this money? There is an old woman next door; her housekeeper was strolling her around one night like she was at a carnival." G took another sip of the healthy concoction; his eyes narrowed in the direct sunlight.

"It's just the housekeeper. Name is Zosia. Doesn't speak much English, but won't talk anyway. We've tried everything: ringing the bell, stopping at unexpected times, handsome guys…visiting city hall and even bribes. She's tight as a drum." He frowned and then added, "As far as I know, there's no old woman in that house."

"Maybe that's why you got tossed from the Mossad, dude." G laughed. "I saw the old lady with my own eyes one or two months ago."

"When? Why didn't you tell me?" Eliad narrowed his eyes at the news.

"Why would I think to tell you? I thought you knew." G shrugged. "When I was up on the terrace, I saw her taking in the sunset like I was. Around 7:45. She was in a wheelchair pushed by that woman."

"Well, maybe you were drinking some of your mezcal and it was an apparition," Eliad countered defensively.

"No, my friend. I saw her with my own eyes. She wore sunglasses and had a scarf tied around her head and under her chin…like this…" G tied a fictional scarf under his chin.

"Next time you see her, let me know?" Eliad shook his head in a disapproving manner.

"I'm not working for you, dude. You go ring the bell and tell the woman she has a deal on the table. I mean, she's like a million years old, and I'm sure she'd want some cash before she croaks."

'Okay, G. I'll check it out." Eliad seemed miffed at the news.

"I want to be able to swim naked in the pool and have sex on the fucking lounge chair without people snapping photos of me," G said in a saucy tone.

"Well, until we do, keep your speedo on." He surveyed him with a critical eye. "I'm glad you're back to doing yoga."

"What's that supposed to mean?" G's tough veneer quickly crumbled.

"You need to get back into fighting shape, that's all," he said with a dose of Israeli honesty.

G looked down and shrugged. "I may have gained some weight on the farm…"

Eliad reached out and patted his stomach. "Some weight?" He grabbed a handful of G's belly and smirked.

"Fuck you! Don't touch me!" G glared.

"Don't get upset."

"I said don't fuckin' touch me." He was red-faced at the indiscretion.

"Sorry, but I'm the only one around here who tells you the truth. You don't want to hear it, fine. Okay." He smirked again. "G, you look amazing! Your abs are so fucking tight!" He sneered.

"Do you pride yourself on being an asshole?" G raged. Eliad always knew his Achilles' heel to keep G under his thumb, and he went for it.

"Yes." He smirked.

"Well, that's for me to decide, I'm the one they're paying to see, not you!" he said petulantly. "I'll get back into shape."

"If it wasn't for me, you'd be in *National Enquirer* with a dad bod. That's part of my job too."

G turned sideways and looked in the mirror across from the dining room, grimacing at his paunch. He heard his phone buzz. It was his assistant, Karolina.

"Hi G, how was yoga?" He heard her Southern-tinged accent when he picked up. She had proven to be an efficient and dedicated assistant through lockdown, and even now, she managed to run his life without a hitch despite living in Atlanta. She had moved back and rekindled an old romance in Buckhead that looked to be heading for an engagement. G knew he couldn't get on without her and told her she could work remotely at full salary. She had been thrilled at the news, and his generosity only seemed to make her work harder. There were few people G trusted completely, but she had proven her loyalty over time. She was also incredibly proactive, and he felt that she knew what to do without having to be asked. He would tell her he was getting back into shape, and he knew she would work with Maria to have diet and vegan snacks delivered to the house. She would up the yoga to three times a week without bothering him with the scheduling details. She booked his travel plans and table reservations and became friendly with all the important maître d's in town. She also kept him on schedule, always texting and reminding him of his appointments. He had received a text just minutes before that he had a conference call set up with his manager Ryan about tour dates. If he was lazy, she found him; if he dozed off, she sent Sant to wake him. G was generous as could be when someone was in his inner circle and doing a great job. He threw money, bonuses, and expensive gifts at his staff, and they all sported new, gold Rolexes and Cartier Love bracelets after Christmas Day.

G knew he could trust Sant and Karolina, and Maria of course. Eliad was another story, and the jury was still out on him. Eliad had been G's head of security when he did his first Israeli concert in Tel Aviv; his commanding presence and unwavering confidence had caught G's attention. Eliad literally picked up a fan who rushed them to get a selfie and tossed him off like a fly. He flaunted his machismo and physical size, and his aloof and arrogant attitude had G feeling a bit intimidated yet protected. He also looked super cool like an action hero, and G liked his posse to look the part. Sant, who was out of shape, was a bit embarrassing in that department, but he was given a pass as he was considered family. Sant had taken an immediate dislike to Eliad when he was hired, and while he didn't voice his opinion often, he noticed that Eliad was always doing things that infuriated G. On G's part, it was hard to say Eliad wasn't tough, professional, or didn't look the part for security. Although he often overstepped his bounds, deep down, G knew he needed the extra push when it came to his diet and exercise and forgave Eliad for his blunt indiscretion.

He was lost in thought as Karolina asked if he wanted her to order lunch—she would often call take-out places in Miami from Atlanta.

"No, no…. This will be my last good meal before I officially go on my diet. I smelled Maria's empanadas, and I have no self-control." G laughed.

"I can smell them over the phone, too." Karolina licked her lips at the thought. Maria was one incredible cook, and Karolina had enough of her home cooking to understand G's plight.

"I did make a dinner reservation tonight at Katsuya at the SLS Hotel," she said. "They only have six or seven outdoor tables, and I booked them all."

"Great. I'll go with Sant," G agreed.

"Ryan wanted to know if you are in the mood to have Lena and Jasmine with you tonight?"

"I'll play it by ear. Thanks Karolina. How's Atlanta anyway?"

"I've had enough family time to last me a lifetime." She laughed through the phone." Oh, and I FedExed you the cover design layouts for the new CD and tour posters. The shots are awesome. I think you'll be very happy."

"That was pre-tour when I had a six pack. Now, I've just been drinking them," he said in a self-deprecating fashion.

"You always get into shape. Are you enjoying the house? Sant said it's a fantasy," she asked.

"It's really perfect except I need to buy the property next door though for some extra security." G looked over and could hardly see the roofline from the dense foliage obscuring it.

"Well, if anyone can, you can," Karolina stated firmly.

"Thanks, have a great day." He clicked off the call.

"Hey Gabi." Sant was the only one to call G by his childhood nickname Gabi, short for Gabriel.

"Ryan's on my cell." He waved the cell phone as he grabbed a handful of corn chips and shoved them quickly in his mouth, yellow crumbs creating an abstract pattern on his black T-shirt.

"Thanks, tell him I'll be out in a minute." G walked over to the gleaming Wolf stove, took a small ladle from the drawer, and tasted a steaming spoonful of the soup.

In the mirror, he saw Eliad turn and smirk at him breaking his diet. Eliad was always there, always watching. There was something normal about this for G. He had always had a protector. He needed and craved it as it was a childhood pattern.

Yet, if truth be known, his protector had also been his abuser.

Chapter 4

Zoom was definitely one of the silver linings of Covid. No longer did Liz have to dress to the nines, battle traffic to attend superfluous business meetings in midtown, or fly to LA for the weekend at the drop of a hat for a celebrity fitting. When it came to talking to a relative in the convenience of one's living room, sweatpants and Clearasil triumphed over lipstick and vintage couture. Before her afternoon Zoom meeting with her mother and Ira, Liz had decided to splurge on some Banza pasta which she often made with a simple but delicious *aglio e olio* recipe. She navigated her sliver of a kitchen and first filled the aluminum pot with tap water. After letting the water boil, she stirred in a pinch of salt, reached into the small cabinet above the sink, plucked the distinctive orange box, and poured its contents into the angry bubbles. Banza was pasta made from chickpeas offering a high in protein and lower carb solution, but it had the taste and mouthfeel of wheat pasta and was certainly a culinary upgrade from ramen. She always made her favorite *aglio e olio*, garlic and oil, recipe the first night of her period since it seemed to comfort her. She had gotten her now-favorite pasta recipe in Milan from an old boyfriend, well, not exactly a boyfriend.

The dashing Giovanni Vissonti had cornered her at an after-party at the exclusive Bulgari Hotel during Milan Fashion Week three years earlier. Their week-long affair had started off with Bellinis, progressed to walking hand-in-hand for an animated tour of Piazza del Duomo and riding on the back of his BMW motorcycle, and culminated in a weekend of fabulous sex and home cooked pasta at his beach house in Forte dei

Marmi. It had been a perfect weekend. She hadn't been one to engage in multiple trysts or affairs, but his sparkling blue eyes, silver-haired temples, lean, muscular physique, and low-key humor had her letting her guard down. He was passionate, handsome, and utterly romantic and the CEO of a men's luxury fashion label. The only problem, she realized once the weekend ended, was she hadn't asked if he was married, and the answer had her kicking herself for her naivete. Despite the omission and the realization that certain Italian men were both dedicated to home and family as well as their mistresses, she at least managed to extract his incredible *aglio e olio* recipe and the secret to its preparation. Standing by the stove in only a towel, his taut muscles rippling with downy fur, cooking the pasta like a pro, Giovanni revealed the secret: the trick was to use a half cup of water from the boiled pasta and add it to the simmering mixture of sliced garlic, extra virgin olive oil, salt, and pepperoncini, creating a sublime golden liquid. Topped with a bit of fresh parsley, it was pure heaven. A twirl of al dente pasta followed by a bout of romantic Italian sex. "*Fantastica!*"

Even though Giovanni had a hard time understanding what all the fuss was about his being married, Liz consoled herself each month with the memory of his Olympic oral abilities and the recipe, which she considered a better parting gift than a Florentine gold bracelet or a French eau de parfum.

Once she strained the pasta and added it to the golden sauce, she poured it into a large bowl and sprinkled some extra pepperoncini on top. She sat Indian style on her sofa just as Roy's handsome face appeared on Liz's MacBook Pro, looking airbrushed even by Zoom standards. As a makeup artist, he used his contouring skills on himself, and he appeared fresh, angular, and smooth. Originally born as Raoul Diaz in San Juan, he changed his name when he first moved to LA and dyed his hair platinum blonde. He had started out doing makeup for drag queens and porn shoots, and word soon spread that no one knew how to gloss over "ass blemishes" better than Roy La Roy. He dubbed himself "Queen of Ass Contouring." Once he started doing legitimate hair and makeup jobs, his previous experience came in handy as more than one actress needed to diminish the appearance of cellulite, an early varicose vein, or even a herpes outbreak. Liz immediately knew how talented Roy was, as he could take the frumpiest-looking millennial actress and give her smoldering eyes, a much-needed mole on the lip, or high cheekbones where there were once none. They became fast friends when he did her makeup for free for an ill-fated date with a handsome but depressed scriptwriter after a shoot.

"You're prettier than any actress I know, you're too smart to be in front of the camera," he declared, "but your hair is a nest and a fashion emergency." From that moment on, they had been friends and co-conspirators.

Liz had called Roy even before she called Cary, and he was both thrilled and flabbergasted at her news.

"Is this the Lady of the Manor?" Roy arched a plucked eyebrow.

"Yes, the Lady of the Studio Apartment with the oven open so I don't freeze to death!" Liz shook her golden mane.

"You'll be in Miami soon enough, and I'll be there with you, doll. Just say the word, and I'll be your houseboy." His eyes sparkled at the thought of languid pools and olive-green palms.

"If there is a house. I am still trying to confirm this isn't a scam." Liz snarled her lip.

"It's real. I have a good feeling about it all." Roy shrugged.

"And why is that?"

"It's too ridiculous *not* to be real." Roy laughed, blasting Wham! in the background.

"Wait, Mom's on the other line. I'll call you back…gotta go," Liz said as she clicked over to her mother's FaceTime. Given her mother's condition and treatments, Liz had gotten in the habit of picking up after the first ring which Roy was used to as well.

They first spoke about the doctor's report on her chemo as Liz inhaled the last of the pasta and washed it down with a quarter bottle of inexpensive Pinot Grigio she had stocked in the fridge. She soaked up the remaining sauce from the bottom of the bowl with a piece of semi stale crusty bread and then took the empty bowl and her computer to the kitchen, still talking aloud to her mother as she made an espresso with almond milk. She stirred the ceramic mug, standing and shivering in the tiny kitchen, wrapped in her favorite, antique, Japanese shawl; the computer was placed on the counter next to the stove, so she could still see Linda while they talked. She turned up her oven to 450 degrees and left the door open to try and stay warm. While she knew she shouldn't have and that turning up the gas wasn't safe, she gave in every once in a while, especially when it was below eighteen degrees outside.

"I can't wait for Miami, with this no heat situation," Liz moaned.

"I can't wait to visit myself," Linda declared.

"So, Mom, what did you mean last night about…the photographers?" She looked directly into the screen to see Linda's reaction.

"Well, I've been racking my brain because there has to be something, *some* reason this woman left you the house," Linda opined.

"Villa."

"Okay, fancy-schmancy, villa! So, it got me thinking."

"And?"

"The only thing I could think of was," Linda paused dramatically, "when you were born, Dad and I were living in our first apartment in Little Neck. There were a few times when I was pushing you in the stroller, I saw a man holding a camera with a long lens taking our photo."

"Taking our photo? You mean you and me?" Liz couldn't believe her ears.

"I guess," Linda stated as if it had been a normal occurrence.

"Did you ever tell Dad or call the police?" Liz was incredulous at the news.

"It was a different time; people didn't think about all these crazies back then. But, every year around your birthday, I would see the same man across the street, by the park, or by the apartment. He would snap a few photos and walk away before I could catch up to him. I told your father, and he just said it was because I was so pretty and not to worry about it. So, I didn't."

"Always around my birthday?" Liz became wide eyed at the thought.

"Yeah, around January seventeenth. In fact, when you turned five, I wondered if the guy would show up again, and he did. So when I saw him, I waved. He took some photos and walked away really quickly. I'm not sure, but maybe that has something to do with this Elsa Sloan Barrett leaving you the house?" Linda offered casually.

"Mom, this totally creeps me out big time! If what you are saying is true, then maybe, just maybe, this man has been following me since I was born. Is that what you're saying? That I've had a lifetime of…stalking?" Liz let out a gust of air and was so cold she looked to see if she could see her breath. "I'm not adopted, am I? Is that next on the list of your… confessions?"

"No, you are certainly not adopted. I have the stretch marks to prove it." Linda patted her stomach for effect.

"Maybe he's out there watching now?" She walked over to the window but just saw a homeless person lying prostrate in the park. "Do you think they're going to kidnap or kill me?"

"No, absolutely not. I am one hundred percent certain of that," Linda exhaled.

"Why would you say one hundred percent certain?" She stood behind the drapes and looked out in a paranoid fashion.

"Well, when I got to thinking about the man with the camera, something crazy popped into my head. I hadn't thought about in years and years."

"A lot has been popping into that head of yours. It's like a popcorn machine. What's next?" She emitted a sardonic laugh.

"When I was growing up, my mother always said that I was the most beautiful baby and that I could have won beauty contests," Linda went on. She wove stories like Liz, not in a direct line but a wavy one.

"Mom, every mother says that."

"But I really was. She would always say that people would stop to look at me in the stroller," Linda paused, "and that I was even offered money to be in an ad campaign for talcum powder."

"Okay, so you were a really cute baby. So what?" Liz wanted her to get to the point.

"But now, I vividly remember her telling me that I was such a pretty baby that…people used to stop the carriage and take my picture," she suddenly revealed.

"Really? Pictures?" A shiver shot down Liz's spine.

"Someone was taking photos of me too. Maybe it's because we're both so gorgeous." She laughed in a gravely tone.

"Yeah, real beauty queens!" Liz pursed her lips.

"I don't know, maybe there is a connection."

"Now, you're totally freaking me out, like there's some generational stalking going on," Liz said in a wavering voice.

"Well, nothing ever happened to me, and no one ever left me a villa in Florida. So, stop complaining," Linda opined.

"Mom…this is, well, a bit disconcerting, but if you remember anything else, anything…Please let me know, okay?" Liz pleaded.

"Of course." Linda paused looking at the news. "When is our next Zoom with Ira?"

"Later today at 4:30. Be on time, he's very busy."

"Okay, call and remind me!"

"Fine." Liz shook her head. "I cannot wait to get the hell out of here. Uncle Ira said that Elsa even provided me with money for plane tickets and a hotel room."

"It seems she really wanted you to go and enjoy her home. Let's think positively about this. I told Marion, who lives down in Surfside, about it, and she didn't believe it. She said North Bay Road is like the Fifth Avenue of Miami! She thinks it's a scam." Linda rose from her lounger chair.

"Aunt Marion thinks everything is a scam." Liz bristled at the mention of Marion's name as she rarely had anything positive to say. "When I was talking to Cary last night, he asked if the villa is on the water. I said I didn't know and that I'd ask Ira. Seems that the bayside houses are where the real money is." Liz finally closed the stove door and turned off the heat, not wanting to be overwhelmed by gas. "You don't think the house is on the bay, do you?" Liz asked softly. "Because, if it is, he said the waterfront houses are in the fifteen-to-twenty-million-dollar price range."

She heard her mother suck in air at the thought. "You're kidding me, that much?"

"Can you believe it?" Liz shook her head.

"Well, don't get over excited. Let's hope it is, but it's still wonderful if it's not," she cautioned in a motherly tone.

"Let me go, I'm going to call Delta. Do you think it's safe to fly?"

"Wear a mask and a shield, and fly first. That's how Marion's daughter and husband fly down to see her. I think it's pretty safe, but be careful! My friend Dotty, who lives in Bal Harbor, told me Miami is a shit show, and no one wears masks down there. So mask up when you're there." Linda pointed a manicured finger at her over Zoom.

"I will, Mom. So, you think I should go?"

"I have a few more questions for the man, but of course you should go. For twenty million dollars, I'd go to Mount Everest in a wheelchair." Linda cackled. "And if I was well enough, I'd beat you to the airport. I cannot wait to get the second shot, then I'll be packing my bathing suits and shifts. It does have a pool, no?"

"Ira mentioned he thought it did, but if there is one, it would have to be fixed and refilled."

"I cannot imagine how dirty and smelly it all is, but don't look a gift horse in the mouth…." Linda sipped a bottle of Poland Spring.

"Mom, can you please try and be just a little positive?" Liz shook her tawny mane.

"How can you say that? I'm totally positive."

"Okay, gotta go. I'll call you at 4:20 to remind you about the meeting." Liz ended the FaceTime and decided to shower, change, blow dry, and try to tame her slightly, unruly hair so she would look good for the Zoom meeting, the prospect of bayside real estate dancing in her head. She turned on the shower, hoping the hot water would create some much-needed steam heat, hung up her Japanese robe on the hook in the bathroom, and breathed in the cold, peppermint air that crept in from a crack in the window. A house in Florida? Someone must be playing a joke on her, especially on one of the coldest days of the year.

Chapter 5

Liz looked at her iPhone and paced, trying to dim her nerves as she considered Linda's original suspicions and Cary's negative concerns that cautioned her not to get overly excited lest it all be a scam. Not to mention the villa was in Miami Beach, not Boca Raton or Palm Beach, and Linda was a tad paranoid about the area being safe. While Linda hadn't been to Miami in years, she had lasting memories of the glaring headlines from the crime-ridden days of the Mariel boatlift; they all left deeply imprinted memories of gang hits and South American drug wars. Liz tried to assure her that things had changed since then and that the area was experiencing another boom, but her mother was fixed in her ways and instructed her to install a new alarm system. She ran her fingers through her freshly blown hair—which was now straight and layered, giving her the look of a *Charlie's Angels* castmate—and pulled on an oversized, vintage, Ralph Lauren Polo Bear sweater she had bought for virtually nothing the previous year in a thrift store in LA. Soon after, the sweater had become a coveted fashion item, and the prices exploded like bitcoin. As a top stylist, she had been one of the people to reintroduce the classic Polo Bear sweater, and she realized that the real bargains in more temperate places like LA or Palm Beach were thrift stores stocked with vintage and unused winter clothes once a Northerner had relocated.

Liz walked into her shoe box–sized living room and stood by the dirty, soot-stained window for better reception before calling Linda to remind her the Zoom call was in ten minutes. She put her MacBook on a few stacked books on top of her tiny coffee table and accessed the meeting. She took in Ira's wiry gray hair and kindly lined face as it came into view on the slim screen. His deep voice seemed fatherly and comforting to her as did his seemingly prosperous, paneled legal office. In recent weeks, Liz and her mother had a lot of Zoom calls with Ira, and she had come to trust his calm manner and depth of knowledge. Everyone they spoke to in Miami who knew of Ira Reznick said he had a reputation as one of the most trusted lawyers in South Florida and there was no way he would or could be involved in a scam. The Reznicks were a high-profile couple who were part of the fabric of the community; Sheila Reznick, Queen of Hadassah! Once Linda heard that Shelia Reznick was involved in the Jewish women's charity, that was good enough for her to provide the ultimate seal of approval. However, Linda was no pushover and wanted to have all her questions answered before Liz made the trip to down to Florida to see the estate, especially during Covid.

Once they accessed the Zoom link, they made pleasantries, and Ira enquired about Linda's treatments. He was happy to hear she had only one remaining chemo session and was scheduled for the Covid vaccine. Ira sensed Linda's hesitancy and came prepared for the meeting; he held up the large, official-bound will for mother and daughter to see.

"I had my office send you both a copy of the will by FedEx. Here it is!" He opened to the title page, which indicated it was a formal legal document with Liz's name front and center, and held up a few other pages for them.

"You'll be able to review it before Liz comes down, and I'll go over all the details with her in person as well before we see the villa," he said matter-of-factly.

"Well, that certainly looks official." Linda nodded and mollified at the hefty legal document in his hands.

"It is."

"Ira." Linda took out a yellow legal pad of questions she had scribbled to look official and also remind herself. "I wanted to know how long were you representing this Missus Barrett for?" Linda put on her bifocals, giving her a more serious look.

"Fifteen years exactly."

"And you said you never met her?" she queried.

"Linda, I know this is hard to believe, but I would say eighty-five percent of my meetings are now by Zoom or telephone call. Some of my clients live here, and some live internationally. I see some clients in person, but I have not seen many for years on end. Now with Covid, it's almost all virtual," he explained.

"I see." Linda nodded. "And you really have no idea why she left the villa to Liz?"

"Again, there are many wealthy widows living down here who have to make decisions about their estates at the end of their lives when they don't have any heirs. Some leave the bulk of their fortunes to charity, but I have seen it all—bequests to butlers, staff, pets, and friends. Doris Duke, one of the wealthiest women in America, famously left the bulk and control of her fortune to her Irish butler Bernard Lafferty, and the designer Karl Lagerfeld left a substantial part of his fortune to his cat Choupette."

"These people are crazy." Linda shook her head in disbelief.

"No, because they are wealthy, they are not considered crazy but eccentric. Elsa Sloan Barrett may have been a bit eccentric, but she was lovely and sane. And she left this villa to your daughter. It is an extraordinary opportunity, if I don't say so myself."

Hearing Ira's conviction, Liz looked out on the ice-covered branches of the sad trees in the park and wondered how she would ever adjust to vibrant palms. She looked down at the questions she herself had scribbled on a piece of paper.

"Ira, Cary, my boyfriend, asked me to ask if the villa is bayside. He said the houses there are more valuable," she said softly.

"He's correct. Not only is it bayside," Ira intoned, "it's something like two or three lots. Liz, Villa Pompeii was a famous house back in its day. I've never been inside, but it is considered one of the grandest mansions on North Bay Road. The land alone must be worth twenty-five or thirty million dollars."

"You're kidding me," Linda gasped.

Liz immediately became weak in the knees. The idea of a house being worth that much money and nearly in her grasp seemed otherworldly and impossible. But here was a man, a serious man with an impeccable reputation, telling and showing her and her mother proof it was real. She tried hard to believe it but was having trouble digesting it. Ira then held up the black-and-white, xeroxed survey of the land he had gotten from the town files and pointed to a drawing of an outdoor pool, a greenhouse, and the tennis pavilion. Liz mentioned to Ira that she had been on the tennis team in college, and he thought it was more kismet. He offered to have his office and his assistant Marilyn help her with travel arrangements down to Miami. Ira would meet her at the airport, take her to lunch, read through the specifics of the will, and show her around the property. It all seemed so outrageous and normal at the same time. She and Linda thanked him profusely before they hung up, then she walked into her small galley kitchen and put on a kettle for jasmine tea. Ten minutes later, she saw Linda's incoming call for a FaceTime.

"Hi Mom, that was wild," Liz said." I can't believe it's on the bayfront."

"I'm so happy for you, baby. You seem to have won the lottery!" Linda exclaimed. "And you'll never believe this!" She was bursting with excitement.

"Believe what?"

"Well, when Ira mentioned there was a tennis pavilion, it jogged my memory, and I ran and got out your old college scrapbook. I looked back at some of the old clippings and the stories about you." She held up her daughter's white, leather-bound scrapbook.

"And?" Liz continuously tried to get her mother to the point.

"Remember? There were two." Linda flipped to the faded newspaper stories glued into the book. "One was in the paper in LA. The other story was in the *Miami Herald*. Liz, the *Miami Herald*!" Linda shrilled and pointed.

"So?"

"So, you don't think that's a coincidence?" Linda acted as if they won the lottery with this information.

"I don't know what to think anymore, but yes, it is sort of strange." She sipped some water after downing the tea.

"Well, maybe tennis has something to do with it?" Linda offered brightly. "Maybe Elsa Sloan Barrett saw the article in the *Miami Herald*?"

"You think? But that was years ago."

"I just think you'd better not forget to pack your suntan lotion… and your old college racquet! Well, now I'm convinced…. When do you think you want to go down?"

"Next Friday, so I can be back for your last chemo appointment on Tuesday. Ira's putting me up at the Edition."

"That's so nice." She paused. "Liz, something tells me this is going to change your life," Linda declared.

"For the worse?"

"No, for the better. I think it's high time *we* got the hell out of New York." Linda paused.

"We?" Liz laughed.

"That's right. We! And don't forget to pack that cute, old tennis skirt. You know the one with the pleats."

"Mom, are you sure and one hundred percent comfortable now?" Liz asked nervously, as if the wrong answer would pop her high like a pin would a helium balloon.

"My dearest daughter. I have only one thing to say… *Run*, don't walk!"

One thing was for sure, despite all their original doubts, after seeing the will and hearing about the eccentric rich, her mother was already mentally packing and sending Liz to the land of sunshine and oranges.

Chapter 6

She couldn't believe she was actually in Miami. The first thing Liz noticed when she deplaned and looked down at the airport floor, was the black onyx, speckled terrazzo inlaid with golden bronze shells and sea creatures. Terrazzo, of course! She was now in Florida, and everything seemed a bit more stylish and whimsical. Liz had listened to her mother's advice; she tuned out Cary's overly cautious remaining concerns and decided to roll the dice and forge ahead. When she discovered Ira's office was paying for a first-class plane ticket, it was the sprinkles on the ice cream cone.

"Broke and flying first? What's next, bankrupt and flying private?" She laughed to herself. It had all been a reminder of her past life, a pre-Covid world of work and travel; the absurdly early 7 a.m. morning flight out of Kennedy Airport and the even earlier Uber ride to the airport had Liz setting her alarm for the first time in months, and the 4:30 a.m. wake-up was just as jarring as she remembered. When she arrived at Kennedy Airport, the American Airlines terminal seemed deserted and ghostly. Once she boarded the 727, checked her carry-on in the overhead bin, and buckled herself to her first class seat, she passed out from sheer exhaustion despite her uncomfortable N95 mask. She had seen a glimpse of herself in an airport mirror in her plastic shield and mask and thought she looked like an original cast member of *Star Trek*. She thought about how strange the world had become as she dozed off. She only woke up when the pilot indicated they were landing in Miami and the stewardess firmly asked her to put her seat back up and buckle herself in. The frigid, dark, and chaotic city she had just left seemed a world away as she looked out the plane window, seeing the white clouds part and contrasting the turquoise sea below.

"Am I crazy to be doing this?" she questioned herself, rolling her carry-on luggage onto the terrazzo floors and peering into the crowd to find a familiar stranger. Looking like a long lost relative, Ira Reznick met her in baggage claim. His six foot four inch frame seemed to balance a prodigious belly spreading over a white belt, and she hadn't realized he would be so much taller in person. He waved, and she could see his smiling blue eyes which seemed to match his light blue hospital mask. She quickly made her way over, wheeling her secondhand Louis Vuitton rolling suitcase and satchel. She may have lived on Avenue A, but she always had the good stuff when she traveled. She had carefully bought each piece in thrift and used clothing stores in LA and Palm Beach when she was flush after a shoot or job. She removed her plastic visor and lowered her mask for a moment to say hello.

"Uncle Ira!" She waved.

"Liz! It's so nice to meet you. You're even prettier in person." Ira gave her a small elbow bump. "Wait, I'm probably not supposed to say that these days. I guess I'm too old to know what's PC." He shrugged.

"It's so nice to meet you in person too, and thanks for picking me up! Are you sure you're comfortable inside the airport?" Liz mentioned and smiled at his light blue, old-school Izod shirt under the zip-up sweater.

"Don't worry," he said. "Sheila and I have been vaccinated. The only good thing about being sixty-nine and living in Florida is that it's the land of milk of magnesia...and vaccines!" He chortled.

She finally put her clear visor into her oversized, vintage YSL handbag after they entered the baggage area and walked towards the exit.

"No checked luggage?" He looked around.

"I just brought carry-on. I'm here for the weekend to check out the will and the house, sign all the papers, then I need to get back to New York for Mom's last treatment." Liz smiled, instantly comfortable with Ira and he with her. They walked outside, and Liz immediately felt the warmth of the sun, stopping for a moment to take it all in and soak in the morning's warm rays.

"How's Mom?" he asked.

"She's getting better. After I get back, I'm going to take her to get the second vaccine in a week or two. Once I do that, she'd love to come, if this is all real." Liz paused. "Half my friends and my boyfriend still think it's a scam or that there's some sort of catch!" She mentioned with nervous energy.

"Oh, it's real." Ira checked his classic, stainless-steel-and-gold Rolex Perpetual Datejust as they walked across the pathway to the garage area. "The car's in the lot that way." He motioned.

"I thought you might be hungry, so I had my office make a reservation at a place I think you'll like," he said. "It's called Call me Gaby, and we can go over everything before we head to the villa. My daughter and granddaughter love to go there when they're in town visiting; they have the best pizza." Ira insisted on taking Liz's rolling luggage from her out of the terminal to the parking lot. The drive to Call Me Gaby on Washington Avenue flew by as Ira explained more in-depth his working relationship with Elsa and other wealthy clients, most of whom had hired him by word-of-mouth.

"Miami, after all," he said, "is a small town. Everyone knows who's who."

Liz nodded and said she and Linda had also vetted him that way through close family friends who lived in Miami and that everyone seemed to agree he had a flawless reputation for being smart, discreet, and loyal and was a nice guy to boot. Ira smiled and revealed he always thought having a good name was the most important asset, given his unique childhood. His parents had been born in Poland, and his father met his mother in a Red Cross camp after the war. She had been in Bergen-Belsen and weighed only ninety pounds when the Allies liberated the notorious concentration camp. After desperately trying to find their relatives before learning they had been murdered, his parents married, emigrated, and settled in the new state of Israel where Ira was born. His family were proud settlers of the new state; his father had fought in the

War of Independence. His father's one remaining cousin had settled in Brooklyn, and in the 1950s, his parents decided to join what was left of their family in the US and decided to uproot once more. They all had to adjust to another, totally new land, new climate, and new language, but Ira adapted quickly despite the awkward teen years. He was tall but shy and his photographic memory gave him a leg up on all his exams. By the time he graduated high school, Ira was the valedictorian of his class, and his height allowed him to play basketball which helped him on his college applications and earn a scholarship. He eventually attended Harvard Law School, and when he graduated, he met his future wife, Sheila Goldberg, at a dance in the Catskills where he was working as a waiter during the summer. After dating and quickly getting engaged, his future in-laws, who lived in South Beach, persuaded him to set up shop in Miami so they could see their daughter and eventual grandchildren. Ira decided he'd had enough of cold New England winters, and it didn't take long for him to agree. He and Sheila moved down after their wedding. Ira mentioned to Liz that Miami reminded him a bit of Tel Aviv with the white deco buildings and subtropical climate. Not to mention, the large amount of Holocaust survivors and pensioners who had relocated there to enjoy their golden years. His parents also decided to move down to Miami for that reason, and they lived there well into their eighties. Once he had set out his own shingle, older survivors who knew Ira's parents sent him business, and he developed a reputation as a smart and caring young man who allowed the pensioners to pay over time. Ira and Sheila eventually felt secure enough to start their own family, and over the next few decades, they raised their daughter Lara and son Mitchell, first in a small walk-up on James Avenue and then on tony Hibiscus Island as his practice grew. It had been a good life. They loved the weather, their friends, and the lifestyle; best of all, it allowed Ira to play golf on most days at the nearby La Gorce Country Club. Not to mention, you couldn't beat the income tax situation!

When they arrived at Call Me Gaby, Ira parked the car in a nearby lot, and they walked to the chic outdoor restaurant. He gave the female hostess his name and reservation and waved to the maître d' who seemed to know him. Liz noticed that only half the patrons were wearing masks; it seemed that her mother's Covid rumors were true. Florida, apparently, was a bit more oblivious to the pandemic, and the popular Republican governor, DeSantis, was more pro business and anti-shutdown than the rest of the country. Ira gallantly pulled out Liz's chair and once seated, they perused the menu. They both decided on toasting with some wine, even though Ira said he usually eschewed during lunch. The waiter brought two glasses to the table—a glass of Chianti for Ira and a glass of French rosé for Liz. They removed their masks at the table and clinked glasses.

"Congratulations, Liz. I'm really happy for you." Ira beamed.

"I still can't believe all of this." She smiled, happy to be eating outside in the warm sun rather than shivering under a heater.

"It's unusual, but these things do happen. I think I mentioned I once worked on a will where someone once left 2.5 million dollars to their poodle. That was a bit more complicated because the kids were left with nothing." He laughed.

"I don't want to be annoying since I know I asked you before," Liz asked for the last time, "but you really don't remember who recommended Elsa or how you met her? I thought that might give me a clue or two on why she left me the villa." Liz sipped the pale pink liquid which seemed to blend with her lovely skin and looked around. She took in the colorful, chic, patterned pillows and the tiny chirping birds dipping their beaks into the tiny birdbath fountain. It felt like an authentic European restaurant with alfresco dining and long, luxuriating afternoon meals. This was certainly a world away from ramen and sitting outside in the freezing cold; no wonder everyone was moving to Miami. The fluffy clouds above had created some cover, but it seemed surreal to Liz to be sitting outside without a hat or gloves in December. They made small talk as the waiter brought out the first courses, a delicious white truffle pizza served on the simple wooden board and simmering meatballs for Ira in a small steel pot.

"This is amazing, Uncle Ira. I do love the vibe here…it kind of reminds me of the Florida version of Ivy at the Shore in Santa Monica.

I used to go there a lot on business." She shrugged. "When I was still working."

"Sheila loves it there, too. You're right," he said as he looked around. "I do see some similarities." He sipped the ruby red liquid.

"Regarding Elsa…" He paused and got back to the subject at hand. "I remember she called my office about fifteen years ago. I had a profile in *Ocean Drive* magazine. They did an article on the top Miami lawyers, and I got a lot of referrals from that. At the time, I simply thought she found me because of the article, but she never outwardly mentioned it. I did think It was odd that she didn't want to meet in person; I assumed she was old and infirm, but she didn't balk at my rates," he explained.

"Why did she first call you?" Liz looked at him coolly. Ira was the age her father Joe would have been had he still been alive. The realization saddened her, and it hit Liz just how much she missed her father and yearned for a father-figure in her life.

"Why does anyone that age call a lawyer?" Ira also took a piece of pizza with his fork and knife. His simple gold wedding ring settled into the ridge of his finger. "Estate planning, wills, plots, those sorts of things. I really thought she was an elegant old bird and enjoyed speaking with her on the phone. She was always very lovely, and she also seemed up on things, politics, the news, etc. She didn't live in the past. The only time I really started to take notice of her was when she mentioned being ill and started talking about putting the villa in trust. I was intrigued, and since Sheila and I had plans to attend a cocktail party at another client's who lived near her on North Bay Road, I decided to drive by the house. When I did, my mouth dropped open." He spooned a plump, luscious meatball in tomato sauce onto his plate from the small metal pot.

"Why's that?" Liz raised an eyebrow.

"You'll see. The survey I sent you doesn't do the property justice." He nodded.

"So, explain the five-year thing to me? I don't quite understand." Liz put on her vintage Chanel sunglasses after the sun burst through the passing clouds.

"Elsa told me she wanted you to experience and enjoy her home and not make any rash decisions about selling it. She was savvy about real estate prices and the market and didn't want the house to be a teardown."

"So why five years?"

"She actually asked for my advice on it. She put enough money aside for the taxes on the property for five years, which are relatively inexpensive at eighty-five thousand dollars a year."

"That sounds like a lot to me." Liz looked wide eyed at the figure.

"Well, if the house is sold, the new owner would have to pay two percent of current real estate taxes—that's where they get you in Florida. Two percent of thirty-five million dollars is a lot of shekels." Ira smiled.

"I see." Liz toyed with her pizza crust.

"She also put aside a million dollars a year—the bulk of her estate—for you to run and upgrade the property as you see fit, as well as a small stipend for expenses."

Liz's eyes widened. "Really? That much?"

"It's a big property and in total disrepair; you'll have to be smart in what you do. Even with that much money, you can only spend it on the property—not on yourself. I approve the bills." He smiled, and his eyes twinkled.

"Seems like you both thought of everything!" Liz laughed.

"She really wanted you to make it your own, and we both thought that after five years, you would know what you wanted to do. By the way, you only have to be there six months and one day to become a Florida resident. After five years, you can sell the property, keep it, or rent it out. Once you officially sever ties and move, you would no longer have to pay New York state and city taxes, which I advised her would be a fortune, after becoming a Florida resident, It's a very smart plan, if I say so myself." Ira's kindly eyes crinkled at the creases.

"So, you even figured out my tax savings if I sell or rent. You really are my Uncle Ira now." Liz laughed.

"Yes, that's why you hire Ira Resnick. I saved you millions of dollars if you ever decide you don't want to keep the house. That being said, you could also make a fortune renting it after the first six months, which would be my recommendation. Anyway, this all seemed to please Elsa. I think she knew the house was overgrown and run down, and I'm sure it hasn't seen a paint job in seventy-five years."

She smiled; her pale turquoise eyes danced. "I still don't know why Elsa would go to all this trouble for me?"

"It seems that she wanted you to know about her and her story. Here…" He pulled out a manilla envelope from his briefcase. "I have something for you."

"What's this?" Liz asked wide-eyed as she looked down at the wrinkled manilla envelope. Her name was inscribed on the front in floral, old-fashioned penmanship. "Can I open it here? I'm scared." Liz smiled nervously.

"Of course. Liz, there is nothing to be scared of." Ira smiled.

Liz tentatively opened the yellow manilla envelope. She withdrew a faded, old, Florentine-patterned book.

"Oh, look." Liz flipped through the pages and saw the handwriting. "This must be Elsa's diary.

"Maybe when you read it, you'll understand why she left you the house." Ira nodded.

"Are you sure she has no relatives? No one?" Liz looked a bit flush with excitement.

"She told me she was quite alone in the world except for an old, faithful Polish housekeeper, a maid named Zosia. She is paid by the trust to work there for as long as she wants, and she gets her health insurance paid for. She speaks very little English," Ira said in an informative tone. He was thorough and professional which Liz appreciated.

"Wait. You mean she left me a mansion with a housekeeper who doesn't speak English?" Liz raised an eyebrow.

"Here, I bought you a Polish-English dictionary, too." He handed her a small Berlitz book he had brought along in a small, brown paper bag.

"Seriously?"

"Seriously." He chuckled, "Look if want something you just translate it and write it down and give it to her…" He flipped to a page and put on his bifocals. "Eggs…*Jajka*."

"*Jajka*. Okay this is going to be fun. Zosia, I want some..." She flipped through the book looking. "I want some *tampony*."

"What's that?"

"Tampons, Uncle Ira! Tampons!"

He laughed out loud. She started flipping through a few of the pages of the diary as they continued lunch but decided on reading it all later. Once they finished eating and had espressos, Ira took her through an additional copy of the will and pointed out specific paragraphs and highlights. He then took out a platinum American Express card from his worn leather wallet to pay for the bill. Ira Reznick was clearly successful, but he was low key, not flashy and had that rare combination of high-low that appealed to Liz. Her father Joe had that quality. She sadly thought the two men would have been friends if they had known each other.

"Thank you so much for lunch." Liz smiled politely and looked down at the diary. "And for this! I can't wait to read Elsa's diary!"

"Ready?" Ira stood and looked at his client intently as he walked around and pulled out her chair. Liz Galin was really pretty, funny, and one lucky girl. She stood, put the diary safely in her handbag, and gulped the last of her wine to steady herself. She looked directly into the brightly shining Florida sun.

"Ready whenever you are." She smiled. "North Bay Road here we come."

Chapter 7

Unlike New York, Miami has always embraced the "car as an extension of themselves" culture as people spent more time in their cars and ultimately spent more money on them. Everywhere one looked, there were racing and luxury cars in vivid Miami shades: canary yellows and sizzling tomato reds. The owners themselves often embodied their vehicles, the way some people looked like their dogs, in what was known as "Miami Style." They were impeccably groomed with architectural stubble or ample cleavage, poured into tight jeans or miniskirts, tinted sunglasses, wore the requisite Chanel or Gucci accoutrements, and of course, sported the ubiquitous Florida tan. Often, though, the price of the car proportionally outpaced the cost of the real estate. Someone driving a Ferrari, Aston Martin or a Lamborghini could arrive home and park it in front of a modest, two- or three-room bungalow with five or six similar cars vying for spaces. Parking in Miami was at a premium and would often create tension with neighbors as cars of every model, color, and flavor poured onto the streets, jamming into driveways and making up spots.

Ira was no exception when it came to his car of choice. While he didn't opt for something young or flashy, his Mercedes-Benz was his baby, pristine and well cared for. He had it primped, detailed, and waxed every other week, and he drove smoothly like a seasoned captain at the helm.

The transition from South of Fifth to the more residential La Gorce seemed to fly by in stages. Seedy liquor stores turned into boutiques and orthodox Jewish day schools. As Ira's gleaming, black Mercedes-Maybach made a left onto Alton Road, it was lined with comfortable, respectable, Mediterranean-inspired and art deco homes with a few, newly constructed, glass box–style houses thrown in for good measure.

"Now you'll see what North Bay Road is all about!" Ira said proudly as the car turned into the enclave and started to slow. Liz's eyes started to widen once they passed the sterile Mount Sinai hospital complex. Her spine rose as she took in the huge, gated, palatial mansions to her left and the beautiful, aqua bay beyond the mansions. She quickly noted each property was built in a different architectural style and reflected the tastes of the wealthy over the last hundred years. However, it seemed that most of the homes dated the 1920s and '30s when the Mediterranean and Spanish revival was the rage. There were Roaring '20s–Mediterranean mansions; midcentury modern, sleek, low-slung houses dotted with palms and geometric patterned walls; curved, deco-powdered confections of the '30s in white, yellow, and frothy cream; and A-frame edifices with white marble drives that looked like they belonged in Vegas.

Multiple construction projects loomed with cranes overhead indicating another boom was well underway. Everywhere one looked, there were the ever-present construction crews, legal and illegal teams and equipment, not to mention the startling and omnipresent bed of noise. The burly crews also posted bold notices about trespassing and sported twenty-four-hour cameras as all were worried that the coveted, and limited, equipment would disappear overnight; even the construction teams needed protection!

In the last decade, white, stark, modern mansions had sprung up like tropical weeds, offering a new aesthetic and taking advantage of the sun and bay views with their office building–sized sheets of glass and teak framing. Another thing Liz noticed was that one thing all the bayside houses on North Bay Road had in common were the gates: gates, gates, gates, and more gates. There were large, metal, filigree gates; oversized pillars topped with ornate carved pineapples above polished mahogany; electronic, metal sliding walls; and ominous, industrial steel, modern ones with digital keypads. They existed as not only a protective barrier but a visual one that plainly communicated, "This is a rarefied world. You can look from the street but cannot enter. Don't come too close. Keep out!" Liz sat silently from the passenger seat, taking in this new world.

"So, you said your boyfriend is a doctor at Mount Sinai in New York?" Ira enquired. "The hospital is even walkable to the villa," he mentioned.

"I thought they were somehow connected, but Cary said they aren't. It's been hard not to be able to see him, especially while I have been caring for Mom. He is basically the King of the Covid Wing," Liz lamented a bit.

"That must be hard…" Ira nodded in a fatherly fashion as he started to slow the car. "Well, we're almost there. I arranged for Zosia to meet us and open the house for us."

"I cannot believe the house comes with a housekeeper." Liz marveled.

"She's been working there for thirty years, and the only thing she seems to know how to say in English is 'where is my check?'" he joked, and they both broke out laughing.

"Wow, this neighborhood is really something." She craned her neck at the array of mansions. "I never imagined it would be this…" Liz struggled for the right words.

"This what?" Ira turned. She saw herself in the reflection of the green lenses of his gold wire Ray Bans.

"This *rich*." She laughed. The car pulled down the street, and Ira slowed as he approached her new home.

"Speaking of rich…" He motioned to the white, modern mansion ahead on her left. "There's new money like your neighbor's house over there, which was just sold to some Latin pop star, and there's old money…" He idled the car dramatically before making a left on the property and pulling in, "like yours. Here we are… Welcome…to Villa Pompeii." He turned to see her expression, and his eyes glistened.

Liz gasped and held her chest as she was confronted by the regal, high, rusted, rod iron gates. The massive, gated estate literally took her breath away.

"You're kidding me!" she whispered under her breath and turned to Ira with misty eyes. "You're kidding me, right?"

He let out a deep gust of breath. "This my dear is, as they say in the old country, the real schmear!" Ira whistled as they drove into the car port area past the huge, Renaissance, white marble fountain featuring a naked woman with angel wings in glorious repose placed in the center of the courtyard. She stared back at Liz with pursed lips and vacant eyes surrounded by hovering and concerned winged cherubs. The olive-streaked and black-stained marble basin was filled with thick leaves and century-old, decomposing storm debris. One could imagine it cleaned and with working water spray, but currently, it was under solitary, neglected duress.

"I have a lot of wealthy clients and have been to some of the nicest homes on the beach, and this well, this, Liz, is…next level." He craned his head as the car came to a stop.

It was one of those clear, perfect Miami days where the blazing sun had broken through the clouds, but it wasn't about the weather, it was about the optimism. Liz was breathless as she stared at the outline of the palatial villa and its faded, sun-bleached and undulating terracotta tiles set against the thickly slathered, foundation concrete and climbing bougainvillea. The electric pink and light orange canopy was such a visual pop against the aqua sky it was hard to look directly at it without sunglasses. The villa's roofline seemed to go on indefinitely, and in some faint part of her brain, she heard violins playing a concerto.

"Is this really mine?" She shook her head.

Ira looked at her dumbstruck. "Well? What do you think?"

"I don't know what to say and…and I've never been good at… speechless." Her legs buckled under her a bit, but she steadied herself against the Mercedes. She tightly squeezed her eyes shut, getting accustomed to the new sounds: birds, swaying palms, and silence—no cars, fire engines, or New York street noise. It was the sound of privacy. *It's the sound*, she thought, *of being rich.*

"Liz?" Ira saw she was in a trance. "Liz, dear."

"Yes?" She turned, and he saw a lone tear streaming down her face.

"Are you upset?" Ira cocked his head.

"I'm…not." She gulped. "I'm…just blown away and in shock." She turned from the massive fountain and regal edifice. "Why would a woman I have never met do all this…" She turned, her eyes pleading for answers, "for me?"

"I'm not sure, but I have a feeling you'll find out. For the time being, I'll tell you what I would tell my own kids; just try to relax and enjoy it." Ira patted her hand in a comforting, fatherly way. She shook her head in disbelief, trying but still not able to accept the advice. An eerie, deserted gloom added to the overwhelming sense of faded grandeur and encroaching jungle.

"It's…" She turned to Ira, feeling impossibly like a little girl. "I don't know. It just feels…too much."

"Like, you-don't-want-it-too-much?" He looked at her with a fictional question mark hanging over his head.

"I don't know. At first, I thought it would be a normal, cozy house, then maybe something on the water, but I certainly didn't expect this." She slowly rotated taking in the entire house and the vast estate. "Did you?"

"I've driven by a few times, but this is the first time I've been inside the gates. I see what you are saying though. It's literally quite enormous." Ira turned and saw a small woman. "Oh, that must be Zosia. She said she would open the house and say hello but give you some time alone to go through it alone."

They both surveyed a squat but diminutive figure waiting on top of the stairs that led up to the massive oak doors. Ira waved. "Hi there," he called out.

"I thought you said she doesn't speak English?" Liz asked, confused.

"I had my legal assistant call the Polish society here and hire a translator. Her name is Sara Samplawska; here is her number if you need something really important." Ira handed Liz a small business card which she put in her jeans pocket. Zosia was standing in place, her thick arms hanging at her side like a toy soldier. She looked small and dour. Her faded kerchief and worn apron would have seemed out of place and anachronistic anywhere but Villa Pompeii.

As Liz and Ira approached the house, she bobbed and gave a small curtsy. "I, Zosia. Witamy!"

"Zosia, it is so nice to meet you." Liz extended her hand which was ignored. Instead, Zosia promptly handed an envelope to Ira.

"What is this?" Ira looked at the crumpled gift.

"*Klucze.*" Zosia motioned for them into the inner courtyard.

"Keys." He shook the small, crumpled envelope and heard the jangle of the keys.

"Well, it's very nice to meet you," Liz gushed.

"I go…. I see you Monday, Miss," Zosia said without emotion.

"Zosia, I have so many questions," Liz started talking as Zosia walked past her towards the garage area and her small apartment.

She turned and bowed again. "*Witamy*! *Piekna.*"

"What is *piekna*?" Liz smiled and whispered.

"*Piekna…Piekna*?" Ira scanned the dictionary. "A beauty."

Zosia walked towards her rusted Honda.

"Zosia. Come inside, please?" Liz offered.

"No, *panienka.*" She bowed again. "You new…Miss Elsa," she said downcast, a few translucent tears appeared as she pointed to the interior of the house. "Kitchen. *Jajka. Mleko.*"

"Eggs?" Liz called after her. Ira was impressed as Liz was clearly a quick study. Zosia nodded yes as she quickly walked away.

"Well, she seemed sweet." Ira shrugged. "And milk and eggs in the fridge."

"Sweet but a bit creepy, no?" Liz craned her neck as Zosia got into her old Honda and drove out of the gate. It all seemed so surreal as Liz and Ira walked into the house in a dreamlike trance. As they walked slowly through the arched doors, they first encountered an open-air, symmetrical, Moroccan-style, inner courtyard with graceful arches surrounding a reflection pool which only contained rainwater and debris.

"Oh, this is so glamorous." Liz's eyes widened as she scanned the well-proportioned outdoor courtyard room. The sandstone arched pillars were lined in circumspect glamor facing their symmetrical partners on all four sides, suggesting a royal harem or grand Moroccan *hotel particular.*

One imagined Parisian models on a rúnway lifting their birdlike arms in diaphanous silk sheaths to an exotic beat.

"It reminds me of a shoot I did for *Vogue* at La Mamounia." She viewed the grandeur of the '20s architecture. "I cannot believe how beautiful this is. We could be in North Africa, Spain, or Italy," she said like a little girl in awe of a new doll propped high on a store shelf.

They stood in the center of the courtyard, taking in the graceful cream carved arches etched with vines and acanthus leaves that surrounded the entry area. Ira shook his head at the amazing sight and then led the way to the next set of massive wooden castle-like doors to enter the interior of the villa. They were studded with black, rod iron rivets, and he pulled hard to open them as he motioned for Liz to follow him.

"Here we are and…" He sighed. "And there it is."

"There's what?" Liz asked somewhat perplexed as he stopped in his tracks looking down at the entry floor. Ira pointed down at an ancient, inlaid, black-and-white mosaic floor in reverence; the figures of a spiny lobster engulfed by an octopus came into view as she approached the remarkable sight. He stopped and took an old black-and-white faded photocopy of a mosaic out of his briefcase, held it up to the light and compared it to the original floor in front of them.

"That's super cool." Liz shrugged, not quite concentrating and instead looking ahead at the grand curved stone staircase.

"It's more than super cool, Liz." Ira looked up at her and pointed with awe. "It's history." He handed her the photocopy.

"I don't understand." Liz glanced at the photocopy. It looked like it was taken from a 1930s newspaper article.

"It's a mosaic floor originally excavated from Pompeii." Ira approached it as his voice declined an octave.

"Are you serious?" Liz took in the modern looking black-and-white floor and compared it with the photocopy. It was intricate and incredibly realistic.

"It looks like it could have been done today." Liz smiled at Ira and marveled.

"Elsa made a provision in the will that if you ever sell the house, this mosaic floor must go to the museum in Pompeii lest they want to tear it down."

"Wait!" Liz cocked her head in astonishment. "The villa comes with a mosaic from Pompeii? Real Pompeii? Like spewing-ash-and-volcanoes-covering-people Pompeii?" she exclaimed in wonder.

"Yes, Liz. Hence the name Villa Pompeii. Get it?" Ira smiled broadly.

"I'm quickly getting it, but I'm trying hard to believe it." She stared intently at the beautiful details.

"It's quite famous and very, very valuable both from a financial and historical perspective. It's a provision in the will," he repeated. "It was a fairly extensive legal issue I had with the museum over the years to avoid a lawsuit; as long as you keep the house and it's intact, it's yours to enjoy alone."

"Between Zosia and the floor, it's like living in an ancient museum. She's as old as Pompeii." She approached the mosaic from above. "I cannot believe what this floor must have seen."

Ira knelt down and ran his hand over the braille-like ancient mosaic and the repetitive black-and-white diamond motif. "Yes, it seems somewhat surreal."

"Death and destruction?" she offered.

"Why not look upon them as…love stories?" He looked up at her, his blue eyes clear and young despite his lined visage.

"Love stories? I didn't realize you were a romantic, Ira?"

"Why yes, love stories throughout the ages. It's something Elsa told me I'll never forget when we were talking about the mosaic. She said she always hoped it would end up in the hands of lovers who were entwined together forever. She added that's what she had always hoped for."

"Did she ever find that?" Liz asked, a bit bewildered.

"I think by the way she spoke of it, she didn't. But she did say, and I quote," he said, mimicking Elsa's upper-class accent, "'I hope our dear Liz enjoys it and finds that everlasting, eternal love.' That's what she said. 'Everlasting, eternal love.'"

"She said that? Elsa?" Liz cocked her head.

"She said that!" Ira nodded.

"Wow, Elsa was one happening lady." Liz's eyes sparkled.

"Yes, she was." Ira stood with authority. "Now let's go inside and see her house!"

Chapter 8

The Zoom was to take place at 3:45, breaking what would have been his prime-time afternoon reverie. G hated afternoon meetings as they interfered with the perfect location of sun over the deep end of his pool and achieving his more perfect tan, but he didn't want to appear to be difficult given his recent work schedule or lack thereof. Karolina had insisted it was the only time his manager Ryan could take the Zoom since he was back in LA where it was three hours earlier. She had mentioned he had a school appointment for his kids and a meeting afterwards.

"LA is a shit show, be glad you're in Miami!" Ryan Palermo offered a MacBook picture perfect view of his Malibu balcony. He was recently divorced, and although he had just turned fifty, he had a baby face that had people thinking he was in his early thirties. Ryan was handsome, smart as a whip, funny and worked like a madman; best of all he could hang and party all night with his clients and still make the breakfast meeting at the Polo Lounge by 8 a.m. His ability to deliver and also socialize with his clients was why he was considered one of the most successful managers in the business, and also divorced. As his ex-wife Haley would tell you, his career and choices were not conducive to married life, not to mention the bevy of young ladies he could never say no to.

"We're starting to float some tour dates. We think things look like they're going to open up by next September." Ryan sipped his latte as he nursed his hangover. He had been out on a bender the night before with a notorious rapper and had overindulged as usual to wake up with the room spinning and a strange model in his bed. "How's the new album coming?"

"I'm a bit blocked on the songwriting." G shrugged. "I only have one I like so far. I've scrapped the rest."

"Do you need some inspiration? I can hire you some. Miami is full of it," he said. Ryan had an old school guys guy approach to the business and felt client service extended to every sort of inappropriate activity. While he danced on the knife's edge of risky and un-P.C. behavior, when it came to work, he was a tough task master to his A-list clients many of whom needed a healthy dose of babysitting after all the partying.

"I'm fine. It comes to me when it comes." G shrugged.

"Well, I think you should start working with Chantal on choreography. We need a new, fresh look. Until then, the strategy is to keep you in front of the press. Stephanie and the PR team have some good things lined up." He downed the latte.

"Okay." G shrugged while drinking his own green smoothie.

"She has you on Joe Rogan's podcast which has huge numbers and best of all its remote. She also is setting up a local cover, *Ocean Drive* magazine." He popped an Advil.

"That sounds cool." G put his iPhone on FaceTime and paced the cream stone deck area of the pool with his tanned bare feet.

"They want to shoot you at the new house. Stephanie and I also thought we would introduce your new look, and we think it needs to be super Miami." Ryan waved his hands dramatically.

"What's super Miami?"

"You know, something all white, maybe with some Versace thrown in. You get it." Ryan visualized.

"Yeah, I do." G looked out at a super sleek, high tech, silver VanDutch 40.2 yacht slicing through the bay.

"How's the diet?" Ryan asked.

"I prefer the term 'lifestyle shift,'" G explained. "Good, I guess. I upped the yoga. Now I'm jogging and just eating sushi, salad, and juicing. I'm down a solid ten."

"I knew you'd do it. You always do." Ryan smiled broadly at the news.

"You know what I always say, 'I'm just a fat kid who's thin' or even better, 'it's not how thin I am, it's how fat I would be.'" G laughed. "I told Maria she had to stop cooking. Maybe once a month I give in. She and Karolina just order in salad or sushi for me here." He lit up and took a drag of a spliff. "It's so fucking boring."

"Well, you look better already. I'll have Stephanie go over all the details, send over Carmine to do your hair, and start getting the look down for the cover."

"Who's the writer?" G paced nervously. "Do they know the rules?"

"Look, we've gone over this a million times. You can't tell them not to ask about your childhood G. We can only make suggestions, like 'we want a forward looking piece' or 'Why go there? Everything's already been written.' Even though it hasn't." He punctuated the word "hasn't."

"Don't remind me." G grimaced.

"Sorry." Ryan tread softly knowing it was a sore spot.

"I know, but these people are snoops. Remember the one last year where they sent the reporter to the orphanage?" G grimaced.

"I get it, but this is a lifestyle piece. I don't think you have anything to worry about. *Ocean Drive* is super glossy, it's not investigative journalism," Ryan said optimistically.

"Sounds good, I guess." G shrugged.

"How's the new place? Are you enjoying it?"

"It's just what I needed." G smiled brightly.

"Good. Karolina told me you had some trouble with a paparazzi that tried to break in."

"Yeah, but the police got him, and they deleted the photos."

"G, you have to keep your clothes on." Ryan scratched his balls which was ironic since he was sitting on his deck without a shirt and in boxers.

"I was more worried that I looked fat." He shook his handsome head.

"Keep up the diet and keep your bathing suit on. I can't pack stadiums with a pot belly." Ryan offered the model walking by in a micro thong a hit of his spliff which she bent over and inhaled.

"It's so fucking boring." G grimaced again.

"You'll find out what boring is when no one shows up to your tour dates." Ryan gave the model the five-minute sign.

"That's not going to happen," G said in a forceful tone.

"We all need to do our part brother. Glad you're off the rice and beans…and you also need to get laid," Ryan scolded.

"That's my business."

"No, that's my business. It's show business baby, remember? Show and business!" Ryan voice went an octave higher. "Stephanie and I will set up a night out with Bebe Blanchet. She's my new client, and she's hot."

"I hate that shit," G said defensively.

"You gotta get out of your damn house of yours. You know the rumors, baby." Ryan paced on the terrace of his beach house and then walked to his bar, pouring some 1942 over ice with a lime even though it was only 11:30 in the morning LA time.

"Hair o' the dog." He lifted his glass and toasted as the blonde model named Brandee moved back into frame. Ryan reached over and snapped her thong. G shook his head at Ryan's bad behavior at his beach front divorced man cave.

"Don't remind me." G looked out towards the bay and the distant skyscrapers looming in downtown Miami.

"Reminding you is my job my brother," he said with little emotion. "You think J.Lo doesn't understand the value of a little arm candy?"

"Okay." G shook his head and looked at the sparkle of the sun against the distant glass towers, and Brandee's toned and spray tanned twenty-one year old ass.

"Set it up."

Chapter 9

After the Great Miami Hurricane of 1926 and the financial devastation following the height of the Great Depression, Carl Fisher was desperate to sell his North Bay Road mansion. Unfortunately for him, there were no buyers despite its apparent grandeur. In fact, he was so desperate to sell his opulent estate that he actually sent a letter to Edsel Ford offering the house to him at an insanely low price, who politely declined. Not deterred, Fisher sent him a second letter asking him to at least take a look at his beloved property, which he also rebuffed. Fisher was never able to sell the estate and eventually lost it to foreclosure along with the rest of his fortune. Located at 5020 North Bay Road, the three-story Renaissance bayfront palazzo is still considered one of Miami's most prestigious estates. It has 270 feet of bayfront and a marina for a large yacht. It features twelve bedrooms, a grand double staircase, nineteen baths, a five-car garage, hand-painted ceilings and gold leaf walls. Best known for its eighty-five foot observation tower it is now replete with an elevator. Built by architect August Geiger, it was commissioned and owned by a man who in his prime had everything, not to mention an island named after him; Fisher Island which he traded seven prime acres for Commodore Vanderbilt's two-hundred-foot yacht *The Eagle* in a card game. According to public tax records, Fisher's North Bay Road estate was sold in 2017 for $16.5 million. In 2005, the Miami market once again plunged, and the grand estate was sold in 2008 for only $7 million to savvy Italian developer and race car driver Ugo Columbo. After extensive renovations, it was recently offered on the market for $40 million. Emblematic of the booms and the busts Miami has endured, things have constantly changed on North Bay Road, but the view remains constant.

Liz and Ira stood in awe before Elsa's grand staircase, bowled over by the fluidity and graceful curve of the endless wrought iron filigree banister and the stained glass topped rotunda above. Interestingly the actual construction of the stairs had been done in a rough-hewn concrete which Liz thought was quite chic as a contrast to the overall gilded extravagance of the estate. Someone had amazing taste when they designed this castle back in the day, she thought. To the left was the cavernous living room with rows of arched palladium French doors leading to the bay view and a commanding fireplace mantle as tall as a sentry guard and carved from frothy, whipped Provençal limestone offset by the dark polished oak paneling. The high arched doors mirrored each other on both sides, and they wandered through the grand reception rooms and over the threadbare silk Orientals and then into the vaulted dining room with a huge, circular, 1920s, black wrought iron chandelier.

"Sort of like King Arthur's Court." Ira shook his head in awe. They both took in the remarkable and elegant layout and reception rooms off rooms. There was even one smaller room dedicated to just the china; rows and rows of formal Limoges, service and dulled silver in leaded glass fronted and cedar cabinets.

"This house could use twelve maids though." Liz sighed at the dust an inch deep on a pair of marble topped consoles.

As they took in the overall grandeur, they came upon a small bedroom off the kitchen which appeared to be a maid's room. It looked as if it had been recently converted into a sleeping area with a sagging daybed and a solitary aluminum medical walker, a worn wheelchair and some random medical equipment which lent a depressing air.

"I think they must have turned this into Elsa's bedroom toward the end when she couldn't walk up and down the stairs." Ira surmised, surveying the bottles of prescription pills lined up like soldiers. Liz quickly peeked into the room as if she were intruding on a private moment and then balked at entering the room as it smelled of rancid antiseptic and the medicinal smell seared her nostrils and reminded her of her own mother's recent cancer treatments. Liz also scanned an array of mundane prescription bottles on a small nightstand and Elsa's name sadly reinforced the reality that this has been a real woman's room; flesh and bones and immediately wanted to back away. Ira walked over and picked up one of the bottles and also confirmed the name was indeed Elsa's. While the small room boasted a bay view and French doors, it brought home the humanity and finality that a real person lived and most likely passed here.

"Let's come back." Liz backed out with a sad feeling. She needed fresh air and a change of scenery to counter the stale odor and medical banality which signified the finality of Elsa's life.

"I want to see the upstairs." She tried to put on a good show.

As they walked back to the main entry foyer, Liz noticed an unobtrusive, dark paneled door next to the staircase.

"I wonder what's in there?" She pointed. They were both feeling the same thing as Liz walked over and nonchalantly opened a carved mahogany door which boasted a carved coat of arms. The grand letter "B" for Barrett was raised and clearly inscribed in the center of the crest on the door and she had noticed it elsewhere. The graphic icon was unobtrusively implanted in fireplaces, dentals, fireplace mantels and brass doorknobs throughout the villa owing to what must have been quite a large ego or the prevailing trend of the period when someone commissioned such an imposing estate.

"Wow, what is that?" They both poked their heads into the seemingly dark interior as they opened the door. There was an old fashioned electric light switch to the left of the doorframe which most likely hadn't been used in eighty years. Ira switched it on and voilà, it worked as the frosted glass sconce illuminated the interior and they were shocked to find a small mechanical elevator. It was only six feet in diameter, but they could see it had been operated by a pulley and a stained, thick, plaited rope which became apparent when turned on.

"Wow, this is from the year one!" Ira shook his head. He had never seen anything quite like it; a manual elevator.

"Look how beautiful it is though!" Liz was taken with the romantic, hand painted interior walls, in turquoise and white chinoiserie design of an ancient Chinese palace. If one looked close enough there was a small figure of a young woman, a princess on a Great Wall motif, standing on a parapet. Had it been Elsa? She had blonde hair, blue eyes and looked strangely familiar. Had the architect implanted Elsa's image throughout the house as they had done with her initials?

"That's incredible." Ira put on his bifocals. "That could be you!"

"I wonder what they used this for?" Liz asked.

"I am sure the staff used it for luggage when guests arrived. It's quite a piece of history and I have never seen anything quite like it." Ira marveled at the ingenuity.

They both shrugged and closed the door and then started to ascend the grand staircase and when they reached the first landing, they encountered a gilded, Louis XVI sofa upholstered in faded, turquoise damask which faced them under a huge palladian window. It was perfectly frozen in time as if no one had ever taken the time to sit on the plumped-up cushion as they were too busy taking in the scenic view of the Bay although time had the fluff sagging a bit, like an aging movie star who eschewed having her eyes or neck done.

Ira led the way as they walked through cavernous rooms, and it reminded her of the Gritti Palace in Venice or a grand decaying palazzo overlooking the Grand Canal. And now it was hers; she couldn't wrap her head around the idea of it.

She and Ira walked down the bedroom wing into what was the grandest master bedroom on the floor. The double doors opened to reveal It was done in faded turquoise and disintegrating white silk which seemed to be a constant design theme and had a vaulted ceiling and a rococo bed with hanging drapes and tarnished golden gilded angels above the canopy. She was overcome with the beauty and tarnished old age of the room. The light reflected off the Baccarat crystal chandelier casting prism rainbows against the ornate moldings. She spotted a cobweb in one corner and shuddered.

"This must have been Elsa's master before she became too infirm," Ira said as he glanced around the room all done in elegant and feminine French antiques and a graceful and birdlike Louis IV writing desk. Layers of dust and grime covered the sills and the furniture.

"Oh look, there's a terrace as well." Liz looked beyond the decay and walked over to the view, opened one of a series of French doors with the slim and feminine bronze door handles onto the terra cotta terrace fronted by a regal, sculpted stone balustrade.

"The view is so beautiful." She smiled. "And you can see all of downtown Miami!" She beamed.

"Yes, I live on Hibiscus Island…it's in that direction." He whistled. "Wow, this is really something Liz." They both stood silently taking in the panorama and how remarkable and stunning the vista to downtown Miami was. It felt like one was on a tropical vacation only minutes from reality.

Finally, they both walked back in the bedroom, Ira closed and locked the French doors and they quietly looked at the closet area and then the grand master bath all done in white and pink veined marble with gold fixtures. The arched, closet doors boasted aged, silvered, and speckled mirrored glass cut in triangles and brass rivets in the shape of tiny rosebuds. Every faded detail was fit for a queen.

Suddenly, Liz stopped dead in her tracks. Ira could see she had turned an eggshell-white and was suddenly transfixed in place.

"Liz, are you okay? You look like you've just seen a ghost!" Ira said, somewhat alarmed. She breathed heavily and then she steadied herself against the wall and gulped and pointed. There on the bathroom hook, hanging limply against the door was the exact same Gloria Swanson robe she had back in her apartment in New York; raised bird of paradise, dragon pattern, fringes and all.

"Liz what's going on?" Ira noticed her heavy breathing and instant pallor.

"I…see that kimono style robe hanging on the bathroom door?" She gasped.

"Yes, it's…old but pretty." Ira shrugged.

"Ira, you have no idea, but I have the exact same one back in New York. How can that be?" Liz froze in place.

"Well, women are always showing up wearing the same outfit." Ira made light of it and shrugged.

"Yes, but not from the 1920s. No, this is different, Ira. I bought mine in LA in a thrift store, and the man who ran the store said it was owned by Gloria Swanson. I go to thrift stores all the time for my work as a stylist, and I have never seen another. I'm sorry, but I am totally freaked out." She cried softly.

"Over a kimono?" Ira shook his head.

"You don't understand; it's too much of a coincidence. There is no way we could have had the same robe, Ira." She shook her head and suddenly looked like a lost little girl. "I think we need to go." She emitted a low dry sob.

"Over a robe?"

"It's not that! There is no way we could have the same one, it's impossible and too much of a coincidence." She shook her head. "Look, it's all hand done." She pointed and tried to explain, "Can we go to the hotel? I'm feeling creeped out!"

"Sure, if you really feel uncomfortable." Ira seemed perplexed but softened at her apparent distress.

"I…just need some time to gather my thoughts." She walked over and inspected the robe. It was the exact replica of the one she had in her apartment down to the rich colors and silk needlepoint and as she ran her hand over the lovely, faded silk and her spine ran cold as it had a faint smell of lavender as hers had. It was also hand done, not machine made and there was no way it could have been done by another person, factory, or atelier. It had to have been done by the same person.

"I mean this was handmade almost a hundred years ago and it's exactly the same. And has the same smell of lavender." She turned and shook her head in disbelief. "I thought mine had to be one of a kind."

"Okay, okay. I think I get it." He paused. "I'll drive you to the hotel and we can meet back here tomorrow." Ira nodded.

"Thank you, Ira. I really appreciate it, you're the best." She immediately brightened and kissed him on the cheek at the thought of a clean separate and safe hotel room. They both walked back into the bedroom area expecting to see a ghost or Elsa standing there but the room was empty and serene, beams of sunlight streaming through the luminous French doors. Ira looked toward the French writing desk and noticed an envelope on the leather blotter.

"Liz, hon, come over here." He beckoned.

Liz approached the desk and also saw a plain cream envelope. In elegant calligraphy, she saw her name in beautiful penmanship. Elizabeth.

"She must have left it for you. I recognize her writing as she always sent me handwritten notes."

"Should I?" Liz picked up the envelope and hesitated opening it.

"Yes, go ahead." He nodded.

Liz opened the letter tentatively.

"Well, what does it say?" He looked over her shoulder.

"It's very nice. It says, *'Dear Liz,'*" Liz read aloud, "*'Welcome. I hope you will enjoy the villa. It's yours now, should you want it. I hope you do. Elsa. Ps. Remember, it's all about the view. It might change yours.'*" Liz looked up at him and paused. "That's strange… She said it's all about the view."

"Yes, I heard you."

"What do you think it means?"

"From a lawyer's perspective, I think it means you might learn something from the things you will see. For example, the view. Look, I have no idea Liz, but it seems to me you'll find out soon enough." Ira nodded.

"This is crazy weird like she is watching me. I am totally freaked out." Liz tried to smile but it was all too overwhelming. "Can we go now?" She pleaded.

"Okay, let's get you to the hotel."

Chapter 10

Art deco is derived from the French term "arts decoratifs" originally introduced in France before World War I. The movement became a global phenomenon when it was heralded in the International Exhibitino of Modern Decorative and Industrial Arts in Paris in 1925. Its forward and thoroughly modern design elements reflected a new world order propelling it to become a wildly popular and international trend influencing everything from fashion, film to architecture during the 1930s and '40s. During this period hundreds of art deco hotels were constructed in Miami's South Beach making it the largest collection of deco inspired hotels in the world. All were built in a myriad of derivative styles; streamline moderne, nautical moderne, med-deco which celebrated not only travel; trains and ocean liners but offered a cleaner more modern aesthetic marking the joyful exuberance of new technology. Gone was the more traditional, richer, darker sensuality and formality of the Spanish and Moroccan revival of the Roaring '20s summed up by Alva Johnson, Addison Mizner's Biographer as "Bastard-Spanish -Moorish-Romanesque -Gothic-Renaissance-Bull Market-Damn-The-Expense-Style" which preceded it. Often whimsical; stripped down and unadorned, the art deco aesthetic also offered an antidote to the strife of the Great Depression through its streamlined optimism and sensuality. In Miami, particularly, it also naturally seemed to coexist with the sun and the surf offering weary vacationers an aspirational and sun washed experience with its new white, wide-open spaces, clean curved lines and glamorous marble inlaid or terrazzo floors.

Over the next few decades, a newer wave of eye-catching and fantasy-like development debuted in the 1950s with famed hotels like the Fontainebleau and the Eden Roc which noted architect Morris Lapidus described as "too much is never enough" taking the deco inspired hotels to new heights with new luxury. Many years later, when tastes once again changed developers swooped in to try and demolish many of these architectural gems and replace them with modern high rises and condos and a preservationist campaign headed by a forward-thinking interior designer Barbara Baer Capitman took form to designate the Deco district as a historic district. Due to her unwavering perseverance, forward thinking leadership and conservationist efforts many deco jewels and the essential character of Miami were saved from the wrecking ball and a bust of her likeness overlooks the sea on famed Ocean Drive and 10th Street.

The Edition, which opened in 2012, was the famed hotelier Ian Shrager's latest Miami entry. Originally built as the Seville hotel in 1955 its clean, stark and cubist white celebrated the area's deco tradition mixed with '50s glamorous fluidity. It features two outdoor pools and an indoor skating rink, and the iconic lobby is emblematic of Ian's successful vision; an all-white Miami fantasy that celebrates the newer modern aesthetic but pays homage to the classic whimsical Miami architecture.

Liz smiled in a relaxed fashion as she and Ira walked through the airy lobby towards reception as if encountering an oasis after days without water. The clean white modern vibe was exactly what she craved, and the curated vintage mambo and salsa music had her thinking about a different time when women paraded in mink stoles and pointy peau de soie pumps with their families on holiday vacations. She was so taken with the décor; it gave her a creative thought that maybe she could make over one of the rooms in the villa in a similar all white scheme. Liz thanked Ira profusely as he checked on her reservation and she bid him goodbye as he kissed her on the cheek. He gave her his business card and cell number and left for a late afternoon appointment and dinner after retrieving his car in the circle entrance. The bellmen had taken her luggage from Ira's trunk and put it onto a cart and whisked it up to her room as she held Elsa's diary tightly to her chest which she had retrieved from the bottom of her bag. Something told her the answer to all she was looking for was most likely in the volume.

Once checked in and given electronic key cards, the high-speed elevator took her to the eleventh floor where she walked to and opened the door to an ocean view suite and tipped the young bellman who deposited her luggage on a folding stand. Her mouth literally dropped open as she entered a huge suite with a dining room and a cavernous modern living room and floor to ceiling windows overlooking the dramatic coastline. Off the living room was a generous bedroom, walk in closet and bath with a white egg shaped white modern bathtub. There had to be some sort of mistake, she thought. She couldn't afford or ask Ira to pay for this as this suite was fit for a movie star or high-profile investment banker. She had just wanted a nice clean room and hadn't expected to put Ira out and took a few beats before walking over to the cordless phone and pressed talk and the front desk button.

"Yes, Miss Galin, how can we help you?" She heard Julie at the front desk's lyrical voice over the phone.

"Hi, yes. I just checked into room 1105. But it's not a room, it's a suite. I…well, I think there may be some sort of mistake? I just thought I was getting and paying for a regular room," she said in a low voice. She knew Ira and the estate were footing the bill, but this was much too extravagant!

"Of course, let me check please." As Julie placed her on hold, as she checked on her accommodations Liz paced looking at the aqua coastline beneath her feet and saw the myriad pools strewn across the coastal path next to all the white deco hotels lined up like white uniformed soldiers. It was a beautiful and welcoming tropical sight after a freezing winter in her tiny New York city shoebox on Avenue A and it was no wonder thousands were decamping from the Northeast for Florida per month.

"Hi, Miss Galin." Julie returned on the call. "Yes, that's correct. I double-checked, and the room was upgraded to a suite. We hope you like it," she said enthusiastically.

"Why thank you so much, I love it!" Liz struggled to find the right words. "Can I ask why I got an upgrade, though?"

"Yes, it's courtesy of Mister Reznick and Missus Barrett. We hope you enjoy your stay."

The words "Mrs. Barrett" struck her. "Oh, I love it. Thank you so much. It's absolutely beautiful." She had never stayed in a suite before as it was the kind usually reserved for her celebrity clients when she was working on a job but never her own. Liz tried to process the information. Why was this all happening, being treated like a princess by a man she hardly knew and a woman who was supposedly dead? It didn't make much sense. She looked around at the modern fantasy of white and beige and saw there was no one in the room or even the closets. She walked to the suite's entrance and fastened the modern silver lock above the door and then walked back into the living room, diary in hand.

"Just be thankful." She took a deep breath and shook her tawny locks again. "Be thankful for the gift you are receiving." She opened the mini bar and almost decided against the small bottle of white wine, knowing the markup would be prohibitive but then she decided to splurge since she was only paying for incidentals. She took the wine, twisted off the top, grabbed a wine glass, and settled into a comfy, modern white divan with the letter and the diary, Elsa's diary. Clearly, Elsa had given a great deal of time and thought to her plan. A diary! She had wanted Liz to know her and her story. At first, she hesitated; what would she learn? Would it be banal and saccharin or too personal or upsetting and cast a pall over "the gift" as she now called it. She removed the faded diary from the manilla envelope and the moment she opened up the floral cover and saw the elegant and neat penmanship she felt connected to this woman and transported to another place and era. She brought the modern glass goblet to her lips as she sipped more white wine savoring the smooth and tart notes as she opened the hard surface of the diary and a musty lavender emanated from the pages, which brought an image of the identical silk kimono hanging on the bathroom hook.

She started to read...

ELSA

—The Grove -1933

Today was so hot and humid, not that we don't see those oven days here, but this one, the temperatures would have burnt a chef's souffle. I have always felt that life's decisions, the major ones, remind me of the Robert Frost poem we had read at Miss Harris's… "The Road Not Taken." However, sometimes it's not always your choice, but one that is thrust upon you by circumstances out of your control or events that unfold and prompt you to take the one you might not have chosen. Therefore, I don't know if I totally agree with Mr. Robert Frost, despite his Pulitzers, intelligence, and creativity. My choices seem almost chosen for me.

"Elsa, whatever you do, be nice and mind your manners. And don't forget to make some lively conversation when he arrives, like you do with your foolish friends," Daddy said as he paced the gloomy, ornate drawing room of our Florida mansion in the Grove. He cut his Cuban cigar at his leather topped partner's desk, his large belly heavy with discontent.

"Why are you so intent on my being so nice to that old man?" I bristled at the thought of his conservative suspenders and salt and pepper whiskers and put my Photoplay Magazine down on my lap. I was trying to do my best Fay Wray imitation in the glass window; that sexy winsome look and then the horror of King Kong's adoration; the proverbial beauty and the beast. Was there coincidence in small events like this?

"You look so pretty in that dress and Beaulah did a beautiful job on your hair." Mother smiled, nervously lighting up a

Lucky Strike. The gold lighter wouldn't light, and her hands replied violently to get the flame going. "I just think what your Daddy means is…"

"What Daddy means is I should throw myself at him because he's still rich. Isn't that so? You think I would be interested in someone like him? Am I chattel to be sold to the highest bidder because everyone is on a bread line?" I said with a tad more insight than I am given credit for.

"Now listen here Elsa…" Father wagged a burly finger at me that felt like a child's punishment; sent to bed without any dessert.

"Now dear, what Daddy means is that, well, we want you to be smart, that's all. The last few years…." Mother paused and went on. "The house is rented, and we are leaving in a few weeks for Sarasota. I know you don't want to miss your friends here. You know you don't have to go, that's all."

I made a face, grimaced, and nodded in hard supplication. I do know my fate too well, even though I'm only nineteen. Life hadn't been the same since the market crashed in '29. Daddy had lost what was left of his fortune, but it hadn't started just then. The Big Blow, as they called the hurricane of 1926, flattened the beach leaving twenty-five thousand people homeless. The MacArthur Causeway connecting Miami and Miami Beach was submerged under 6 ft of water and even the dome of Daddy's friend Carl Fisher's famed Flamingo Hotel blew off, an eerie sign of things to come. It was the year it had all started to unravel, wiping out Daddy's get-rich real estate firm which had defined the Florida land boom. At the height, he boasted at dinner parties that parcels of swamp land were sold daily at ten

71

dollars an acre to out of towners who were lured by sunny dreams of weather and escalating land prices and the promise of a better life, making big profits in the process. The first few years we lived in this spooky Victorian in the Grove, the chauffeur would take me each morning in the big black Duesenberg to Miss Harris's school for Girls in Miami. I remember at that age being terrified of being alone, but I made many friends, and I might say over time I became a somewhat popular girl in school. They all complimented me on my natural blonde hair and mother always had me turned out in expensive turquoise and white silken bows and the very best Parisian fashions. I am devastated at the thought I will have to leave for Sarasota, and I will miss dearly my best friends Lily, Celia, and Flora and their autograph albums and movie magazines. I'll miss Beulah, our doting maid, and I'll even miss that one strange girl in the grade below, Cora Smart. She is on scholarship and is poor, but she is smart as a whip, like her name and I like her sarcastic humor. Her mother is a waitress, and she lost her job and word has it someone who might be her real father was paying her tuition. The other girls give her the air, but I like her company. I will miss her too. If I go, that is…the road diverging.

It is abundantly clear I am being used as bait for Mother and Father's ambitions, and yes, desperation, yet I am quick enough to realize I have little choice but to oblige as I don't view backwater Sarasota as an option, but I will put up a good ruse.

"Don't be foolish. You're not a spring chicken anymore and Leland Barrett has taken a shine to you," Daddy proclaims and puffs.

"I think he's handsome in a commanding sort of way."
Mother joins in and tries to be optimistic.

"For an old man." I am not going to make this easy on them.

"Yes, but he's one of the few people that's actually made
money during the Depression," Father lectures. "When
everyone else was buying and selling residential real estate in
Florida he was buying the thing that matters most: banana,
orange, and pineapple plantations in Cuba and Costa Rica"

"I hate bananas," I say in a deliberately petulant manner.

"You'd do well to bite that tongue of yours, girl," Father
lectured.

"You'd do well if I married him," I counter, perhaps a bit
fresh. I don't really mean to be.

"Honestly, I'm not going to lie to you girl," Father said,
"unless you want to end up in a swampy backwater of
Sarasota, that's where you're going, because that's all we
can afford now. Even Carl is selling his show elephant Rosie
and his mansion on North Bay Road, and I hear there are
no buyers."

Suddenly, there is the sound of the silver and navy Packard
rumbling round the turn and the crunch of the gravel in
the drive. Anxiety and trepidation overwhelm me for the
moment. Yet, for some reason I also flutter. Deep down I
know I am developing a certain type of power that can be
exerted over the opposite sex. It is something the other girls
have remarked on at the tea dances and formals I love so
much. Now I look at my father, nervous, downtrodden,

and weary mother still pretty but worn at the edges. She hasn't had a new dress in over a year, and I know I have the ability to solve their distress and perhaps my own. It is not untrue that I use the skills I learned at Miss Harris's and decide to summon my inner boldness, to pull back my shoulders, erect my posture and be the very best version of myself; a Miss Harris's girl. I can do this. After all, I know deep down there is no chance I am moving to Sarasota.

I walk over to the large gilt, smoky mirror and look at myself for a long time in the reflection. Am I a girl or a woman? Pretty or plain? Strong or weak? I think I know the answer to these questions, but I don't want to appear overly vain.

"Where are you going dear?" Mother asks nervously.

"Give me a moment." I walk into the powder room and suddenly decide to remove the girlish satin ribbons from my hair. Decidedly too girlish, I adjust my shoulder length bob I had fought with my parents about and then walk back into the main salon. Mother is clearly not happy about my new look, but they both rise the moment Leland Barrett enters the room.

"Ladies" he removes and tips his hat. At thirty-six, he looks sixty with his salt-and-pepper beard neatly trimmed and his huge bulk overwhelms. He smells of sweat, vetiver, and sharp tobacco. At six foot four, he is somewhat a bear of a man, and his testosterone is both impressive and fearful. He is, however, what is called a man's man, and he dwarfs father who is more than equipped as a figure of masculinity.

"Lorene." He kisses Mother's hand in the continental fashion. "Looking lovely as ever." I hear the silky words flow like a white silk evening scarf over a notched tuxedo lapel.

"Now Frank, do you see Leland's lovely manners?" Mother titters more than remarks.

"All due to Father who went down on the Titanic. *Refused to get in a lifeboat and escorted all the ladies aboard with a kiss on the gloved hand," Leland exclaims.*

"Well, chivalry is not dead."

"Leland attended Yale, and I'm backwater. Well just that's what you get as a child of Kentucky chicken farmers." Father laughs nervously.

"Nonsense. You have more than I have…a beautiful wife and daughter." Leland looks around at the reduced circumstances, a few items like the gilded harp have been sold and no houseman, only dear Beulah to serve.

"Elsa, do come here and say hello to Mister Barrett," Mother calls, her throaty southern accent more pronounced.

"Leland," he insists. "Elsa, why, you are looking like a beautiful rose on the vine not yet plucked." He smiles revealing small, pointy tobacco-stained teeth.

"Why thank you…" I pause knowing my power. "I'm not accustomed to such compliments," I say knowing it is not true.

*"Well, then you haven't been around the proper company."
He looks me up and down like an ice cream cone in summer.
I blush as I see him take in my bust to my hips.*

*"Were you blonde at her age as well, Lorene?" Leland
Barrett cannot take his eyes off my hair.*

*"Why as a matter of fact, I was. It runs in the family. It
runs through the mother's genes you know. I assume when
Elsa has children, they'll be towheaded as well."*

*"Lovely, just lovely." he looks at me like any acquisition
in his ever-growing portfolio. Am I to be coins, a rare
stamp…a new phonograph?*

*"Frank, do you have a moment for me in the library. Men's
business, that sort of thing."*

*"Lorene, will you have Beulah bring in some good bourbon
and a bucket of ice and two glasses?" Father says in a
commanding voice. He knows now he has the upper hand
for good bargaining like he always taught me.*

"Of course, dear."

*"I think it's high time we retired to the library," Father
declares in an overly jovial manner, like he has a winning
lottery ticket.*

*"Good idea. I have a man's proposition for you and your
family," Leland boasts, "which I do hope will be well
received." Leland Barrett licks his lips as he looks at me. Is
he trying to find the real me? He won't by looking.*

"You know, traveling to the Caribbean can be somewhat lonely," Leland adds with a lustful laugh.

"But profitable."

"But profitable." He claps Father on the back. *"And I need someone like you."* The bargaining of the deal begins.

"Someone like me? How so?" Father looks up, inquisitive.

"Someone I can trust to oversee the shipping company here in Miami. You know…family. I need something else which we can discuss more in the library. You know men's things."

"Of course, why this sounds marvelous, just marvelous. Doesn't it, Lorene…Elsa?"

"Yes, quite interesting." I look at the two men as if I am seeing a silent reel with dramatic players. I am in and outside of it at the same time.

"Her head is in those movie magazines," Daddy says as he kisses the crown of my head lovingly. That said, I feel the grip on my arm knowing it will leave white prints as he adds for good measure. *"But she's a smart girl though, always makes the right decisions."*

Chapter 11

The moment the wheels of the plane touched down at Kennedy and bumped and skidded onto the runway, Liz was confronted by the overwhelming gray. Gray, gray, everything looked dead, depressing gray. Gone were the cobalt blue skies, the vibrant turquoise of the bay and the pop of the avocado green swaying palms and the unrelenting and intermittent sunshine. She saw her own reflection in the small, frosted plane window and her slightly forlorn smile as she digested the sober slate skies, muddied charcoal-tinged snow and pearlized ice and shivered at the sight. She had popped a quarter Xanax before takeoff which made wearing the white N95 mask and shield a bit more bearable but couldn't wait to remove it as she unbuckled herself. Ira had kindly approved a first-class ticket home and she luxuriated in a larger plane and a fully retractable pod.

Once the plane pulled into its assigned hub, she struggled to take down her roll-on and satchel from the overhead compartment and was helped by a swarthy middle aged, married man who tried to engage her in conversation. The stewardess wagged a finger and cautioned him to keep his mask above his nose and Liz politely thanked him but turned away as she saw he was staring lasciviously at her cleavage. Why did it seem that all the men that flirted with her were married overgrown frat boys, playboys, or bad boys? What kind of look did she have? Was it suggestive or trashy? Was her sweater that low cut or too tight to warrant such a look? Perhaps she would need to start wearing cardigans and Elsa's pearls if she found a strand in the villa? Ira had been coy on the subject of her personal effects which he said had been removed from the house and kept in storage and were not part of the will. Fine enough.

The thought of the Japanese robe still had Liz somewhat reeling but she had visited the villa a few more times with Ira during the day, getting accustomed to the property and Zosia's stolid and somewhat invisible presence. She always felt more comfortable when the sun was beaming, and the turquoise of the bay calmed her. She knew once she had the large and gracefully shaped swimming pool repaired and put into shape and the house cleaned and painted, it would be truly luxurious and relaxing. After a few visits and reading more installments in Elsa's diary she felt a bit more comfortable about the woman who had left her house and her possible motives. She had concluded after reading a portion of Elsa's diary that she was a lovely person who most likely faced her own difficulties despite her wealth and station and difficult economic times.

Ira's idea that she could rent the house and keep the income during the off months also seemed like the smartest idea. She also knew her mother craved some warmth and promised that after she finished chemo and received the second vaccine, they would both head down for a much-needed rest and vacation, however, the terms of the will; the six-month, five-year stipulation had her hemming and hawing a bit before actually signing the papers. She wanted to have a final, real chat with Cary about his feelings and plans as she knew deep down that he was not too happy at the recent turn of events but had been working the entire weekend without a break. Ira understood and said there was no rush once he saw her off to the airport, but the expectation was that she would get back to him that week in a timely fashion. She could see he thought she was a bit nuts at even thinking about it, but she always trusted her gut.

She stood patiently in the line on the jet and looked at the time on her iPhone as she waited until the crew opened the door to the plane. Everyone seemed anxious to exit and there was palpable tension in the air as people jostled for position. Was it Covid or did they have real jobs to get back to, unlike her? She placed her satchel and handbag on the rollaway and exited into the terminal as the married man looked after her with a wolfish grin prompting her to walk a bit quicker following the exit signs. She loved that she had no checked luggage which made exiting the airport so much easier and was planning on ordering an Uber to the city. She took the sterile escalator down to the baggage area and clicked on her Uber app ordering the more economical Uber X. It read eight minutes. Eight minutes later, it said seven minutes. That was the only issue she ever had with Uber, but, despite any small issues, it was one of her favorite life changing apps. She waited inside the terminal until she saw the car in close proximity to the airport on her phone and then zipped up her parka as it finally arrived. Once she saw the slightly battered Nissan Altima pull up, she stepped outside into the frigid weather and felt attacked by pin pricks and needles of ice. The driver barely turned and just popped the trunk, indicating that he was not about to get out of the car to help her in the frigid weather.

"Nice!" She thought to herself as saw her breath. "He's not getting a good rating" She struggled to lift the roll-on and managed to get the luggage inside the trunk and then opened the door, pleased the interior had a plastic separation.

Welcome back to New York manners, she thought as settled into the back seat and tried Linda to let her know she safely landed, only to get her voicemail. Then she called Cary and got his voice mail as well. "Nice, no one was home! Working of course!" She had tried Cary the night before but couldn't seem to reach him and it had been frustrating that they had not been able to connect in real time given his shift. The subject of committing to five years in Miami as a full-time resident had been somewhat avoided as she was getting the lay of the land, but now she knew she had to face the music. The will needed to be executed and she only had a few days grace period yet deeper questions about their relationship loomed; what would it look like after Covid was over? Would Cary consider moving to Miami, given how much the property was worth and that it could secure their future? If not, was he at least willing to make concessions about visiting and coming down more often on weekends when she was there and restricted from coming back to New York given the residency issue and the counting of days? There was so much to consider. She was lost in thought as the Uber battled the bumper-to-bumper traffic and finally arrived back in Manhattan, through the packed, dismal tunnel. The driver then took the FDR downtown to Alphabet City and she glanced at the gray, churning river which looked as if it had icy chunks floating in an arctic regatta. There was something nice about being home, but the landscape looked bleaker and emptier than when she left. New York City was always bustling and packed but now seemed actually deserted. Where was everyone?

Once the Uber exited the drive, all she saw was homeless people. The news reported that the Defund the Police movement had made New York City the recent crime capital with a mayor who seemed blasé about the uptick in murders and violence. Linda had told her to be careful and stay away from the myriad protests now competing for attention and often turning violent. There were pro-Trump rallies and anti-Trump protesters near Trump Tower and Black Lives Matter protests erupted after the devastating murder of George Floyd. People were angry and divided and it seemed to be only getting worse.

The moment the car pulled up in front of her small tenement building she saw the ominous police tape sealing off an area by the curb. The neighboring building entrance was blocked off and residents had to walk around the area and speak to a police officer to gain entry to the building.

"What the hell?" she grumbled. The driver waved and popped the trunk, and Liz got out and removed her luggage. It had a surreal quality as her home now looked so small and squalid after the grand dimensions and faded opulence of Villa Pompeii and the sleek clean luxury of the Edition. She removed her rollaway luggage, closed the trunk, and then approached and asked the sturdy Dominican female police officer in her tight-fitting pants standing guard what was going on. At first, she shrugged and said that a grandmother who lived in the neighboring building had been hit by a stray bullet from a shootout. She then added softly that the granddaughter had witnessed it, called 911, yet to her horror the older woman had been killed instantly in front of her very eyes. It was more than a daily occurrence as the shootings and murder rate were on the rise with slacker legislation and bail laws. New York, once the greatest city in the world, was now wounded and bleeding as well and had seemingly turned into a war zone and every day there were daily stories of its imminent decline. The rich felt attacked by the left and were leaving for tax friendly states like Florida and Texas and the millennials were off to Brooklyn and Hudson Valley to bake bread and to tend their gardens and raise organic carrots. Liz shook her head and used her key to gain entry to the tiny foyer and ancient, crooked staircase. The dirty marble stairs were cracked and painted over and sloped slightly to the right, throwing her off-kilter. She was lucky she lived on the second floor as she lugged her bags up the stairs and couldn't imagine living on the top floor. Her arms hurt and she had to go back down to get the satchel; no secret elevators here and no one to help her.

She heard the familiar click of the multiple locks unlocking and opened the door to her apartment as she inserted her jangling keys. Once she gained entrance, it seemed smaller than ever and when she saw her breath, she knew something was dreadfully wrong. She immediately walked over to the radiator and turned the knob to make sure it was on full heat, but it was stone cold to the touch. Liz ran over to the window and saw the repair truck outside to the left of the building, shook her head in disbelief and then ran downstairs and stood for a few moments to catch the attention of the two unshaven workers who slyly looked her up and down and smirked at her slight tan she had gotten by the hotel pool in her bikini. They seemed blasé about the problem and told her that the boiler had broken down once again and they were waiting for a part to fix it. Damn her slumlord landlord! He was more than aware that the building needed a new heater but all he did was patch it every winter. The heat would hopefully be turned on later that evening they explained. "Hopefully" wasn't exactly encouraging with twenty-degree weather. Liz couldn't believe it, but deep down she could. She went upstairs and didn't even bother unpacking.

"Mom, you'll never believe this," Liz groaned into the cell phone in her tiny kitchen after her mother finally called her back.

"I'll believe anything at this point." Linda shrugged, blasting a talk show audience clapping and cheering at some sort of free prize, most likely a cleaning product. The sound was deafening as if they had all won the lottery.

"I'm getting in the car and coming out tonight," Liz muttered.

"That's so sweet, I can't wait to see you!" Linda exclaimed.

"Me too…" She gulped, her voice breaking.

"What's wrong Liz?"

"I'm scared….an elderly woman was shot and killed next door by a stray bullet in some shootout, and there is no damn heat in the apartment. I came home to protests, and the only people I see are the homeless," she said tearfully. "I'm living in a crime scene."

"Oh, I can believe it with this mayor! Another typical day in NYC." She sighed. "Come home as soon as you can! Did you sign the papers yet?" Linda asked hopefully.

"No, I was waiting to talk to Cary."

"Don't be a fool. Sign the papers, Liz. This is a sign for sure!" Linda admonished.

"I thought you told me to wait to talk to Cary about it and not to make any rash decisions?"

"That was before I heard about this shooting and well, I also heard Myrna's daughter Mindy just got engaged." Linda snacked on some popcorn as she spoke. "They were only dating for six months, and it all happened during Covid!" She drove her point home. "If Cary loves you, you can work it all out."

"Mom!" Liz groaned at the news. At a certain age, dating and engagements had become competitive and equally important a topic as Covid or the upcoming election.

"Get the house, then get engaged. I call engagement 'dating with presents,'" Linda explained.

"Mom, what has come over you? I thought you would have said the opposite," Liz said in a shocked tone.

"Liz, Cary has to try too. It can't be all you. In fact, my mother once told me that it won't work unless the man loves the woman just a little bit more," Linda explained.

"I can't believe what has gotten into you." Liz was even more confused by her mother's new stance. She was from a generation where one did not make a move without asking "the man" first.

"You've been dating Cary now for over two years and he hasn't put a ring on it," Linda offered her new point of view. "I'm just thinking about what's best for my daughter now, and after seeing the iPhone photos of the villa you sent me, I'm one hundred percent. If you marry Cary, you know I would be thrilled, but right now, I think your future is more secure with a twenty-five-million-dollar house than a guy who won't commit," Linda said matter-of-factly before munching on another handful of popcorn. "He's doing what's best for his career and you need to do what's best for you," she added.

"Wow." Liz paced the apartment, shivering. She couldn't believe what she was hearing. With her friend Myrna's daughter getting engaged, she thought her mother had just reached her breaking point.

"Sign the papers Liz, and send a photo of the signature page back to Ira. If Cary loves you, he'll follow you to Miami. If he doesn't, there are plenty of fish in Biscayne Bay." She laughed, her husky signature laugh permeating through the phones.

"I think you are getting better! My old Mom is back!" Liz congratulated her.

In fact, there was something nice and cool about her mother's new "fuck it" attitude.

"That's right, and did you call Roy yet? I'm sure he'll give his eye teeth to be invited!"

"I will."

"Don't dillydally! I know your father would tell you the same thing, 'run, don't walk!'" Linda commanded. "Drive carefully!"

Liz hung up and decided to get her car out of the lot and hoped the battery hadn't died in the cold. She locked the apartment door, schlepped her luggage down the rickety staircase and hailed a cab to the lot as she heard the workmen laughing behind her. *Mom's right*, she thought, *There's only one thing to do and that was sign the papers*. If Cary wouldn't come live with her, she would do the next best thing and invite Roy to move in with her. After all, what was the point of having a gay best friend if it wasn't to watch late night Bravo shows, tan by the pool, and live in a bayside villa in Miami. She immediately dialed Roy, and he picked up after the first ring. She regaled him with her update, and he couldn't believe her neighbor had been shot; it was a sign for sure.

"I do have some great news I wanted to run by you though," Liz said.

"Don't tell me you're calling with a job? I'm down to my last thirteen hundred dollars," he said in a voice she knew meant he was at the end of his emotional and financial rope.

"Better." Liz laughed.

"What could be better than a job? The only thing I can think about would be a date with that hot Latin escort I hired when I was still making money," Roy complained. They often talked about how some people were getting richer and richer during Covid yet so many were falling off the financial cliff.

"How does living with me in the villa in Miami sound?" Liz offered with glee.

"Honey, I thought you'd never ask." He chortled over the phone making a snorting sound that broke them both up.

"And it's better than your hook up."

"Better than Raoul's expensive, hard thang? How can that be?" Roy said in a sarcastic tone.

"What I'm offering is hotter and more gorgeous, and best of all Roy… you don't have to pay for it!"

Chapter 12

When Carl Fisher started developing Miami in the 1910s and '20s, he and his cronies like Knowlton Collins, Newt Rooney and Leland Barrett differed on many things. The one thing they could all agree on was they wanted Miami and Miami Beach to be "Jew free." Two decades later, the Nazis took it to the next level with a term *judenrein*, which meant "cleansed of Jews". In the shameful history of segregation and racism, both Jews and Blacks were not welcome at a majority of the finest hotels on the beach and the owners weren't exactly discreet on the subject. Hotel signs boasted "Always a view, Never a Jew." In fact, the antisemitic policies were only outlawed in 1949 and African Americans workers on the beach were forced to leave by 6 p.m. and have transit papers as late as the 1930s. Overtown became the "colored ghetto" as a vibrant community grew around stars like Louis Armstrong, Billie Holiday, Ella Fitzgerald, and Josephine Baker who had to go "over town" to sleep as they were not allowed to stay in the segregated hotels and nightclubs they were performing at.

There were, however, those brave souls that stood up to racist bullies like Fisher and Barrett.

In a tense standoff in 1935, the New York Giants had booked Fisher's famed Flamingo Hotel for their spring training, but two Jewish players Harry Danning and Phil Weintraub were denied entry on arrival. Only when General manager Bill Terry threatened to move the team to another hotel were the Jewish players allowed to stay. Blacks themselves were not welcome as guests on the beach until in the 1950s, when legendary and trailblazing performer Frank Sinatra broke the color barrier for his friend Sammy Davis Jr. at the Fontainebleau by insisting to owner Ben Novak that he accept him as a guest. In a strange twist, the hardened racist Carl Fisher had originally purchased two-hundred acres on the famed eponymous Fisher Island from Dana Dorsey, Florida's first African American millionaire, lest it be turned, in his mind, into a black ghetto. However, contrary to the founding fathers' intentions and in an ironic twist, Miami's historic South Beach eventually morphed into a largely Jewish area for retirees and Holocaust survivors who came from the northeast for the balmy weather and the lower cost of living. Some would return to New York in the summer months prompting the moniker "snowbirds." Little did Liz think she was one of them, but once she accepted and signed the terms of the will, Ira congratulated her she was now an official "snowbird."

Taking her cue from Linda, Liz had signed the paperwork and the will and had it notarized within two days of their conversation. Ira was delighted by the quick response and assured her that he would have advised his own daughter to do the same had she been lucky enough to have been offered such a rich bequest. Her late evening Zoom with Cary was something of a tense standoff, but even he thought, despite his personal feelings, when push came to shove, she would be crazy not to do it,. Cary was, however, very detail oriented and did insist on reading the will and paperwork and she was grateful to have another set of eyes on it, especially his. The next day after digesting it, he sighed in a martyr's fashion and said it all looked on the up-and-up and ready for her signature. Cary was evasive about her becoming a resident but did say he would think about spending more time in Florida with her and wanted to finish out his residency at the hospital before he took any real time there. And while he understood the need for her to spend over 183 days in the state to become a resident, he thought Ira's idea of renting the villa the other half the year was an ingenious way for her to make money given her tenuous profession. His only input was to have Liz doublecheck she could rent the villa after six months of possession which Ira assured her she could. His biggest complaint was she was able to visit other states but not spend any time in New York during most of the year.

"We can always rendezvous in New Jersey," Liz quipped in her usual humorous offhand fashion although Cary did not think this was particularly funny. Her accepting the bequest and agreeing to the terms had indeed put some distance between them as a couple but for now she had the green light. Linda also insisted she and Roy fly down immediately to get the house in order, lest something derail this chance of a lifetime and poo pooed Liz's fears about the spooky robe incident and actually yelled at her daughter over the phone.

"What? You're going to give up twenty-five million dollars because of a *schmatte*? Give me both robes. I'll put them on at the same time and dance through the house like Madam Butterfly." Linda cackled. "You must be crazy! Don't look a gift horse in the mouth!" Liz always got a kick out of her mother as she was always a font of old school homespun expressions and the cancer had not diminished her personality one bit, perhaps even enhancing it as she was now in her "I don't give a shit phase." Liz knew Linda was also looking forward to spending time in Florida once she had the second vaccine and nothing was going to stop her, and she had also made Liz promise to start on refurbishing the outdoor pool as job number one! "Why should someone else enjoy it and not us? Now you go and get what is rightfully yours!" she declared.

"But why is it rightfully mine?" Liz asked.

"The woman left it to you, so it's rightfully yours. It's like if you went to a holiday party and the hostess put an extra slice of brisket on your plate. Are you going to turn it down? It's on your plate so eat it, baby!" Linda urged with motherly love.

The next few weeks were spent packing, trying to find a tenant to sublet her apartment and Zoom calls with Linda and Ira going over details large and small. Liz Zoomed and squared things away with Linda's doctors and also managed to get her second vaccine appointment on the books. She offered to delay going but Linda insisted and said her friend Marion would take her to her last chemo treatment and vaccine shot and then she would come and stay at the Villa in Florida. There were no if, ands or buts when it came to Linda making up her mind.

Roy handled the plane reservations with Ira's efficient secretary Marilyn and after a frenetic two weeks they had accomplished enough and crossed off the major things on their list to actually feel good about leaving and spending the rest of the winter in Miami. Once this was done, she hired the moving companies to pack up her vintage clothes and collection of handbags, which she bubbled wrapped and labeled for good measure.

After weeks of hard work and planning, the day of the official move arrived and Liz stood in the center and looked around her apartment, stripped of her personal effects, and couldn't get over how small it looked once it was emptied.

"I have been living in a freezing shoebox all this time!" She frowned. She walked over to the window one last time and peered out the window spying a homeless man lying in the park, shook her dirty blonde tresses, picked up her rolling luggage and headed downstairs for the airport. In fact, she couldn't wait to high tail it out of there and didn't bother looking back. The drive to Kennedy seemed to be in slow motion but when she arrived the winds whistled dramatically with an icy undertone as the Uber pulled up and she spied Roy in front of the Delta terminal. She smiled broadly and waved, ran over, and hugged him as they both navigated their respective pieces of luggage. They laughed and high-fived at his appearance as Roy had put together his "Miami Vice" look sporting an unstructured white blazer, white vintage patent leather shoes with large gold side buckles he had bought in the thrift shop in Hudson and a pair of oversized Tom Ford sunglasses he had splurged on when he was making money, not to mention a long rapper chain over his unbuttoned aqua shirt to the navel despite the cold. He looked handsome and fabulous, and all heads turned as the good-looking duo put on their masks as they entered the terminal. Two young Bay Ridge guys heading for a weekend at the Fontainebleau nodded and clapped as Roy sang the Will Smith song "Miami" sotto voce before they boarded the plane on the way to their southern adventure.

Chapter 13

The late afternoon flight to Miami International Airport was uneventful and Liz was a bit disappointed to be landing in a cloudy rain shower, but Roy's innate optimism prevailed. Roy always had a "glass half full" vs. "half empty" personality and declared "get over it *Mami*, it's just a sun shower." It was one of the things that endeared him to Liz from the moment they met on a styling job two years earlier in LA.

It had been to create the look for an indie movie actress up for an Independent Spirit Awards LA. Layla Stephens wasn't mainstream but she had earned the distinction of being one of the Queens of the Indie movie scene and while not classically pretty and an actual Jolie-lead, she was known for her outré and forward fashion choices and Liz always seemed to be able to pull a rabbit out of the hat for her and keep her au courant and the editors guessing. Whether it was an obscure Twiggy inspired boxy, geometric pantsuit from the '60s or an original Debbie Reynolds chiffon costume from a secret fashion vault she had access to off La Cienega, Liz was her go -to stylist. When Layla's regular hair and makeup person ended up taking a Disney Movie premiere for real money the day of, the agency recommended their newest addition to their roster, Roy La Roy. It was love and laughter at first sight and Liz knew that opposites did attract. Roy always made friends and conversed wherever he went and enlisted a cute guy to help him with their suitcases on the luggage carousel and then slipped him his card with a smile and a wink. Liz marveled at his ability to flirt with anyone from flight attendants to macho Uber drivers. It was a skill she needed to work on, and he was constantly pushing her to dress sexier and be a bit more open to strangers which she often declined to do.

Once they collected their luggage in baggage claim, they ventured out of the terminal and Ubered over to the estate. Zosia had gone home but left the gate open and a new set of keys hidden in a terracotta pot next to the entry stairs. Liz then took Roy on a tour of the villa and the property. He had seen iPhone photos, heard about and imagined the grandeur of the estate, but nothing prepared him for what he was about to see; it was more overwhelming in person as he had grown up poor as a church mouse in old San Juan and the thought of a villa in Miami was almost too much to bear. He fanned himself and fell to the floor a few times at the faded opulence and imitated Bette Davis as Margo Channing in *All about Eve* when he surveyed the graceful arches in the courtyard, the ancient mosaic, and the hidden elevator. Roy's favorite room was the circular breakfast pavilion which he thought was Palm Beach chic and fabulous. As they walked up the grand staircase to the bedroom wing, Roy fanned himself again and when she opened the door to the master his jaw dropped open at the bay view, terrace, and the ornate, princess-style canopy bed with golden cherubs.

"Fasten your seatbelts, it's going to be a bumpy night," he repeated Margot's famed line from the classic film as they both laughed. Liz took in the master bedroom and was relieved that Zosia had done a rather nice job both cleaning and dusting and was pleased with the new, crisp plain white sheets and fresh pillows and pillowcases she and Ira had instructed her to buy. The controversial robe had been sent to the dry cleaner and was tucked away at the back of the closet under plastic and Liz felt much safer and secure now that Roy was there with her. They dropped off their bags by the large, mirrored beaux arts armoire and before unpacking decided on a light, celebratory dinner at Sushi Garage. They would be meeting Ira and Sheila the following night at Joe's Stone Crab to celebrate the start of her new life and sushi always helped keep the waistline in check, not that either had a problem with weight but why tempt fate? Roy took out his shaving kit and cosmetic bag from his luggage and brought it into the master bath and marveled at the pink marble and gold swan fixtures. Even the affixed soap dishes were created in the shape of scallops; golden shells to hold the French milled lavender soap. Roy claimed his sink and set all his products out on the veined marble ledge in size order and freshened up with a bit of moisturizer, eyeliner, and a bit of mascara. Roy's gender-bending style and handsome face was often compared to Maneskin's lead Damiano David who still managed to look masculine despite the eyeliner, the earrings, nail polish and spangles. Liz often pointed out she used less makeup than Roy as she only applied a bit of lipstick and ran her fingers through her loose tangle and walked down the grand staircase to wait for the Uber while Roy primped. She had a sudden surge of elation as she surveyed the mansion and felt like a Princess and the luckiest girl in the world as she sauntered into the main salon and flipped on the light switch which reminded her of a renaissance palazzo she had visited in Florence during a junior college break; the old master paintings in carved ornate gold plaster frames and the richness of the deep scarlet walls suggesting a royal Medici bank account. Was all this truly hers? She still could hardly believe it. She made her way over as if in a trance, picked up a heavy, tarnished, sterling silver ashtray in the shape of a seashell, turned it over and saw the .925 sterling stamp and then passed her hand over a heavy, gold old fashioned lighter. Much of the furnishings were in a heavy, outmoded, and antique style but she imagined Elsa during the Great Depression entertaining her lady friends and silk dresses and long ropes of pearls as they sipped their tea or perhaps let loose with a jazz band on the veranda and heard the strains in her head.

"Liz? *Principessa* Elizabeth!" Roy's hearty voice filled the cupola from atop the staircase and brought her back to reality as he soon joined her in the entry foyer completing a 360 fashion twirl. His "vintage Don Johnson look," a turquoise V-necked T-shirt and white suit created a sense of whimsy against the chiaroscuro of the dark renaissance furnishings and lighting. The Uber was already on the way and they both gazed at their surroundings in disbelief and delight. Once they saw the car pull into the grand circle they put on their masks and sat in the back seat as they made their way toward Sunset Island and Roy flirted with the handsome Cuban driver.

After an animated and light meal at Sushi Garage with too much hot sake, Roy paid the bill and they returned to the villa incredibly tipsy. Liz locked the gate and after climbing the staircase holding onto the gilded banister, they both burst through the double French doors of the master and literally collapsed into bed falling into deep slumber next to each other before the new luxury springs had a chance to recover.

Through her dream state, Liz heard Roy's light breathing and processed a jumble of ornate moldings and Linda running through the house in the flapping, dragon kimono in Kabuki makeup, before descending into darkness.

A direct laser ray of golden morning light found Liz's right eyelid like a surgeon's scalpel. Her lid fluttering to the orange heat and opened widely as she adjusted to her new surroundings and as the room came into view. She was immediately proud that she had conquered her fear of sleeping at the villa the first night, with Roy at her side gently snoring as she tapped his naked shoulder and woke him.

She scanned the room and noted that nothing had happened in the dead of night, no sounds or ghosts or boogeyman or women for that matter. The ghost of Elsa had not dramatically appeared. She smiled as Roy's naked rump was exposed as the blanket had fallen off. She and Roy had shared hotel rooms before on jobs and it was nothing new to see each other naked or negotiate a bathroom and a sink. The old master bathroom suite and boudoir had more than enough room to accommodate both, and there was an old-fashioned porcelain tub with claw feet under a star shaped Moroccan-style stained glass window in cobalt blue glass which Roy immediately co-opted when he finally managed to wake up and get out of bed. He was totally comfortable walking around naked as a jay bird with not an ounce of modesty and then ran the bath and got into it for a luxuriating soak. Roy had a dancer's body, and his naturally lean and mocha skin was a gift to his Puerto Rican heritage. Liz admired his natural grace as his dark, velvet, muscular, hairless legs dangled from the porcelain tub.

"The hot water pressure here is really good, *Mami!*" Roy said, thinking he was now in a five-star hotel and was in a joyous mood as he could not believe his good luck. Just the week before, he had been staying at his ex-boyfriend's house in Hudson, crashing on the lumpy nubby sofa, fighting over the tiny bathroom, and skimping on Swanson frozen dinners. The small Victorian was freezing and only had one bedroom and one bathroom, and they were at each other's throats by the time he left.

After brushing their teeth and lounging in the bathroom Liz and Roy once again made their way down the grand staircase for breakfast as Roy mimed being a King and then a Queen and then had Liz in hysterics as he tried to climb the metal banister to pretend to slide down the railing. If it was the 1920s, Roy may have made a great silent film actor with his handsome, elastic face and upturned aquiline nose and soulful eyes framed by thick, artistic arched brows. Their moods amplified at the grandeur and excitedly they made their way to the old pantry and kitchen where Roy placed his prized possession, his Nespresso machine which he had put in his luggage and schlepped from NY and installed in the pantry. He also bought a few sleeves of vanilla espresso as a present for Liz with his few remaining funds as a housewarming gift which he took out of a small roll-on suitcase and placed it next to old '30s ceramic striped blue and white ceramic canisters. With the sunshine streaming and windows and doors now open to the outside patio the villa seemed a bit smaller, less intimidating, and more manageable. They scavenged the shelves and were delighted and surprised that there were a few new containers of Dannon yogurt and blueberries and a bowl with hard boiled eggs that Zosia had put in the old fridge. It seemed like the ultimate luxury to have someone buy them anything, let alone staples. Roy went to the old white fridge with metallic script on the door and opened the old-fashioned handle and reached in and removed a lone hard-boiled egg from the clear bowl, his eyes dancing at the sight as if he discovered a rare diamond. He peeled the egg, popped out the yolk into the trash and ate the egg white with some salt and pepper he sprinkled from ornate, baroque sterling silver shakers he found on the counter.

"I would sell these for a few months' rent in Hudson." He laughed at his good luck as he admired the heavy sterling cast weight. They sat at the small cafe sized table in the pantry and Liz sipped her coffee as they both checked CNN and the *New York Post* online. Roy stretched and yawned and if on cue both rose and ventured outside, opening the French doors to check out the balmy weather as it was a beautiful seventy-nine degrees and they both high-fived each other as they took in the blinding sunshine. Roy jumped up and down with adolescent enthusiasm and they both ventured over and then sat in the sun on ancient, faded wicker chairs, drinking their espressos in ornate china cups Liz had washed out from one of the cabinets. She delighted in her plain vanilla yogurt and they sat as they looked out at the bay. Each commented how lucky they were and how fabulous it would be when the pool was in working order as they finished their simple breakfasts and then lay back and enjoyed the heat of the early morning sunshine, closing their eyes in a dreamlike fashion soaking in the rays and vitamin D. Afterwards, they went back upstairs, decided to put on their sneakers and gear for a neighborhood hike and bounded down the steps; a veritable workout in and of itself. As they exited the villa they stopped and admired the graceful arches of the open courtyard and the wild unpruned orange trees before opening the gate, deciding on a long walk to take in the neighboring estates.

Roy hadn't seen the neighborhood during the daytime and wanted to get the lay of the land as the warm golden sun cast an optimistic haze. A lemon filter of light had the happy duo gawking and whistling at the grand estates bordering their own, the array of luxury cars and formidable service groups, from gardeners to the omnipresent construction crews. They thought it another world entirely as they walked to the end of the 4000 block, made a left and a sharp left onto the traffic on Alton Road and stood on the bridge viewing the white and pastel mansions. Suddenly Roy had tears as he looked out over the bridge and took in the bay view.

"What's the matter?" Liz put her arm around him.

"It just suddenly reminded me of when I was growing up in San Juan, you know the palm trees and all. When I was young, we were so poor that I had to share sneakers with my brother, and now, the thought of living here in this mansion…well, I…" It was hard for him to get the words out.

"I know, I feel the same way." Liz hugged him closer "It's another world."

"I'm so lucky to have you as my best *Sugar Mami*." He thanked her and turned and she saw the tear leaking from one eye as he kissed her on her cheek and hugged her close. She hugged him back and they both smiled again as they gazed at the opulent whitewashed homes and gorgeous wide open bay. Most of the waterfront homes boasted an array of speedboats, toys and bayfront pools and Roy was in heaven taking in all the luxury, trying to make sense of it all. Liz turned to her friend and saw his aristocratic profile and hard gaze at the "haves." It was all well and good to view it from afar on TV or see it on a page in a glossy magazine, but she knew for them it was different. They weren't used to the private boat slips and gardeners and live -in help. In fact, given their professions they always knew their place behind the camera, helping someone else look good and they both knew in the end, despite the weekends in Cabo and Palm Springs, they were the worker bees! They loved what they did, but the fact was they were the glorified help, and they knew it and had come to accept it. Now they were thrust into this rarefied world in a singular motion like a quill pen dipped into ink and swirling it onto a crackled and aged and burnished parchment page. It left an indelible impression, and they were in it now, experiencing it even if only for one night and they didn't want to give it back or go back to their walk up, cold water flats or their friend's couch. It was as if Linda was beside them saying "Why should someone else get to have it or enjoy it?" They took a moment and looked at a sleek yacht sail by with young teens already blasting the music and claiming the day. Roy put his arm around Liz as they turned and headed back to the villa. They would do this together and they would enjoy it and be appreciative!

After all, like the song, they weren't just going to Miami. Now, they were living it.

Chapter 14

"It's yoga time, *Mami!*" Roy declared brightly and snapped his slender golden-brown fingers as they arrived back at the villa retrieving fresh, fluffy, white towels out of the guest bathroom and his small speaker which he threw into a straw beach bag. They both walked outside down to the bay with the music blaring and smiling that they would have a free-wheeling yoga dance party on the dock.

"I have it!" He shrieked in delight as he looked at his playlist and motioned for her to wait and thus experience his genius. Of course! The moment called for none other than vintage Madonna and started dancing to her greatest hits "Like a Virgin" then "Ray of Light," but when their favorite "Vogue" erupted over the speaker, they fell into sheer joyous movements. The music started pumping as they both high-fived again and within minutes they were both lost in the beat and the streaming sun. Liz removed her T-shirt and swiveled her thin hips and she looked sexy and elfin in her tiny metallic bikini, her ropes of chic Jen Miller charm necklaces, swaying in unison to her movements; an elegant, free-spirited gamin.

Thinking someone was a welcome guest or at home in the neighborhood was the last thing on Eliad Shiraz's mind as he and his security team reviewed their video cameras and footage which extended illegally onto their neighboring property and immediately called the Miami police. He couldn't believe his eyes at the camera footage and reported "crazed hippies," intruders or squatters dancing like freaks at the notoriously vacant Villa Pompeii. Miami police are Southern and often tasked with keeping the spring break crowds under control, but they also take the poshest addresses in Miami seriously and two squad cars arrived within minutes of the call and drove onto the property after pushing through the gate which Roy and Liz had left partially open. The squad car parked past the dormant fountain as Eliad and his team arrived from next door and they all bounded behind the officers after they quickly introduced themselves. Each walked single file on the left side of the moldy, regal property, sidestepping tangled vines and gnarled roots of the overgrown tropical forest to get to the back, bayfront dock.

They heard the music blasting before they emerged on the back lawn just at the moment where Roy came behind Liz in her bikini and cupped her high breasts from behind, imitating the iconic move from Madonna's groundbreaking 1990 MTV music awards performance dressed as Marie Antoinette in a revealing bustier. They were laughing hysterically as the men in blue and the security team advanced quickly and swarmed in. Roy and Liz looked up in shock as they saw the officers withdraw their guns.

"Hands up, you are under arrest, young lady. You too." A tall, bulky dark officer withdrew his gun as Liz and Roy froze in shock.

"Wait officers!" Liz looked up, not comprehending, the music still pumping in the background as the police team seemed choreographed to the beat.

The beat pounded.

"I said hands up." Two officers advanced as she put her hands over her head as did Roy who was now officially trembling.

"What's going on here? I don't understand, this is a terrible mistake!" Liz pleaded, wide eyed.

"You are under arrest for trespassing," the squat, ginger haired officer said firmly.

"Trespassing? This is *her* house," Roy stated firmly.

"Wait officers, this is my house, I can explain!" Liz's highlights and golden streaked hair seemed especially untamed and sprang into anxious action.

"Can I put my hands down? I'm getting tired." Roy's eyes pleaded and they motioned yes.

"Your house?" The handsome African American officer cocked his head at the news, his symmetrical features and square jaw matched his formidable physique.

"Yes, please put your guns away, you're frightening me." Liz looked like a little girl at that moment.

"Well, that's our job, we're the police," the ginger officer said, appearing a bit gruffer than he had intended.

"Haven't you heard of Hispanic Lives Matter?" Roy cracked.

"Roy, please…" Liz glanced at him with serious eyes.

"You can put your hands down for the moment." The handsome police officer looked at his partner. "I don't see any concealed weapons." He smiled and observed.

"In a bikini?" Liz couldn't believe what she was hearing.

"Liz!" Roy sniped back at her in an exasperated fashion.

"So, are you a relative or something?" The officer looked them both over and noted they looked like two, attractive and stylish adults not homeless squatters. His chiseled face featured high cheekbones and kindly brown eyes topped by thick brows.

"No, but the house was recently left to me by the former owner, Elsa Sloan Barrett," Liz declared.

"So, you're related to her?" he asked.

"No."

"Then, how do you know her?"

"I don't."

"Someone you don't know left you this huge mansion?" The ginger officer shook his head.

"I know it's hard to believe, but it's true," Liz explained.

"This house has been deserted for years. We have every reason to believe they are trespassing or squatting on the property," Eliad spoke over the police. "Or are fans who will harass my client."

"Look, I can prove it to you…let me call Uncle Ira." Liz was optimistic but panicking. "Can I use my phone?" She indicated with her shoulder her cell phone was on the edge of the towel.

"Who is Uncle Ira?" The good-looking officer cocked his head.

"My lawyer."

"So, your uncle is your lawyer?" He continued the line of questioning.

"Well, he's not really my uncle. I just call him that." Liz shrugged.

"You're digging a bigger hole, Liz," Roy hissed under his breath and shook his head.

"You expect us to believe you were left a house by someone you don't know?" The handsome officer's tight curls glistened in the overhead sun as he shook his head in disbelief.

"And your lawyer is not your uncle, but you call him that?" The ginger haired, stocky officer stated vigorously. "Makes sense to me!" He licked his lips at Liz's nubile body and laughed out loud. "Maybe she's expected back at the looney bin," he whispered to his partner.

"Please let me call Uncle Ira," Liz begged, still in shock. This was not what she was expecting on her first day in Miami!

"I've never heard such crap," Eliad sneered.

"Fine, make your call." The officer reached down, picked up Liz's phone on the towel, and handed it to her.

Liz smiled and thanked him. It was quite a spectacle and despite the standoff they were all subconsciously shaking their bodies to the "Vogue" lyrics on a loop. It was hard not to.

Liz picked up her cell phone and dialed the number, but it went to his voicemail.

"He's not answering," Liz said in a panicky voice.

"Sure, honey come with us, you can explain all this at the precinct." The ginger frowned and then said the dreaded words. "You have the right to remain..."

Her phone rang, the sound of the ringer piercing the air.

"Wait!" Liz shouted. She had always resented Linda's constant intrusions but not now. "It's my mother. She can explain."

"Boy, can she." Roy smiled at the ginger officer who he thought checked out his package in the bathing suit. "You don't know Linda."

"Please?" Liz begged.

"One last chance." The nice officer grimaced.

"Hi Mom," Liz answered the phone "Stop…I'm here with the police. Yes, the police. Can I put you on FaceTime and you can explain about the house and Uncle Ira? The police think I am trespassing in my own home!" Liz indicated she was going to turn the phone around so her mother could FaceTime. "Here guys, I'm putting you on with my mother, Linda Galin."

Linda's red and angry face appeared on the smaller screen.

"What in the world is going on there?" Linda said with fury.

"Your daughter and her friend are trespassing or squatting in a mansion on North Bay Road, ma'am," the ginger officer explained, the noise from his walkie-talkie going off made it a bit hard to hear.

"Now you listen to me, that villa is her house! I am her mother Linda Galin. Today was my last day of chemo, this is giving me major tsuris… Do you know what that means?"

"Not exactly?" The African American officer raised his eyebrow in a question mark.

"It's Yiddish for distress," Linda explained. "Now what my daughter is saying is true, the villa was left to her by Elsa Sloane Barrett, and you are trespassing on *our* property. Unless you want a serious lawsuit, I suggest you leave right now or I am going to call our lawyer down there, Ira Reznick!" she said the name with the regal emphasis of an empress.

"Wait, Ira Reznick is your lawyer? Why didn't you say so?" The two officers instantly looked at each other in fear and confusion.

"I did!" Liz was now gulping for air and crying.

"You mean *the* Ira Reznick is Uncle Ira?" They nodded at each other sheepishly at the news.

"He was just honored as Man of the Year by the police force down here." The handsome officer shook his head in acknowledgement.

"You see, and he has all the legal documents." Linda seemed self-satisfied.

"Oh, I have a copy of the will in the library," Liz said nonchalantly, remembering Ira had put a bound copy on the old Napoleonic desk in the library.

"Why didn't you say so? You have a copy of the will?" The two police officers looked at each other somewhat amazed and perplexed and then angrily at Eliad. At that moment, G sprinted onto the property in only his bathing suit and flip flops.

"Stop! Guys, what are you doing?" G Alvarez waved his hands, out of breath.

"Wait, who is that undressed man in a banana hammock?" Linda said as she surveyed the scene from her iPhone advantage.

"I'm the neighbor." G Alvarez waved. "Hi, nice to meet you."

"Wait, you know her?" Eliad looked perplexed at his boss under his aviators.

"I saw them both last night on the dock at sunset; I wanted to stop by and say hello. Then I just saw this commotion from my balcony."

"You saw them?" Eliad barked.

"Yes, her and him." G pointed. "How could you not know?"

"I did know…that's why we are here. We've had security issues with stalkers," he explained to the police."

"Yes, there was a recent incident and report filed." The ginger officer nodded.

"Wait, Liz… It's G Alvarez," Roy whispered in a tone that suggested he was ready to pass out or fan himself.

"Liz, what's going on there?" Linda raised her voice as Liz shushed her.

"G who?" Liz leaned in.

"'G Alvarez," Roy whispered loudly.

"I don't know who G Alvarez is," Liz said under her breath, shaking.

"You don't?" G smiled in a downcast way at the news.

"I don't care who he is, tell him to put on some clothes." Linda's voice emanated from the iPhone.

"Okay, Miss Galin. Can we see the will you said you have? Then we will be on our way." The handsome officer wanted to wrap things up.

"Mom, I'm going to show them the will. I'll call you back." Liz clicked off the phone and started walking towards the villa and the line of palladian doors. G walked quickly to her side to catch up with her.

"This is all a big misunderstanding. I am so sorry; we've have had some issues with fans trying to break into our property by going over your gate," G tried to explain. "When…when did you move in?" He smiled.

Liz stopped in her tracks and looked at him coldly. "So, you're the one who called the police?"

"I didn't, he did." G pointed and frowned at Eliad.

"But they work for you, he works for you? That one!" Liz pointed to a smirking Eliad.

"Yes. He's my head of security and they're the police." G wasn't used to being dressed down. It brought him back to his days at the orphanage, and anxiety swept over him quickly like a wave.

"Why do you need so many?" Liz squinted angrily.

"Because he's famous, Liz," Roy said.

"Well, I am sure you are very famous in your world, but your security had no right to bust in and try to arrest me." She bursts into tears. "They scared me."

"I am so sorry." He shot darts at his head of security, "Eliad, I think you owe this woman and her friend here an apology. This was not the way to meet a new neighbor." G tried to calm the situation gone awry.

"You should all be ashamed of yourselves. Harassing a single woman and a gay man in bikinis." She gulped. "In my own home of all places. Just wait till I tell Uncle Ira."

"She gets this way when she's mad," Roy whispered to G. "She's like a volcano; once she erupts, she'll be fine." He looked him over and licked his lips. *He's hot*, Roy thought.

"Wait till I tell my boyfriend about this." Liz walked furiously. "He may not be famous, but he's a New York City doctor and frontline hero."

"I am so sorry. I...well, this is a terrible way to meet." G shook his head.

"I want you and your sorry excuse for abs off my property. You almost gave poor Roy here a heart attack." She pointed angrily at Eliad.

"Can I make it up to you?" G looked at her lovely hair and stunning pale blue eyes.

"I don't care who you are or who you think you are, just because you are supposedly famous you can't treat people like shit." Her anger was building.

"'Look, I am truly sorry. Hopefully one day I can make it up to you."
He looked down.

"I doubt it. Officer, the library is this way." She pointed to the handsome officer. "Only you! You're the only nice one. Come in, and I'll show you the will."

"Thank you, Miss. We are very sorry for this mishap. It was an honest mistake; we're just trying to keep you and all your neighbors safe," he said meekly.

Liz and the officer walked past G into the vast villa. They passed through the reception rooms through a mahogany carved archway to the library. Liz walked straight over to the massive Napoleonic desk. The officer looked in wonder at the grand architecture and opulent furnishings and emitted a low whistle. In the center of the regal desk, she picked up a copy of the thick bound will on the leather blotter. She flipped to the notarized title page as the police officer looked around and then at her name and signature, and Ira Reznick's law firm stationery and signature. Liz showed him her passport from the flight since it was in the desk drawer to make it all official.

"Well, I am truly sorry to you and your friend." The officer shook his handsome, well-proportioned head.

"Roy," she repeated.

"Roy," he repeated, "And congratulations, this is some place." He looked at her with his kindly brown eyes. "I'm Officer Adams. Here, I'll write down my number if you ever need us."

"Thank you, I doubt it." Liz softened but was still angry at the intrusion as the episode definitely reinforced the idea that she and Roy were lesser-than and undeserving.

"If I were you, I would put the will somewhere safe. I wouldn't advise having it just lying around." He smiled brightly.

"Thanks." They both walked out towards the terrace, and Liz saw that G and his security team were getting ready to leave the property.

"Mr. Shiraz." Officer Adams pulled up his impressive torso and flashed Eliad a stern look. "Next time you call the police and waste our time, I suggest you have the facts straight. The house is indeed hers, and I think you owe Ms. Galin here an apology," he stated firmly.

"I'm very sorry, I had no idea," Eliad said but did not appear apologetic.

"It's your job to know, Eliad." G shook his head angrily. "We're very sorry. Please accept our apologies, and welcome to the neighborhood."

"You guys do know you could have a lawsuit on your hands for what you just did? I want you and your thugs off my property now." Liz fumed as G shook his head again.

"I promise I will make it up to you." G was steaming mad as he walked ahead of a sheepish Eliad. The two officers shook hands with Roy and Liz, and Officer Adams congratulated them both again as he took down his mask. His wide, bright smile gleamed against his ebony skin.

"Call us if you need anything. I left my number on the desk," Officer Adams offered. "Again, we are very sorry for the mishap, and enjoy your new home."

"Now, he is a dreamboat." Roy looked after him as he hooked back his walkie-talkie and exited the property. "Maybe we should orchestrate a break-in and call him back." He looked after him with his hand on his hip.

"I've had enough drama for the year." Liz fumed.

"I cannot believe what just happened and that you live next door to G Alvarez. The property is worth more already." Roy laughed. "He performed at the Super Bowl with J.Lo. He's famous for his abs. And you just *crushed* him; I mean, I was feasting on those abs."

"Then you go out with him. How dare he!"

"Okay, you made your point. Let's finish our dance party and lay in the sun; we have a few hours before we need to meet Uncle Ira and Aunt Sheila at Joe's Stone Crab," Roy said as if it were his family and villa.

"Wait till they hear this one." Liz shook her head, knowing she was going to find a way to get back at her neighbor and his henchman.

"And can you believe it? It's only day one!"

Chapter 15

The cut crystal ashtray barely skimmed Eliad's head and a singular knifelike shard lodged itself into the pale gray venetian plaster wall before falling and crashing to the floor into a thousand, glittering pieces. G was incensed and red-faced as he unleashed his anger at his head of security and a huge fight ensued with Eliad threatening to quit. G knew to push it only so far as he wanted to avoid Eliad leaving under unseemly circumstances and possibly revealing unsavory things to the press and apologized for throwing the ashtray, but he was still fuming and wouldn't speak to him for days. G had wanted to meet some neighbors, and the girl next door and her friend looked cooler than most of the residents he saw entering and exiting their estates in their Bentleys or walking their maltipoos in their designer velour sweats. The girl Liz and her friend seemed fun. In his loneliness, he was excited by the prospect of nice, younger neighbors and even thought that they might end up being friends yet Eliad, with his brusque manners and approach, had just dashed that idea.

G had always thought of himself as happy and even-tempered on the surface despite being troubled, and was a typical Taurus the bull, calm until he wasn't and then when he got angry the steam literally emanated from his ears. After the anxiety and panic attacks he experienced on the farm in Colombia, he had been considering seeing a therapist and this latest episode only confirmed his anger problem. He had gone only twice when he lived in New York to a Dr. Klinkov, a trained Freudian therapist who was referred to him by his manager Ryan after a terrible episode of drugs and alcohol. He promised Ryan after a brief hospitalization he would make an appointment with the older therapist who told him that depression was "anger turned inward." He was very smart and insightful, but he touched a nerve and G hadn't been ready to delve into the part of himself that was injured, mortified and angry, not to mention intensely lonely.

Much of his feelings and emotions had been pushed away or buried and his story was not a new one; in Colombia it was already an urban legend. The hard public truths of his youth were seemingly whitewashed by an array of publicists and handlers and his own desire to claim a more normal and respectable childhood had been received with slight scorn by the press and adoring public yet, everyone forgave him due to his incredible talent, his endearing smile, and the fact that in his native country he was one of them. So, what if he was prone to putting on airs? The rumors circulated even more as he tried to avoid the subject of his childhood entirely. The only person who really knew the entire truth was Sant…and Ryan. He and Sant had lived the hardscrabble reality together from a young age in the orphanage. They would often laugh, drink together and eat their favorite foods at the fanciest restaurants in Miami but neither ever discussed the past, much the way many holocaust survivors buried their trauma after the war and wouldn't discuss the horrors even with their closest family. As G was maturing, he was starting to realize that not dealing with his issues and problems were catching up with him and he needed to get his emotions under control, or better yet deal with them. The facts were painful to admit even to himself and made him feel unworthy and perhaps if anyone knew the real story, he would be an object of pity or scorn and perhaps even incapable of being loved. The facts were the facts and couldn't be changed despite every cleverly crafted PR release; his mother Josefina had not been a waitress and starving artist as put forth to the press, but had been a common street prostitute who had died from AIDS through sharing needles. G had grown up seeing a constant stream of men come and go from their dinghy one room apartment in the barrio and he never knew who his father was. Josefina, who was of Afro-Latino heritage, only said that his father had been a Dutch tourist, hence G's green eyes which she was always proud of. Due to her erratic behavior and activities which ranged from loving to beatings, G became extremely withdrawn and shy often hiding in plain sight. He would leave their one room flat early in the morning and stay out late to avoid the range of male johns who were often creepy and violent and the drug paraphernalia and the stray needles, which he was deathly afraid of. The morning he found his mother dead from an overdose and prostrate on the dirty mattress he sat for hours with her body weeping before calling his landlady as he knew what was in store for him and within days he had been sent to a public orphanage in Bogota. The conditions were appalling with little heat in the winter and no air conditioning in the humid summer. He was slight and handsome, and the older boys abused him on arrival and one morning when he went off to the showers he was tackled and held down by a group of older boys and beaten by a wooden broom handle on his bare ass. His cries for help luckily did not go unnoticed, and he was saved by a large heavy-set boy called Santiago who threw punches to get the gang off him and from that day they were best friends; the family he never had always ready to do for the other. Santiago had suffered himself; his own parents and grandparents having been gunned down by the rebels when they were visiting their relatives in Puerto Cachicamo and from that moment on he used his height and girth to shield himself and then his best friend G for the mean, spartan life they were subjected to.

G's smile was always his best gift besides his voice and the kindly Mother Superior Maria Victoria who ran the orphanage took pity on him. She adored the impish little boy and tried to find something or a skill that would save him from a life of squalor and despair. When she found out G could sing and had the voice of an angel, she encouraged him to join the church choir and when he sang "Ave Maria" a cappella in the chapel, the nuns gathered to hear a miracle and he knew at that moment, he was home.

A performance at a nearby church on Christmas Eve led to the Mother Superior being called by the assistant of Arturo Garcia-Nerada, a noted record producer who had it in his mind to create a boy band of virtual street orphans. Arturo was widely known and successful in Colombia but hadn't had a hit or new star in the last few years and was living off a fairly moribund reputation. However, on a trip to Medellin, he had come across two beggar boys singing for change in the street, and he instantly had the idea of a boy band made up of huerfanos. He knew if all the boys were truly talented the public would fall in love with the poor orphans and from that moment Arturo scoured the country to find his "five." The name came to him in a dream and was a perfect marketing ploy; La Sistema…The System. These five boys because of their talents and looks, without any background or advantage would beat the system; and all the local teenage girls and boys, waitresses, teachers, and bus drivers would be cheering for them to do it.

A friend had heard G sing a solo that Christmas Eve and called Arturo with the lead. He had already picked his four band members and the press was building around each choice. Of all his concepts and ideas, Arturo knew by the initial interest and press that he had solid gold on his hands as the public had fully embraced his concept even before the first single drop. His last pick, Matias Sanchez was a soprano meant to round out the group and he was a country boy who had won numerous talent contests. With the announcement of him joining La Sistema his picture was already starting to appear in the Colombian press and with his movie star looks and beautiful voice he would also become an international star, but nothing prepared him for the innate looks and the searing multi-range voice of G Alvarez. When Arturo met him and heard his voice he was transfixed and thought the young man a veritable angel. His smile was magnetic, his apple green eyes could be seen from the last row of the chapel, and he had an impish way of smiling that highlighted true dimples. G had a magnetic vulnerability and his talent mixed with his beauty and sadness would have the public eventually wanting not only to know him, but to protect him.

After Arturo went to hear the boy sing it all happened very quickly as Arturo was still regarded as one of the most successful record producers in Colombia and he immediately arranged an audience with the Mother Superior and had his wife Carmella along to ease any concerns. Sister

Maria Victoria was thrilled that young G was to be in such capable hands and all the sisters were delighted little G would be on the road to fame and fortune and of course, saw it as a once in a lifetime opportunity. It was all secured when Arturo also made a healthy donation to the orphanage.

Then…nothing.

Arturo was traveling and G and Sister Maria were perplexed yet anxious with the lack of movement and no announcement. A month of painful waiting seemed torturous. Had Arturo been serious or had changed his mind? G and Sant sat at the poor wooden dining table each night, downcast thinking nothing good would ever come to them then out of the blue, Arturo's lawyers called and sent over all the promised documents and paperwork, and it was all spelled out in black and white. G would be signed to La Sistema for a seven-year deal; he would be moving into a group apartment with the other boys in the band in an upper middle-class part of town and his earnings would go to Arturo and clothes, food and rent would be deducted. Once the debt was paid, he would receive 49 percent of proceeds into a trust account he would receive at age twenty-one which Sister Maria Victoria would oversee. All trips would be chaperoned, and G would be required to take his high school courses with the other students and turn up and work six days a week studying and rehearsing.

There was cause for cheer and celebration at the home and Santiago was happy and thrilled for his best friend, but deep down was sad and depressed as he knew his own life was a dead end as he knew he had no special talents nor did he excel at his studies. G sensed this and promised once he was successful, he would come back and get him, and this promise was sealed with a finger blood oath pricked by a pin. Sant nodded, hugged him, and gave a mournful smile and said little thinking it would never happen, but G always knew he would keep this promise in his soul as Sant had been the older brother he never had and his protector.

Life was about to change for G, and it did so rather quickly. He and the group moved into the large apartment with the four other boys, a low rise but prosperous brick apartment building in the affluent Rosales neighborhood. At first, he thought he would be welcomed by the other young men given their similar backgrounds but after a week he had deep anxiety that everyone was competitive and out for themselves. His only friend was Paco Hernandez. He was tall, and, skinny and underdeveloped and had the hint of a mustache and they sat together quietly at dinner while the bigger kids rough housed and played video games.

Everything seemed normal yet the constant pressure to perform seemed to slowly mount and eat away at all the boys. Arturo could be generous and warm one minute and hard and cold the next and when they started taking their act on the road, he seemed to reward some boys and mock others. This tension created a competitive working environment Arturo knew would make the boys succeed, at a price. He thrived on the attention that each of the young boys lavished on him and enjoyed that they all tried to curry favor with him as he would deliberately shine his light on one boy making the others all feel insecure. He started telling each individually in rehearsals and in the recording studio that if they didn't work harder, they were easily disposed of and replaced and would single out someone to compliment and someone to belittle, and slowly the boys started to turn on each other.

At the end of a grueling summer Arturo ramped up the pressure as the tour was around the corner and started to take his favorite of the week out from a sumptuous dinner and regale them with tales of their future fame and fortune. The next day he would tell them to pack their bags if they were off key or missed a synchronized dance move. G was the least complimented and the least criticized and almost felt invisible. One day after a solo in the studio when he hit a particularly high note he was surprised when Arturo invited him back to his suite in the hotel for a late supper. Arturo could be charming, and G looked up to him as a father figure he never had and was thrilled when Arturo told him he could order anything he wanted on the room service menu, and he gladly ordered a hamburger and fries. After they both enjoyed dinner and talked about his future career. Arturo asked G to come to his side of the dining table to show him a view of the group's dance moves on his phone he had recorded…and that's when he first groped him. G was frozen in fear as Arturo's hands explored his young body which he knew was wrong and tried to pretend it never happened, but worse things would be forced on him over time. He would, however, always remember that was the night when the abuse started. None of the boys ever spoke to the others until much later that they were all victims of Arturo's lechery until years later they would reveal that they all felt that they had been singled out or made to feel they themselves had caused the abuse to happen. Arturo Nerada may have been evil, but he also covered his tracks well; his wife was on hand during the tours, often out with the boys and shopping and it all gave a most respectable appearance. In order to also add a spice of Latin machismo to the equation Arturo boasted of "making men" of the System. He had done this with his previous groups and word traveled on the tour that Arturo got his young men laid. Before the first concert Arturo had all the boys up to his grand hotel suite and insisted they all have sex with the two female prostitutes he had hired as a bonding exercise.

"I want to make sure you are all men before you go on stage." He declared and each young man was required to lose their virginity in front of everyone. G was terrified when it was his turn but when the buxom country girl started fiddling with his cock and offering her high breasts, he became hard and did the deed as Arturo just sat in an armchair watching and stroking himself and taking photos. It was however turned into a proud moment for the boys, each one having taken one of the two women. When they went on stage they lost their fear; despite the sick attempt at bonding they had nowhere to go but up. Little did they all know that within months of the first tour and album single release, La Sistema would break out into the world's most popular and successful Latin boy bands with crossover appeal. When their first single hit the airwaves the title alone *"Mi pena"* (my pity) had young girls weeping at the angelic voices of the five handsome orphans and G Alvarez's singular and heartbreaking solo. When he reached the vocal zenith with the words *"have pity on this poor, broken soul"* the girls swooned. Arturo also knew that each young woman had her own fantasy young man which is why he had chosen different looks and body types. He knew that some liked the swarthy cockiness of Nicki Lopez or the lean, six pack and muscular biceps of Matias Sanchez. Yet everyone could agree that little dimpled, green eyed, and handsome Gabi, G Alvarez, was the group's breakout star.

Chapter 16

Sheila Reznick stepped out of her gleaming, vintage chocolate and beige Cadillac Deville but also out of central casting and lived up to her name with a pavé diamond-and-gold Cartier watch on a pink alligator strap and a flowing zebra patterned muumuu. She did a 180-degree turn in the grand courtyard arriving in a ghostly gray-white cloud of cigarette smoke. Her bleach blonde crash helmet was perfectly coiffed, and her mahogany tan led the way, looking more like an aging cheerleader who had comfortably settled into middle age with all the trappings. She wore an eternity band of half cut round diamonds that sparkled in the Miami sun and suggested a healthy, long-term marriage and motherhood all rewarded by her successful, loving, and appreciative husband. Liz and Roy immediately embraced her like an old friend and proceeded to give her the grand tour and unlike their own reactions, she didn't seem overly impressed at the faded grandeur and alternatively gasped, rolled her eyes and muttered the occasional "oy" when she saw the peeling paint and sagging mattresses in the bedrooms, adding "The way some people live!" for effect.

Ira had been right; Sheila was part den mother, part therapist, and part Scout/cheer leader. Liz and Roy were highly impressed with her ability to focus on not the opulent or vast interior but the goal of making Villa Pompeii into a livable, rentable home and property. She wandered from room to room with purpose, opening up shutters and pulling dusty drapes to let the sunlight in. After the exhausting tour, Sheila stated she was "going plotz from all the stairs." On the drive afterwards back to their favorite restaurant, Call me Gaby, she made a proclamation which made a great deal of sense; first and foremost, the mansion needed an in-depth cleaning. "A hundred years of neglect would not do," declared the Jewish mother who often did the white glove test in her own home. She recommended a professional cleaning team she and her friends had used for larger projects and had an in with the owner Milton Weitz who ran the service, and they would get a discounted friends and family rate and VIP attention! She pointed out it was important that they had insurance and were bonded lest anyone break or steal anything. However, that was not first and foremost on her mind as they settled into a courtyard table for a long overdue lunch.

"So, tell me?" Sheila Reznick rasped and exhaled creating perfectly circular smoke rings as her substantial gold charm bracelet clinked against the chardonnay filled wine glass. A little fourteen carat gold telephone with tiny seed pearls as the dial dangled from the gold link bracelet and added a sense of old school glamor and whimsey.

"Why isn't a beautiful girl like you married yet?" Sheila lowered the boom peering suspiciously at Liz through her oversized Gucci Sunglasses. She wasn't someone who held back exactly like her mother, charm bracelet and all.

"She always went for the bad boys," Roy offered a knowing glance.

"Until now." Liz forced a smile, not entirely comfortable being put on the spot.

"Oh, I see. So, you're driving your mother crazy, like my Lara did. When she was your age, she dated a drummer with dirty hair who picked her up for dates on a motorcycle. Every time, I had a little heart attack. Then she got smart and met a nice lawyer, and the rest is…her-story." Sheila toyed with her little gem salad.

"She did, too." Roy confided. "Liz met Cary, a nice, Jewish doctor. Short auburn hair, not balding, and a resident at Mount Sinai. Every single girl's mother's dream."

"Well." Sheila sighed. "Your mother must be kvelling, like I am with my Lara. At least you know he's not a fortune hunter!"

"But she doesn't have any money!" Roy sipped his bellini.

"Roy, hello, I'm here." Liz waved. "I can talk for myself."

"Sheila, I'm the one who will tell you the truth!" Roy laughed.

"I can tell, Roy, you and I are going to be besties," Sheila said in a gravelly sing-song voice. "I just love you already. I love him already!" She turned and readily admitted to Liz.

"Roy La Roy at your service. I'll come do your makeup free, Sheila"

"Oy, what a lucky break."

"We'll have to do away with that blue eyeshadow, but I will modernize you, Sheils. Grrr. You will be fabulous. Ira will have to double the Viagra dose." Roy extended his hand to create an erect penis in the air, and Sheila let out a hearty laugh.

"I haven't had a makeover since *Three's Company*, but that Suzanne Somers still looks good, and I hear she boffs her husband at least once or twice a day." Shelia confided.

"You know it's the Thighmaster. I use it." Roy turned all his attention to Sheila as he was obsessed and couldn't hold back.

"Hello," Liz gave another slight wave. "Remember me?"

"Liz, so now that you are the landed gentry, as they say on *Downton Abbey*, you have to be careful of fortune hunters." Sheila leaned in and whispered conspiratorially.

"Fortune hunters?" Liz sipped her sangria.

"Honey, that spread of yours is probably worth at least twenty-five million, maybe thirty now that the market is so hot. We live on Hibiscus Island, and it's like hotcakes…brokers knocking on the door every five minutes. All you 'New Yawkers' finally packing it in and getting smart. I gotta tell you the lifestyle in Miami is second to none, second to none. And North Bay Road, well I needn't tell you honey, it's like the Fifth Avenue of Miami. All these celebs live there: Barry Gibb, Phil Collins, Ricky Martin. In fact, I just heard that Cindy and Rande bought a house on the street as well. Esther Percal did the deal."

"And G Alvarez." Roy looked at her and raised a plucked eyebrow.

"Who?" Sheila looked perplexed at the name.

"G Alvarez." Roy confided.

"Never heard of him." Sheila blew out a perfect smoke ring that hovered in the air like a UFO.

"Neither did she! He's a famous Latin singer. He did the Super Bowl halftime show with J.Lo."

"Who watches the Super Bowl? Maybe Ira. The point is they all live on North Bay Road, and now you do too. So here is the plan." Sheila sipped her glass of dry Chardonnay.

"What is the plan? We love being told what to do." Liz also sipped her floral and fruity sangria.

"You need the cleaning service this week. They'll come in and spend days, and I mean days, cleaning that place. The way some people live! Why that house hasn't seen a real cleaning since the '30s, I'm sure." She blocked out her well-manicured hands "Clean, clean, clean! Clean the carpets, the bathrooms, the drapes, and the shears. Let the sun in. I would also get new mattresses and sheets for the master and a few guest rooms. I'll tell Ira to approve some new linens and bedding as well." She sipped her wine and sighed. "Once it's cleaned, and that will take a while, then you can see what you want to do. I'll also get my friend who lives on North Bay, the Zarcos, the son works with Esther, very successful you know those 'Jewbans'"

"Jewbans?" Liz looked at Roy.

"Jewish Cubans... He's adorable and smart Jason. Lovely family! In real estate! I'll ask him to get their gardeners and pool people over. That's what you do, kids. Clean the whole damn thing up and make it livable. Honey, you are now officially a Miami celebrity too, only no one knows it yet." She puffed. "Except me, Sheila Reznick."

"Sheila Reznick." Roy clapped his hands in delight "Twirl!"

Chapter 17

Liz lay in bed and sighed after what she thought was a particularly "painfully boring" group dinner with Roy and his new designer friends at Kiki on the River and flipped through all the newly installed streaming services and shows and declared there was nothing to watch on TV despite the ever-expanding list of shows. She was annoyed since she had found dinner tedious with a pretentious and shallow crew Roy had orchestrated and had wanted to find a new series to make up for it to no avail. That was one of the few downsides of Miami; while a fun and sexy scene it also attracted a multitude of overt partiers and suspect transplants who were more transient and surface in nature than those she had interacted with in New York. The sun and surf culture seemed to attract weekend revelers which often erupted into spontaneous group dinners where friends or acquaintances would bring additional guests without asking. Liz had a jaundiced view of what she dubbed "randoms" and "grifters" those who tagged along expecting everyone else to pick up the check and loud vapid dinners where no one got to truly know or talk to anyone in depth and certainly never expect to see each other again. Liz was miffed that it had been one of those ever-expanding group dinners as Roy had presented it as the exact opposite and she just sat there, sighing a bit too loudly.

Roy whispered, "What's the problem?"

Liz just shrugged and offered, "I thought I was over having to deal with people who wear stone washed jeans and women with bustiers and high hair…. It's not the '90s."

Liz rolled her eyes at his displeasure. Her only issue with Roy was that he was a social butterfly who loved a constant crowd and an audience whereas Liz preferred smaller and more intimate interactions. Roy disagreed and scolded her for her aloof behavior and "snobbishness," but she stood her ground describing her personality as more "social-slash-antisocial." It had also been a busy and exhausting week and she had been just looking forward to a relaxing weekend and not having to entertain people she did not know or care for and had a number of stressful events to deal with. There was so much to do getting the house ready yet the one thing on which they could both agree was that Sheila was a saving grace. Liz was grateful for the older woman's guidance as renovating an old estate and running a vast home was not exactly in her wheelhouse and she was still dealing with lingering issues from New York. Besides Cary's constant irritability, she had sublet her New York City apartment to her college friend Pamela who now called once a week to complain that there was no or little heat in the flat which made Liz feel extra guilty that she could see her breath in the frigid bathroom. Her tone was angry, and she blamed Liz for not disclosing the poor heat situation when she sublet her apartment. Liz apologized but countered that it was a normal Lower East Side rental and explained the heat only came on when the temperature fell below fifty-five degrees and that the landlord had set it to that temperature, despite her innate feeling he had set it lower. She felt badly at the thought of shivering Pamela and a bit guiltier counting her blessings as she took the call on the terrace overlooking the bay. She could hear the memory of the rattling pipes in her own head as she saw the gleaming white yachts glide by and bikini clad revelers.

It was a clear Monday morning, and Sheila's extensive house cleaning service and team of six promptly arrived at 8:30 am and started work on the property in a professional way with museum style gloves and light blue booties. It would take two weeks working round the clock to get the house up to a level of "Jewish mother approved cleanliness" and Liz had spent the day supervising the details of the work needed to be done. She oversaw the ancient, stained and moldering striped mattresses being carted away and thrown into a vast metal container Sheila had rented and placed near the garage. By early afternoon it was almost full with disintegrating moth-eaten silk sheers, draperies, moldy old beds and stained and smelly carpeting. Delivery services were arriving at the same time replacing new box springs and hygienic mattresses but before they could be installed the empty bed frames also needed dusting and vacuuming as the underside of the beds revealed years of thick dust, hair, cobwebs and lint and the remaining good condition drapes and shears sent out to the dry cleaner. Sheila, who laughingly called herself an interior "dreck-orator" had wisely suggested replacing the ancient moth eaten and disintegrating silk drapes and upholstered furniture with a polyester that looked exactly like silk but would not be perishable to moths or the humid weather. It was actually ingenious, and Liz started to understand what owning a home on the water and its issues and responsibilities entailed. A full-time crew of landscape gardeners now showed up daily and worked weeks to prune and trim back the overgrowth and replace some of the paving with a green AstroTurf on the bayside, which Liz also learned many of the larger mansions used to mimic lawn that would ordinarily turn brown due to the salt water. There was so much to do and so much to learn as work on the estate had officially begun.

Each day it was a cacophony of sound and disarray as different groups descended on the property. There were the cleaners, the gardeners, the pool people; a new sound system and installing Wi-Fi and cable. There were carpenters and craftsmen who laid the tiles and grout and a fountain specialist who had to get the ancient fountain working and bubbling again. Liz and Roy enjoyed the company on the property yet there were always so many decisions to be made; should the old pool now have chlorine or a new saltwater system that was better for your hair and skin? They chose the saltwater one. Did they want to replace the seagrass or use the synthetic grass between the paving stones on the bayside due to the salt water? They chose the synthetic. Each day brought hours of problems and solutions. Yet, Liz always joked it was "Uptown Problems; the problems of the one percent." The pool and the Wi-Fi were the most urgent. Her plan was that she and Roy would pay extra out of the budget to upgrade the Wi-Fi with technology and modern plugs so they could work there as opposed to having to go to Starbucks during the day for service. Linda would come down in March once she had her second vaccine and felt well enough to travel and a working pool was a gift to her mother. With so much going on and adjusting to her new life, Liz, was disappointed that Cary had not yet visited but she did know he was working in the ER on the weekends and promised he would when they gave him some much-needed time off. With the Covid crisis there were few nurses and doctors to spare and that was more important, but Liz still felt somewhat emotionally neglected and literally fell into bed each night weary and exhausted, her to-do lists getting longer and longer.

When it came to staff, Liz and Ira agreed that they would continue to pay Zosia full salary but only needed her on the weekends to shop for groceries and, as she found her a bit strange and weirdly silent and thought a generous, yet limited schedule would be the best idea. She had come with the house and they both wanted to honor her service and loyalty to Mrs. Barrett, but Liz found her at odds with all the work being done and knew that she viewed the cleaning and the renovation work as somewhat insulting due to the unspoken tension and dramatic grimaces. Liz felt the less she was there to offer frowns at the work being done, the better.

The next day, on a rare break, Liz FaceTimed her best friend Lucy in LA to give her the grand tour and all the improvements being made. Lucy was enthusiastic and oohed and ahhed over the regal architecture, the bayfront views, and the new pool marble dust, and she promised to come with her husband and baby for spring break vacation.

A few days later, the house was finally starting to take shape and Liz was thrilled. That evening she planned to stay in with Roy and celebrate by ordering in chili from Joe's Stone Crab, snuggling on the bed, and watching *The Real Housewives of Atlanta* on the new TV that Ira had approved. It was as if they were in a time warp; the black flat screen against the painted boiserie. Roy waved his hand in the air as he just couldn't get enough of Atlanta Housewives Nene Leakes and Kenya Moore and got out of bed to do a diva impression.

"Twirl, twirl, twirl…" He insisted they watch reruns. "I just love the drama." He would eat popcorn and spill it in the bed, and after an episode they would call Cary and then fall asleep together or stay up and watch Andy Cohen on *Watch What Happens Live*, where Roy dreamed of being a guest bartender.

Linda called her separately and put her on the spot wanting to know why Roy didn't have his own bedroom. Liz was too scared to sleep in her room alone and Roy had become a surrogate protector, but the subtle message was driven home by her mother. She needed a real boyfriend or fiancé in her bed, not a friend. They had settled into a lovely schedule and most evenings were spent playing the occasional board game, watching the latest series on Netflix and binging on the *Bachelorette* episodes until Roy decided they would go out on the town and Liz would grumble and eventually give in.

It was a typical Thursday evening and Cary was out for a rare outdoor dinner with doctor friends when Liz decided to open Elsa's diary which was next to her bed on the marble gueridon nightstand. Liz read aloud and the installments were as intriguing as any *Housewives* episode.

Elsa

Miami 1936

The miscarriage was not taken well, not even by my parents. Mother was her dutiful self and lightly caressed my hand like I was still her toddler and Father said the right things in the hospital, but in the end, it appeared I had let everyone down, first and foremost my husband. No one is saying anything outright, but I can tell they blame me with subtle accusations. "Perhaps I shouldn't have run down the staircase! Why were you still playing tennis in your early trimester? Maybe I should have eaten blander foods." No matter what the doctor says to the contrary, they are fixed in their opinions. Mother sits with her rosary and wrings her chapped hands and says she prays for me; the look of love mixed with disappointment and despair…a cocktail of fear almost too much to bear. Two weeks ago, when Leland returned from his orange plantation in central Florida and found out it had been a boy, he became belligerent and angry. His eyes stormed and he drank a prodigious amount and now refuses to speak or go near me. It's as if I have gone from his golden girl to his sworn enemy with an act I had little or no control over. He is now staying out late carousing, and then retires to his own bedroom across the hall without a word to me. He doesn't inquire as to my feelings or wellbeing at all. Each night, I think he might want to start again yet, no matter how sweet I am, he does not visit my bedroom. I know at this point what my wifely duties entail and while they are not pleasant, I have been schooled to accept and submit. I am cementing a long-standing business deal and I certainly don't want to let mother and father down as I know how much they are looking forward to a grandchild, not to mention their livelihoods depend on it.

Then this Monday Leland left without a word to me, only leaving a half-scribbled note that he was off to a tour of his banana plantations in Costa Rica. I had seen his suitcases and trunks piled high near the service elevator which gave me an indication, but I was only presented the missive by Gerard, our houseman, this morning. It seems a somewhat convenient escape to nurse his wounds. Mother, who is quite devout, sends Sister Beata weekly. She came after the baby died to console me and say the last rites. She sits with me to pray for our marriage, our union, and the future fruit. Yet, somehow with his overpowering presence gone I feel free again, younger. I don't want to admit it out loud, but the solitude turns into a much-needed vacation, after the tears of course.

It had been a struggle from the very beginning. The marriage had been a hasty affair with a huge party thrown at Villa Pompeii, more akin to a museum than a home. Mother arranged it with Leland's secretary, and we had over four hundred people in a tent with classical violinists from the New York Philharmonic for the ceremony and with my input, a swing band for the younger folk. Leland created a speakeasy in the library for an open bar which was the only thing he had insisted upon. Although Leland is Episcopalian as was Father, he indulged Mother's "interest in the Papacy" as he calls it and agreed upon a priest who married us in the ceremony after he had given a healthy donation to the church. I wore a lovely white lace gown and a beautiful silk veil and long white satin gloves. Mother lent me her pearl and diamond drops and Leland gifted me a beautiful and expensive diamond and platinum parure which I wore to the party. It elicited a few "oohs and ahhs" from the ladies. There were the obligatory speeches and even Leland toasted to my "golden loveliness."

After the guests left by 2 a.m., we retired upstairs, and I paced nervously. Mother had told me things and I was a bit of a wreck as I waited for him in my lace peignoir. I remember looking into the mirror of my pink marble bathroom, and thinking I looked adult for the first time with my eyeliner and rouge. Yet, all I shall say is with Leland there is and was no romance or sweet talk. I shan't get into the details, but it was a very hasty business-like affair, which suited me fine, but his mood did not. Over the next few days before we left for Europe on our honeymoon, we found out just how different we were; he likes moody darkness, I like the sunlight. He prefers solitary activities like stamp collecting and golf, I am desperate for dances and tea parties. I am, after all, still in my twenties. Father was in his glory when I moved into Villa Pompeii, yet I always feel the mosaic from Pompeii portends things to come, a certain sense of disaster. Despite this It is considered one of the finest houses on the Bay and Leland had spared no expense as a bachelor and had virtually handed over the design and the appointments of the villa to the architect. He had just wanted a mansion worthy of the Barrett name and future progeny and his non-involvement most likely added to the Villa's grandeur. August was a fine architect who had been recommended by Carl and his unerring eye for detail and grand proportions made the estate coupled with the view, an extraordinary result.

Our first year of marriage is marred by a few highs and lows as well. I am thrilled Father is working again and they moved into a respectable house on the dry side of North Bay Road in the 5000s. When he does visit, he and Leland are able to conduct business in his library. Now with a healthy salary mother has her own observatory and even a small swimming pool, not to mention new dresses. What should have been a lovely time has been marred but the stain of disappointment and I am seemingly the culprit.

With little to do and my husband somewhere in the Caribbean, I have decided to take on a bit of decorating and charity work. A few teas here and there and I shall redecorate my bedroom under mother's tutelage with a turquoise and white motif which seems to lift my spirits. Mother thinks a new bedroom might entice my husband upon his return, but I have a sense of hopelessness and gloom. I feel like I am relegated to a losing horse in the stable; well fed and groomed but neglected and hardly ridden. I know, however, not to complain. We have food in our mouths and live in a palace. Most of America is struggling for a piece of bread and a job.

Chapter 18

They resembled miniature, reflective pterodactyls; the sight of them flying above immediately sent shivers down Liz's spine. The drones came dangerously close and then flew off in a violent turn to the left of their property, indicating where they had originated from and where they were returning home to. Liz and Roy were sitting on their new teak lounge chairs getting some afternoon sun by the sparkling refurbished pool after it had been marble dusted and filled, and were Facetiming with Lucy in LA. They were all wide eyed, as if Martians had landed.

"What the hell is that?" Liz looked skyward in a panic as one of the three silver drones accidentally hit the capacious leaves of a looming, verdant palm tree and fell to earth in a dramatic nosedive. She and Roy ran over and surveyed it as if it were radioactive, and as she looked down realized what it was, she grabbed the fallen drone that had hit the dense leaf and flung it to the newly installed AstroTurf. She looked up at the other two drones making their way back to the property next door in fury.

"This is not to be believed! First, they try and arrest me and now they are spying on me with drones!" She raised her voice, fuming. "I'm done! I'm going next door," she raged to Roy.

"No, you are not!" Roy leered at her as if she were insane.

"Yes, I am, and you can't stop me and I'm going to kick that Israeli dude's ass," Liz commanded.

"I think he can take you." Roy laughed. "With his pinkie. He's built like steel, and he knows how to be mean to people, and while that's very exciting to me, I'm not sure you're up to it."

"Are you coming or not?" She stared at him, drone in hand, drawing herself up tall. She threw her old vintage *Fleetwood Mac* concert T-shirt over her bikini top. Roy silently put on a tank and slipped into his navy and tan linen espadrilles, and he silently followed her as they both marched quickly next door. Roy knew when Liz got into her angry zone there was no stopping her and he wanted to support her, and at the same time was excited to check out the mansion next door. What was going on there? The gate was open for a delivery and Liz and Roy walked through onto G's estate. Despite their anger, they marveled at the light and clean lines of the modern masterpiece on the bay.

"Okay this setup is cray cray…" Roy shook his head. "The decor is so narco-porno! Rich." Roy drooled.

Within seconds, they were surrounded by a security detail.

"I want to see him!" Liz fumed at two men in black polo shirts who appeared suddenly before her on their walkie-talkies.

"Me? You want to see me? I'm so flattered." Eliad Shiraz smirked as he emerged from the inner office in a skintight black T-shirt which showed off his chiseled physique. Black hair sprouted from the chest and armpit area and his stubble seemed to glisten in a way that swarthy men often do, men who know they reek of sex and power and use it as a weapon. His cockiness was his aftershave.

"Yes, you!" Liz fumed.

"And why's that?" he said with arrogant assurance. Roy could feel the tension between them and looked down at his crotch. Did he detect a boner? Was the man having an erection over their interaction? *Now, that would be amazing sex*, he thought.

"Here!" Liz held up the drone in an accusatory move.

"Why do you assume it's mine?" Eliad curled his lip in a cruel fashion.

"Just seeing the other ones fly back to your property like homing pigeons," she said angrily.

"We were just testing out some new drones for fun and it was never meant to make a right turn. I'm so sorry," he said in an offhand way that indicated he was not sorry at all.

"You're always saying you're sorry but you're not. If I see one of these on my property again, I will not only call the police, but I'll call the press and tell them all sorts of nasty things which Roy here will be happy to corroborate. Do I make myself clear?" Liz had her hand on her lovely hip, her hip bone thrust forward.

"Suit yourself." He yawned in her face.

"Where's your boyfriend?" She looked around to see if G was about and marched forward not waiting for his response. Eliad called after her and ordered her not to go back but she disregarded him as she followed the music that was blasting over the outdoor system.

"You're not allowed back there," Eliad called angrily after her again. She turned and flipped him the bird and he actually laughed as she rounded the corner of the mansion to the backyard area. Eliad followed quickly and she felt his dark, penetrating eyes on her behind. Suddenly she stumbled upon an interesting sight as G was sunbathing naked on the lounge chair listening to his rival Maluma, his competition blasting on Sonos. She couldn't understand the lyrics, but the combination of the modern mansion and the Latin beat seemed both sinister and sexy. Her rage built as she walked through the back area and saw all the electronics and toys. She gained a vague idea of the lyrics as she saw her naked neighbor's body writhing to the beat.

Liz walked back quickly and felt a shiver as she intruded on G's naked reverie.

Roy followed slowly and fanned himself when he saw the oiled and tanned naked man on the lounge. His pelvic area moved sensually to the beat and his privates seemed to flap in the opposite direction. G's eyes fluttered open suddenly. He looked up in shock and blushed as she took her iPhone and snapped a quick photo of him naked. He quickly sat up and covered himself with a towel. She had to admit it to herself that he looked good, tan and in shape, and she looked away when she saw him looking.

"Hey, that's not allowed!" He pulled himself up, angrily.

"Do you want me to confiscate her phone?" Eliad asked. "Or call the police for trespassing?"

"No, wait!" He sat up wrapping the towel firmly around him.

"I'll call the police!!" She threw the drone at him. "Now you know how I feel." She pointed a finger angrily.

"Can you please delete that?" G looked at her and her iPhone pleadingly.

"Let's just say it's my insurance policy," she threatened.

"Meaning?" Eliad walked closer.

"Meaning, I want the spying stopped." She turned to both men, fearless and in anger.

"Spying?" G's vivid jade eyes twinkled in the sun as he flashed his trademark impish smile.

"Your spy, Mr. Darth Vader over here, is sending drones on my property." She fumed. "I assume you will tell me you don't know anything about it?"

"I don't, and I apologize." G shook his head again at Eliad in anger.

"The two of you are always apologizing," Liz cried.

"I'll have a talk with him," G said in a low voice, he was clearly upset at the news.

"If it happens again, do you know what will happen?" Liz approached his lounge chair.

"It won't," G said in a low, disappointed voice.

"I will call a press conference and the police and tell them the two of you are having naked orgies here. The photo will be great proof," she threatened.

"It might be good for my reputation." He offered a wry smile.

"I don't think your fans would be so impressed if I processed this photo and sold it to the tabloids." Liz smirked.

"I'm not so sure, Liz." Roy licked his lips.

She turned and glared at Roy. "Whose side are you on anyway?"

"I think my abs are better. I've been doing an extra two hundred a day since you insulted me. By the way, I could have security get that." G shrugged.

"I already texted it to my mother for safekeeping. And I could tell the police you assaulted me." Liz doubled down.

"You win." G shrugged. "Look. I don't want to fight. I promise you I will get it all under control." He pointed at Eliad "And it won't happen again. Eliad are we clear?"

Eliad nodded in a barely acceptable feigned smirk.

"Can we be friends, good neighbors?" G's eyes twinkled. "Can I offer you something to eat?"

"I'm too angry to be hungry or thirsty" Liz fumed.

"Hangry?" He offered.

She paused and laughed unexpectedly. "Look, If we are going to be forced to live next to each other, can we at least respect each other's privacy?" She frowned.

"Like popping in when I'm naked and taking photos?" He shook his handsome head.

"Uggggh, you are so frustrating. Let's just call it a truce and not see each other, okay? Now that we're even." Liz smirked as well.

"Even." He reached over, and they both shook hands.

"Are you sure you don't want to stay for lunch? I have sushi coming." He smiled.

"Liz?" Roy pleaded. "I'm dying for sushi."

"Traitor, let's go." She frowned at Roy. "You can't buy me off with a California roll! Have a great day, and don't burn down there." Liz laughed out loud. "By the way, use some more suntan lotion…. I can assure you, you won't use up the bottle."

G looked down and grimaced. "You may have a right to be mad, but you are mean," he said.

"Not as mean as Darth Vader over there. We're going, aren't we, Roy?" She turned to Roy and started to walk off without him. As she walked past Eliad, she stopped, made a face, stuck her tongue out at him, and continued on. He shook his head as she marched off.

G looked after her and smiled then laughed to himself. She may have had a photo of his balls, but she had a pair of cojones as well. Sant emerged and brought over a spliff for G as he picked up his guitar from the adjoining lounge chair and started strumming.

"Ella es feroz." Sant smiled as he opened a bag of plantain chips.

"Yes, she's fierce!" G shook his head and started a chord and singing the words "Ella es feroz."

"Wait. That's it!" G's eyes suddenly popped and danced in the light.

"What?" Sant looked a bit confused and heavier than usual as he munched on the golden chips by the handful. "Ella es feroz. She's fierce. The lyric, that's it, Sant! You are a genius." G stood up, the towel falling off him. He stood naked and kissed him on the cheek and sang *"She's fierce. She's fierce. Ella es feroz."* He picked up his guitar and strummed. *"She's the boss…. She's the force…. Ella es la jefa, ella es un fuerza. She's the boss…. She's the force…."* He sang and strummed.

The words came tumbling out in concise lyrics as G in his creative spark and, unabashed in his nakedness, started swiveling his hips and dancing to the imaginary beat interpreting the lyric as he usually did with his songwriting. It didn't happen very often but when it did it was magic. Sant got it as well and started beatboxing and dancing with G. Both were laughing and dancing at the new lyric as Eliad watched from the inner courtyard. He took out his iPhone and snapped a few shots and shook his head.

Little did both know that in less than a year "She's Fierce" would be his biggest international hit on all the charts, and the *Fierce* tour and album would be heralded as G Alvarez's biggest crossover moment.

Chapter 19

Perhaps it was the mention of a sushi lunch, but Liz and Roy ordered their own sashimi platter from Sushi Garage which was delivered beyond the gate an hour later. They decided that after binging on pizza and pasta the night before, sashimi sans rice would set things straight in the diet department. Roy enjoyed setting the massive dining room table and they ate off the formal gold edged china and the array of silver cutlery which had been recently hand polished by the cleaning service. Liz looked down and noticed the large engraved "B" on her spoon for the miso and felt the weight; the sterling was heavy, rich, and formidable and it must have cost a fortune. Liz ran into the pantry and opened the old-fashioned fridge and took out a bottle of inexpensive rosé, which she artfully unscrewed. She would have preferred a cork but liked the under ten dollar price tag more than she liked a cork! A glass or two was needed after their confrontation with their neighbors which seemed to both simultaneously exhaust and exhilarate them.

"You could have been nominated for an Oscar with that performance," Roy congratulated her as they unpacked the sushi containers and set it out on the Limoges. "I love that you are fearless, but don't you think the blackmail photo was taking it a bit far?!"

Liz shot him a withering look and he knew to drop it. He did comment however that he thought G was extremely handsome and "boyfriend" material, but that Eliad was just "sex on a stick" and thought Liz should go over for a quick shag in the gatehouse.

"He knows how to fuck—I am telling you." Roy licked his lips as he ate the tuna sashimi. "What I would give for that hot Israeli!"

"You are so immature." She shook her tawny locks at him. "I think he's gross."

"That's the whole point. You would hate yourself so much for doing it that he would abuse you and debase you as he pounded away, and you would have the most amazing orgasm." Roy licked his lips salaciously.

"Why don't you go over since you're so interested," Liz scolded him.

"Maybe I'll bring over a pie and see who bites. Cause I'm Miami sexy!" he snapped his fingers and started belting out vintage "Ice Ice Baby" by Vanilla Ice to punctuate his thought.

"Okay, Ice, can we change the subject? All you talk about is sex, it's so boring." Liz rolled her eyes.

"And you never talk about it." He looked at her like she had three heads.

"I have more important things to think about." She smirked as she plucked the diary from her beach bag.

"Okay. Fine." He paused. "I think it's Elsa time!" Roy savored the installments. Liz sat at the head of the dining room table and opened Elsa's diary. She decided to read the entry out loud as if it were another installment of a Netflix series as Roy opened the packets of soy sauce into a small crystal and silver bowl. Her eyes lit up and sparkled as she found a passage where she left off. Liz was starting to understand Elsa; she was no longer a figment of her imagination but a real woman with flesh, bones, and feelings. She was complicated and young and had her own relationship issues.

Just like she did.

Elsa

Miami -1934

It is actually a little bit of heaven having the swimming pool and the bay all to myself, but I have to admit the nights have become a tad lonely. Father and Mother came last night as they do most Sundays for dinner and always seem so proud of the villa. Father enjoys his wine and whiskey and feels at home selecting bottles from the wine cellar which were cleverly hidden behind a bookcase during the first days of prohibition. Leland kindly showed him his "stash" and told father to help himself when we were in the first salad days of marriage. I am not sure if he would show him anything now, perhaps the door. He and mother permanently have a worried air about them. Could all this be temporary if I do not provide, as the English say, "an heir and a spare?" They are proud but the subject of the miscarriage has been carefully avoided. Mother has a damp, dispirited scent about her with Leland gone. Clearly, the situation cannot remedy itself with my husband away and blaming me for the loss. However, it was not mentioned, and we discussed lighter topics; Claudette Colbert's lovely dress in It Happened One Night, *which she thought would look well on me, the allure of Mr. Gable's mustache. Father thinks he stole the idea from Adolphe Menjou and can't forgive his appropriation of the whiskers. And then, of course, more serious news of Hitler and Mussolini meeting at the Venice Biennale. All in all, everyone is doing their best despite the hangover.*

I am also quite lucky that I have a standing weekly tea date with a girl I had known at Miss Harris's, Flora Davies, who also married an older man and is now sporting a lovely five carat diamond ring and the name DeJonge (pronounced de-young.) Her husband Arno is in the tin business, has done well during the Depression and they bought a grand pile on neighboring La Gorce Island. As young married women we became "in the family way" around the same time yet unlike me she has successfully carried to full term with a beautiful baby boy named James. I adore him and it does not make me sad to see him but only reinforces that I or we now need to keep trying to achieve our goals. I am willing to do whatever it takes to achieve that goal although Leland and I are clearly not as well suited or likeminded on the subject.

Like most young marrieds, I originally had hopes that Leland and Flora's husband Arno would be friends or maintain a certain sense of civility for our sake but there is some undisclosed tension. There always seems to be an obstacle of some sort with Leland. Everything is put down to him not being a people person, but I suspect there is more, he is that difficult. That said, I quite adore Flora and we have lunch or tea switching off at our respective homes, once a week which I greatly look forward to. Leland doesn't quite care for Flora and just flees to his library when he sees her with a perfunctory "You're looking well" Over a tense dinner he often queries why I need to "see people." I just smile and say, "because you're so busy."

Flora did put on quite a bit of weight with the baby and her husband who she lovingly calls "Daddy" arranged a weekly tennis instructor from the Bath Club and we have lessons on Thursdays on her court and at our home on Tuesdays to swim in my pool, since she does not have one. Leland nods silently when I asked if we could split the associated tennis costs and Arno hired an older instructor, a Mr. Sven Jones, an older man who puts us through our paces with our wooden racquets in the early morning heat. It is essential to play before 12:00 in Miami and my back hand has improved greatly, as has Flora's. They are constructing an indoor tennis pavilion so one can play in the late afternoon heat which should be done soon. I suggested this as well to Leland who waves his hand, which means if I want it I could have it. It's all rather a bit excessive, since Flora isn't naturally inclined towards tennis, but we do have fun and the lessons have also helped us to trim down to our pre-baby weight.

Just yesterday….

I had Gerard drive me over to Flora's house in the Packard. I am only allowed to use it when Leland is out of town and not about. I always feel very grown up sitting in the back seat and having Gerard open the door as we drive into their gated entry. We are like two parakeets, Flora and I; pretty young things in gilded cages going from one gated home to another. We do feel safe and well cared for though. Gerard opens the door as I step out into the bright sunshine of the courtyard, he hands me my tennis racquet and a canvas bag with my initials on it that contained a day dress, shoes, a hat, and gloves and of course, my strand of pearls which had been packed by dear Beaulah who knows the schedule. It was an overheated morning and I do remember seeing a different car in the drive; an old '20s black Ford that was dusty and somewhat rusted, not at all well cared for like our Packards which are highly buffed. Gerard said he would be back to pick me up at four in the afternoon. Of course, I thank him before he drives off out of the gate.

I walk through a set of filigree iron gates into a beautiful entry arcade and through the house out towards the lovely backyard. Her home overlooks Indian Creek and one can see some of the new hotels inching skyward and looming in the distance. As I walk towards the hedge and the court… suddenly, I have a jolt. Flora is playing tennis with a young man! The first thing I notice is his glossy black hair and then his light flashing eyes as he looks up at me…. long, dark girlish lashes and a brilliant white smile. He possesses that athletic lankiness that reminds me of a younger and swarthier Bill Tilden. He looks so handsome and tapered in his V neck and tennis whites; his trousers beautifully pressed, I think I shall always remember the perfect crease. How does a man achieve a perfect crease? He waves in a genial fashion and Flora comes running.

"Do come and meet our new instructor. Good old Sven was in a motor accident and busted up his knee and so he sent one of his younger associates in his place." She offers dramatically.

"Will he be okay?" I ask, not caring. My eyes are delighted to see a young man of about our age, but he doesn't look like any of the boys I had met with his high cheekbones and lashes and olive skin.

"He'll be fine." She laughs. "Let's hope he has a very, very long recovery." She giggles and whispers. "Meet B. this is Elsa?" She says all this in a nonchalant way, but I could tell she is proud and excited that we have a younger, more attractive instructor rather than the gnarly old Sven. We are both married to men much older than ourselves, and it is so nice to interact with a young man about our age as we lead such sheltered lives.

"How do you do, Missus Barrett!" B. flashes a high wattage smile and waves. The moment I see the white teeth and his slightly crooked smile I am suspended in air and time. There is a snap, electricity in the air and for the first time I feel a frisson. I must be truthful, now, that while I had had crushes and movie star fantasies, I have never seen a boy, a young man I had connected with in the flesh I admired.

I am hot and damp and took a gulp of humid air, trying to force a smile and yet I only could get out a simple "how do you do."

"Oh, let's not be so formal with the Missus title" Flora insists. "We don't imagine ourselves our mothers!" Flora's laugh rings out.

"Flora and Elsa will do."

"Yes, Flora and…Elsa" I like the way he repeats my name. He stares at me for what seems like an eternity as I take in all of him, like swilling a cold lemonade on a hot summer day. It is a brief moment, but I can detect he might feel the same way.

"Now," he says as he starts the drills. "Flora and Elsa, let's start with the forehand and then the backhand." He reaches into the pocket of his whites and removes a ball and suddenly I am so overcome.

I will always remember standing with my legs apart and smoothing my white tennis skirt waiting. The moment he hit the ball towards me, I remember swooning; it is all too much. And I must admit it wasn't the heat of the day, although I pretend it is that form of heat as he comes running.

Chapter 20

February turned into March which suddenly turned into April with a swiftness that occurs only on vacations and doomed and fleeting romantic interludes with great sex and no relationship potential. For Liz, it was hard for her to believe the passage of time and the idea she was now truly getting accustomed to living and enjoying life in Miami which was somewhat shocking to her New York centric, neurotic sensibilities. Mornings were filled with yoga and long walks taking in all the estates and the constant sunny weather and lifestyle put her and Roy in an easy and relaxed mood. They were starting to make friends they both agreed on in town and made plans to see people once everyone was vaccinated. There were so many people relocating to Florida that it felt like the winter Hamptons, and all joked that with the Governor's Republican politics it was the land the Covid had forgotten. Most people did not wear masks and groups of stylish Latins kept the chic, outdoor restaurants packed and overflowing with cleavage, miniskirts, and magnums of French rosé. She and Roy had gotten into the habit of Ubering over to the more sophisticated Faena Hotel in the early evening for drinks or lunch and then dinner afterwards they walked Collins Avenue to the Edition, where they met up with a mix of diverse friends, old and new. The outdoor restaurant Matador became one of her favorites with a chic sophisticated vibe and fresh farm to table food. A few men with requisite chunky Rolex's would always approach her if she was at the bar, but it was soon evident most were married, looking for a weekend fling. Linda had called with an enthusiastic report that she had gotten her vaccine appointment and she and Roy were looking forward to having her down at Villa Pompeii to celebrate and spent time readying what would be Linda's bedroom across the hall.

In early April out of the blue, Liz received a call from her LA agent LeeAnn, confirming her first styling job for a TV advertising campaign. Due to Covid, most of the production was being done remotely by limited crew and Zoom, but the actors still needed in-person wardrobe, hair, and makeup. She was able to recommend Roy as the makeup artist and, they both celebrated once they were officially booked; they would be working together again! Roy took care of the JetBlue Mint reservations to LA, and they spent the weekend packing and excited to return to the West Coast after almost a year! They made plans in advance to see Lucy and her baby in Brentwood and shopped for an array of over-the-top baby clothes for the baby girl Jasmine, settling on a pair of expensive turquoise baby sized cowboy boots.

The takeoff to LAX was smooth and the skies clear but a few hours later it turned terribly turbulent over the Rockies and Liz took an extra half a Xanax to calm herself but knew she would be a bit woozier when they landed in LA. When they finally deplaned, she was so drowsy she fell asleep in the back of Uber and woke up forty-five minutes later happy to once again be checking into Shutters. Upon arrival and check-in Roy had the concierge make them make a dinner reservation for an outdoor table at their favorite Ivy at the Shore in Santa Monica and Liz fortified herself with a room service espresso to counter the effects of the medication. As she stepped out onto the outdoor terrace overlooking the bay they were thrilled to be back in town, despite the sixty-five-degree weather and sheltering clouds.

Lucy arrived earlier at the restaurant looking plumper, exhausted, and frazzled from her new mommy duties and after a haze of hugs and kisses, immediately started downing cosmos and they noted she had already had two before they arrived. A diminutive and buxom brunette she had a hearty laugh, big twinkly brown eyes, and an honest way with words, especially when she was drinking. She also seemed more attractive with her post pregnancy glow and got them smiling and talking as she complained about her now enormous breasts were, tender and filled with mothers' milk.

"I'm so over this," she said but showed pictures of Jasmine and beamed at her daughter's fair hair and dimples. They all sat under the aluminum sky and ordered their favorite fried chicken and drank flights of cosmos, caught up and laughed until they closed down the restaurant. It was so nice to know that while Covid and lockdown may have separated them physically for almost a year they had naturally picked up right where they had left off, despite the variants and the ongoing intrusion of masks and social distancing.

Besides the LA weather forecast, another cloud remained looming as well as Lucy pressed for an update from Liz on her relationship with Cary. Since moving to Florida, Liz felt even more disconnected from him, and their nightly calls seemed to trail off to one or a two a week and even then, it felt like it was becoming somewhat of an afterthought. She was particularly bothered that he had not managed to come to Florida once and that they only had one long tense weekend together in the city when they had both received their first vaccinations. When she had stayed over his apartment, he seemed a bit cranky and disconnected, and was short tempered with her about how messy and disorganized she was. In her mind, he had always been a neat freak and she had put it down to his bachelor ways, but lately he seemed extremely unbending in his personal habits. She wasn't exactly thrilled by his regime and rules; he only slept on the left side of the bed, her shoes had to be removed before entering the apartment, and she was only allowed to use her own set of towels, not his, not to mention he was constantly Purell-ing every chance he had. For all their being apart, the sex was even lackluster and he seemed preoccupied in the act. She had complained to her mother about it but in typical Linda-fashion, her mother had tried to gloss over the issues.

"It's a stressful time," Linda noted and her decision to move hadn't helped matters and then added they hadn't spent much time together as a couple due to Covid and her treatments and were just starting to get to know each other again. When Liz told him about her booking in LA, Cary was happy she had landed a styling job but also seemed irked she

142

was able to travel to California, but visiting New York now presented a problem with her establishing Florida residency and the counting of days. He complained that her being able to only visit New York in the summer months seemed especially difficult and she countered he had not visited Florida! He then countered back he was a resident with no time off. It seemed to be an endless game of verbal ping pong each hitting the other back. His obvious lack of interest in her and in Florida set her teeth on edge. Nor did he seem interested in talking about the villa and its restoration. Cary made it constantly clear he preferred cold weather, hated the sun and humidity, and also threw out constantly that he had no intention of moving to Miami, was dedicated to New York and Mount Sinai, and establishing a career in the northeast. It seemed like an impossible standoff but in the end Liz did what she mostly did which was delay a serious discussion. She knew if she were officially single again, she would have to start the dating process all over again at thirty and that was something she was not prepared to do just yet, and not without a real push. Roy, it seemed, didn't have these issues as he frequently met men he liked at the gym or bars and wasn't under a ticking biological clock for children. He wasn't a fan of Cary and thought he wasn't handsome or interesting enough for Liz, but he held his tongue as much as he could as he felt his offhanded criticism annoyed her. When Lucy pressed for details Liz held back her fears as she just wanted to have fun after such a stressful lockdown, and only mentioned that her and Cary's relationship seemed a bit stalled.

When they arrived on the West Coast, the LA styling job proved less interesting than she had originally hoped for though she and Roy were happy for the work and the paycheck. She had wished it would have been glamorous or creative, but it turned out to be for an ad campaign for a menopause drug company. She was tasked with bringing an assortment of size fourteen to sixteen jeans and chenille sweaters to the set for the older plus-sized models. The big news came when the ad agency creative director asked her to find some plain linen summer dresses as an alternative. She wanted to add a bit of her signature cutting edge flair, but knew that might not fly as the brief was for a mass target who were

JC Penny and Walmart gals. The shoot was slow and dragged on but she and Roy and some of the crew lingered at the Kraft service table each day chatting and snacking on fattening chips and guacamole the chef put out for the team. At least the food was good and plentiful, and she was flattered that she was circled by a really cute twenty-something with an array of ghoulish tats and a man bun, but demurred and felt like a cougar when he hit on her. Roy encouraged her to have a fling with the handsome Millennial, but Liz shut it down as she usually did; casual affairs were not for her and she just flirted, smiled, and felt flattered that he found her an attractive older woman. Roy just raised an eyebrow and cautioned her that "if you don't use it, you lose it!"

Once the shoot was wrapped, they happily moved on to their mini vacation, as they always did.

She and Roy checked out of Shutters, picked up Lucy after a visit with Jasmine, then drove their rented car from LA to Palm Springs. Lucy had offloaded her baby with her mother-in -law who was more than happy to accommodate and spend time with her granddaughter. Lucy loved her girl to the moon and back but as a sleep deprived new mother, she needed a weekend away from bottles and formula and was desperate for a good massage and a Cosmo. They had all booked a room at the stylish and mid-century Parker and were looking forward to a fun weekend of lounging by the oval pool, drinking cocktails, and laughing their heads off and Liz and Lucy left Roy at the intimate Jonathan Adler designed hotel bar as he was chatting up the buff bartender and went hiking together in Joshua Tree. They both caught up on love and life on the desert trails. Lucy was Liz's constant, her Girl Friday and female confidante, and the truth finally came pouring out over the dusty desert trail filled with prickly cacti and omnipresent Joshua Trees.

Lucy Cardone hailed from South Orange, New Jersey, and had been her roommate junior and senior year at UCLA. They shared an easy rapport with a similar sense of humor despite their different paths and while she was prone to breakouts and weight gain, cellulite and sported an off-center nose, Lucy always had a myriad of boyfriends as she knew how to connect and make the person she was talking to feel like the most special in the room. She had perfected the art of looking directly into her subject's eyes and asking people about themselves; understanding that a conversationalist was actually not about what she had to say but had discovered people loved to talk about themselves and in the end would think she was scintillating. It was an innate talent, and she had a series of boyfriends before dating and then marrying her Senior college beau George, a solid Midwesterner who was in computer sales. She wasn't thrilled to hear the news about Cary once Liz started to open up about the real issues on their hike.

"Flexibility is important, and he seems to be very set in his ways," Lucy cautioned, swilling her water bottle in the hot sun as they hiked in the sweltering heat. Lucy's honest words seared, and Liz looked forlorn at hearing the obvious as they walked past the omnipresent cacti in the blazing heat and caves with ancient hieroglyphics that looked like modern UFO drawings. She walked the rest of the trail in silence, Lucy's assessment buzzing in her head and knowing that she was right. Later that night, they both sat outdoors at the iconic rat pack steakhouse Mr. Lyon as Liz opened up and ranted to Lucy a bit over another round of cosmos; the Covid year had been extra harsh for her; she had basically lost her career, was tending to her mother's cancer treatments, and she and Cary were essentially kept apart because of it. Until the news about Miami, her life had seemed rather bleak. Lucy's brown eyes swelled with tears, and she patted her best friend's hand.

"I want you to have that great love, Liz. You deserve it!" she exclaimed. "You of all people shouldn't settle." She laughed and added, "And no one who is five foot nine, a size two, and is as pretty and funny as you are *needs* to settle!" She boosted her friend with the truth, and they clinked glasses.

On the JetBlue flight back to Miami she heard Lucy's words ring and echo in her head, *You can't force a relationship, Liz. You're the opposite of a collision course. You and Cary seem to be going in entirely different directions.* The part that hit her hardest was when she admonished, *You can't be with Cary just to make Linda happy, that's no way to live!*

As she landed in Miami, she was even more nervous. After a great deal of pressure and complaining, Cary had promised to come down the following weekend, and she now had growing anxiety that this weekend would really either make or break their relationship. She pushed the thought from her mind as she and Roy wheeled their luggage out of the terminal and called an Uber to North Bay Road once they touched down at Miami International. She smiled and looked out the Uber window at the Causeway appreciating the towering, swaying palm trees and a group of sexy Cuban ladies passing by in a cherry red BMW convertible. She was happy to be home, in sunny Miami.

Saturday arrived in a gust of humidity that frizzed even the straightest hair and she and Roy slept later due to the hum of the air conditioning and layering heat, happy for the day off and to be back in the Villa. While they were away, the master bedroom had been painted a chalk white and they both felt a bit dizzy at the smell of fresh paint, although the pristine white of the room in the morning sun made everything sparkle. She looked over at the digital alarm clock and saw it was 10:30 and managed to get out of bed and motivate, her arm pins and needles from sleeping in a bad position. She'd had too many cosmos in the airport and a mini bottle of Chardonnay on the flight due to turbulence, and after all the snacking and liquor in LA and Palm Springs she knew she needed a reset. Roy tossed and moaned and wouldn't wake up, looking like a teenage boy after discovering the liquor cabinet. She looked out at the bay and the clear weather and decided to go for a jog. She begged Roy to come but he moaned and demurred and put the pillow over his head. He was having a "bed-in," he groaned and wanted to catch up on a new Netflix series, *The White Lotus*.

She bounded downstairs into the kitchen and nodded hello to Zosia, somewhat pleased to see the plodding familiar housekeeper. She had come to consider the old Polish retainer a comforting and familiar sight on Saturday mornings, like the faded wallpaper in the maid's room or the linoleum tile in the back pantry. Zosia had put some cut fruit and hard-boiled eggs in the fridge and a pot of black coffee was brewing on the counter in the Mr. Coffee machine Sheila had given her as part of a housewarming gift basket. In the first few months, Liz had tried to engage Zosia in conversation but now realized she was part of the house the way the limestone fireplace or the fresco above the library dental was part of the villa. She didn't know whether she was shy, slightly off or just plain reserved, but Zosia was as impenetrable as steel and as deep as a curb. They had come to accept each other, though, and what was best; Zosia knew her place, working a few hours week and lived over the garage on the weekends. It was actually somewhat calming that she had to make little or no effort with her, though Zosia was the type of person that didn't embrace or like change, hence her more recent facial grumbling at the cleaning crew.

Liz sipped some pulpy orange juice and walked outside through the French doors into the bright sunshine. It was clear and hot early, and she walked back through the enfilade of rooms to the entry courtyard past the Pompeian mosaic, plugged in her EarPods choosing to listen to old Stevie Nicks as she walked out the imposing gate thrilled to be back and eager for a solitary run.

She started briskly down North Bay Road past a few lemon stucco mansions and modern masterpieces hidden behind gates and groomed hedgerow. After seven minutes she came to the end of the street and made a right and a sharp left, crossing the small bridge on traffic heavy Alton Road which connected the adjoining side of North Bay Road. She stopped to look at a seemingly lethargic manta ray hovering in the shallow water and then made a sharp left into the 5000 block once again. The homes were stunning, and she never tired of the varied architecture; a tower here, a rotunda there, pastel colored rose gardens edged with manicured boxwoods in bloom.

She started a light jog and passed the burgeoning construction teams and cars shoehorned in to benefit possible empty space. A few workers whistled at her back side. Suddenly she felt the presence of a body quickly approaching behind her as she turned and saw the lean muscles and biceps and a potent smell of sweat, tobacco, and old school Paco Rabanne. Eliad Shiraz quickly advanced on her like a pouncing jaguar and then slowed down his jog as he looked over and smirked.

"Glad to see you're back in town," he said in his cocky fashion.

"You are the last person I want to see and I find it creepy you are keeping track of my comings and goings." She slowed.

"Well, not all your cummings." He licked his lips.

"Gross. Pig!" She slowed down more and rolled her eyes.

"Don't you want someone to run with…to push you?" He looked at her intently.

"I'm fine on my own," she stated blankly and purposefully.

"You know, I like your spunk." He smiled.

"I hate yours."

"Maybe it's a love-hate thing?" He quickly fell into rhythm beside her.

"Eli…?"

"Eliad."

"Whatever your name is. I understand you have a job to do. So just do it, and leave me alone. I have no interest in you," Liz said defiantly.

"You don't? I see the way you look at me." He smiled in what he thought was his own version of sexy.

"You're an egomaniac." She couldn't believe what he was saying.

"No, I see it." He smirked again.

"And how's that?"

"Let's just say it's the way you and your friend look at me." He rested with his hands on his hips, the tight Lycra of his shorts highlighting his impressive bulge. There was no way he didn't put himself on display on purpose with those shorts.

"He can look at you anyway he pleases, I am sure he does, but when I look at you, I have only one word for you." She squared off with him.

"And what's that?"

"Contempt." She laughed a little.

"That's a little harsh, don't you think?" He wiped the sweat from his brow.

"I really enjoyed being…alone." And then she added, "You're everything I hate in a man."

"Sometimes that works for me." Eliad gave her his best smoldering look.

"Clearly." Liz stopped in her tracks and motioned for him to run ahead of her.

"Fine, suit yourself. Your loss," he said gruffly, his accent becoming more prominent in his anger. He put in his EarPods, grimaced and started to run. He wasn't used to women turning him down, but Liz only saw one word when she looked at him: trouble.

She did look up and after him as he strode away and as much as she hated to admit he was sexy in a mean, "I'm going to abuse you sort of way." Roy was right and she felt a tingling between her legs at the thought.

No! Absolutely not. She stopped herself. *That might be fine for Roy, but it would be the worst idea of my life.*

Chapter 21

Liz found Roy having taken a page from G, wearing only his EarPods, sunbathing nude while listening to the Bee Gees and undulating to his Miami playlist. Liz rolled an eye and threw a towel over him over his privates as he raised his midsection. He looked up and smiled and sang.

"Really?" She raised a sweaty eyebrow from her run and stripped off her tank and leggings in the blazing sun and plunged into the deep end of the pool in her sports bra and panties.

"Well, you're not much better in that getup." Roy sniffed.

"You'll never believe who I just saw!" Liz rolled her eyes, lying back and putting her elbows on the ledge of the pool behind her with her face in the golden light.

"Who? Barry Gibb? I keep walking by his house waiting to see him. Nobody had better hair!" he sang and blasted the music.

"I wish. Darth Vader tried to pick me up." Liz tossed her tawny mane as she unleashed it from her ponytail and soaking the back of her head. "Gross!"

"And?" Roy peered at her.

"And nothing. I told him to leave me alone." She made a face like she tasted something spoiled.

"I *vant* to be alone!!!!" Roy put his hand on his forehead imitating Garbo. "I cannot believe my timing was off. If I was with you, I would have told him I needed a little…Israeli invasion."

"You're depraved."

"And you'll never meet a man with that attitude." Roy pointed at her.

"Who says I need a man; I have a boyfriend," Liz offered.

"That's right, *boy* not man!" He rolled his eyes.

"Don't remind me." She sighed and tacitly agreed and waded back in the shallow end of the pool and then got out, dried herself with a terry towel and then lay down on the lounge next to Roy. She smiled at the strong sun and the warmth enveloping her as she checked her phone for the time and then for texts. After she answered Linda, she plucked Elsa's diary from her beach bag as Roy sat up.

"It's diary time!" she said in a sing-song voice.

"No, let me do the honors!" He reached over and grabbed the diary and proceeded to read the words in his version of an upper-class accent.

Elsa's Diary

Miami 1934

I enter or shall I say, sashay into the breakfast pavilion, which in my opinion has a whimsical edge due to the life-sized ceramic leopards and the tromp l'oeil tented ceiling. My husband prefers things all paneled and gloomy with cranberry velvets and dimly lit blackamoors which is why I am surprised to see him there. The peaked, striped tent design was an element August, the architect included and must never have been run by Leland as I cannot imagine he would ever have approved anything so light-hearted. In fact, it is my favorite room in the villa yet there he is, a veritable apparition come to life. I wrap myself tightly in my lovely Japanese silken wrap I had purchased in Paris on our honeymoon which I secure around my morning dress. It gives me a sense of false comfort, yet I adore the elevated and artful stitching so much that when I first saw it in the shop on the Left Bank, I bought two.

Roy stopped reading in his tracks as the words sank in, and he and Liz locked eyes.

"Liz, she bought two!" He stared at her.

"I know. Wow," Liz repeated as they both looked at each other and raised their eyebrows together in unison.

"Roy, mine has to be the companion piece!" Liz said totally startled.

"But how?" he asked.

"Keep reading…" she commanded.

> *I thought I would never see such fine handiwork again. I first spotted the robe on a mannequin in the window of a small French Vietnamese seamstress shop on the Rue Jacob and Leland looked at his pocket watch and harrumphed as I insisted I go inside, and he waited outside the shop as he usually did but didn't question that I had bought two. It was the only lovely memory of the* honeymoon, *I must say.*

> *I rub my red eyes for effect as I am shocked to see him sitting upright, erect and posture ready at the breakfast table reading the Miami Herald and I instinctively wrap the robe tighter. I survey the table strewn with plates and silver. He had seemingly downed a sumptuous breakfast of sausage and eggs and barely looks up at me as I enter.*

> *"Leland. How nice to see you." I regain my composure quickly channeling mother's Southern Charm. "When did you return?" I ask sweetly.*

> *"Last evening." He continues reading without looking up.*

> *"And how was your trip?" I feign avid interest.*

> *"The same as always; the natives are lazy, good-for-nothings…. The rum is the only thing worth anything there."*

"Now you know I don't countenance that kind of talk in my home. If Beaulah should hear it would be very upsetting," I say softly.

"It is my home," he sneers. "And Beaulah is lucky to have a roof over her head and bread in her mouth," he snarls at me, and I instinctively jump back a bit.

"Yes, your home, still no need for that kind of talk." I pause. "It's nice to have you home." I try to be polite and enthusiastic, I really do, as Beulah walks in with a hot tea and lemon on a silver serving tray. I am embarrassed she had only walked in moments after his slur.

"No it's not," he harrumphs.

We sit in stony silence. I try with him with all my heart, I truly do; however he is unrelenting in his frosty temperament and it sets the tone for his arrival. We barely speak.

Sunday, Leland decides to join us for dinner when my parents arrive this evening. Father and Mother virtually fall over themselves in ecstasy at the sight of him despite my report on his icy behavior. Needless to say, I am not pleased. It is somewhat encouraging but nevertheless disconcerting when he makes his proclamation before he and father retire to the library for their whisky and to discuss the shipping updates.

"I am glad you are all here," he says aloud and adds, "and on time." He looks at his own father's gold pocket watch. Leland is terribly punctual and holds everyone to account if they do not show up on time or adhere to his rigid schedule.

"I have consulted with Dr. LeFevre, who was Fisher's physician after his son died. Of course, he was as beside himself as I am."

"Yes, just terrible, Leland." Father nods in sympathy.

"That's Mister Barrett to you, until she," he rails and points with accusatory aplomb, "procures an heir," he bellows. "And then we can get back to pleasantries again."

"Leland, you mustn't speak to Father that way. There's no reason for unpleasantness," I admonish him softly. "We will give it a college try, not that I was allowed to attend college, but I shall."

"And if that doesn't work, you will all be in Sarasota." He sips his wine. "I have already purchased a lovely Victorian in town where the Sloans can all retire should our efforts be unsuccessful. You won't go homeless or starve," he says with supposed beneficence.

"So be it," I say calmly. "Perhaps Sarasota is my destiny. I was going there anyway."

"Perhaps it is." Leland stares me down with steely reserve, waving his large hand in a dismissive way as he has a habit of doing with the cowering staff. Only this time it is with me, his wife or am I now relegated to staff since I did not perform? Father and Mother look down into their soup bowls, and I actually go from feeling badly to feeling betrayed.

"You can see for yourself your daughter's arbitrary and distempered personality," he states with a steel countenance as he threatens with his red rimmed eyes.

"I have consulted with the doctor, and he wants you on a strict diet and no exercise—no riding or tennis—and each morning, you shall have your portion of cod liver oil. In the afternoon after bedrest, I have hired a Swedish masseuse, Missus Inga Eriksson to massage your abdomen. I am willing to go through this one more time before I buy myself another filly."

"Lovely," I state, looking at Mothers' downcast eyes in dismay and mentally packing for the other coast. Father is intent on his wineglass, and Mother makes meaningless conversation.

"Cod liver oil is known to have a wonderful result." She nods in agreement.

"Thank you, Mother," I whisper sarcastically.

This evening before Mother and Father leave, we climb the stairs in silence. I go into my boudoir and secretly take my wedding gift from own jewel box: a geometric deco diamond bracelet and necklace set in platinum and put it into a small, scarlet, silken pouch and silently hand it to Mother for safekeeping. The small drawstring is the color of blood exactly. Blood money.

"For Sarasota," is all I say as I hand it to her, with no emotional attachment as it is all a business deal, and these are the proceeds. She frowns in a downcast way.

However, despite her look of surprise, she doesn't tell me to keep it.

Chapter 22

The only thing Cary seemingly liked about Florida was Eric Clapton's 1974 classic *461 Ocean Boulevard*. The faded sleeve of the old-school album cover he had in high school showcased a classic white sun washed Florida home which Clapton had rented during that period as it was close to his recording studio when he was recuperating from a bout of heroin addiction. The album title, house and iconic palm tree on the cover art is often mistaken for Ocean Boulevard in South Beach but the property was actually farther north in Golden Beach. It is notable that Clapton rented the house before many other popular artists considered Miami as a creative recording alternative and the album remains one of his most popular and enduring featuring the now classic "I Shot the Sheriff." Soon other artists arrived for the sunny shores and weather and the cultural fusion, from the English-born Australian Bee Gees to Cuban American Gloria and Emil Estefan who have since made Star Island their home. Miami has since been an international cultural melting pot influencing the sights and sounds of the barrier reef island and then globally. Since the success of the eponymous *Miami Sound Machine*, Miami is now associated with an influx of Latin rhythm, and the Estefans are often credited with mainstreaming Latin music paving the way for other artists ranging from Selina to Ricky Martin to G Alvarez. As many like to note, the Cubans and South Americans brought the drums and the beat, and the Afro Caribbeans brought reggae, calypso all to create a truly uniquely memorable "Miami sound."

Cary had jumped through hoops with his hospital schedule to organize a trip to Florida and once settled in on the plane, tried to relax inserting his EarPods listening to his playlist. He was not a fan of reggae or Latin music and his taste leaned only towards classic rock. Liz could only tolerate a quarter of his playlist and joked that the Clapton, the Grateful Dead, and Boston were too "frat boy" for her. He countered that if she were a "Dead" fan she would be the perfect woman but had concluded it was hard enough to find someone with enough things in common and didn't expect her to share his musical passions. He had managed to get the weekend off at the hospital with a white lie saying he had a family wedding and while he told her he was excited to see her he mentioned he only wished her villa were in New England or the Berkshires, which set her teeth on edge. The iPhone photos and the videos she had sent seemed incredible and he was thrilled for her, just less thrilled for himself.

"Florida!" He shook his well cropped head with distaste. He looked around at the other passengers in coach and saw a glint and array of gold chains and gold rimmed sunglasses, tracksuits, and man bags. Why did everyone look like Vanilla Ice and Miami Vice together? *Vanilla Vice!* He laughed to himself and thought to tell that to Liz, but then thought again. He knew she would take it as a criticism or slight as she always did when he poked fun at Florida or her new home. As a doctor he was also baffled by the state's lenient Covid policy, yet it seemed Miami, Boca Raton, and Palm Beach were also overflowing with vaccines while the rest of the country was struggling to get it. Perhaps, it had something to do with the Trumps moving there, but maybe that was another conspiracy theory!

He tried to get comfortable in his seat but was also feeling uncomfortable emotionally as his feelings about Liz were causing him a certain amount of anxiety lately. While part of him was looking forward to spending time with her now that she was vaccinated, he also recognized they had drifted somewhat. He looked at his iPhone and switched it to airplane mode as the captain made his announcement describing the flight time, the weather and ordered a wine from the stewardess after takeoff, sipping it slowly and thinking about their strained relationship.

It was the little things that were getting to him as well, a bit miffed that Liz wasn't planning on meeting him at the airport as there were certain things he expected a girlfriend or a fiancée to do. When he asked, she said Ubers were easy to get and also added that she was supervising a team of workmen getting the pool back in working order which was almost complete. Liz seemed excited he was finally coming for the weekend, but it all seemed rather slapdash and thrown together for his taste. Cary would have loved nothing more than a home cooked meal and dining-in but she mentioned she had booked some of her favorite restaurants from the eternally romantic Casa Tua and lunch at the hip Setai. The deluge of New Yorkers had made getting a reservation virtually impossible and she and Roy boasted of their reservation prowess, which also slightly annoyed him, highlighting their differences; that he had a social girlfriend who loved to go out on the town, and he was a homebody who loved to eat and entertain in.

Cary had taken the early morning flight to arrive in time for lunch and was starving and half expecting a welcome lunch or buffet when he finally arrived. He was less interested in a tour of the mansion than he was a bagel, a scoop of tuna salad and a platter of nova upon his arrival yet Liz had not managed to orchestrate a meal. She ran out to see him in the courtyard and gave him a warm hug and kiss and then asked him what he wanted to order-in, as Roy brought out a stack of paper take out menus. He oohed and ahhed a bit about the grand house as he knew he should but grumbled internally. He thought of his late mother Paulette and knew that if his father were flying to meet her there would have been a veritable feast on the table waiting for him when he got there. It was one more strike against Liz and Miami. Once he changed into shorts and a shirt, he looked over the menus Roy had given him he chose their favorite, Sushi Garage where he ordered a few rolls and chicken teriyaki skewers.

At the estate next door, G was sitting by his pool after a particularly sweaty rehearsal with his choreographer Chantal as he knew his management team were starting to plan tour dates and ideas for the show even though Covid had decimated the touring industry. While he loved his Miami respite, he was starting to get itchy to get back on the road again as was his management, not to mention the hefty fees. He wrapped up his session, air kissed and hugged Chantal and walked out to the pool with his iPhone and was thankful for the particularly humid free day and the translucent bay, as calm as glass. Chantal waved goodbye as Sant handed her a cash envelope and he decided to get out his paddle board from the pool house, walked over and threw it into the tranquil bay. He stripped off his tank in one easy motion and hoisted himself down the gleaming chrome ladder now hot to the touch into the translucent water. It felt cool and invigorating after the grueling dancing in the sun and he wet his hair as he threw his head back into the clear ripples. He loved paddling on the board out on the bay and taking in his neighbor's estates as it all looked so vastly different from the water rather than land. Once paddling out, he stood on the board in perfect balance, but a cigarette boat came out of nowhere with a photographer snapping away at him.

"G, hey, look here?" The waterborne paparazzi shouted and took what seemed like an endless number of photos before jetting off; his reverie was broken and he realized he was never truly alone, and it rankled him. He looked down and was happy his abs were tight and once again knowing that the photo would show him in great shape and not at all flabby. Indeed, the diet, exercise and self-restraint had been working, as he looked at his modern mansion from the bay and took its clean white lines and the sparkling windows and reflective glass and was proud of the sight and as he paddled out, he noticed from the shore that his next-door neighbor's lot was twice as big and featured a tennis pavilion and a greenhouse.

Lucky girl, that Liz, he thought to himself. Each day he and his security team observed an influx of construction teams arriving on the property sanding, plastering, and painting and while the noise bothered him, he decided against complaining. Eliad had run a search on his new neighbor, and it seemed she was a fashion stylist and not from a particularly wealthy background. They all couldn't figure out where she was getting the money to renovate the old place as they were baffled at the teams of gardeners and workmen who seemed to be working around the clock. The gardeners had done a very nice job pruning back the old growth and restoring the villa landscape to its former glory. He decided to paddle in and to get a better look at the other improvements as it seemed the pool had also been filled. From the distance, he was able to make out the renovated cherub fountain now spouting water into the deep end of the pool. As his board approached the house, he saw Liz on a lounge chair next to the sea wall overlooking the bay, tanning, and reading a magazine. She looked simple and elegant in her saucer sized sunglasses but also slightly bored and annoyed for some reason. He paddled closer and decided to try and charm her.

"You don't write, you don't call…" He waved and forced his widest and most brilliant smile, which always had his fans and the reporters, women and men alike, swooning.

"You scared me." She glared at him from above. "Lucky I had my top on!"

"I'm not!" He joked, standing and paddling in closer, sucking in his stomach for better effect of his now visible cuts on his abs.

"Gross! My boyfriend just flew in, and he's coming down for a swim at any moment." Liz deliberately yawned and flipped a page of *Vogue* nonchalantly for effect.

"That dweebie guy?" G hit back, upset she was impervious to his charms. His smile was said to melt ice cubes, yet she was the impenetrable ice queen.

"How do you know he's a dweeb?" Liz sighed.

"You see, even you think so." G smirked.

"No, you just said it. He actually does something *worthwhile*; he's a doctor." Liz flipped more of the glossy pages in an attempt to show she was bored by the conversation.

"So, a musician who sells out stadiums and entertains millions of people isn't worthwhile?" G countered.

"I didn't say that…." She yawned. "You did."

"Touché… You know how frustrating you are?" He squinted in the sun, his hands running in the rippling water at his side.

Cary walked down and emerged, walking past the pool to the seating area at the edge of the bay. "Hey babe, lunch should be here soon"

Liz looked up and noticed he was wearing an unstylish, short sleeved Hawaiian shirt, and his legs were milky white and hairy. Liz grimaced at the sight; his fashion choices and untanned skin in contrast to G who seemed to have been born to the water and sun. Cary's shirt pattern featured repeating Hawaiian girls in grass skirts. Really? She raised an inner eyebrow; she would have to have a fashion intervention.

"Who's this?" Cary squinted into the sun at the handsome athletic man on a board talking to his girlfriend, adjusting his gold wire Ray Bans which highlighted the red in his auburn.

"This is my next-door neighbor, the one I told you about," Liz said matter-of-factly.

"Hi there." G waved in a friendly fashion. "I was out boarding and decided to stop by and say hello."

"Oh, so you're the guy that called the police on her." He frowned and turned to her. "Is he bothering you again?"

"No, he's fine, he just doesn't understand...things."

"What things?" G smiled.

"Like privacy," Liz muttered.

"No, I just wanted to," G paddled in, "make you an offer."

"An offer?" Cary's ears perked up.

"Yes, I would like to buy this house and combine it with mine," he spoke directly to Cary.

"Wow, that's interesting." Cary shrugged and thought about a quick sale and the money involved; a way out of Miami!

"Well, I'm sorry to inform you, it's not for sale," Liz countered.

"It's not?" Cary looked at her as if she was crazy.

"Just name your price." G beamed at them confidently.

"I said it's not for sale," Liz repeated.

"Forever?" G was a bit stunned at her resilience.

"I didn't say forever, but it's not in the cards now," Liz said in a curt tone.

"So, you are saying we might as well get used to each other. Hey, I'm G, by the way." He looked at Cary.

"This is my boyfriend, Cary." Liz fake yawned again.

"The doctor?" G smiled.

"How did you know I'm a doctor?" Cary was trying to catch up.

"I told him you do something worthwhile." She smiled ruefully.

"Wait, you're G Alvarez?" Cary looked stunned.

"Yeah, why?" G perked up.

"You know who he is?" Liz looked at him sideways. Cary looked at his girlfriend like she had three heads.

"He's, well, I'm a fan. I thought your Super Bowl performance was amazing!" Cary gushed.

"Wait, don't tell me you are going to ask for an autograph. Gross," Liz sneered.

"I love your version of Frampton's 'Baby I Love Your Way.' I have it on my playlist when I work out." Cary nodded enthusiastically.

"Wait, that's your song?" Liz gulped.

"Uh huh." G smiled slightly.

"Oh right, you're famous." She shrugged.

"Is that a bad thing?" He paddled forward.

"Is that my fave neighbor G Alvarez?" Roy sauntered down to the dock to join the group as he adjusted his navy terry Orlebar Brown polo and his Tom Ford sunglasses.

"You remember Roy, my best friend. When the police came?" Liz fake yawned again.

"I thought your boyfriend was supposed to be your best friend!" G was now enjoying this.

"You know what I mean." Liz looked frustrated.

"No, I don't." G smiled again.

"G, I love your nose stud. You look HAWT." Roy posed as he saw the glint of the tiny rose diamond nose sparkling on the left side of his nostril.

"I'm sorry I intruded, but if you ever decide you want to sell, let me know. I'm the natural buyer for your place," he said matter-of-factly as Cary shrugged in exasperation thinking *If she could get top dollar from a Latin pop star; how could one not at least entertain the offer?*

"I think that you should think about it," Cary whispered loudly.

"I think you should stick to the Covid wing," she said angrily.

"Sorry. I was just trying to…"

"Look," Liz glared at G, "I know you have had your eye on my property for a while, but I'm here to stay. You and your thugs need to get used to me and stop harassing me. I'm not going anywhere."

"Okay, okay, just wanted to plant the idea." He started to paddle. "So, you're not going to invite me in and show me what you've done with the place?"

"I think your drone footage would be sufficient."

"Liz, you don't have to be so rude." Cary shook his head.

"Cary, please, for the last time, stay out of this." She shot him daggers.

"Just saying." He shook his head. He wasn't used to her acting this tough.

"'Maybe you two want to go out with G." Liz frowned.

"That would be fun. I have a table at Casa Tua tonight. Why don't you all join me as my guests, my treat?" G offered.

"I would love that!" Roy planted his hand on his hip.

"No, that's where we are having dinner tonight," she said in an exasperated tone.

"Okay, sorry to intrude. Nice meeting you all, and Cary, thank you for your service." G started to paddle away and then turned. "If you ever change your mind."

"Have a nice life!" she yelled after him.

Cary was stunned as he could not understand what had come over her as she was usually so nice and polite; he thought her behavior was tacky, bordering on tawdry.

"Liz, I don't get it." Cary looked at her like she was a stranger. "I've never seen you act this way. Why do you hate him so much?"

"I have a better question?" Liz turned with a rare fury. "Why do you like him so much?" She picked up her copy of *Vogue*, stood up in a huff, and walked into the house.

"Roy, would you do me a favor and set the table? I'm sure Cary wants to have lunch here *before* I sell it," she stated. Cary followed her across the lawn like a lost puppy, trailing and not quite understanding the fuss and even more confused as to why she wouldn't entertain a solid offer for the property. It only reinforced his feelings that he was oblivious about women. She managed to get to the elegant veranda lined with antique wicker chairs and couches when he said he was sorry. Liz turned and looked at him with a critical eye.

"Burn that shirt."

Chapter 23

Later that evening when tempers had cooled off a bit, Liz dressed in a simple, electric blue silk, off the shoulder Ramy Brook top that set off her cobalt blue eyes and hair, and Cary had redeemed himself with a classic white button down, jeans, and Gucci loafers. Tensions were still a bit strained as they Ubered to Casa Tua, but as they sat in the romantic outdoor garden and the overhead lights twinkled, they held hands and their issues seemed to dissolve as they sipped glasses of rose from their bottle of Whispering Angel. Cary carefully avoided the subject of their afternoon visitor, even when G walked over with his best friend Sant and then sent over a magnum of rose. He sat at a nearby table attracting a great deal of attention and more than a few diners walking over and asking for selfies with him. He seemed happy to accommodate his fans and gracious at that and the waiter indicated that G Alvarez had sent them a large magnum Liz waved and mouthed "Thank you. You shouldn't have." She acquiesced. "That was sweet of him, I guess."

Cary waved quickly, nodded, and looked down at the menu and knew better than to address the subject. He just reinforced that the villa was remarkable and was glad she was enjoying living there and asked a few questions about the cost of the ongoing renovation. The waiter first brought a beautiful amuse bouche of chilled leek soup and then shared a delicious fettuccine with black truffles and parmesan appetizer. The two basked in the romantic ambiance; spending the first part of the evening talking about the tragedy of Covid and Cary's overwhelming responsibilities. Liz patted his hand and had tears in her eyes as he described the elderly patients and those with underlying conditions who had passed under his watch. It made everything else seem trivial.

Cary switched the gloomy subject back to the villa, and Liz filled him in on many of the new responsibilities of being a homeowner on the water. He listened diligently without looking at his phone texts as he usually did, happy the afternoon tiff was behind them. After dinner and eschewing dessert, Cary ordered his espresso macchiato and promptly paid the bill.

Liz avoided G's table as they walked out of the restaurant hand-in-hand but felt his eyes on her back—or at least she felt that she did. They exited the restaurant and turned left to walk to Collins Avenue, taking in the array of deco hotels and visiting, young crowds most who were not wearing masks and seemingly oblivious to the pandemic. He stopped in front of the Raleigh Hotel, now under construction to kiss her and in that moment, she was appreciative for his solid frame and soft, confident lips. It had been a while, but later that evening they made love in her bedroom, and she was happy to have him back in her arms. While there weren't fireworks, it was pleasant, and she felt safe and secure with him sharing her bed. He lay on his back and saw the golden cherub above the four-poster bed and joked they were having "a ménage à trois." Liz laughed and wished that she could capture this moment of ease and humor forever.

"You really hated that shirt?" He laughed afterwards, lying back on the feather pillow. "I bought it for you, you know."

"It's like a Midwestern frat boy puked over it with that pattern." She laughed out loud.

"Okay, okay. I was trying." He frowned.

She stroked his tight cropped, wavy hair. "I know, and I appreciate it, but it needs to go into the bonfire of bad taste."

"I'm very happy for you, and this villa is amazing." He looked up at the European moldings and the elegant and simple new draperies. "Have you found out any more about the woman who left you this place?" He stroked her luxurious locks.

"Here." She reached over for the diary on the nightstand. "I'll read you where I left off. I'm getting to know her and honestly, the strangest thing…" She looked at him with her beautiful baby blues.

"Yes?" Cary asked, looking at a text on his phone while Liz picked up the diary and prepared to read the passage aloud.

"I've learned she's a lot like me."

ELSA

Miami Beach, 1934

I have accepted my fate of a loveless marriage. I am after all, despite the optics, the sole support of my family during the Depression however, I never like the "meanness" that accompanies certain situations no matter the agreements in place. On a rare social evening, Leland insisted we attend a party the Knowlton Collins were having at his latest hotel on the beach last Thursday evening. Word had it he had divorced his wife Charlotte and married his secretary. It was business of course and no one turned down an invitation from Knowlton, who besides Carl Fisher, was widely credited with inventing Miami. Even Leland, who was loathe to admit it, would never have dreamt of not attending. It was a command performance among a certain group; the prevailing thought that if one wasn't there one may have thought one wasn't invited etc. etc.

Leland and I both gritted our teeth in attending as we both despaired of certain social obligations for different reasons; he isn't too partial to people and I to pretense. Leland also is not miserly, which is one of his only good qualities and he did insist I buy a new frock for his reception. I went to the boutique on Lincoln Road and chose a lovely French Lelong with beautiful hand stitched chiffon and subtle crystal beading. I think I look good and wear the substantial string of golden pearls he gifted me for our engagement. When he sees me dressed in my finery, all he says is I look "suitable" as we walk down the grand staircase together in stony silence. We each sit looking out our car window as Gerard drives the Packard across the bridge. It will be a typical developers evening; we are all summoned to christen his newest hotel and to meet the latest Mrs. Knowlton Collins.

There before the Grace of G-d go, I think knowing my replacement is most likely in the wings as well. Carl Fisher had also left his wife Jane for his secretary years before when his son died and the parallel hangs in the air like cloying, heavy French perfume.

When we arrived at the hotel, I forget the name now—there are so many…it is a glistening deco confection that seems to float like a yacht rather than firmly planted in the sand and earth. Gerard helps me from the car, and I exited in a swirl of my tulle wrap, not my own husband. The hotel seems rather sleek for Knowlton who is known to throw every extravaganza and extra glitz into his projects not to mention pet elephants and dancing girls as they have all taken a page from Carl Fisher's antics and Knowlton has become quite the showman. As I look up at the freshly painted structure, I notice a sign which sets my teeth on edge: "Always a view, Never a Jew."

These signs, "Restricted, Gentiles Only," dot the beach and always made me think of my classmate at Miss Harris's poor Esther Reigenstreiff whose family had escaped prejudice in Germany only to see this here. Terrible. I am about to say something to Leland when I turn, and a vision takes my breath away. There is B! He has his arm linked with his wife, presumably a sweet but rather disappointing looking girl who is heavy with pregnancy and has a sheen of sweat on her rosy cheeks. Honestly, I had been expecting a bit more given his dashing looks. Is that awful of me? Probably. He freezes and then quickly nods but I can see the pain evident in his eyes when he sees we are entering the restricted property. Flora had told me in confidence B. was Hebrew and has changed his name to be hired at the club. Now I understand fully.

We are smart enough to slightly nod with our eyes but not acknowledge each other and I do see the pain as he grips his pregnant wife and ushers her along. Leland surveys them from afar.

"Jews, wops, the place is becoming overrun. Greasy fucks, the lot of them." He shakes his head. He only sees what he wants to see or maybe he is jealous of B.'s elegant and lean gait, slim hips, and glossy jet hair.

And then, just like that, B. looks back at me for a moment and smiles. Although we are both trapped in our own ways, in that instant I have hope again. Perhaps it is the sight of his white teeth against his olive skin and the swaying palms above the new building. It is a sign for me and in this very moment I know I have given myself over to other thoughts which are not considered ladylike. And when I walk past the insulting sign, I have now made up my mind and yes, it does give me a pep in my step.

Leland grips my arm tightly as I am after all his property as we enter the shiny lobby and take in our set, a mass of the tidy and confident during these dark times we see the usual suspects; the wealthy socials and some hangers on…

but that is always to be expected as well as a few surprise guests thrown in for good measure to ensure the party is considered très amusant; a famous female pilot or aerialist or Ziegfeld beauty. Knowlton peppers his events the way a good chef seasons a stew with different ingredients only, tonight the cuisine served here is rather bland fare.

Here we are milling about drinking champagne and laughing as people are now round the corner begging in the streets! Just yesterday, I saw a mother and her children on Lincoln Road sitting there in the hot sun with a sad handwritten sign and I opened my purse and gave her a silver dollar for food. She had a bottle and I hoped she would feed her sweet children with the money I had given her and oh, what I would have done for one of her brood! I push aside my thoughts as I have become quite familiar with that exercise.

Once inside, Leland and I walk directly to congratulate Knowlton and then off to the bar. I am a tad surprised that he brings me over a glass of champagne before disappearing with Knowlton and his cronies. Sometimes I am taken aback by the niceties, but I always know in the back of my mind that to Leland appearances are everything. His wife without a champagne flute? Well, people might talk. I am left to fend for myself as I usually am and am suddenly happy when I spot an old acquaintance across the room from Miss Harris's, Cora Smart. Her name was always a source of laughter for the girls at school as there was nothing smart looking or chic about her, although she is clever and a dear. I walk over quickly.

"Cora, how are you, my darling?" I must be making a fool of myself fluttering over, so happy to see a familiar, friendly

face and breathing a deep sense of relief as it is someone from my past. "It's been almost two years since Miss Harris's," *I say in a breathy voice.*

"*Yes.*" *She reaches up with her cheek, and we gave each other a slight kiss.* "You are looking as beautiful as ever Elsa, of course." *She surveys my dress and line of pearls.*

"And you, pray tell?" *I giggle, touching her elbow and the hem of her capped sleeve.*

"Well, to my mother's surprise and delight, I am finally engaged." *She smiles, baring small crooked yellowed teeth and a tiny diamond ring almost as small as to be a chip. Cora had been sweet but had always been quite unfortunate looking. Some people took her looks to mean she was insipid or slow, but she is neither and actually quite sharp like her name suggests.*

"She thought I was going to be an old maid." *She shrugs.* "Unlike you...who was destined for a grand life!" *she says in a low voice, without any bitterness.*

"Congratulations, I am so very happy for you," *I say.* "And my life is not so grand, Cora, I am here to report," *I whisper.* "And who is the lucky fellow?"

"John Ackerly. He used to work for your husband but..." *I see she is struggling with her words a bit.* "After the incident, he now runs the food and beverage for Knowlton, I mean Mr. Collins, at this very hotel."

"Firstly, congratulations. I am so happy for you. I'm not sure I know of any incident," *I ask wide eyed.*

"The girl who was found," she paused, lowering her voice, "murdered in Stiltsville. In the bay."

"I have no idea what you are talking about. Where is Stiltsville? Though it all sounds positively gruesome," I say my head suddenly throbbing like a thumb instantly bruised by a hammer.

"You didn't hear? Why, it was the talk of Miami until it was all hushed up." Cora looks about as we were discussing unmentionables.

"Hushed up? I have no idea, Cora."

"Well…" She gently takes my arm and walks me to a quiet potted palm. "Since you seem unaware, there was a girl who worked at one of your husband's bars in Stiltsville. It's an area built over the water where people can legally drink."

"Oh, I see." I think how clever, given it was Prohibition. How was it Leland owned bars there, and I know nothing about it?

"Well, let's just say, she was a woman of the evening, a working girl, they called her. She was found dead and the police, well…" Cora pauses. "I hear she was pregnant and ended up floating in the Biscayne Bay with her throat slit. They closed the case to avoid any scandal."

"Are you sure Leland owns a bar in that place? He never mentioned it to me." I look down at the new terrazzo floor noticing the bits of silica mixed in the marble chip glistening as my head spins.

"Poor Elsa." Cora suddenly reaches out and puts a loose tendril into place. "I don't believe you were raised to truly understand men. They have always put you on a pedestal."

"I'm finding out the hard way," I say bitterly.

"Yes, I am sure." She shakes her head in a way that says she understands but feels sorry for me. Then she fills me in that her intended, John, had initially cooperated with the police but was summarily fired, and when he was about to speak to the press, Mr. Collins suddenly called and offered him a job but stressed he did not approve of his employees ever talking to the papers. She whispers that was why they were able to get engaged, "It is hard enough to make ends meet, but now with a steady paycheck, we are able to announce our engagement. I really shouldn't be saying anything more. Promise me you won't, Elsa. I'm just looking out for you as you always looked out for me in school when no one gave me the time of day and here was the most popular girl at Miss Harris's being nice to me and all. Well, it meant a lot. I always looked up to you and thought you should know." A benevolent tear appears in her eye.

"Thank you, Cora, you are a dear. I always thought you were, well, misunderstood. I don't know anything about this, but I know my husband and that's all I need to know," I say. "Thank you, you are a dear, dear friend." Then, I decide to make a bold move. I feel free after seeing Knowlton's awful sign and Leland's abhorrent behavior.

"Will you meet me at the Bath Club one afternoon for tea?" I ask, thinking I know much less about my husband than I should.

"Oh, it would be so lovely. I have always wanted to go there, the Bath Club. How marvelous." Cora beams.

"A Miss Harris's reunion, we shall call it." I force a smile, my brain going a million miles a minute.

Something tells me that I will find out more which could help me in my escape.

If only things turn out this way…sunshine and not the lull before a tropical storm.

Chapter 24

Liz was somewhat relieved when the weekend with Cary ended and he packed his things into tight, neatly regimented squares in his carry-on and high tailed it back to New York. Despite his kisses, entreaties, and the one lovely dinner on Saturday night, the visit had been decidedly underwhelming. She confided in Roy that she had found him entirely annoying and argumentative, the sex banal and his views on Miami antiquated verging on prejudicial. His extremely conservative nature, once considered an asset, was now looking more like a liability. Still, deep down she knew that Cary was a catch and wasn't ready to decide on the relationship, and her damn age was starting to become a factor in her decision making. She felt the pressure of her childbearing years weighing on her and didn't want to let fear creep into the equation but it was eating away at her foundation. The thought of being single and "out there" again was decidedly less attractive at the moment to her than accepting Cary's drawbacks; and certainly, she knew she had hers…not to mention wanting to disappoint Linda who was ill and craving a grandchild. She felt she was almost at the finish line with Cary and rationalized he did have many good qualities. Roy listened and didn't say much which also spoke volumes, his silence and eye rolling indicating he wasn't a fan of Cary's. All he said after her entire rant was "He looked like he was going to an insurance convention in Orlando with that shirt!"

Liz shook her head in agreement but also recognized that despite his crankiness, Cary had tried a bit and that meant something to her. She knew that his breaking away from the hospital had also taken a great deal of work and negotiation and that he would have to work two weeks straight to make up for it. She tried to rationalize that he was a typical guy who just happened to have bad style. It all weighed on her like a lead blanket at a dentist's office taking X-rays, however, she put her feelings on the back burner as she had other pressing obligations.

With Cary's departure she was now readying the villa for another important guest, her mother. She took out her Polish English dictionary from the utility drawer in the pantry and approached Zosia on her Sunday workday, pointed to the words "mother" and "visits" "wizyty matki" and they silently walked up the grand staircase to the room down and across the hall from the master and designated the guest bedroom for her mother's arrival. Liz and Zosia managed to pry open the door, which seemed a bit stuck after a century of closure, poked their heads into the gloom and inspected the sealed bedroom. It had a darker motif and had clearly been a man's room, perhaps Leland's room she spoke about in her diary as it had a masculine and regal feel, yet it had been shut away and had fallen into aristocratic disrepair. Liz almost avoided giving this room to Linda but given her medical condition she wanted her mother nearby and this bedroom offered close proximity with a certain degree of distance since it was located across from hers yet still off the main corridor. As they both entered the room, the air was heavy and thick with dust and cobwebs and showed just how much decay had set in over the decades. She walked over and immediately pried open the shutters, dismayed by the room's moldy condition. As the light poured in highlighting the ray of dust in the air, she appraised the particular bedroom and frowned at the ornate Empire furniture all boasting an intricate wood veneer with gold and brass filigree and metal mounts in the center and at the sides depicting acanthus leaves and crowns. Roy held his nose as he quickly ducked his head in but said it was all original Napoleonic antiques and while not their style was most likely worth a fortune to the right collector or dealer. She would have to call Ira to get approval for a new mattress and have the room painted, not to mention removing the moth-eaten draperies all done in elaborate disintegrating heavy royal blue silks with the traditional bee pattern, gold fringed taping and faded gold tieback sashes with elaborate tassels. Liz took in the oppressive furnishings and immediately thought white sheers and a simple chalk white paint job and white bedding with gray piping would do the trick and she would have the intricate oriental carpet cleaned. She estimated that this would all take two and a half weeks approximately just in time for Linda's arrival.

Happily, her mother had gotten a good report from her oncologist and awaited her second Covid vaccination appointment in early March. The first shot had her with a slight fever and chills and her arm sore to the touch. The second one was scheduled weeks later and hopefully would take just a day or two to get back to herself and when she felt better, she would start to pack for her vacation in Florida.

"Mama's coming, and nothing can stop me now!" Linda declared. She added, "I gotta get the hell out of here! New York is as cold as a witch's tit." After all the treatments, she was delighted and ready for her holiday fantasy and to inspect her daughter's new home and thrilled the pool was now in working order. Liz offered to fly back to New York to help collect her, but Linda wouldn't hear of it; she was flying down with her best friend Marion who was also heading down to her co-op in Surfside. Marion would pick her up in Great Neck and they would travel together, and both had booked an early morning Delta flight which would arrive by lunchtime. Roy and Liz would meet them at the airport, which was more of a command than a request. Despite her mother's larger than life personality, Liz was thrilled and proud to be able to give her mother a vacation fantasy by the newly renovated pool after all she had been through. Over the weeks and months, Liz had sent her mother a daily and weekly account of the renovation work by emailing iPhone photos and samples of the new furniture and paint chips and she was not only supportive but thoroughly impressed with the amount of work her daughter had done to upgrade the old estate. She was eager to meet Ira in person and also meet Sheila, who had been such a help although Liz had said they were so similar she thought they might butt heads. However, no matter Sheila's imperious personality she had also been a font of information and local resources for which Linda was grateful.

Two weeks breezed by and Sheila, the cleaning service, and Zosia had created a fresh, clean guest bedroom. Despite the dark antique furniture, the sparkling new bedding, duvet covers, and white sheers lifted the heaviness of the previous decor and it could have been any suite in a villa hotel in the South of Italy or France. The night before Linda arrived, she added a small spray of fresh cut yellow roses in a beautiful Lalique vase she had found in the China cabinet and a spritz of perfume added to the femininity. New towels and sachets and lavender soaps gave the ancient ensuite bathroom a facelift as well and she hoped Linda would love it.

The highly anticipated day arrived, and Linda called last minute before they boarded the flight and insisted they now *not* pick her up as Marion was renting a car and was going to drop her off at the villa instead. Liz bristled at the thought of having to see "Aunt" Marion who had always been difficult and high maintenance her whole life however Liz knew she had no sway over this decision. She would have to put up with "Aunt" Marion's backhanded compliments and sharp observations. She never knew why Linda had chosen such a difficult best friend but had come to the realization that they both loved verbal sparring and lived off the competition. Once the navy Honda pulled into the driveway, Liz knew exactly why Linda had told her and Roy to stay put; Linda wanted to show off! Of course! It was so her mother to orchestrate the grand tour and she realized by dropping her off, it sealed Marion's invitation.

Marion Stern was the definition of the word "yenta" and part of her mother's inner circle of friends. She flaunted a towering black lacquered bouffant style hairdo which was achieved by weekly visits to the beauty parlor and was a twice divorced widow whose first husband Seymour had been best friends with her father Joe. Liz often referred to Marion's choice of coiffeur as not a hair-*do*... but a hair-*don't*. While they had been friends for years, Liz considered Marion a "frenemy" who was equally as opinionated as Linda but far more annoying as she was petty and competitive and not exactly subtle about her choice of zingers and mean spirited bon mots. She stepped out of her car immediately frowning at the grand estate and gave Liz an air kiss with her mask in place. She nodded dismissively at Roy and immediately looked around with a haughty, critical, and probing eye as if she wanted to confirm that what Linda told her was indeed true. As Liz and Roy took them both through the vast estate Marion offered subtle complaints and few compliments and an air of negativity.

"Oy, I'm going to plotz from all the stairs." She huffed and puffed. "It reminds me of the Boca Hotel—the old part." She also stated annoying comparisons; "It reminds me of my friend Phyllis's house in Palm Beach. She can never find enough help to dust all the rooms." Throwing out the example of their one truly wealthy friend whose husband had made a fortune in the Velcro and zipper industry.

Linda was also overwhelmed at the size of the villa and had a similar reaction to Liz when she first saw the grandeur of the property and rooms. She summarily dismissed Marion's claims with the wave of her newly manicured hand.

"Marion, Phyllis lives in a shack compared to this." Linda arched a plucked eyebrow and countered in typical fashion. It seemed Marion only wanted to stay long enough to see the basics and was annoyed at how fabulous it was and when she finally had enough declared she needed to get to Surfside before the bagel store closed, which everyone knew was a lie.

"Liz, the only thing about Florida you have to get used to…is the bagels are terrible here because the water here isn't as good as New York water." She air-kissed everyone and grudgingly offered a "Mazel Tov" before she left and then added the ever-annoying statement "A house without a man isn't a home!" to which Linda responded "Cary, her doctor boyfriend, was down last weekend! And remember to tell that to your own daughter who is also single and three years older than Liz." She sniffed as they all walked Marion to her rental car and saw her off, out of the gate.

"Women are the worst," Linda declared as she fake smiled and waved after her out the gate. "She's just jealous because you have it all and her daughter Mindy is a *mieskeit*."

"A Mies-what?" Roy asked as he raised his eyebrow.

"Mies-keit. Pronounced like the word kite," Linda explained. "It's the Yiddish word for someone who is plain or ugly, often referred to a woman." Roy and Liz laughed and took Linda on a tour of her freshly spruced up room and the newly renovated pool area. The new aqua tiles under the stonework and new teak lounge furniture made it all seem like a luxury resort. Linda kvelled and professed it was "five star fabulous" and literally had tears in her eyes as and pointed to a lounge chair which she declared was her spot. The trio walked the house and the property for over an hour with Linda taking a few small breaks sitting here and there as she was tired now more often due to her treatments. There was so much to take in and Linda savored each antique in the villa's interior and ran her graceful hands across the polished, marble, and intricate surfaces and moldings. She loved everything but took an instant dislike to Zosia.

"She's an anti-Semite. I can tell," Linda declared.

"Mom, how can you say that? She's been nothing but lovely!" Liz countered.

"The way she looks at us, she wants to start a pogrom."

"You are insane, but I love you." Liz deadpanned. "She's actually very nice; I think all the work in the house is a bit overwhelming for her. We only have her coming Saturdays and Sundays now and doing some light cleaning and food shopping," Liz offered.

"Just keep her away from me." Linda was one of the most opinionated women and was known for instant like or dislike of people, which she rarely changed.

"Come, I want to show you one last thing which I know you will love." Liz and Roy walked her across the far end of the property and supported her mother at the elbow to the enclosed tennis pavilion which was still untouched. Liz pulled open the old screen door and pushed in towards the entry foyer. Linda oohed and ahhed as she entered and saw what was inside.

It was as if one was walking back in time imagining a gaggle of flappers congregating round the bar after a round robin of tennis matches tinny jazz music on the old-fashioned radio. It reflected 80 years of dust, mold and cobwebs but still retained a golden patina of refined sport and the aura of an aristocratic private gentlemen's club. There was a long, oak bar; once polished and gleaming now covered in a layer of dust and grime and a panel over the bar was a mural painted by the renowned J. C. Leyendecker, the famed '20s American Illustrator, featuring monkeys having cocktails and swinging from palm trees and dotted with whimsical bananas, coconuts, and pineapples.

"It really is quite wonderful, a mini Monkey Bar." Liz thought of the chic watering hole in Manhattan that Graydon Carter had transformed and brought back to life in the Hotel Elysée. The pavilion was a veritable time capsule of the 1920s; old wooden racquets hung in rows on the walls and old lace up sneakers seemed fossilized and disintegrating from the heat and their age. There was also a peculiar smell of aged sweat and mothballs as the indoor structure hadn't been aired out in years.

"Well, this is really something." Linda looked around at the old school sports motif and laughed. "Ralph Lauren would have a field day in this place!" She commented as she walked up to a ledge of tarnished trophies and ran her hand over a silver engraved loving cup. Liz left Roy and Linda at the bar as she wandered off to the far end of the court to check the window which had been nailed shut with a rough wooden board to see if it had a bay view. She would talk to the workmen the next day to see if they could pry it open and air out the place. Linda sat on the high leather red leather stool pulling it from the bar and sat caddy corner to a portrait out of a 1930s movie casually looking up at the portrait of the dark handsome dark-haired man, his hair slicked back with pomade, his toothy white smile and his V-neck white tennis sweater. Suddenly, Linda did a double take.

"Liz, come quickly!" she called out and gasped for air as she immediately paled and looked as if she was about to faint.

"Liz, your mom wants you now!" Roy looked concerned and called out as she rushed from the other end of the court to the bar.

"Mom, what is it? Are you feeling okay? Do you need me to call the doctor? You're white as a sheet!"

"Liz…" The blood had drained from her face.

"Linda, what is it?" Roy swooped in concerned.

She held her chest as she wagged a finger at the portrait above the bar.

"That..." She could hardly get the words out.

"What, Mom? Tell me!" Liz surveyed the situation as if she was crazy or feeling ill.

"That portrait! It's..." Linda looked up and pointed to the portrait of the man in tennis whites. He was standing with a racquet and his dark glossy hair contrasted the white sweater.

"It's what, Linda?"

"How can it be? It's my grandfather...Ben!" She shook her head in disbelief.

"Liz, I told you there was a family resemblance." Roy batted his eyes.

"Mom, really? You're imagining things." Liz scoffed.

"No Liz, that's Ben. My grandpa, Ben Brody!" She gasped again. She went up closer to inspect it and viewed the small, dulled bronze plaque on the frame.

"You see, 'Benjamin Brody, 1939.'" She pointed and read aloud. "What the hell is a portrait of my grandfather doing hanging over the bar?" She turned and shook her head.

They all looked at each other in disbelief.

Liz thought back to the diary and "B."

Ben Brody. Of course!

And at that moment things started to fall into place.

Chapter 25

"Well, we all should have guessed..." Linda shook her head over their celebratory dinner on the balmy terrace of Matador discussing their fairly incredible discovery, her hazel eyes sparkling at the news.

"You don't think she left it there as a clue for us?" Liz asked, looking exceptionally pretty under the sapphire evening light.

"It looks like it's been there for years, so I am not so sure," Roy added.

"Either way, Elsa and Ben clearly were an item. Now this whole thing is starting to make a lot more sense to me." Linda seemed relieved and more at ease now that there was a clear connection at hand. The vintage mambo music added to the optimistic ambiance as well as the flourishing palms and hanging plants and Linda sat looking serene and beautiful in a simple cream silk long sleeved blouse and ivory slacks sipping a glass of chardonnay. If one looked at her no one would have believed she had been ill or recently completed chemo in fact, strangely she looked healthy and vibrant and had put extra care into her wardrobe and wore a lovely line of pearls that gave her the look of an aging Miami social doyenne. Liz also admired her mother's favorite, vintage gold charm bracelet she was wearing which she noticed was similar to Sheila's but a bit more ornate. It added a bit of old-world glamor to her look, and she remembered playing with the array of little charms as a young girl. Joe would often add a new charm to the bracelet for a special anniversary or occasion or closing a big contract; there was the tiny dangling gold treasure chest which actually opened to three tiny sapphires and a ruby and the miniature gold tennis racquet with the white pearl in the center to mimic the tennis ball. Everything seemed to be coming back to tennis, even the little things.

"So, if Great-Grandpa Ben is B. in the diary, why all the secrecy? So what if they were doing the nasty?" Liz asked bluntly.

"Liz, I didn't bring you up to talk like that," Linda admonished. "I'm sure in those days people didn't discuss those things, it wasn't the 'me generation' like it is today," Linda explained with a small wave of the hand. "People lived through the Great Depression and did what they had to do to support their families. It must have been incredibly hard."

Linda sipped her gin and tonic and reminisced a bit about her grandfather Ben. He had it all; he was so handsome and was considered to be one of the great tennis players of his generation. Of course, she added, in typical Linda-fashion, that it ran in the family; Liz had gotten the tennis gene but didn't have the desire. Linda rolled her eyebrow again at Liz's consternation as she added, "Or the ambition." Liz shook her head at the slight as Linda went on to say her Grandpa Ben was on the verge of becoming truly famous but had to put aside his tennis career to support his family and that his religion didn't help at a time when many of the tournaments and clubs were restricted.

Liz sat back and marveled at her mother's resilience with new eyes and was so happy she was getting back to herself again. Luckily, her hair had not fallen out due to the cold cap treatment and was now freshly dyed back to its original blonde and swept back into a small chignon. People had always commented that Linda in her youth had been a dead ringer for Lauren Bacall and she had a similar personality as well. The low, husky voice and the stunning Slavic eyes created an alluring persona and she had been a real beauty but had given up her modeling career and her dreams of being an actress when she met Joe Galinsky. It was love at first sight and despite some early TV commercials and ad campaigns all Linda really wanted was a husband and baby. Maybe it's because her own father Sidney had died fairly young in a car accident on the mountain roads in the Catskills and her mother Gloria had never remarried. It had been a true love affair and it had been a hard life for her mother without a husband or father as well as for Linda, who grew up without elder male attention. She always felt she had an empty void that made her feel as if she had missed out. Linda had attended high school in Forest Hills; her books always pressed closely to her sweater set and had dated a few eligible young men at the dances she attended, but no one really sparked her interest until she spotted a handsome man in one of her acting classes and the attraction was magnetic, pulling them together. Everyone in class thought that Joe Galinsky was "school of Tony Franciosa" and once they made eye contact that was it. There was no one as dashing as Joe and his half Italian and Jewish roots gave him an earthy sensuality. As for Joe, he could not get over the lithe, blonde beauty he saw sitting shyly with her script trying to memorize the small part she had gotten in *The Little Foxes.* Joe had inherited his father's pale blue eyes and his mother's olive complexion and had the most beautiful glossy hair and the creamy skin she had ever seen on a man. He had gone to City college and was an aspiring actor and his family was supportive of his dreams but were nevertheless concerned about his ability to make a living. His tough Lithuanian father Harry took him aside and cautioned that with a girl like Linda he would need some stability, but Joe just shrugged his imposing shoulders as he wasn't about to sell out and stated firmly that neither he nor Linda cared about money, that they could "live on love" and that was not about to change for anyone or anything.

The first year they were married they did just that and Linda worked in the cosmetics department of Saks Fifth Avenue so Joe could go for auditions. The newlyweds scraped together what little they had, and Linda made do with chopped meat sloppy joes which they extended for the week by adding pasta and rice fillers. Despite the occasional hunger pangs, they had such fun together and their tiny studio apartment in Little Neck was filled with laughter and joy. They celebrated when Joe got his first off Broadway play and the part of a handsome janitor who sleeps with his middle-aged landlady. *The Upstairs Wife* had mostly mixed reviews but the *Daily News* theater columnist had singled out Joe for his raw sensuality. They toasted at a little Italian on the Lower East Side and splurged on spaghetti carbonara and a bottle of chianti and that night they made passionate love and Linda would later find out that her dream about being a mother had come true even though it was unplanned.

Yet, sometimes dreams have a way of working for you or against you and Joe's father was diagnosed with liver cancer and died quickly. Sadly, there was no one to support his younger brother and sister and when Joes' mother lost her job in the Italian bakery after slicing her hand causing nerve damage Joe knew he had to put his career on hold and help the family; it was the Italian and Jewish way. It was also especially critical now that Linda was pregnant. After a brief reflection and discussion with his wife and mother-in-law, it was only natural that Joe go into Linda's family's small insurance business, and he gave up one dream for another. Gloria's Uncle Louis had taken control of the two-man office years before when Sidney had died. He was a lifelong bachelor and welcomed Joe into the business with open arms. He also saw in Joe with his charismatic personality a natural talent for sales and his ability to close a contract with people based on his charm and good looks. As Joe had used his stage name Galin in the theater, Louis advised him to do the same in insurance as well…why create problems as a great salesman was about having a blank slate and then filling in those blanks! Under Louis's tutelage Joe took his new job seriously and viewed each sales call as an audition and played the role he thought he should and played it to the hilt. If the person were middle class Irish or Italian, he played the Italian card. If the call was for a wealthy family his accent changed and he was the working college man. If the woman was a Jewish housewife in her split level, Joe peppered his conversation with Yiddish phrases. He read his audience like a charm and gave each his best performance. He was the handsome everyman, and he knew it and after six months he was making real money on his commissions to now support his family and the baby on its way. Everyone said Joe and Linda were the movie star couple and when Liz arrived, she was one of the most beautiful babies anyone had ever seen with her platinum blonde hair and the most stunning blue eyes rimmed with gold.

Roy chewed on an olive. "I never knew you and Liz were so interesting. Tell us more about Ben?" Roy looked at Linda dreamily as she continued the family history.

"Well, my grandmother Sarah told me that when she was first married to Ben, he had been a ball boy and then a tennis instructor and worked this way through school and the Depression with lessons for rich people and their clubs to pay for it. He had won a tournament or two, but in those days, the name Bromberg was considered a real liability and couldn't play in certain clubs in Florida and Long Island. So he changed his name to Brody."

"Similar to Dad." Liz nodded.

"Yes, the family name was originally Galinsky then shortened to Galin." Linda shrugged. "It was going to his stage name, Joe Galin, but it also worked much better in the insurance business."

"Now that's a real makeover. Sort of like Roy La Roy!" Roy batted his eyes and his long lashes cast a shadow on his high cheekbones.

"Yes. My grandparents lived in Miami, and when my father Sidney was born, Grandpa Ben won a big tournament and went on to play at the US Open and advanced in the finals. The final match, however, was on Yom Kippur, and Grandpa had to give up the match and the title if he won. He wouldn't play on the Jewish high holidays," Linda said proudly.

"Did he regret it?" Roy asked, munching on a piece of pita with green pea hummus.

"No, he said it was his proudest moment of his tennis career. When my father was a baby, Grandpa Ben decided to go into insurance to support the family and built a nice, small business and brought in his brother-in-law, my Uncle Louis. It was a nice family business. When my father Sidney was old enough, he worked with Uncle Louis who then supported us when he died. When I married Joe, as I told you, he also worked for my uncle who took him under his wing. In many ways, both Ben and Joe ended their dreams early to support their families. Joe did a great job; that's how we were able to afford Great Neck and Russell Gardens, and Liz was brought up with everything—sleep away camp, braces and so on," she said proudly. "She had all the lessons, skating, dance, then tennis as well. I did feel badly that Joe had to give up his acting career, but he never complained. Every time I brought it up, he would wave his hand and said he made the right choice and never looked back; Liz and I were more important than his acting career." She teared up. "That is true love, giving of yourself, but I knew deep down he was disappointed. Joe always said he was going to go back to the theater when we were settled, but he never got the chance once he got sick." She reflected. "It's my only regret!"

"Mom, Dad loved you. He loved you more than that." Liz took her cool hand.

"That's what I want for you," Linda said forcefully.

"Well, Cary doesn't seem to want to give up anything at this point for me or Florida." Liz frowned.

"Then, as much as I hate to say it, maybe he's not the man for you." Linda shook her head squarely. "There has to be compromise, and I always say Liz, and I know you hate when I do, because it's not P.C these days, but in my book the man has to love the woman...just a little bit more," she paused for great effect sipping her cosmo, "if it's going to work."

"I agree!" Roy said in a saucy tone. "I always want him to love me a little bit more." They all laughed.

"It's the secret to a great relationship, and you deserve that. You too, Roy!"

"You found that Mom, but maybe I never will." Liz looked downcast.

"You will. I know it, I feel it. Just like I knew you were destined for great things and a great love."

"Well, she evidently took after her great-grandfather Ben. They do look a bit alike, you know." Roy observed.

"Yes, they do! Especially the eyes."

"It all makes so much sense now. Elsa and Ben had a thing, and I haven't gotten to the part, but it is clear Elsa was in love with him and that's why she left me the house." Liz put two and two together.

"So what part are you up to now?" Linda asked.

"The part where B., your grandfather Ben, is starting to give her tennis lessons."

"And other kinds of lessons as well," Roy added.

"He obviously had good taste," Liz said. "I wonder why he didn't end up with Elsa and live with her."

"I would have moved my ass right in." Roy sighed.

"We know…you already did," Liz ribbed.

"Touché!" They clinked glasses.

"Oh, this is all so romantic!" Linda exclaimed.

"Do you think your grandma Sarah knew?" Liz asked wide-eyed.

"If she did, she didn't say a word to anyone. In those days, men did what they wanted."

"It hasn't changed. He was considered so handsome that I'm sure all the women were running after him."

"And maybe some men too!" Roy said.

"With you, everyone is gay." Liz pursed her lips.

"I don't put it past any man." Roy winked. "It's like that famous Robin Williams quote. 'G-d gave men both a penis and a brain but unfortunately not enough blood supply to run both at the same time.'" The two women laughed out loud. Roy was indeed very funny and entertaining.

"I cannot wait to get home and read the next chapter in the diary," Liz said smiling.

Linda insisted on picking up the check while Liz ordered an Uber. The drive home seemed more energetic and optimistic now that the bequest of the villa seemed to make sense and dictate such a large gift.

When the car arrived at the entrance to the villa on North Bay Road, Liz opened the new electric gate with the small battery-operated device she now kept in handbag and the Uber pulled into the grand driveway. The driver whistled at the imposing estate and the fountain which had been cleaned and put back into shape. It was now officially working with champagne-like spray and bubbles tossed into the air. The dinner had been cathartic, and they all felt self-satisfied as they were finally getting to some sort of sense of closure. The trio walked into the kitchen and Linda put up a pot of boiling water for tea and they all sat around the new white marble knoll kitchen table she had recently splurged on and snacked on

Linda's favorite Milano cookies. Liz then ran upstairs to fetch the faded floral diary on the nightstand, which she brought downstairs, and they sat around the table as Liz flipped open to the last entry she was reading.

Suddenly, her eyes lit up as she started reading the next installment. "Guys…I think we hit paydirt."

Chapter 26

Elsa

Miami, 1935

I must be a terrible person or a good person who occasionally does bad things. Either way, I am now doing what I want and doing it knowingly. It is not untrue, as I unburden myself to you, dear diary, that I am betraying my husband and his strict orders while I am doing it. And the thought of that does haunt me, but I am in no position to control myself.

My tea with Cora at the Bath Club was eye-opening to say the least. One thing about Cora is that she is a bit of a chatterbox. When I plied her with some illegal champagne and orange juice, it loosened her tongue, and she seemed quite comfortable telling me all about Leland's nefarious activities in Stiltsville. I blushed as I heard the unseemly things that went on there; it was as if a whole parallel world exists, and I am so sheltered from such unthinkable possibilities. It makes sense, though, that a man such as Leland would take what he wants without a thought and in Miami there is so much opportunity at hand, both high and low. At first, it doesn't make sense to me why he would stoop so low, but power and ego define some men and they lose their heads, quite literally and the mind and body often betray common sense and who am I to judge? No one has schooled me in love and desire, only obligation, duty, and strict protocol. I kissed and thanked Cora for her tutorial, signed the club bill and left back to North Bay, only my view of my husband and the bay was different than when I left hours earlier. Imagine finding out my own husband runs a brothel and a gambling den of iniquity all in one social tea!

After a tense month and Leland's constant silent disapproval, he suddenly left as quickly as he arrived on a business trip to Cuba to look at some sugar cane plantations; not that he owes me an explanation as he comes and goes as he pleases without any regard for me and my feelings. I only knew he would be leaving the villa when I saw a large stack of his luggage trunks on the landing outside the service elevator door. Of course, I assume there are other reasons for his trip as I had heard him laughing one afternoon from the recesses of the library on the phone with one of his cronies offering a vulgar description of a famous brothel in Havana where he is planning a stag dinner. Perhaps it is his total disregard for me and his intense personality, but I breathed a heavy sigh of relief when he departed early Monday morning. He barely said goodbye and offered neither an explanation or any whereabouts, only a perfunctory "Continue your regimen and I will see you when I return." He then turned his immense back and snapped his fingers at Gerard and the staff to take his bags and steamers to the car which they did in short order and sent them down in the service elevator, a newfangled contraption that was installed with a manual rope pulley system which is quite ingenious. All I know is I now feel a lightness of air. I spent this morning luxuriating *in bed and feeling a sense of relief…. Yes, release at not having his gloomy and oppressive presence about!*

Now that I am free to do what I want, I immediately call Flora and ask for tea and tennis. I don't want the help talking or saying anything about my whereabouts or activities which have been so restricted with Leland about, so I ask Gerard the driver to drive me to Flora's for tea and say I will be staying for dinner and will ring him later this evening. I carefully dress and wear a silk day dress, my pearls, a lovely fuchsia hat and white kid gloves, with pearl buttons, for I know I will borrow tennis clothes at her house. Lovely, dear Flora often sighs at Leland's harsh edicts and sweetly knows not to ask too many questions. Her husband, while older, adores her and she realizes she is lucky when I inform her that Leland has banned our lessons, but we both know I am in no position to fight with him.

I telephone in advance and tell her Leland has left for Cuba and she gives a long knowing sigh. When I arrive, she giggles and immediately lends me a tennis outfit and racquet after we spend some time viewing James in his nursery! I so appreciate having a friend whose actions and intentions are loving, intuitive and unspoken as she kisses her dear boy in his crib. What little plump and cherubic cheeks he has as I look at dear mother and son and wish it was me, but no matter my wishes it hasn't been my destiny at this point! I must say although I am sad for my circumstances, I am truly happy for Flora and beam at the loving scene before me. Once he falls asleep and she tucks him in, and we close the door to his room, and we are off on a tour of her new tennis pavilion which has just been completed and I change in the changing room. Perfection!

I am amazed as we enter the newly constructed pavilion. I am given over to an unusual smell of glue which Flora says is due to a new type of flooring, yet it does make me a bit woozy until she opens the large windows for the bay breeze. I help her as well with this task as there are so many in symmetrical rows as we unlatch them all and move the windows skyward, the air diluting the harsh smell through the screens. I glance up at the pulleys and the retractable roof and the shade which allows one to play in the afternoon without the sun beating down and the oppressive heat, not to mention avoiding an unwanted and noticeable sunburn. It is ingenious and I will commission one for our estate as well.

I think I must have planned it all along; the coquettish makeup in anticipation of a flirtation with B. before he finally arrives. After I change, Flora and I mix gin and tonics at the newly installed and well stocked bar which fortifies my nerves knowing there is an underlying excitement and tension. I also think it is telling that Flora clinks glasses with a toast "to life and love." While she was never considered a beauty, Flora has the most amazing quality of making you feel like you are the most special person in the room. I think her talent lies in her listening skills, always intent and interested and never looking over one's shoulders as many people do.

At that moment B. walks in with his slight jaunt and those startling blue eyes against his olive complexion, a rare combination. He is both cautious and gracious when he sees I am once again in attendance. I almost take his good manners for a lack of interest but then he looks at me when Flora goes off to the loo and says in an exasperated manner "Finally!" with his gorgeous, crooked white smile, eyes skyward. I laugh and upon Flora's return we spend the hour practicing our backhand strokes and volleying on the newly installed court. And then I do something that I shall never forget. I don't know where I get the strength to do it.

I lie. I telephone my home and say I am staying for an early dinner and that Flora's driver will take me home.

After the lesson, I change and kiss Flora on the cheek and I time walking out with B. He holds the door for me and smiles at me as we walk into the outer courtyard. It is apparent we have missed each other. He asks where my driver is and I say he must have fallen asleep again in the heat and he graciously offers me a lift, which I gladly accept. He holds the door for me as I step up on the running board and get into the front seat. We sit quietly after he cranks the car and then he starts telling me about himself a bit more. I want to find out more. His eyes light up when he mentions he is eager to attend college on a scholarship and is saving money with his income from the lessons. In tennis circles he is known as Ben Brody, having changed his name due to certain discrimination and I nod as Flora has already told me of his exotic Hebrew background. He reveals that he hails from Harlem in New York and that he has always been athletic and followed the sun and the surf to Florida when his parents both perished in the flu epidemic. He had at first been a busboy, then a lifeguard and a golf caddy before having a natural inclination for tennis. He worked as a ball boy picking up the game and making contacts in the sport and his dream of college had been put off due to his financial situation, yet I notice he carefully avoids the subject about his wife, which honestly sends me a bit more into a frenzy.

As we drive onto North Bay Road he turns and asks if I want to see a beautiful view. I nod yes, knowing it was a conspiratorial move and I would never blurt out "you are the beautiful view" but he is. He smiles somewhat sadly, I think, as he drives his old jalopy onto the end of the gravel road, and we sit quietly together looking across the bay. It is indeed beautiful and bucolic yet deep down I am nervous and comment that it is all so lovely and make inane and frivolous conversation that there are so many new buildings being constructed on the opposite side, with another huge estate being constructed at the parcel at the foot of the bay. The construction site to the right of where we sit is silent on Sundays and we are silent as well for a moment and then he looks directly at me with his penetrating eyes and smiles and tells me he thinks my eyes look like the bay. I blush and tell him I think his does as well. He runs his long, tapered fingers on the dashboard and asks me questions about Leland and how long we had been married. I take a deep breath at the question. How should one answer something so personal yet so important in what seems to be a hint to things to come. All I say is "too long." We both laugh and he shrugs and rolls our eyes a bit and then, just then, he turns to me and at that moment it is as if a physical electric force, a power greater than my moral sense pulls us together. We kiss and it is unlike anything I have ever known or will ever know. That first kiss, so innocent and mixed with desire.

I must say, it has created a certain havoc in me; this place, this carved out moment is our time and place. And I will lie each time to the driver, to Flora, to myself, and yes, to each other. And each time as we become more acquainted with each other, it becomes more casual and more desirous. And each time I know I will go further because it has become unbearable and yes, I have to admit it…not a decision to take but an uncontrollable, unrepentant act that is driving me to ecstasy and hopefully not to my downfall.

Chapter 27

Carl Fisher may have been the founding father of Miami, but Crawfish Eddie was the pioneer and unofficial King of Stiltsville—that is until Leland Barrett usurped him. Despite the apparent sunshine, Stiltsville is even a shadowy place today and few who are alive remember its origins, or as Somerset Maugham once quipped, "a sunny place for shady people."

During Prohibition, word soon got out that at the edge of Biscayne Bay the enterprising Eddie had cleverly constructed a shack ten feet above shallow seawater, on stilts and concrete pilings. He had discovered a rare loophole in Miami law that alcohol and gambling were legal one mile offshore, and the police weren't able to drive there either. Eddie's overwater shack became famous as did his crawfish soup called chilau, made from crawfish gathered under his shack and simmered in a pot chased down with suddenly-legal beer. Soon, bigwigs, celebrities, millionaires, and politicians were descending to this new "unofficial" Miami hot spot. It wasn't enough for men like Carl and Leland who owned most of the real estate and respectable hotels to sit on the sidelines when such a rare and lucrative opportunity presented itself; they also wanted in, and within months competing shacks started popping up. Leland loved the idea so much he had three shacks each dedicated to a different vice, the first a real functioning bar, the second offering whiskey and gambling, and the third prostitution. Since times were so lean, it was easy to recruit workers and soon out of work models were making their way to Leland's Shack D'Amour by boat to offer services. The girls were easiest of all as most were second rate bathing beauties from the Northeast struggling during the Depression, and they and their families needed to eat. A quick trick in Stiltsville with a wig and some lipstick guaranteed anonymity and a few went on to marry rich men and become pillars of Miami society. Leland put more money and design into his shacks; he was the first to do it right and then the smart Miami set started slumming.

Barrett and his cronies were also inherently rapacious in their quest for more and like most patrician men of their generation they saw an opportunity and as they took it, as they actually thought they were entitled to it. There was a competitive side they admired in each other, and they were the type of men where it wasn't enough for them to succeed, but also for their competition to fail. It was in places like this where connections, standing and deep pockets prevailed, and they took advantage of their inherent privilege without remorse as it also provided them with something as good as money in business: information and blackmail.

The Shack was Leland's chance to finally be known as an innovator, even if dabbling in an array of acknowledged and dark vices. Interestingly, the seediness beneath the surface appealed to him as he was a man of public pride and private greed and lust. He also knew there would always be collateral damage in operations like this, but they just needed to be kept private and he hired a security team to do just that, putting the entire operation under a fake corporate name, bagging, and laundering the cash with the encroaching Miami mafia whom he knew how to deal with. Capone had built a mansion in new neighboring Palm Island, and they met a few times at his bar. While he couldn't countenance his flashy cufflinks and manners, and would never be seen with the likes of him at the Flamingo or the Bath Club, men like Capone were necessary. He also knew given his social standing they were eager to curry favor with him as they knew that by association, even if it was nefarious and on the sly, it burnished their own image. Leland couldn't have cared less and shrugged it off as "just business," and often rubbed shoulders with the more unsavory characters in Stiltsville. In fact, he was so proper that he thought these colorful characters added a bit of spice as long as it was hidden away, and Stiltsville offered the perfect hideaway to conduct his low affairs. Once inebriated, Leland and his cronies drank illegal liquor and sampled the constant array of new girls. The women all seemed to come from places like Wichita, St. Louis, or Alabama and they didn't stop coming; the availability of nubile young flesh was another side benefit and one that appealed to him and his wealthy friends who now had a place far away from probing eyes and inquisitive wives and relatives. Leland loved to play cards, drink whiskey, and have women attend to him in that order. With his women, he preferred to lay back and let them work their magic on him as he did most of the hard work in every other aspect of his life and the girls were eager to please their boss and his friends.

There was something extra special about the new girl he brought back to his room one night after poker. Charlene wasn't her real name, but he never thought it was and what struck him about her, was beside being a tight little piece, was that she actually looked at him with her large brown eyes as she pleasured him, which was a rarity. She seemed to enjoy giving him pleasure and was a natural at it, had a willing body; the heat of her moist bow lips on him in his back room above the deck seemed to excite him as she moaned that she loved it. Did she really enjoy it or was she a smart little actress? He didn't care and over a few months, Charlene became his main girl because she was talented and did dirty things no other woman had ever seemed to do for him. She lorded it over the other girls and he gave her more leeway in her pay and privileges. In the end, however, she wasn't smart enough to keep quiet like the others. In the end, she thought she was special because she was the boss's favorite pump.

One night after she fellated him and proceeded to tell him she loved his taste, she approached him with confidence and told him she was pregnant. He looked up at her blankly from the bed in his room as he processed the information; Leland wasn't someone who reacted to news like this without a measured answer. He let her speak and ramble and she said she wanted more, she wanted to keep the baby and some stability. She thought a man like Leland Barret would take care of her and she was wrong. Leland sat back in bed with his hand resting over his head, looked at her directly. "How do you know it's mine?" he asked and proceeded to laugh in her face.

"I only use my mouth with the others," Charlene answered, as if that line of thinking would make sense to a man like Leland. He wagged a lone finger and told her to get out with her bastard. She was hurt, she begged. She loved him, she never intended to do what she was doing, she explained; she wasn't necessarily a bad girl, she was just trying to get by during the Depression and put food on the table. She knew she wasn't wife material, but she still had hopes. He was cruel and called her a liar and a whore. She was hurt by his laughter and then she became angry, irate. She cajoled him and with no positive response she made the mistake of threatening him, of saying she was going to go to the press. Two days later, Charlene, whose real name was Dorothy Strom, ended up with her throat slit in the bay and a week later her bloated and decomposing body was hauled in by fishing boat nets. There was a small inquiry into her death, but it was soon dropped. It became another case of powerful men protecting other men and their turf. No one wanted to bring unwanted attention to Stiltsville or investigate the death of a common prostitute, not to mention the flowing money and payoffs. Leland Barrett wasn't going to risk anything when his Elsa was pregnant with his heir or if a girl, his spare. Little did he know that only a few months later the fates would have their way with him. And in the end, as he drank his hard, illegal whiskey, he couldn't get it out of his head: his proper, beautiful wife had miscarried and that woman, Charlene, carrying his other child was now dead too.

He went on a drinking binge for a week and fled to a Caribbean whorehouse to forget his troubles.

He never would get over the irony.

Chapter 28

Elsa

1935

Dear Diary,

It's been a few weeks since my last entry, and it is now approaching June. I am dreading the summer heat and humidity. I am already perspiring on other issues, yet I feel I need to unburden myself with what has occurred.

It would be totally unladylike of me to describe in detail all the events that transpired between B. and I and I do feel an overwhelming sense of guilt and pleasure, intermingled of course. I have had many confessions on the subject the last few weeks and have said many Hail Marys and have donated a large sum to the church to assuage my guilt on the subject. I consider it all the height of my nirvana and my downfall, all in one. I try not to regret my actions, but I do; how can I not? When I look in the mirror, I know I am not cut out for such things; the guilt and the repercussions, yet I am doing them and there is no possibility of changing course now or revisionist history.

I was always taught that honesty is the best policy. Is it? And I told my priest, I initiated it, I couldn't help myself; B.'s dark hair, muscled arms, and brilliant white smile created inner havoc, and having been so neglected by my husband I am almost unsure if I possess the self-control. I know it's not an excuse, I don't view myself as a harlot as I was never to be cast in that role, but I must be deeply flawed at the core. And when I promise I won't and then I am around him, I am in a state of constant arousal. Do I hike up my skirt a bit? Yes, I finally can admit it. Perhaps I am…the only word that fits the bill is, desperate. Desperate for love, for validation, for attention, and for some physicality. On reflection, even good girls are desperate for that kind of attention. And maybe it's because I was never that kind of girl. I never let boys take advantage of my good name or take me for a spin and heavy petting in their father's car, and I never would engage in a trip to the powder room like so many of my fast friends. While it is terribly exciting, once B. and I crossed the line, the car seemed too public and too scandalous lest anyone see. It was an ongoing and vexing problem and yet there seemed to be no other good solution. B. has a tiny apartment, and his wife is always at home. I have come to understand from his confessions that he had married her as she was the first good girl he had dated who let him "do it" and she has become pregnant. It isn't loveless but far from his soul mate. I talk to him about Leland and we both know we are trapped, but what to do? Hotels are not an option as Leland's friends own most of them. I feel quite adult contriving to find a "den of iniquity," yet proper married women do not cavort around or even go places themselves, let alone be seen unaccompanied with another man.

The car is risky; the staff or a neighbor might see us. It isn't an issue easily solved; a place to tryst. The car after tennis seems to be the only option and I get used to the hard leather seat and B. and I try to make the small space comfortable during our time together. I do feel some guilt and rather adult after the first time; we went farther and farther until it was uncontrollable and finally, we were one. Afterwards, walking home I felt his love was with me rather than feeling dirty. However, each time I exit the car and smooth my skirt I feel the hot white sun glare on me like a spotlight and know we need to find a better solution for our love and yes, lust.

It has all but consumed my thoughts, a place for us to be together. Then two weeks ago Sunday morning, I was having tea by the breakfast pavilion. Leland was away again, and I was alone in the house when I heard an odd sound by the bay; a motorboat horn. I turned and saw in the distance, out the French doors, that Flora and her husband Arno had arrived at the slip in their beautiful teak Riva. It is highly polished and has the flag of the Netherlands flapping in the breeze. Flora and her husband looked so chic in their straw boaters, with an elegant white and red striped ribbon and they waved happily.

"We knew you were alone with Leland being away again. Want to come for a ride?" she shouted gayly from the boat.

"I get a little boat sick, but why don't you both come in for some tea? The staff is given off Sundays except for Beulah and the gardeners, so it's mostly me and my lonesome. I'll put up a pot of tea, and I have some biscuits and some nice whiskey hidden away for Arno," I happily offered.

"Sounds divine," Flora said.

"Are you sure? I don't want Leland to be angry that I am taking his stash," Arno said. Arno and I quite like each other but I knew there was tension between him and Leland, and he seems almost afraid of him. Yes, that's the word. Afraid. Like I was.

"He'll never know or that you were here. He doesn't ask, and I don't say." I laughed.

And suddenly I have my answer, as they tie the boat to the dock with the long white rope and hop off. I lend a hand to Flora who jumps onto the dock in her gleaming, white tennis sneakers. They rush over to give me a kiss. Then as if struck by lightning, an epiphany is staring me straight in the face.

I am going to see B. on Sundays, and he will come to see me by boat.

Chapter 29

Most travelers to Florida think only about the sunshine, beaches, coconut patties and orange juice but there is and has always been a darker side to living there. Since 1851, Florida has had over five hundred tropical and subtropical storms and is the state most affected by hurricanes, most recently the devastating Ian. In addition to the perilous storms, rising seawater due to global warming, and climate change, future flooding of Florida's coastline poses an existential threat to the State. The tragic collapse of the Champlain Towers in Surfside only underscores that aging construction is affected by parts of Florida that are already sinking, deteriorating, or have become unstable due to neighboring development, creating a panic after the Covid real estate boom among some of the older condo owners.

Floridians overall are obsessed with weather and the weather services and had predicted a major storm due the following week. Roy checked online a few days earlier and hightailed it back to New York the previous week for an advertising job for an older discount fashion brand and to avoid the gathering storm. The job was going to be "a bore and snore" he proclaimed, but it paid the bills and he wanted to get out of town early lest he be stranded, and Liz and Linda drove him to the airport a few days earlier and gave him a warm sendoff.

On the way back from the airport and in anticipation of the storm, Liz did extra food shopping at Publix for supplies; she and Linda decided to hunker down and make the best of it. The weather was still perfectly sunny and clear, a cliche lull before the storm, and then as if a house painter used a roller of dark paint the clouds descended. The winds started to whip and the skies turned an ominous dark gray the color of an insurance office carpeting. At first, Liz thought it might be fun, but as the storm started to build and then rage, she ran to close as many of the long-necked teak shutters as she could. Liz was impressed by the enduring quality of the almost century old teak shutters and the brass latches which reminded her of yachting hardware. As she ran to fortify the windows against the rising winds and spray, Linda lay in bed watching an old rerun of *The Devil Wears Prada* and just shrugged when Liz reappeared. "This house has been here almost a hundred years; I am not worried!" she proclaimed, propped up by pillows, eating skinny pop popcorn, and admiring Meryl Streep's skillful deadpan performance.

It was 11:30 at night when the storm officially bore down and there were otherworldly groans from the sea. The old sailboat on her neighbor's dock was tossed up in the air like a toy boat and landed close to the sea wall. Liz was on the phone complaining about the storm to Cary in NYC when the cell service suddenly went dead. She groaned and picked up the antique phone on the nightstand to find the land lines down too.

"Nice," she commented to Linda. "A power outage during a hurricane!"

"I always thought storms were romantic," Linda offered, scooping up the last kernels of the bowl of popcorn. Weirdly, the cable was the only thing still working, and after *Prada* ended and a short bout with Anderson Cooper on CNN, they both tuned into a rerun of *Pretty Woman*; no matter how many times they saw the movie they both loved the chemistry between Julia Robert's ebullient character and the suave Richard Gere in his prime.

"I'm not sure this movie could be made today, glamorizing prostitution." Liz observed from her side of the bed.

"That's the problem with your generation…. Everything is now so… what do you people call it? 'Woke.' When Elizebeth Taylor starred in *Butterfield 8*, it was scandalous at the time, but everyone wanted to be like her and look like her. People always talk about her eyes, but boy, she had some bust! I never had that kind of cleavage! Now *that* would have been fun. I'm telling you, if she went to the powder room in the movie today there would be an uproar. The whole thing is crazy and makes no sense to me: I never minded it when construction workers whistled at me, I shook my ass more and gave them a show!" Linda shrugged nonchalantly.

"Mom!" She shook her head in disbelief as Linda raised herself from the bed and slipped into her pink bunny slippers shuffling to the bathroom.

Liz was watching the shopping scene in the movie when she heard a crash and a piercing scream. Startled, she bolted up in bed and ran to the bathroom. She found Linda crumpled on the hard marble floor, moaning, lying like a ragdoll. The room was in a blur and then came into focus as she realized Linda had tripped over the tangled wire of a curling iron. She rushed over to her and could see something was dreadfully wrong.

"Mom, are you okay?" she cried.

"I'm hurt." Linda moaned in fear. "I think I broke something." She writhed in pain; the chemo had obviously weakened her, and she suddenly looked diminutive, thin, and bony.

"Call an ambulance!" She moaned.

"Let me get you some ice." Liz panicked.

"No call…please, it hurts. I'm afraid," Linda whimpered, and it broke Liz's heart. But she knew she needed to rally, keep it together and get into action mode. Why did Roy and Cary have to be out of town when she needed them? Here they were in a huge, darkened mansion all alone and in the middle of a crisis. Liz ran over to the old-fashioned phone and panicked as she lifted the receiver; the phone line was indeed dead, and the cell service was also out on her iPhone.

"Mom, the phones are all down!" Liz panicked at having no bars in her phone.

"You have to call me an ambulance," Linda cried.

"Wait here…" Liz starting to panic even more. "Let me get you a pillow and some ice." She ran to the bed, ran back, and gently put a soft pillow under her mother's head.

"I think I broke my hip." Linda whimpered and struggled.

"You'll be fine," Liz lied as she felt herself sweating and looked at her beloved mother writhing in pain. She was almost hyperventilating as she only had one option "I'm going next door."

"No, don't leave me," Linda cried.

"Mom, I have to," Liz insisted.

"Don't, I'm scared." Linda held out her hand.

"We have no choice…. I'll be back as fast as I can." Liz kissed her mother's forehead, sprang into action, and ran downstairs in a total panic. She quickly put on her sneakers, almost falling to the side as she stood on one leg, and then ran outside, where she was overcome by the heavy winds and the pouring rain soaking her from slanted angles. She cursed and ran back inside to get the electric gate opener. As she ran outside again, she pressed the button and waited as the newly installed wall of steel slid open. She ran into the courtyard, past the fountain, and looked up as a bolt of terrifying lightning appeared in the sky. She had always been deathly afraid of the lightning. She wiped the water from her eyes and tried to stay under the overgrown palms as the ghoulish white light crackled and illuminated the vacant night sky. She ran next door as fast as she could. Suddenly, she slipped on the uneven coral stone pavement and blinding red pain seared her knee. She cried out, as it was badly skinned and bleeding, but she had no choice but to run with a slight limp, her sneakers sloshing wet. When she got to G's house it was darkened and closed tight as a drum. She knew she had to try, and she pushed the button on the steel part of the gate again and again.

"Fuck! Please open," she cried as she pushed the buzzer yet again.

Finally, she heard a distinct male voice over the intercom. "Yes?"

"It's an emergency! Please open the gate!! We have to call an ambulance! It's Liz from next door! My mother fell and is injured." Everything came tumbling out.

The gate clicked open. Eliad and another member of the security detail emerged from the interior of the house, surveying their drenched and hysterical neighbor with slight apprehension.

"To what do we owe this surprise?" he said with little or no emotion.

"I don't have time for jokes, my mother fell and is injured, and our phones are down—you have to call an ambulance! Please!" she pleaded, whimpering.

While Eliad wasn't warm or possessed of an endearing bedside manner, he had been used to emergency situations in the army and remained calm and nonplussed when it came to handling a crisis.

"Of course." He turned, and his team went quickly into gear and assured her help would be on the way given their newly installed emergency generator was operational.

"Thank you," she croaked as she gave her address again. "It's 4345 North Bay Road. Thank you."

"Done! They're on their way," Eliad said in a slightly more empathic tone than usual as he offered his help. Liz nodded and thanked him again, then ran outside and back to the villa into the courtyard leaving the gate open for the ambulances. The torrential rains drenched her, and she almost wiped out again on the polished marble floor as she entered the house. She ran up the staircase shouting she was on the way, hopeful her mother would hear her. Bursting into the bedroom, she found Linda frightened and writhing in pain. She prepared a cool washcloth for her head as they both waited for help to come.

Finally, after what seemed an interminable amount of time, she heard the sirens and ran down to meet the masked emergency workers who quickly filed ahead of her to the bedroom with a board and array of medical equipment. After their initial intake and protocol, which seemed to take longer than Liz thought possible, the masked emergency workers attended to a distraught Linda, took her vitals, and then put her on the ominous wooden board and carried her slowly down the staircase. Liz followed dutifully, grabbed a hoodie off the bench, and gathered her purse and mother's wallet on the way out. The red and blue ambulance and police lights reflected on the sleek, rain drenched pavement like a TV crime scene. The workers took Linda's pulse and monitored her breathing. They ushered Liz aside, and she stood in the rain weeping.

Suddenly she felt a presence behind her and turned.

"How is she?" G handed her his umbrella, approaching gently as Eliad stood in the background on a cell phone. He was totally drenched by the rain as was his security staff.

"They're just doing some tests. I think she broke something." Liz gulped as she turned and saw he was now drenched as well.

"I'm sorry. Can I do anything?" he offered.

"That's nice of you to come by." She took refuge from the elements under the umbrella. "Thanks for this."

"You need some company," he said more as a statement than a question.

"No, I'm fine," Liz stated firmly.

"Liz! You need some help." He gave her a doe-eyed look. "You may hate me or dislike me, but I'm your neighbor and I'm not going anywhere." They stood silently in an eerie face off, and finally the emergency staff motioned for her to come in the back of the ambulance as the rain pelted.

"You don't need to." She ran towards the ambulance as they motioned for her.

"Whatever you need." He followed and shouted with a bit of grit.

"You don't have to." She gulped as she started to get into the back of the ambulance with her mother. They handed her a surgical mask to put on.

"I want to help," G stated, the rain drenching his hair and face. "Really."

"I'm fine. I want to be alone, okay? But thank you." She looked at him squarely before entering the back of the ambulance.

He paused, thinking, before confidently saying, "I'll check on you tomorrow to see if you need anything. Okay? Mount Sinai?"

Okay, she thought and paused. "Fine, tomorrow. Thank you!" Liz acquiesced and didn't want to appear rude as she stepped inside and sat in the jump seat and held her mother's hand. She saw G looking after her as the ambulance doors closed behind her. He resembled a drowned puppy and despite her protests she was impressed and appreciated the offer. Would he live up to his word? Out of the corner of her eye she had also seen Eliad on the phone talking to a friend, behind G, and he was laughing.

G seems sincere, but it's probably all an act. And his henchman is still an ass! she thought as they were getting ready to rush Linda to the emergency room. She wouldn't hold her breath that he would keep his word and show up, but she would keep his umbrella. It also happened to be Burberry.

Twirl!

Chapter 30

The stormy night turned into a drizzly, foggy morning which turned into the better part of the afternoon as if it were a play of acts without any intermission. Liz walked outside the hospital and removed her mask, breathing in the thick, humid air with relief as the light blue mask dangled from her right ear. Even though she was Linda's daughter and doubly vaccinated, she was asked to wait outside the hospital once she completed the paperwork given the updated Covid protocol. She was tired, exhausted, and depressed from the evening's ordeal as she walked out of the hospital in dismay. Linda had indeed broken her hip and the surgery had a few complications given her weakened state.

Liz did what she could for her mother, completing the extra paperwork to try and get her mother a private room and to hopefully make her recuperation as comfortable as possible. She knew they really couldn't afford it, but there was no way she was going to allow Linda to share a room with a stranger. When her father Joe was dying at North Shore Hospital, Linda had dipped into their savings to pay for a private room for her beloved husband, and Liz would do the same for her mother. She would call Ira and get a loan if she had to.

As she exited the sterile environment, the hazy daylight blinded her for a moment and she reached into her vintage, fringed YSL bag to retrieve her oversized Chanel sunglasses she had scored two years earlier in a Beverly Hills yard sale. They'd shield her eyes, not to mention she most likely looked a hot mess without sleep or makeup. She walked over and plopped down, grateful for a seat on the hard metal bench in a shaded, covered area while she waited for Roy to meet her. Luckily, Roy had arrived early that morning after the storm cleared and ran to the hospital, and then had taken an Uber in search of coffee and snacks once the surgeon had given them his report banishing them to the parking lot for Covid protocol. The doctor's news was a bit grim; while the surgery had gone well, given her weakened condition, Linda would most likely be kept in the ICU for a day or two for extra observation. Liz tapped the side of the metal bench and shifted her position; the hard backed metal rungs on the bench were so damn uncomfortable and she knew they were going to leave unsightly and embarrassing stripes on the back of her thighs. Just what she needed, thigh stripes to highlight impending cellulite! She was exhausted and hadn't slept yet. She rationalized that had never stopped her before in college where she had always pulled all-nighters, although she had been over a good decade younger to bounce back. She checked her iPhone, glancing at the time and also seeing if Roy had texted her, and thought it might make more sense to go back to the house and wait. Suddenly, a semi-familiar figure appeared looming in front of her.

"How is your mom?" The handsome police officer's broad figure and navy uniform cast a shadow.

"Wait, you were the police officer from…" Liz squinted and remembered he was the nice policeman who had helped her the day at the house when that asshole Eliad had tried to get them arrested.

"That's me," he said with a broad smile.

"She's still in the ICU so we can't see her yet. How did you know about my mom, Officer?"

"I was making my rounds last night on North Bay Road and Pine Tree Drive and saw the ambulances," he said in a kind, caring voice, "So I made a few calls and wanted to stop by and see if you needed anything."

"That's so very nice of you!" She now felt lucky that she had on her sunglasses as she had no mascara and felt a bit embarrassed how she looked with messy hair and with a bandaged, skinned knee as she looked at the handsome officer.

"That's really so nice," she looked up and read his nameplate, "Officer Adams." He was the nice, good looking one who had given her his card.

"I figured I had to make it up to you and your friend; I felt so badly about that day." He shrugged.

"I really appreciate it." Liz nodded as she saw Roy hop out of the Uber and walk over with a Starbucks bag. He smiled brightly and waved and silently handed Liz a cup of black coffee and a small cellophane bag of her favorite madeleines.

"Why don't you just apply these directly to my hips." She laughed. "Roy, look who it is; you remember Officer Adams?"

"Please call me Garvey." The officer smiled brightly.

"I always remember a man in uniform." Roy looked up and joked as they all laughed.

Both Liz and Roy took in Garvey's magnetic presence; his jet skin shone in the direct haze and his massive shoulders seemed to glide under his skintight uniform and hung beautifully against his narrow waist. A sexy combination. It was as if The Rock and Will Smith had been put in a blender with a bit of Jay Z to boot! It was also clear from his broad, white, and lingering smile he seemed interested in someone, but who? After making pleasantries he excused himself to find a men's room.

"My oh my, my, he's just our type." Roy fanned himself and swooned.

"How do you know my type?" Liz deadpanned.

"Your type is anyone better than Cary, so that's your type. He is obviously interested in one of us. Who, pray tell, is it? I hope it's you, but I also hope it's...*me*." He batted his spidery lashes for great effect.

"We shall see, but I agree he's very dashing and handsome." Liz rubbed a tired eye under her glasses.

"And that uniform! HAWT!" Roy sat down next to Liz. They opened the cellophane bag and noshed on their snacks as he got the update on Linda. "Liz, I'm telling you if he asks you out you go! Don't be a fool," he said, caring for his friend. A few minutes later, Garvey appeared once more and reached into his pocket to retrieve his car keys.

"I'm glad to hear your mother is out of surgery." He smiled again, taking off his paper mask. "I need to get back to the station, but let me know if you need anything at all."

At first Liz thought he might ask for her number, but he turned, looked directly at Roy, and asked him how long he was planning on staying in Miami. Roy raised an eyebrow and took a deep breath. He was interested in Roy, not her!

"I think I'm here for the time being," Roy offered.

"That's good to know." He looked down awkwardly at his shoes. "I'm originally from the Bronx, and when I got down here, I never left. You're either for this place or not," he stated.

"Well, I'm all in," Roy flirted.

"Good to know!" They made heavy eye contact.

"You must come over for dinner one night," Roy offered. "I am very good at ordering in."

"Yes, of course," Liz offered brightly. "You must!"

"I would love to." His dark eyes shone brightly as he lingered a beat. "I'm good at cleaning up."

"But in the meantime, maybe we can get a drink one night and you can show me around *MY-Jami*!" Roy seized the moment. Liz marveled at his flirting abilities; she could learn from him.

"A drink sounds great." Garvey beamed at the thought. "Are you around this weekend? I'm off duty."

"Let me walk you to your car," Roy flirted. "You can pretend to arrest me again." They all laughed again, and Garvey smiled brightly as he said his goodbyes. Roy walked him to his police car in the nearby lot. Liz was a bit stunned yet truly happy for Roy. His innate inner ease always broke the ice with people; he possessed a natural gift. Garvey seemed genuinely lovely and someone with wonderful manners and good character. It was strange, she thought, as he was so outwardly macho that that she hadn't given it a thought that he might possibly be gay. It was a happy surprise for Roy. Although, she had to admit she would have gone on a date with him had he been straight. Within minutes, Roy texted he was going for a spin in the police car, apologized for leaving, said he would be back soon, and sent one happy face emoji and one of a pickle. She smiled again; he sure worked fast.

Her phone buzzed, and it was the surgeon calling to tell her that Linda was resting comfortably and they were indeed keeping her overnight for observation. They suggested, given the new Covid rules, it might make sense for her to go back home to get some rest and assured her they would call later in the day with an update. She thanked the surgeon, then looked for the Uber app in her phone.

Suddenly, she heard the roar of a sleek sports car pull up and idle in front of her; it was a gleaming silver Lamborghini, the glint of glamor and new money was undeniable. Inside, G Alvarez sat and waved. She was surprised that he had lived up to his promise; everyone, it seemed, was showing up except her own boyfriend.

"How's Mom?" G asked brightly.

"That's so nice of you!" She offered a small hand wave. "She broke her hip and had surgery, so she'll be in the ICU again overnight, but the worst seems to be behind us, hopefully. Thanks again to you and your team." She paused. "Are you here to get your Covid shot? The pavilion is that way." Liz pointed nonchalantly.

"No, I already got the Pfizer one. I came to see you and to see if you needed anything?" He looked a bit perplexed and added, "Like I said I would."

"Oh, really?" She paused. "Well, that's...very nice of you. How did you know I was here?"

"We called the hospital, and they said the visitors usually wait in this section outside." He looked at her like he would a lost puppy or kitten. He paused. "You look surprised. I told you I would come."

"Yes, no. I mean, I meet a lot of people here who say they are going to do things and don't follow through."

"Well, I always do what I say I'm going to do. The nuns taught me."

"That's refreshing. I'm glad to see it's become a *habit*." She laughed and groaned at herself. "Oh, sorry, that was so cheesy..." She shrugged at the pun and gathered her bag. "Well, I'm going to go home. They don't allow visitors, so I'm going to call an Uber."

"Then I came just in time. Hop in neighbor." He smiled.

"No, really I couldn't," Liz stated firmly.

"And why couldn't you?" He looked at her with a questioning smile. Did the man still have dimples at his age?

"Because," she offered.

"Because why?"

"Because…I don't know." She lingered. "I like hating you, and now you're making that very difficult." Liz looked at him for the first time clearly. He was handsome, but his style was somewhat effeminate and flashy. She couldn't get over a man wearing a silk tiger print shirt, but then again, it was Miami. He was a walking advertisement for Versace and could have played the main character in *Aladdin*.

"Maybe you can try to like…liking me." He smiled again.

"If this is a ploy to buy my house, I told you it's not for sale." She frowned. Why did she always have to get the assholes when Roy was probably making time in the backseat with a hot cop?

"Liz—can I call you Liz?" he asked.

"It depends."

"I'm no longer interested in buying your house." G smiled brilliantly.

"And why's that?" She looked at him coolly.

He smiled again. Why was he always smiling? It was so annoying.

"Because, I already have an accepted offer on the neighbor's house on the other side of me," he said matter-of-factly.

"Wait, you bought that house? The big, ugly, yellow one?" Liz was baffled but impressed.

"Yeah, he's a Cuban businessman, and I offered him ten times what he paid for it. There are still some people in the world who want to make a big profit, you know." He smiled yet again.

"I have to hand it to you; you seem to get what you want one way or another."

"My security team came up with designs for a new plan, so I now have no ulterior motives, can we be friends?" he asked.

"Okay, I guess." Liz shrugged. "I give in."

"Good segue…get in." He paused. "Sorry for that pun, but I am better than Uber and cheaper."

"Are you sure? I don't want to take you out of your way." She smiled for the first time.

"I don't call a hundred feet out of the way. Please." He got out of the car and walked around to open the passenger side door for her as she handed him back his umbrella.

"Okay, okay, thanks." Liz shrugged, thinking Roy and Garvey were most likely making out like teenagers by now and knowing Roy, they were already using the handcuffs. Her "gaydar" was off these days. She thought Garvey was straight, but he turned out to be gay. Then G, who she assumed was gay, might actually be straight. It was all up for grabs.

One thing was for sure; Miami seemed to live by its own rules.

Chapter 31

Cary pulled his weather-beaten, tan Coach weekend bag from the top of his closet with a shake of his squarish head and emitted a small inner groan. The call from Liz at 3 a.m., weeping in the hospital, woke him out of a coma-like sleep. He tried to calm her down despite the hysterics. He'd grown up with two older brothers and knew he was fairly oblivious when it came to women; their volatile moods and reactions and how they responded to events large and small. It was clear to him that his brain was wired in the rational zone while many women and some men, like Liz's friend Roy, seemed to live in a more emotional one. He often had to stop himself from being judgmental to accommodate and navigate ongoing personal and professional relationships and those with colleagues. In his mind, not having much interaction with the opposite sex till high school, he thought women were supposed to be soft, sexy, and accommodating, but he knew so little. He only discovered they had their periods when he was a senior in sex ed class. No one bothered to talk with him about it at home; his own two older brothers were too busy with hockey practice and college boards to give him much guidance and his mother had passed away in junior high school due to breast cancer, so little attention was paid to anything other than sports and medicine. Women were another world entirely and kept out of reach, high on the shelf like the dog eared and worn-out Penthouse Magazine he had kept on the top of his closet under his spare track uniform. His unrealistic views on women and motherhood took shape from foggy childhood memories of his mother setting the perfect table and attending to his father with a readymade martini when he came home from work.

As he grew older, he had little patience when it came to emotions in general and had fallen behind in correcting that flaw. His distant and demanding father had pushed him and his brothers with a rigorous sports schedule and academic excellence knowing medical school was only available to the brightest, most dedicated, and most disciplined. As a doctor he knew that his bedside manner was somewhat lacking, yet with Covid he didn't have much time to think about any of it; it was now all action and reaction in the moment. The kinder and gentler Dr. Cary Simon would hopefully emerge when things calmed down and the pandemic was at bay.

He did know; however, it was serious that Linda Galin had fallen, broken her hip, and was in surgery; G-d forbid there be complications given her weakened state. He knew the right thing to do, what he had to do, and that was to take the next flight out to help and comfort his girlfriend, especially given his medical expertise and oversight. He had also always liked and cared for Linda. She was in many ways the kind of woman he really wanted and needed; totally dedicated to her man and a *balabusta*, a Yiddish expression for the "perfect homemaker who brings together family by caring and cooking for them." He thought Liz could have improved a bit more in this category yet gave her the benefit of the doubt. He knew he had to fly down and help control the situation. It had all just come at the worst possible time, and he had just used his last chit to get down to Miami only days earlier. It was as if someone was playing a joke on him, not to mention Liz slipping in that Roy had flown in first thing and the asshole Latin popstar next door's team had called and offered help. Not that he thought he was interested in her; it was all about buying the house! It was all a ploy, as word on the street was G Alvarez was gay and rumors abounded that he lived with his long-term boyfriend or some such arrangement.

He threw some things in the weekend bag and tossed all his essentials into his leather shaving kit which he zippered quickly. As he neatly folded his undershorts and socks, he wondered whether he even needed the socks.

He couldn't believe he had to go back so soon to the sunshine state. He hated Florida; the sun, the heat and humidity and broke out in splotchy, angry rashes and worse, despised the vulgarity and the showiness of the people. His conservative Canadian roots had him craving winter and hockey season, and his Harvard graduate experience had him aspiring to a New England, Norman Rockwell–style life. New York was where he was going to get his foundation, but he always dreamed of a position in a Boston hospital and a large colonial home in a place like Wellesley, with kids running around and coaching Little League or hockey.

He booked his ticket online and then called UberX for La Guardia and shook his head once more in disbelief. As he looked out the car window to La Guardia he thought about the state of things with Liz; the relationship had come to a bit of a standstill. He had been tolerant and accepted they could not see each other during Covid as she was caring for her mother. This appealed to him as she was obviously a caretaker and not as frivolous as he once thought she was, but then out of the blue this crazy thing happened with her inheriting the Miami mansion. He knew she had to live and declare residency there for six months and one day and suddenly, although he hated to admit it to himself, she had become in his mind "geographically unsuitable." She wasn't going to be able to visit New York because of counting the days and he was expected to fly down to Miami on a whim, which interrupted his residency and caring for his patients. While it was all wearing on him, he decided to fly down and surprise her as he knew it was the right thing to do and perhaps her reaction would make things a bit clearer for him.

When he first met Liz, he thought she could be the one; she was more beautiful than any girl he had ever dated and he was enraptured by her large blue gold-tinged eyes and stunning figure, not to mention she was funny and kept him laughing. He always thought she might be the yin to his yang yet now he had a gnawing feeling it was close but no cigar. Lately, at work, he had been spending more time with a nurse on his shift named Carla Rubio. Truth be told, she was not nearly as pretty as Liz and a bit heavyset for his taste, but she was warm, and they shared the same interest in medicine and their patients. She also loved the Grateful

Dead, possessed a sweet bright smile, and had a big heart. She also loved the Northeast, skiing, and snowshoeing. While she wasn't Jewish, she had mentioned her brother had converted after marrying a Jewish girl. Was that a hint? Perhaps the trip to Miami would be clarifying to him on a number of levels. Either way, he knew he needed to go. It was like the Will Smith song, "Miami," hearing the melody in his head.

Ugh, he thought. *My least favorite type of music but perfectly fitting for my least favorite state in the union.*

Chapter 32

Wynwood Walls, once referred to as Little San Juan, and El Barrio attracted largely Puerto Rican residents who settled there in the 1950s. Forward thinking vision and investment helped the area become one of the great success stories of urban planning and redevelopment. In 2009 the late developer Tony Goldman commissioned artists to create an outdoor gallery of street art for the emerging vibrant graffiti, turning the district into one of Miami's cultural hotbeds and what would turn out to be one of the state's most popular and enduring tourist attractions, while still keeping the area's authentic flavor and feel. Tony was known as a big thinker with great energy and Wynwood would turn out to be his triumphant legacy.

"Hey, where are you taking me?" Liz panicked slightly as she noticed G guide the shark-like, silver Lamborghini right instead of left out of the Mount Sinai parking lot, heading towards Wynwood.

"Isn't my house, I mean our houses, that way?" She pointed backwards.

"I'm kidnapping you." G smiled slyly, slowing for the light. A white Mercedes convertible pulled up, and three teenage girls started honking, yelling, and waving as they recognized G.

"Should I be scared?" Liz surveyed him intently. Was he for real or another well intentioned phony? She was going to find out, as she had enough fake friends and acquaintances to last her a lifetime and didn't need any more, especially a famous one with a seemingly swelled head.

"I'm taking you to Salt and Straw. You've had a hard night." He sympathized.

"I could use some sleep actually." She tried to suppress a yawn. "I haven't slept, and I'm sure I look like something the cat dragged in."

"You look beautiful, and that's my point," he said, turning sideways. "You deserve something sweet before you turn in."

"I do?" she said, not fighting the thought of a scoop of chocolate with hot fudge sauce. Perhaps he had a point.

"You've been through a lot," he said, pumping up his playlist. It was certainly different from Cary's frat house selection of the Grateful Dead and Boston.

"Is that yours?" she asked, listening to the sensual beat and Latin lyrics, adjusting her sunglasses.

"I never play my own stuff. I actually can't stand the sound of my voice," he said softly. "That's my hero Carlos Vives."

"Why is he your hero?" She looked at him inquisitively.

"Well, he is a Colombian success story, and it happened a bit later for him, the singing, you know."

"No, I don't know…are you Colombian?" she asked naively.

"You really don't know anything about me, do you?" He turned and beamed in a shocked way as he turned the car past some downtrodden liquor stores and derelict office buildings as they headed for the causeway.

"Does that bother you?" she asked.

"No, I find it a bit intriguing. Most people think they know everything about me," he offered as a fact.

"What's to know?" she asked in an offhand manner. He was not used to anyone as direct as Liz, as years of fame and fortune had inured him to so many of the basics most people were used to.

"What does that mean?" He tried to understand the question.

"Well, since I don't know anything about you, tell me what you want me to know about yourself." Liz was pointed and direct in her line of questioning as the traffic to the causeway slowed.

"You are very forward Liz…what is your last name anyway?" G seemed taken by surprise.

"Galin." Her gaze was slightly unsettling as she looked at him directly, the blue of her eyes unsettling in a starry gaze. "Used to be Galinsky, but my dad changed it for business."

"Liz…Galin," he repeated with his subtle accent, appreciating her honest approach. Liz Galin, or Galinsky for that matter, clearly wasn't someone who put on airs. It sounded nice as it rolled off his tongue easily and sensually with his Latin accent.

"So, tell me one thing?" She prodded, trying to get more of a fix on him.

"I don't usually like to speak about myself." He swerved the car onto the causeway leading to the arts district looking straight ahead.

"Why not? Are you hiding something?" She popped a Wintergreen Tic Tac that she found lurking at the bottom of her handbag into her mouth.

He laughed nervously. "I wanted to get you ice cream, and now you're analyzing me."

"It's my personality. I'm sorry." She shrugged.

"I think it's, well…" He hesitated. "Endearing. I haven't met anyone like you before."

"Meaning?" She pushed.

"Meaning you are very interesting." He was somewhat taken aback at her directness.

"'Interesting.' That sounds pejorative." She rolled an invisible eyebrow under her large, bug-like sunglasses.

"It's not, it's a compliment." He looked at her, smiled, and then moved his eyes back on the road. She noticed his perfect white teeth. Were they laminates, or was he born with Olympic dental genes?

"Okay." Strangely, she was starting to find his company easy and relaxing. "So, since I don't know you, tell me something about yourself you would never tell anyone," she asked again. She wanted to know if he was real or paper mâché; what was he made of? At this juncture in her life, she had no time to waste on frivolous people, famous neighbors or not.

He paused a beat, and, in that moment, he decided to be his authentic self. He had never met anyone before, besides Sant, who he had felt this comfortable with and with whom he had nothing to lose. He would try another approach than usual, he thought in a flash, as he was always having to put his guard up with the press and his fans. She was neither, and it was refreshing. He remembered what the New York therapist Dr. Klinkov had said in his one pivotal session, that honesty might set him free and alleviate his pain. He knew it was the right way, but he hadn't been ready for it…until now. *Perhaps the outcome will be different if I act differently*, he thought as he put his foot on the accelerator. They both felt the tight speed of the car.

"I was raised in an orphanage in Bogota," he said slowly. "It was hard, but it made me who I am today, I guess." He drove a bit steadier as he told her his story.

"Oh, G." She turned him sympathetically. "I had no idea, that must have been so hard. How old were you?" She appraised him differently with one stroke.

"Seven," he said softly.

"Wow. What happened to your parents, if you don't mind my asking?" She was now truly curious.

"I never knew who my father was. My mother died of a drug overdose. It wasn't an idyllic childhood to say the least." He gulped. He was not used to talking about such things, and Liz sat hearing his truth, never having expected it.

"You're not saying anything," he said, immediately afraid that he had revealed too much.

"I'm just…impressed." She nodded. "You must have had such a hard time, and now you have so much success. It must be surreal to have such an interesting story."

"You have no idea." He cocked his handsome head to the side. He was happy he had taken the risk; she wasn't running away.

"I can't imagine the highs and lows." She marveled.

"You have no idea," he repeated.

"Now I have some idea." She sat listening to Carlos Vives and let it all sink in. She had never expected G to be so real so quickly and seemingly so deeply wounded. She sensed he was shy about it but also that he didn't want to change the subject.

"I suddenly feel like I have nothing to complain about my childhood," she said.

"You don't." He laughed, pulling up to the long light at the intersection. There was traffic and only one road into the arts section. "Where did you grow up?"

"In a place called Great Neck on Long Island. It was a very nice suburban community, and my parents tried to give me everything." She looked down. "I was very lucky, I guess."

"Well, it's nice that you appreciate it, and you're a good daughter." He nodded.

"I try. After my father died two years ago, I sort of became my mother's caretaker during her chemo."

"I'm sorry, that sounds like a lot." He looked at her, impressed as well.

"It is. I miss my dad, but I'm up for the task," she said with fortitude.

"You seem very capable," he said.

"That doesn't sound very sexy. 'Liz Galin is very...capable.'" She shook her luxurious mane, which actually appeared more lustrous despite the lack of a morning shower.

"I think it's a compliment." He added, "Capable is sexy!"

"To whom?" She looked surprised.

"To me." He winked at her.

Really, a wink? she thought as she raised an eyebrow under her glasses in response. "Really?"

"Why are you surprised?" he questioned.

"I never thought I'd hear capable and sexy in the same sentence." She shrugged.

"Well, you know, English isn't my first language!" They both enjoyed the repartee and laughed.

"You are quite maddening, but I may decide to like...liking you." Liz sat back and grinned.

After battling the traffic, G finally made his way to Wynwood, and they took in the colorful and vibrant neighborhood which was packed with people acting as if Covid did not exist. Their conversation was easy and natural as they took in the sights. The new luxury shops and outdoor restaurants were packed and it seemed like a totally normal afternoon, not a global pandemic. G turned and saw a navy SUV pulling out of a spot. He waited patiently and then pulled in only a few doors away from the famed ice cream shop. He put on his sunglasses and baseball cap as he noticed people staring as he exited the car, and then walked over to Liz's side, opened her door, and helped her out. *He certainly had good manners*, she thought.

"You know, you might want to drive a more low-key car if you don't want to stand out?" Liz said in her typical honest fashion. "Unless deep down you really do!" She smirked.

He nodded and laughed. Perhaps she had a point; was he really searching for attention and then pushing it away? Something to talk with his therapist about. They both walked into Salt and Straw and ordered two chocolate chip cones. G happily signed an autograph for the store owner, then put on his Tom Ford sunglasses and baseball hat. They enjoyed their cones as they walked through Wynwood Walls, admiring the colorful graffiti art, chatting about everything and nothing. He snapped a few iPhone photos of Liz making a funny faces against a the vibrant painted graffiti backgrounds. Then, deciding to be a bit bolder than usual, he took a selfie of the two of them and casually put his arm around her. He noticed that she didn't pull away. Deep down, they both knew there was something percolating, an attraction perhaps, and even though she was technically taken, she did not immediately rebuff his advances. Liz felt a natural electricity when he put his arm around her shoulder that she felt that was lacking recently with Cary. She pushed that thought away as it was a difficult comparison, one she was not ready to conclude on.

They walked slowly, finishing their cones, and making light conversation as it was low-key and fun. Liz felt a sense of calm. They window shopped and took a long walk to Off White, and then G fell in love with a colorful Dubuffet at the Rosenfeld Gallery. She loved the ease he had with salespeople and gallery owners. Cary was so tightly wound, and G was interestingly the exact opposite; gentle, with an infectious laughter, and his observations were unique and funny. As they walked back to the car, he stopped for a fan photo and then sensed an overwhelming feeling of joy, one that seemed fleeting, totally unreliable, and yet something he wanted to hold onto. The wind suddenly whipped, and Liz used her sunglasses on the top of her head to hold her loose tangle in place. Something strange overtook him as he looked into her clear blue eyes; lost in the golden circle. He felt as if he had known her before. He wiped his lips with the small white paper napkin and reached over and suddenly kissed her tenderly on the lips.

Really? Liz was more shocked than surprised. A kiss out of the blue from another man, an unexpected stranger. Really?

"Capable is sexy." He looked at her surprised reaction and added, "I'm sorry."

"Why are you sorry?" Liz seemed shocked and perplexed, but a tad happy.

"I don't want to offend you," he said.

"I think you're a good kisser." She paused, then added. "Actually, I'm a bit surprised."

"Why is that?" He looked at her face. It resembled an old-fashioned cameo.

"Can I be honest?" Liz rolled the dice; she knew she had nothing to lose and was enjoying their honest banter.

"That seems to be the way we are starting off," he said, impressed at the fluidity and ease of their interactions.

"I thought you liked men," she said bluntly.

"Really?" He paused. "Not in that way."

"Okay." She saw that she touched a nerve and looked at him anew.

"Why did you think so?" he asked defensively, his face reddened.

"It's just a feeling I got." she said matter-of-factly.

"Why is that?" He tried to quell his anxiety on the subject which was a sore point for him.

"I don't know, maybe it's because you live with a lot of guys, I hardly ever see any women around…and that shirt." She eyed him.

"What's wrong with this shirt?" He pointed and laughed nervously.

"Nothing's wrong with it. Straight men usually don't wear tiger print silk shirts from Cavalli." She observed. As a stylist, she knew her brands.

"In South America they do, and it's vintage." He laughed out loud.

"Even more so." She laughed. "Okay. So let me ask you a question?"

"Sure, hit me."

"Have you ever been with a man?"

"Have you ever been with a woman?"

"No, but I did kiss my roommate in college once when I was drunk," she said with natural ease. "It wasn't for me. You?" She stared him down. G didn't want to lie and in that moment; he hesitated.

"That's a yes obviously." She rolled her eyes; she didn't need a man experimenting with his sexuality on her.

"No..." He looked at her and paused. "And yes."

"I don't understand, but I don't care if you are."

"I'm not gay, Liz," G explained with soulful eyes.

"You don't owe me an explanation." She shrugged.

"No, please. I won't lie to you. The yes was something I was forced to do when I was a kid." He slowed his pace as he spoke to her about this traumatic event. "I was young and in the band my music manager..." He paused for a long beat. Then it all came flooding out. "He abused me. I don't know why I'm telling you this. Up until recently, the only person who knew was Sant, my best friend. We were raised in the orphanage together. Recently one of my former bandmates asked me if it happened to me too. At that moment, I knew we were all victims." He stopped and adjusted his sunglasses and wiped away a lone tear in the process.

"I'm so sorry, G." Liz looked at him anew. "That must have been so awful. How old were you?" Liz now felt a bit bad for being so cavalier on the subject.

"Thirteen. It went on until I was seventeen." G walked down an empty side street as he didn't want anyone to see his tears. "He was my mentor...and my monster."

"I am so sorry, that must have been awful and scarring."

"No, I'm…" He gulped for air and then started tearing up. "I'm sorry. I've never told anyone before." The stream turned into a flood.

"I'm sorry, I shouldn't have asked, I didn't know…" She was kicking herself and felt terrible that she had pushed him on such a sensitive subject so quickly.

"No." His voice croaked a bit. "How could you have known? It's been a secret I have been holding onto for a long, long time." He gathered his composure.

"Well, it's always easier with a stranger." She didn't know what to say and felt so badly.

"I was forced to and blackmailed." G wiped his eye with the back of his hand.

"I see." She looked down and felt like a heel.

In that moment, G tried to control his tears but couldn't. Liz reached over and held him as he managed this cathartic moment. Holding him, she knew something was happening that was special and beyond their control. She thought about Elsa and Ben too. Did it feel this way? This natural?

He looked down. He had finally confided in a woman. What would she say or do?

"I'm a little embarrassed I told you." He smiled in a downcast way.

"No, I'm so glad you did." Liz felt for him. "I'm honored you felt you could trust me. Maybe it's because I'm capable." She smiled. "I want to show you how much it meant that you told me." She looked at his handsome face. It was much more majestic in its honesty and pain. At that moment, she took his face gently in her hands and kissed him. It was artful, beautiful, and passionate. A car went by and honked its horn. They both came up for air and laughed, then kissed again. A car slowed and blasted a song.

It was his song, "Baby I Love Your Way."

Chapter 33

As G veered the sleek nose of his Lamborghini towards her gated drive, Liz motioned for him to park in the circle as she opened the electric gate. The extremely modern sports car seemed even more of a contrast as it entered the Roaring '20s estate.

"Come in. I'll show you around the old place," Liz offered. She was surprised she was having such a nice time and didn't want the impromptu date to end so soon, especially after Roy had texted and asked if it was okay for him to go to drinks and dinner with Garvey. It was sweet of Roy to ask given Linda's condition, and she texted back that he absolutely should, as they weren't likely to hear anything more that evening nor would they be allowed back at the hospital. She mentioned that G had showed up at the hospital and they had gone to Wynwood, to which Roy sent emojis of a smiling face, a Colombian flag, and another pickle and a series of exclamation points which made her laugh.

"Wow, this is really something!" G whistled as he parked the car by the now restored, bubbling, ornate marble fountain, exited the vehicle, and took in the estate. He left the keys in the dashboard and then walked to Liz's side to open the door as he surveyed the villa. He was suitably impressed by the recent restoration work and immediately in awe of the property, and marveled that while it was right next door to his home it seemed a world away. She started to give him a brief tour of the villa and when they reached the entry, despite the beckoning grandeur, he instantly stopped and looked down at the ancient Pompeiian mosaic. He leaned over with the enthusiasm of a young boy with an electric train set as he gently ran his hand over the surface of the dusty ancient tiny stones, much like Ira had done. Liz explained the legend of the mosaic and that if she ever sold the house, it would go back to the museum in Italy. She was also immediately struck that although she had told Cary the history, he had hardly glanced at it or feigned interest when he saw it, and that G was the exact opposite, very animated and effusive on the history and details large and small. Liz gave him an abbreviated tour of the first floor and even showed him the manual elevator which he also found incredibly fascinating, and she loved that he truly appreciated the architecture and the restoration job she was doing rather than just viewing the property as a future sale or investment as Cary had done. As they walked the villa, she told G a bit more about her family and childhood and her father Joe, and how devastated she was when he passed.

"My dad would have flipped over this place," she said as she opened the French, oak doors to the grand, paneled library and immense, carved limestone fireplace and saw the look of deep appreciation in his eyes. As they made their way from the formal dining room to the breakfast pavilion, she looked down at her iPhone and couldn't believe time had passed so quickly. It was already 5:30 in the afternoon. She had called the hospital and left four messages for the doctor to no avail, and then finally received a text and report from the nurse who said that Linda was in stable condition, no new news, and she would be kept in the ICU for observation overnight.

She filled G in on the doctor's report, and he seemed truly concerned and supportive. At that moment, Liz stammered slightly but decided to invite G for dinner, if he didn't have plans. She didn't relish the prospect of spending the night at home alone and Roy being out on the town; she was pleased when she saw G's eyes light up at the offer.

"I would love to! I was just going to stay home writing some music tonight, so this is a real treat." He beamed.

"Great!" Liz smiled. "How about we order chili from Joe's?" she asked. "It's early, but I haven't had anything other than ice cream; I'm starved." Her blue eyes lit up. "I've never had ice cream as an appetizer!"

"That's my favorite, and I'm starving as well." He smiled. "I've been on this crazy salad and sushi diet for my upcoming tour and can't take it anymore." He laughed. Liz looked at him anew but also wondered whether he was naturally this nice and affable or if it was all really an act. She couldn't decide but knew she would find out.

G googled the menu on his phone and asked Liz what she wanted. They both loved the ideas of salads and chili, and he insisted on placing the order. He excused himself to go to the bathroom and quickly dialed his assistant Karolina under his breath to order the food since he knew it wasn't in his wheelhouse. She was always accommodating and also knew not to ask questions. She texted him within minutes that the order had been placed. When he gave her the address, Karolina only added, "Oh, you must be at a neighbor's. Have fun!"

He walked back into the kitchen and gave her the ETA for the delivery. He had originally offered to drive to get the takeout, but Liz told him she would rather hang at the house and wait for them to deliver. She offered him a glass of wine in the interim, which he gladly accepted. He had cut alcohol and carbs on his diet to slim down, but tonight he would relax and indulge a bit.

They both walked into the cavernous pantry to retrieve and open a bottle of cold, perspiring Whispering Angel from the wine refrigerator she had recently installed. G did the honors of opening the wine with an ancient, tarnished corkscrew she plucked from the silver closet and then she poured the French rosé into two large gold and aqua venetian goblets she took down from the glass fronted shelving. "Good teamwork!" he said as they clinked glasses. G offered his Colombian toast, "Salud y amor tiempo para disfrutarlo."

"That sounds lovely." Liz cocked her head. "What does it mean?"

"Health and love…and time to enjoy it." He nodded, his teeth looking extra white in the light.

"I love that." Liz's eyes sparkled. "L'chaim!" She toasted back.

"What does that mean?"

"It's Hebrew for 'To life.'"

"I love that too!" He stood looking at her awkwardly, feeling the connection between them.

G sipped and admired the vintage Hoosier cabinet and the hulking, black cast iron stove and told her it reminded him of the turn of the century kitchen at the orphanage only "the rich version." They laughed as they clinked again and carried their wineglasses out the Palladian doors to take in the view of the bay and the glorious burnt orange and pink streaked sunset.

"We're both very lucky with this view, aren't we?" Liz looked over at G and smiled as they walked down slowly to the dock and stood together taking in the incredible view of the city on the bay sparkling like fallen New Year's fireworks. They turned to walk back, and G gently reached over and took her hand as he led her to the rod iron two-seater lounge chair she had recently purchased, and then they both sprawled out together looking up at the Magritte-tinged sky. She suddenly removed her hand like it had been seared by a burning hot coal.

"Is something wrong?" He looked at her fearful expression.

"I'm sorry. I was just thinking I have a boyfriend and suddenly felt very guilty. I am not someone who does this…kind of thing." She looked down.

"What, having fun?"

"And to think this is all on camera; your security people are getting a good look at this." Liz moved a lock of hair off his forehead. "Maybe they'll send in the drones!"

"Actually, after the last incident, I had them take down any surveillance of your property, so no one is watching. I promise," G explained. "My apologies again; I really didn't know."

"Oh, too bad. We could have given Darth Vader a good show," Liz joked.

He looked at her with fresh eyes and was overcome by her silken skin and beautiful bow lips which were more akin to a silent film actress from the '20s than the current breed of plump lipped, injected reality stars. He leaned in and kissed her again and tasted the wine on each other's lips and it all seemed so surreal and natural at the same time.

"Relax," he said. "It's just fun. I think you need a kiss; I know I do." This time she didn't fight him, as she was experimenting to see how she was feeling versus Cary and strangely, it felt really good. She decided to go with it and reached up and kissed him back. It had been so long without genuine, true affection and attraction. After lounging and cuddling for a half hour, watching the glowing sun sink into the distant skyline, Liz pointed skyward.

"It's the exact same color as my favorite Hermes box." She observed.

G smiled. "Yes, but much less expensive." He really seemed to appreciate her offbeat sense of humor and matched her wit for wit. After lounging and taking in the glorious sunset, she motioned for him to go back inside to start setting the table for dinner. They both knew their connection was natural; and Liz tried to put any accumulated noise out of her mind as she changed the subject to the more important task at hand; dinner. She led the way with gold-rimmed dinner plates, toward the incredible oval breakfast pavilion as he marveled at the simplicity, elegance, and aura of the room, which was less formal than the dining room but chic and glamorous. She bent down to light the beeswax candles she had installed the week before in the two tall gold candelabra of naked women with uplifted arms holding the candles. G looked over and admired her lithe and lovely decolletage and languid arms, appreciating her natural elegance which was highlighted by the room's romantic lighting. They both silently helped to arrange and set the table with Liz guiding him to different drawers in the pantry and glass fronted cabinets. The old glass cabinet doors from the '20s had a slight wave, unlike perfect modern glass which offered no individual character or subtle blemishes. Once the delivery service texted the food was outside the gate, G went to the entrance of the property to pay and tip the delivery man and then brought the bags back into the pantry area, helping Liz take out the plastic containers. She opened the wooden drawers for the cutlery and dinnerware, surveying the rows and rows of ornate silver.

"We have formal…and more formal." She waved her hand over the baroque silverware. G shook his head in amazement at the veritable treasure trove.

They worked as an efficient, synchronized team spooning the salad and chili into the delicate Limoges China chafing dishes she had brought out from the cabinets and laid out the heavy, ornate silver and antique Murano goblets which they brought into the breakfast pavilion. G helped bring in the dishes of salad and chili, working together in natural harmony. He walked back into the pantry to get another serving spoon and peered into the custom drawer, picking up a beautiful but unusual sterling knife. It featured a curved, ornate handle and a carved "B" inscribed in the center.

"What's this?" He looked at it from two angles.

"Must be a fish knife or for buttering crumpets, I have no idea," she offered as he carefully put it back and then walked into the pavilion with extra cutlery. "It's all from another era. When engraved silverware mattered, I guess," she quipped.

"I really can't get over this room. It's amazing." G swiveled his head again at the Roaring '20s architecture and decor of the pavilion. "It's all amazing. You are amazing." He smiled again and approached her in wonder, putting his hands on her shoulders and kissing her gently. Liz was so different from any girl he had ever met, and her villa was also so different from his own modern mansion. He knew that not many women could really appreciate it beyond its intrinsic value, and he felt the real patina of old money intimidate him a bit.

"Thank you!" She looked down then back up at him as she always had a hard time accepting compliments and kisses, but with G it was so natural.

"It was the owner Elsa's favorite room in the villa. It's mine as well," Liz declared and looked around with pride. They stood for a moment taking it all in and then he walked behind her and pulled out her chair in a gentlemanly fashion and they both sat at the oval table, serving each other. Once they settled in, G regaled her with some funny stories about life on the road and how the fans always tried to sneak backstage. He had her laughing when he told her someone had actually hidden in a food cart in hotel room service and was wheeled in. They had an easy rapport, nothing forced, and conversation came naturally as if they had been friends forever. An hour passed quickly, until suddenly Liz heard footsteps and a familiar voice enter the room before he actually appeared.

"Hey, hon!" a familiar voice boomed.

She looked up in complete surprise, realizing G had left the gate open.

"Cary, what are you doing here?" she asked in total shock as she saw her boyfriend suddenly appear and walk into the breakfast pavilion.

"What do you mean what am I doing here?" He looked a bit shocked at the scene he had stumbled into. "You called me hysterical late last night, so I got on a flight out after my rounds." He paused as he pursed his lips and mimicked her. "What are you doing here?" he repeated in a sarcastic tone, taking in the romantic setting.

Liz immediately rose, walked over, and hugged him. She felt him stiffen at her embrace and immediately felt guilty that she and G had had a romantic afternoon. What if Cary had come earlier and seen them on the lounge together? The thought and sense of betrayal had her turning a beet-red.

"This is so amazing of you. Wow Cary, thank you so much." She moved to kiss him, but he moved his head so she landed on his cheek. "I'm, we're having dinner. Come join us." She blushed at the optics, which she immediately realized were not very good.

"How's Linda?"

"They're keeping her overnight in the ICU."

"I see. While you're sitting here, laughing and having a romantic candlelit dinner. Do you want your privacy?" He looked at her with dismay.

"Cary, don't be ridiculous," she said, overtly blushing. "You've met G, who has been such a big help." The awkwardness that ensued was disappointing and inappropriate and Liz felt she needed to put on a show. Deep down, while she was thrilled that Cary had made such an extra effort to see her, she also recognized that she was suddenly unhappy that her date with G was now at an inconvenient end. She was also struck by the similarity of Elsa's diary; is this how she felt when Leland came home and saw him in the pavilion? Cary looked at them with a frown and in that moment the room spun and then came back into focus. Liz saw everything clearly, and she opted for a decisive explanation as the right strategy.

"Cary, it was very nice of G to visit me at the hospital, and he called the ambulance last night when the power was out. I wanted to invite him to dinner to thank him." Liz then kicked herself the moment she said it as she now sounded defensive and always had a way of overtalking in awkward situations.

"I'm just a little surprised." He looked at them both. "You seem to be having a grand old time, that's all," he sneered a bit and stiffened.

"We just ordered in." Liz explained, embarrassed at his over-the-top reaction." Please grab some, pull up a chair."

"Would you like some wine?" G looked up and smiled, trying to break the ice.

"Oh, so now you're the master of the house? Offering me wine?" Cary said suspiciously.

"I was just trying—"

Liz cut him off, "Cary, G was just trying to be nice since you flew all the way here." She walked over and tried to hug him again and casually pull him towards the table.

"Come sit and take a plate. It's so amazing you took time off to be here…. You must be starved!" she said with a forced smile, yet he stood like a soldier, stiff and unyielding.

"Here, did you eat?" Liz brought over a china plate as she tried to smooth things over.

"I'm suddenly not hungry." He waved the plate away, eyeing her suspiciously. His anger rose as he took in the silver, lit candlesticks, good china, and wine-filled wine goblets.

"I see what's going on here. I'm away for a week or two, and he's already moving in." Cary pointed his index finger in the air at G. "By the way, he's not interested in you." He eyed Liz with suspicion. "He just wants to buy this house."

"Cary, that's not true and it's uncalled for. I told you, G called the ambulance last night and stopped by the hospital today. It was very nice of him, and I invited him to dinner, that's all." She said desperately trying to smooth things over.

"'That's all?' With candlelight and wine? You didn't do that for me when I came down! All I got was take out menus!" Resentment from the last trip rose in him like steam.

"I'm sorry, Cary." Liz stopped in her tracks. "You came all this way. I see your point about why you'd be upset, and I do apologize. I honestly thought it would be more fun to go out when you came down, and tonight…well…I was just trying…"

"Screw your apologies. The only thing you made for me was *reservations*," He cut her off and glared, his voice rising. "For him, you're Martha-fucking-Stewart!" he protested angrily, his festering feelings emerging,

"Hey, hey!" G stood. "Don't talk to her like that."

"Cary, I understand that you are upset and came all this way, but you have to chill!" Liz said, her anxiety rising.

"Who the fuck are you anyway?" Cary's anger rose and his face was flushed. He'd flown all the way to G-dforsaken Florida, and this was what he walked into? A romantic tête-à-tête?

"You know nothing about it my man." G rose, getting his back up. He had been used to bullies in the orphanage and knew the only way to deal with them was to beat them at their game.

"Are you fucking him?"

The room spun. Was this how Leland had spoken to Elsa in anger and rage?

"Don't say that," Liz said quietly. "Not in this room, in this house," she said firmly.

"I'll say what I want," he answered defiantly.

"Stop, this is exactly how Leland acted," Liz said shocking herself, a well of anger bubbling up.

"Who the fuck is Leland? Are you sleeping with him too?" He tossed another verbal bomb.

"That's disgusting, Cary. I realize you are upset, but that is over the line." She paused and then made up her mind. "I understand you are angry, but I will not have a man talk to me like that. You need to go, now!" she said calmly and quietly.

"I just flew all the way here, to this G-d forsaken house, to see you, to help you and your mother."

"Cary, I appreciate that but don't you see? You're acting like a complete ass. That's because you don't want to be here in this house with me. You're doing it because you have to," Liz cried.

"Yes, I had to. I thought that's what you wanted." His anger had his face sweating and beet red.

"But now you've crossed the line to insulting! I want someone who wants to be with me, not *has* to be with me, and for the record, your behavior is officially vile." Liz blushed.

"What's going on between you two?" Cary was angry and couldn't contain himself. "Be careful, he's a faggot!" Cary pointed his finger and sneered, "That's the rumor and everyone knows it."

"Fuck you!" G flew into a rage. He ran over and, in anger, punched him squarely in the jaw. Cary's temper exploded, and he barged back at G and threw him across the room. G groaned as he fell backwards and crashed into one of the ceramic leopards which hit the wall and then burst into a thousand sharpened splinters.

Liz screamed, "Stop it!"

Dazed, G summoned his inner strength and rage and lifted himself up. He ran towards Cary and punched him directly in the stomach. Everything seemed to happen in slow motion as Cary hit G in the cheek. They both fell to the ground and rolled into the ceramic fragments, cutting G's forehead and Cary's hand and lip. Liz was screaming for them to stop as Roy and Garvey suddenly burst into the room. Garvey immediately assessed the situation and tried to break up the fight.

"What in the hell is going on here?" Roy shrilled, his hand on his forehead dramatically. Liz was so incensed she lost complete control and became hysterical.

"He needs to leave now!" Liz yelled at Cary with an angry force.

"I flew all the way here for you and this is what I get!?" He glared at her.

"Leave, get out!" she repeated, crying.

"I'm done, you ungrateful bitch!" Cary yelled at her.

"Don't speak to her that way." G moved to lunge at Cary again, but Garvey's massive form got in between the two of them. Cary rose to his full height, frothing with anger.

"You!" he said as he wagged his finger. At that moment, Liz walked over and gathered all her strength, drew herself up and pointed back.

"No, you!" she said. "You need to leave and never come back. You don't love me!"

"I did love you." He looked at the blood on his hand.

"You didn't love me *more*," she said, adding extra inflection.

"What the fuck does that mean?" He picked up a napkin and pressed it to the cut on his face.

"Exactly what I said," she said as she walked over to G and dabbed the linen napkin on his cut. "The man should always love the woman just a little bit more. And you don't."

Cary stood and shook his auburn head. He was hot, flushed, and blotchy and his face was ruddy from the fight. He pointed his index finger directly in Liz's face, but Garvey held him back.

Roy walked over, stood right in front of Cary, and bravely pointed in his face.

"You think you're better than everyone, but you can't even polish her shoes," Roy said.

"Says the makeup artist!" he sneered again.

"I'll wake up tomorrow and be a makeup artist, but when you wake up, you'll still be short, ugly, and a douchebag!" He jerked his head. "Garvey, take the trash out." Roy put his arm around Liz who was weeping softly.

Garvey muscled Cary towards the door. Right before he was escorted out, Cary turned and yelled, "Fuck you all! And fuck Miami!"

Chapter 34

They put in a frantic call to Dr. Perez, despite it being 3 a.m., to get him over the house as quickly as possible. Once G arrived back at his house, Sant was ready to take him to the emergency room at Mount Sinai since the gash on his forehead was deep and wouldn't stop bleeding but knew to call Karolina. She was the one who instructed he send a gruesome iPhone photo of the wound to her, which she forwarded to Dr. Perez, a concierge doctor they had on retainer in Miami. G was unaware he even had a doctor on his payroll, but she reminded them that Ryan had insisted all his celebrity clients have a private doctor on-call should there ever be an issue where they wanted to avoid the emergency room and any negative press. In Ryan's experience concierge doctors were used more than they ever thought they would be when his A-list clients got into scrapes, as the press would have a field day if a female artist went to a civilian doctor for a UTI or a male star needed an antibiotic for an infection—a euphemism for venereal disease. Once again, baby-faced agent Ryan Palermo had been right.

After Karolina called the good doctor's twenty-four hour answering service, the groggy Cuban physician appeared exactly forty-six minutes later. Liz had done a somewhat sufficient job bandaging G up, but when Dr. Perez arrived at the gate, he was still bleeding through the gauze. As security buzzed him through, an immense wall slid open revealing Dr. Perez arriving in a gleaming, jet-black Aston Martin. Being a well-known concierge doctor in Miami had its obvious perks, and he not only treated celebrities but lived like one himself with a collection of sports cars and a former Venezuelan supermodel as his third wife. Dr. Raphael Perez was also successful because he was smart enough not to ask any questions, and viewed G's injury with a nonjudgmental eye. Sporting a sleek black, N95 mask, he disinfected and strapped on rubber gloves, and set up his doctor's bag on the marble waterfall island in the kitchen. As they made small talk he removed the bandage and viewed the wound, then gently sterilized it and injected the area with a numbing agent before giving G three quick stitches as G held onto Sant's arm and shouted Colombian epithets.

"Don't worry, you'll be as good as new in a few days," Dr. Perez said as he asked G for an autograph for his daughter Clara. He then looked around remarked that he had liked what G had done with the place. He casually mentioned he had been over twice before, once to attend the previous resident's New Year's party with Leo when he was in town and the film actor who owned it had splurged on The Gipsy Kings as poolside entertainment, and also for a raucous Art Basel event. Sant brought out a concert T-shirt for G to sign. Dr. Perez thanked him and also casually added that the last time he had been there the dancing had gone into the wee hours, and when he and his wife left, there were nude revelers skinny dipping in the pool. G and Sant noticed the good doctor may have been discreet on his client's medical issues, but he was something of a star fucker and celebrity name-dropper, to which they both shrugged off since he had come in the middle of the night. He waved away the cash tip, but G texted Karolina to send Dr. Perez a jeroboam of Dom Perignon the next day as a thank you.

Afterwards, when he left for Star Island, G and Sant both lay outside on the pool chairs looking over the platinum moon and the twinkling lights of the bay as they smoked a big spliff that Sant had procured and rolled, which calmed them both. G filled in Sant about his day with Liz and the fight with Cary. Sant wasn't one for in-depth conversations but would often listen and offer a ubiquitous "that's cool." They sat for hours, and Sant went inside and heated up some of Maria's frozen empanadas in the microwave and brought them outside on a plate with napkins. They ate them the way they did when they bought it in the food stalls back home in Colombia wrapped in paper, and it was heavenly stoner food. Sant was so happy for G and said he thought Liz was a real beauty and seemed smart to boot. In a rare and honest dialogue, Sant also told G that he thought he should keep his interest with Liz on the down low as he thought Eliad would prove to be trouble, and was glad he had his day off and that Rocky the weekend security detail was on duty. He spoke to him once again that he thought Eliad had been taking naked and compromising photos of him which could end up being a source of blackmail. G sat back, pausing uncomfortably, but finally nodded and said he'd think about what to do. He knew that he had to fire Eliad but confessed he didn't yet have the nerve. It was one of the reasons he needed to speak to a therapist and was having Karolina set up an appointment with Dr. Klinkov in NYC, as he felt like he was close to coming into his own power but needed someone to help him get there and to uncover his authentic self. He knew that Sant wouldn't totally understand as he was resigned to certain things in life, but again offered him his standard "that's cool."

Out of the blue, Sant exhaled the thick joint and added, "Don't you have a photo shoot with Ocean Drive on Monday?" Sant didn't always appear to be buttoned up, but he always knew what was happening and often reminded G of important meetings and his schedule that he needed to attend to.

"Holy shit!" G laughed as they both pointed to his bandage.

"Maybe they can retouch the stitches out." He shrugged as he knew the photographer was indeed showing up on Monday and the writer later in the afternoon.

They both smoked more and raided the fridge for seconds. Sant fetched some of Maria's frozen chicken soup which he put in the microwave and then retrieved the tall, slim bottle of 1942 and poured the tequila over ice. They were both ravenous, laughing and drinking well into the early light as the sun rose on the glowing bay. They had such a nice buzz going that they fell asleep on the loungers by the pool under thin towels and were awakened by the early morning light.

G woke up groaning as his head throbbed, and he knew he needed some more Tylenol for the pain. The pink and gold-streaked sky reflected onto the infinity pool, and instead, both G and Sant stripped down to their briefs and waded into the pool before going to shower for the day.

Karolina FaceTimed at 10 a.m., as she usually did after texting, and saw G downing two Tylenol with water for his pounding headache. She reminded him that he had a Zoom with Ryan, who was in Cabo for a bachelor party. G groaned again, thinking that Ryan would give him shit for the stitches. He knew Ryan wanted to check in on the progress for the Ocean Drive interview and cover, and discuss the upcoming tour. He put on his dark Tom Ford sunglasses, which gave him a sexy, sinister look.

"What the hell happened to you?" Ryan did a double take on the Zoom. "You didn't get into a car accident, did you?"

"No, a brawl." G shrugged.

"A brawl?! G Alvarez in a brawl? About what? Moisturizer?" Ryan cackled.

"Fuck you. For your information, it was a brawl over a girl," G stated.

"Seriously? That's totally awesome!" Ryan was eating a sumptuous array of room service on his terrace overlooking the Sea of Cortez. His handsome baby face was framed with two days' worth of stubble that made him look strangely even younger.

"It's not awesome, I had three stitches, and it throbs like a mother fucker." G pouted.

"You called my concierge doctor down there?" Ryan hoped.

"Yes, Karolina did. Motherfucker has a better car than I do." G marveled.

"That's Miami, baby. Anyway, who won?" Ryan was schmearing cream cheese and smoked salmon on a bagel. Clearly the Mexican resort he was staying at knew who their LA clientele was.

"I did, I think," G said.

"Did you call Stephanie?" Ryan asked.

"Why would I call my publicist?" G looked perplexed.

"Because it's good for your image, G. I'll call her for you." His eyes sparkled at the news.

"You will do no such thing; that will fuck things up. Promise me you won't," G begged.

"If you insist, but I think you're making a huge mistake." Ryan shook his head vigorously in opposition.

"Why's that?"

"G, you have forty-six million Instagram followers. Half of them think you are playing for the other team, and the other twenty-five million think you're a handsome pussy. This is exactly what your image needs." He paused dramatically. "A bar fight!"

"It didn't happen in a bar, and the answer is no. I don't care what people think."

"Well obviously." Ryan shrugged.

"Fuck you, Ryan!"

"Who loves you baby? So, who is she?" Ryan pressed his face close to the camera. He had immature appeal to his clients.

"I'm not telling you; you're going to leak it to the press." G smoldered.

"Don't insult me. I would never say a word, my brother, I promise. Who is she?" Ryan smiled.

"My next-door neighbor actually." He hesitated but knew Ryan was a vault when he needed to be.

"She must be super rich." Ryan salivated.

"I'm not sure." G shrugged his shoulders.

"If she lives on North Bay Road, she has to be rich." He was mentally counting bags of gold bullion in his mind.

"She inherited the house," G stated.

"Then she's rich!" Ryan laughed out loud.

"I'm really not sure. She might be the poor relative."

"Then just be careful she's not a gold digger," Ryan advised.

"I hate to tell you, but she had no idea who I was." G filled him in.

"Yeah, right. That's the oldest trick in the book. Who doesn't know who you are?" He looked at G like he was crazy.

"She didn't." G looked over at Sant on a lounge chair eating a pint of Haagen-Daz and sighed at his huge girth.

"What, is she living under a rock?" Ryan scratched his balls.

"Close to it."

"Well, if she's not rich and doesn't know who you are, then she must be really beautiful." Ryan licked his lips.

"I think so."

"Would I fuck her?" Ryan looked hopeful.

"You'd fuck a mop if it had a blonde wig on it." G frowned.

"You might be right," Ryan said. "So how was the sex? Is she a good lay?"

"You don't have to be vulgar."

"Come on G, I've been waiting for this for a long time. I mean, I'm at this fucked up bachelor party, got a blow job from one stripper, fucked another after my buddy fucked her. Why can't you spill?" Ryan was the ultimate party bad boy.

"It's not my style. You're the nasty one, not me." G shook his head at Ryan's antics.

"Well, it may be time for a little nasty my friend. I usually have to tell my artists to clean up their acts, but with you… It's like the reverse." He sighed.

"I hope you're using a condom," G said point blank.

"Now you're the one lecturing me?" Ryan was spearing another slice of Nova for his bagel.

"Look, you may think I'm a pussy, but I was on tour for years with The System. The motto was always, 'Be good, and if you can't be good, be careful.' And it doesn't seem like you, Ryan Palermo, are being careful."

"Well, let me know when I can meet this vixen." Ryan laughed again then changed the subject to the upcoming tour and went over some of the specifics of the interview. Ryan didn't think he should cancel the shoot, just say he'd taken up boxing as exercise and it went a bit too far. It was a good macho look. G Alvarez boxing!

He hung up with Ryan and was thrilled to see that Liz texted him to see how he was feeling and to thank him. He texted her back asking if he could FaceTime with her on an issue, and he wanted her advice.

"Of course." she texted back with a smile emoji. G FaceTimed her from his lounge chair, and he could see she was in her bedroom propped up against her pillow, her luxurious hair spilling out angelically on the bed. They smiled at each other, and Liz expressed how sorry she was and apologized profusely for Cary's behavior, and then added again what a nice time she had had despite the drama. It had been so nice before the fight, and she did feel badly about his coming to Florida, though his behavior was unforgivable. He filled her in on his late-night appointment and stitches and Liz also informed him that Linda was no longer in the ICU. She was up and taking calls and when she had told her groggy mother all that occurred, she had exploded; no gentleman would ever accuse or talk to a lady that way let alone his girlfriend! She stated that Joe, her husband, would never have talked to her in that manner no matter what they fought about. It was time for Dr. Cary Simon to exit the picture! "Good riddance!" Linda declared, punctuating he hadn't put a ring on it and she had no choice but to keep her options open!

"And she said she thought you were the ultimate gentleman defending me. She was so impressed, and Linda is one tough customer," Liz explained. "I also told her despite feeling a bit guilty, what a nice time I had with you!" She smiled softly, feeling a bit vulnerable about expressing her feelings.

G happily agreed, smiling brightly, and said he felt the same way. He suddenly had the urge to ask her for dinner that night and she immediately accepted and said she would love to, the only caveat if Linda was still being kept at the hospital. Both were feeling they wanted to continue getting to know each other and that there was no need for game playing. G then explained that he had a shoot with *Ocean Drive* magazine the following day and asked her advice whether he should cancel it. He knew she was a stylist and that they had also sent over a few options for looks for the cover. Liz said she would weigh in that evening before dinner and that she would check out the clothing options. Suddenly, she had a creative flash.

"Wait, I have an idea!" Liz said suddenly looking at him over FaceTime. "I have it!"

"Hit me!" G said.

"My ex already did." She laughed. "I think we'll get you a nice raw steak for the shoot." Liz beamed at her idea, which was apparent to her but not readily explained.

"What?" G looked perplexed.

"I think you should go with it! The whole thing, stitches and all. You look really cute and handsome, and I see the purple under your eye now that your glasses are off. By Monday, you'll have a nice shiner. I think we should get you a nice raw steak, a great big gold and pave diamond ring, and an open silk shirt. You'd look super sexy and hot, and here's the headline, 'Hit the G spot!' You told me they booked a supermodel on your boat? Here's the photo op: put her in a gold lame bikini and stilettos and have her tending to your black eye and stitches with a raw steak. It will look super hot!" Liz had the whole visual creative idea worked out in her head; she just needed the specifics on the wardrobe.

"Liz, do you know what a genius you are? Ryan's gonna love it." G smiled broadly at the creative concept.

"Who's Ryan?"

"My crazy manager. He always wants me to push it," G explained.

"Tell Ryan, Liz is in town! The new G is coming out—but not in that way." She laughed.

They both did.

"I'll pick you up at eight if you can. We can go over photo picks of the fashion options for the shoot over dinner." G smiled broadly. "And please send your mom my best wishes if you get to speak to her."

G smiled that now he had a date and Liz all to himself with the crazy boyfriend out of the picture. Now, where was he going to take her for dinner in Miami? Where would be fun, sexy, and new?

He would have to put in a call to Karolina and get the lay of the land. He didn't know the restaurants and even if he did, he didn't know how to make a reservation for two.

Chapter 35

Four days later, when Liz picked Linda up at Mount Sinai and they checked out of the hospital, both were floored when they found out that G had actually paid for her private room. It was such a grandiose gesture that at first, they sat not believing it.

"Well," Linda said looking up in the back of the ambulance they had hired to take her back to North Bay, "there is only one thing to do and that is to invite the young man for a home cooked meal."

Liz had hastily prepared Elsa's room on the first floor for Linda and had it thoroughly cleaned, although they did not have enough time to paint it. She would have to make do with the faded and peeling floral wallpaper once Elsa's prescription bottles and walker and other personal items had been removed. Zosia had actually done a good job of dusting, mopping, and waxing the hard wooden floors till they sparkled and shone, and Linda didn't care about the grandmotherly feel, she was just happy to be home from the hospital and seemed more content lying on her new bed and box spring looking out at the turquoise bay through the French doors which lifted her spirits. Once she was back at the villa Liz handed her a cookbook to scan for recipes as she didn't think G would spark to her mother's stuffed cabbage recipe, but she often fell asleep with the book on her chest. They settled on Liz preparing her mother's famous chicken soup recipe which they all savored one night around Linda's bed. Liz put on her best smile and tried to be positive despite the fact that her mother's decline was apparent to all who saw her. It seemed that within the week Linda looked not only frail but seemed to have shrunk; now seeming small and taking on the appearance of a delicate porcelain china doll.

Over the next few weeks there was a constant flow of visitors and workmen which seemed to buoy her spirits and given the proximity of her room to the kitchen and breakfast pavilion, Liz, Roy, Sheila, and Ira were able to sit and spend time with her each week. Linda's annoying friend Marion also visited weekly but despite her bragging and forceful personality, Liz was now able to see a devoted friend who was thoughtful and caring and brought her the little things that Linda enjoyed; black and white cookies and bags of goldfish which she noshed on.

Linda was also pleased when Garvey visited with Roy, and she told him she thought his beau was "dashing" and that he reminded her of her Joe; handsome and thoughtful. At first, Linda didn't quite know what to make of G as his profession and Latin culture were a bit foreign to her, but after one conversation she thought he was terrific and gave her stamp of approval over and above his incredible generosity. She also noticed that he and Liz seemed to have a real connection, which pleased her, and she was thrilled their relationship had heated up so quickly, taking her mind off of the breakup with Cary. Both knew it was best to take it slow, however, they were drawn to each other constantly on the phone, texting and going out for lunches and dinners falling into a natural flow. Over the next few weeks, G dutifully visited Linda and would come early before he and Liz went out on the town on their dates.

There was, however, one lingering problem which they both avoided at first. It was clear G was spending most of his time over at Villa Pompeii when Eliad was on duty and felt awkward about him knowing too much about their developing relationship. While he did sometimes invite her over, Liz also avoided going to G's house as well for the very same reason and felt that there was an elephant in the room; a large one named Eliad Shiraz; the end result felt like they were sneaking around.

G and Liz drove back from a date at Superblue and dinner at La Petite Maison on Brickell and as the car approached both houses, she could tell he hesitated about inviting her back to his mansion, given Eliad was on duty that evening. G drove the Lamborghini into the circle next to the bubbling fountain and turned off the lights, and they made out like teenagers. Liz thought of Elsa and Ben in the front seat of his old jalopy and that the parallel of spending the time in the car was eerie, yet she wasn't ready to have him stay over with her mother in the house.

"Spending time with you has been amazing, G." Liz drew back from his kiss. "But I do think we have one lingering problem." She looked over at him softly but directly, as she wanted to address the issue at hand.

"What? Do I need a mint?" he asked seriously.

"No, do I?" They both laughed.

"Well, now that Cary's out of the picture, I have to get rid of the *other* guy," Liz explained.

"I didn't realize you were dating someone else?" G looked down immediately dejected.

"No, not a boyfriend, your head of security, Eliad. I don't like him or trust him, and I feel like we are avoiding going to your place just because of him." She put it out there.

"I know." He nodded as he took in the news slowly. G wasn't one to confront situations, and it was an issue he was working on with his Zoom sessions he had recently set up with Dr. Klinkov in New York, especially after his conversation with Sant.

"I'm…well, I know I need to remove him. I'm just…I'm afraid to fire him. Sant hates him too."

"Why's that?" Liz frowned, bracing for the worst.

"Sant feels he's taken some compromising photos of me when I wasn't looking. Nothing terrible…maybe some naked ones."

"That's crazy, G!" She shook her head in disbelief. "You can't have a head of security around you can't trust. You have to get rid of him and fast." Liz was incredibly disturbed at the news.

"I don't know how. I think he's a bad dude, so I guess he has the upper hand." G revealed in a vulnerable voice.

"Then let me get back the upper hand." Liz said, "I have *no* problem being the bad cop."

"No, I don't want you to have to get involved," G protested.

"But I am involved."

"Okay, okay. You're right, I have to get rid of him…but what do you think is the best way?" He gripped the wheel, suddenly looked like a little boy in his pj's before bedtime.

"I'll come up with something smart."

"You're very capable." He smiled. "And sexy."

Liz kissed him good night. "Thanks for dinner." She paused. "Wait!" She looked back at him before she exited the car. "I just had an idea, and I think it's as good as the *Ocean Drive* cover. I know exactly who to talk to about it, so don't worry! Our friend Darth Vader will be gone in a month." She opened the car door, turned, and smiled brightly. "Then we can really have some fun."

"You really are a dream come true, do you know that?" He motioned her back to the car and kissed her again. "I want you to know that ever since I met you, and we've spent time together I feel, I don't know…" G revealed. "Whole."

"Back at you!" Liz leaned over and kissed him, then touched his lips with her forefinger and exited the car. "Don't worry about a thing! No one messes with the Galin women." She laughed as she walked into the courtyard and heard his car rev up and exit the gate. She looked back and waved as he turned his car around in the circle, and then closed the gate and the front door behind herself softly. She walked through to the maid's room and checked in on Linda, who she saw was gently snoring, and tiptoed in and turned off the TV. She looked at her mother with dreamy eyes and closed the door gently behind her before heading to her room. Once she arrived at the second landing and into the long hallway, she noticed that Roy's room was dark and that he was most likely out with Garvey or staying at his place. They had become a hot and heavy item and Roy often stayed over at Garvey's, as he had a small first floor walkup in a deco building below 5th. Liz knew that Garvey still most likely felt more comfortable being with Roy at his place and while it was a small studio, it allowed them more freedom and intimacy than having to be quiet behind a closed door across the hall. Everyone, it seemed, was running around like teenagers!

Liz walked into her bathroom and washed the makeup off her face, looked in the mirror, appraised herself, and dabbed a small amount of Vaseline on her eyes and cheeks. She thought about G and Eliad. She would get that asshole out of the picture and, best of all, he wouldn't know what hit him!

She seemed calmer now thinking through her plan and realized she had been so busy she hadn't read Elsa's diary the night before. She crept into bed and picked it up off the nightstand, but as she went to the next entry she was suddenly perplexed. The latest entry and the ones that followed were new, and written in a different pen color, a distinct black rather than faded blue. She also did a double take and noticed that it was dated only months earlier, and was shocked when she saw her name. Liz sat back and read with renewed interest.

Why had Elsa skipped to the present?

Chapter 36

Elsa

July 5, 2020

Dearest Liz,

As you can see from the entries and the dates, I thought I would never see or write in this diary again. However, here I am so many years later and it feels like forever and yesterday all at the same time. Given the events that transpired I gave up on the diary so many decades ago, and in many ways on myself, and have spent the intervening years in France.

I've recently been diagnosed with this awful cancer. As I am very, very old, I don't think I have much longer, my dear. I am not sad, but I do think it's time to tell you all that has transpired and hope when you find out you will understand all my actions and the reasons behind them. I have given it a great deal of thought, the bequest to you, as I tidy my affairs with dear Ira. After confession today I have decided it is time, as I am sure you are already quite curious. It might be hard to write it or read it, but I promise you it is far worse to relive it, I can assure you.

When I think back on that fateful day, I still feel the panic. It hasn't softened and dulled over time, yet I break into a cold sweat no matter how many years pass, how many novenas said, or how much charity donated.

Nevertheless, it was that muggy and humid day that sealed my fate. I remember when I woke up in the morning it was oddly muscle-ache cold and it made me think about the year I remember most in Boston before Father decided on moving us South. I recalled the chilly days and the winter frost and lace snow pattern frozen on the windowpane in our old town house on Beacon Hill. That was my only lasting memory of Boston before Miami. I do remember thinking at the time it was so odd for May and that I needed a cashmere or a wool sweater in the early hours but had none to put on. I knew like most days the clouds would burn off and the afternoon would once again be sunny and dry.

The weather was indeed a harbinger, and although it was decades ago, I can still feel my pulse racing. I was caught up in the moment and could think of nothing else. It was Sunday, the day B. was coming to see me by boat! Leland had left two days earlier. Although he never told me where he was going, his trips usually took anywhere between seven and ten days so I felt like I had an adequate reprieve. Yet, whenever I saw his suitcases and trunks stacked in the hallway by the service elevator my heart jumped a bit more. I could tell whether it was a long or short trip by the number of alligator cases stacked and I was thrilled to see there were more than usual. I also knew other things that made B. and my time together precious and perhaps sweeter. I was also in another form of panic, one I thought I would be able to navigate. From my cycles it appeared that I was once again pregnant.

257

Perhaps Leland had been right about the awful tasting cod liver oil and the deep painful massages. It appeared I was in the family way but far from rejoicing. The baby was clearly B.'s, as Leland still hadn't made an attempt to visit my bedroom. Yes, Liz, this may come as a shock to you, but B. is Ben Brody, your great-grandfather…and you are my great-granddaughter!

Liz sat back a bit shocked, but in many ways not. Of course, now it all made sense. How could she and Linda have not put two and two together? The realization that Elsa was her great grandmother and not Sarah was an incredible revelation, but how, and why, hadn't she known, or Linda? There had to be more, much more. She now tore through the diary at an even more rapid pace.

Elsa

Miami

I hadn't said anything to Ben, given his wife Sarah was due within the next few months. It was almost too much to bear knowing I was having our love child inside me. I didn't have any doubt it would be a boy who would look just like him with those eyes, those beautiful blue gold-tinged blue eyes. Yes, dear Liz, my great-granddaughter! It is a secret I have kept my entire life, but it is part of your history. Now is the time before I pass.

Liz was a bit stunned but also noticed that there was a water stain on the page. Had it been a tear? Liz could hardly believe what she was reading.

Elsa

Dear Flora had been complicit and the perfect accomplice in our love affair. I had never said a word to her, but she told me she knew, and it was quite apparent she was happy for me knowing what a tyrant Leland was. She then revealed why Leland had cut her husband socially. It was not a surprise and yet a source of pain and embarrassment for me; he and his cronies had found out that Arno's father was of Dutch Jewish descent and with that they had socially blackballed him. It didn't matter that his mother was a baroness or that he had been schooled at Oxford. I hadn't known and apologized but this only seemed to give Flora wings to help me fly. The DeJonges had three boats and the motorboat was available to Ben and I. I am not sure if Flora ever said anything to her husband but perhaps he knew and approved.

With Leland gone, I sprang into action like a wild cat. I called and left a message at the Club to book a lesson with Ben and yes, at the time, sadly, it was one thing to be a member and another to work there. It was always the same message I left at the gymnasium.

"Mrs. DeJonge would like a lesson on Sunday." This way Ben knew the proverbial coast was clear. I wanted that day to be a day of love and sensuality where we could talk things through. I knew that once I finally enticed Leland and he found out I was in the family way he would restrict my activities further and perhaps his trips as well and it would be impossible for me to see Ben. For this, I was prepared, but I also wanted my dear Ben to know the truth. I was also so very, very young. Did I think one day he would leave his wife and baby for me? I didn't dare to hope but

yes, deep down I thought he might, perhaps when we were all older and wiser…yet it was quite a naive notion. It was a silly thing to be hopeful about, that I would wait and he would wait. All I knew was that one day, when Leland would be too old or infirm, perhaps there would be a way Ben and I could be together. The last thing I thought would ever happen occurred and changed the course of my life and yes, dear Liz, yours. The end result is so hard to hear, the thoughts and sadness never leave. I will go into all the details as Father Pavado thinks writing about it will ease my burden, and I think it has.

But now as I once again write dear diary, I feel that joyful moment as I see Ben waving and motoring in…

Chapter 37

Eliad Shiraz never thought he'd be invited to Villa Pompeii, yet here he was standing in front of the grand edifice and pressing the old-fashioned door chime. It was a sound he would forever associate with intimidation and old money. He had to hand it to that girl Liz; she had good taste. While she had cut him and ignored him the day of the Ocean Drive shoot, there was a moment he saw her looking at him, and he knew she thought he was sexy despite her actions. Most women did and it was a game he played often, succeeding in his multiple amorous quests despite their initial reticence.

He surveyed the newly groomed property and admired the antique oversized terra cotta pots flanking the dark oak front door, which was dotted and pierced by black iron rivets, suggesting a Tuscan castle. The pots were planted with simple yet luxurious lemon and orange trees and reminded him of the courtyard in the sumptuous, Ottoman-period, Farhi house, as the landscaper had procured mature trees which gave the impression they had always been there as opposed to having been planted the previous month.

While the villa was intimidating, he knew he was too. He had wisely worn a professional yet tightfitting black polo for the occasion and was sporting his dark Persols, giving him the look of a professional wrestler, bodyguard, or assassin. He knew the trick was to wear his polos one size too small which highlighted his incredible physique. It was a trick that worked at bars with attracting women and putting men off balance.

Suddenly, her flamboyant best friend Roy appeared, answering the door and looking him over in an intense way that was slightly suggestive.

"Welcome back! Do come in and I'll show you into the library." He tossed his handsome head and led the way. Eliad had no idea what the visit was about but felt it might have something to do with the fact that G was spending a lot of time with Liz. They did so away from the mansion and G gave no indication whether the relationship was just friends or more. He knew not to push G in this area as he had become overly testy due to Liz's ongoing, heated outrage and he couldn't ask Sant since they detested each other and rarely spoke. He had a faint idea of why Liz had softened, most likely due to his coming to her mother's rescue, yet it made him uncomfortable that they were becoming close. One thing he knew for sure was Liz couldn't stand him and unlike most women, wouldn't give him the time of day. He wondered what she was going to say to him. Perhaps he could finally seduce her, although he thought the chances of that happening were slim. However, Eliad had always succeeded in a department where most men failed, and he wouldn't put anything past a spoiled girl from Great Neck. He had done his internet research on her and knew her type, and thought back to his first summer job in the States and of the married woman he had seduced in her Kings Point mansion while the husband was downstairs in a card game smoking a cigar. They had made love against the bathroom door, and no one was the wiser.

As he entered the villa he looked up at the gilded, vaulted ceilings and was doubly impressed with the grandeur and proportions. The home had been freshly painted, the Venetian plastered walls artfully repaired, and marble inlaid floors polished to a high gloss. The simplicity of the work being done was akin to cleaning a rare jewel and putting it into the right setting, allowing it to sparkle. Eliad knew a thing or two about this as his grandfather Siggi had been a jeweler in Hungary before the war and was a Holocaust survivor. He had been one of the lucky ones who bribed his way off a cattle car to the gas chambers with loose diamond stones hidden in his pockets before escaping and emigrating to the Holy Land. He was an artisan who then founded a kibbutz, picked up both a pickaxe and gun and fought in the war of independence. Eliad had grown up in his grandfather's small jewelry shop in Haifa and heard the stories and prided himself that he came from tough stock. He was also now known as a sabra, a native born Israeli and new breed that sported the confidence of their hard-earned homeland. He entered the army at seventeen and with his athletic prowess and build led complex missions in Gaza. He was tough as steel and this visit with Liz, the enemy, was easy as pie compared to night raids into Gaza and blowing up tunnels risking life and limb and worse, capture. He followed Roy into a black and white marble tiled vestibule that led to two large carved ornate oak doors he threw open dramatically. Eliad noted that the meeting was to be held in the library, which suggested a formal matter at hand.

Eliad assumed as much but was surprised to find an older, imposing gray haired gentleman instead of Liz sitting at the regal desk. He knew the man was successful from his posture and chunky Rolex and the fact that he didn't rise but offered him a seat with the gesture of his large hand.

"Mr. Shiraz, thank you for coming on such short notice. Have a seat." The man motioned confidently, adjusting his bifocals.

"And you are?" Eliad offered a strong hand.

"Ira Reznick." He peered at him over his wire frames.

"So, you're the famous Uncle Ira?" Eliad smirked and flexed his rippling biceps for effect.

"Yes, and I consider myself lucky to have such an appellation." Ira sat taller, equal in height to the younger man, who he judged to be about six foot four and in ironman shape.

"So, please tell me why you've asked me here?" Eliad frowned.

"As Ms. Galin's lawyer, I know from Liz that you gave her a great deal of trouble when she first moved in. I spoke with Officer Adams, who will be joining us shortly." At that moment, Garvey walked in from the side door of the room flaunting his impressive, pressed uniform and physique. He was equally as burly as Eliad, and they respected each other's size and girth; a testosterone fest one could actually smell in the air with an underlying competition of sweat and cologne.

"Please, Officer Adams have a seat. I believe you know Mr. Shiraz." Ira indicated.

"Yes, we have met before." Garvey looked on with little emotion.

"Wait, what's going on here? Do I need a lawyer?" Eliad asked suspiciously.

"I don't believe so but up to you," Ira offered slowly and with great authority that only age can bestow upon a person.

"Mr. Shiraz, I am here to deliver the news that your position as head of security for G Alvarez has been officially terminated," Ira said point blank.

"'And who gave you that authority?" Eliad grimaced in a tense voice.

"Please!" Ira said, waving a hand towards paperwork on the desk. "Give me a moment to explain. You see I have two paper files on either side of me?"

"I have eyes to see, my friend," Eliad sneered.

"We're not friends." He paused. "The first file on my right contains your termination letter from Mr. Alvarez, who I am representing. He asked me himself to set up this meeting," Ira continued.

Eliad was furious at the news. Of course, they were all in cahoots. He had been a fool not to expect as much.

"It also contains a severance check for one hundred and seventy-five thousand dollars, which is equivalent to your yearly salary." Ira explained. "If you sign the NDA, the non-disclosure agreement here, and allow us to delete any compromising photos of Mr. Alvarez in your phone and computer, the check is yours. It's quite simple. Officer Adams can oversee that you do it before you leave."

"I don't have any photos," Eliad lied.

"I have sworn testimony from another employee and friend, Santiago Velasquez. He not only saw you take naked photos of Mr. Alvarez when he was asleep at the pool or sunbathing, but he also overheard you bragging to a friend that you could never get fired because of it."

"Go on," Eliad commanded the dialogue with extra bravado.

"The other file contains some interesting paperwork too," Ira said softly.

"Hit me." Eliad frowned and braced himself for what was coming next.

"The file to my left contains a request for a restraining order from Ms. Galin stating that you threatened and harassed her repeatedly. It is signed by Officer Adams. If the restraining order is indeed filed and granted, I can assure you will have a very hard time, Mr. Shiraz, of finding other employment in your chosen profession." Ira offered a glacial smile as he delivered the news.

"Fuck you both!" He stood angrily and reddened. "This is blackmail!"

"It takes a blackmailer to know one." Ira smiled again.

"I would suggest you calm yourself and sit down." Officer Adams fingered his holster. "We don't want to add threatening a police officer to the complaint."

"Why are you doing this?" Eliad's usual olive complexion paled.

"I think it comes as no surprise since this is your line of work that Mr. Alvarez and Ms. Galin are seriously dating."

"Well, that is a surprise." Eliad smirked.

"Meaning?" Ira asked.

"I didn't know he had it in him." He rolled an eye under his dark sunglasses.

"That's not your business," Ira said, putting on his bifocals.

"I need to talk with my lawyer," Eliad said in a gruff tone.

"Of course, Mr. Shiraz, but I'll save you the time and money. It comes down to just a simple choice: the lady or the tiger. If you do not choose file A, Officer Adams will immediately take the paperwork to the police station." Ira leaned back smiling. "Oh, and one last thing. I checked, and it appears your visa has expired, Mr. Shiraz, which means you are working here illegally. If the restraining order is indeed filed, you will be immediately extradited and sent back to Tel Aviv." Ira paused. "I know the weather is a bit humid this time of year."

"Well, it seems you have thought of everything Uncle Ira," Eliad spewed. "You know, would have made a great member of the Mossad, that's for sure."

"Who said...I wasn't?" He winked to Garvey.

Eliad, sighed. He had done enough missions when he knew it was time to retreat and he also knew a formidable opponent and a good deal when he saw one. He quickly took file A off his desk, flipped through, and fingered the check; $175,000 was a large amount in one lump sum. He asked to see the second file. Indeed, there was a signed and detailed restraining order. He knew he was in the US illegally and assumed Ira had deep connections in immigration. After seeing both options and reading the paperwork, he decided to sign and keep the check. He may have looked tough, but Eliad Shiraz wasn't a fool. This lawyer Ira Reznick had tied things up as tight as a drum, not to mention a uniformed police officer present for it all. He opened his phone and deleted a file of photos showing them both in the process.

"I think you made the right choice." Ira smiled "By the way, we do have a nice parting gift for you to keep things tidy. There is room at the Edition Hotel booked for you for two nights, so no need to go back to the house. Mr. Velasquez will pack your things and send them over. Officer Adams will kindly provide door-to-door service to the hotel, and he can help you delete the rest of your file as well when you get there."

"I promise I won't turn on the siren." Garvey smiled.

"Good day, Mr. Shiraz. One last thing, you can mention your employment with Mr. Alvarez on your resume; however, he will not provide a letter of recommendation. We just want to ensure everyone moves on with their lives. I suggest you don't pull any more shenanigans with your future employers. Word gets around you know."

"Tell that to G." Eliad stood and smirked.

"At my age, I have learned that sometimes rumors are true, and sometimes they're not. Good day, Mr. Shiraz, and good luck to you. Officer Adams will see you out and to the hotel."

"Fuck you both." Eliad took the check and waved it at them.

"Shalom, Mr. Shiraz," Ira said in his mother's authentic Israeli accent. "Go in peace."

Chapter 38

G's relationship with Liz unfolded, as did with the one he had with himself. The past few years as he started to become ultra-successful, if he were truly honest, he hadn't reached his full potential as an artist, a businessman and in his mind, a fully developed person. Deep down he was ashamed of his lack of formal education and more often than not felt intimidated by those he met and interacted with; college educated players in the entertainment industry who were all sophisticated, polished and wore their degrees and backgrounds like silk shirts or cashmere sweaters draped effortlessly around one's shoulders. There were the intellectual female writers in their cat's-eye glasses, the bro-ey agents and managers and especially the arrogant Producers who viewed themselves as top of the Hollywood food chain, all who seemed to have not only gone to college but many to Ivy league Universities while he barely had a high school education. Names like Brown and Penn were peppered in conversation around agency boardrooms with foreign sounding titles like the Wharton School of Business and USC film school. It was true that all whom he met were extremely complimentary about his talents and fell over themselves with great respect in meetings and events, yet he often felt left out in conversations about larger issues and even the finer points of a business deal which were addressed only to his manager Ryan. It was as if they overlooked him, made him feel invisible at the conference table; a handsome face without anything worthy to say or add. At first, he was happy to sit there being talked about as a product not a person but after a few years he knew he needed to up his game and be able to offer his own astute point of view and garner the respect he deserved.

His personal journey for self-improvement started with his love of historical biographies and the understanding that many of the great artists and statesmen were also self-taught or came from similar disadvantaged backgrounds. He was particularly influenced by Neftali Ricardo Reyes Basoalto better known as Pablo Neruda, the Chilean poet who had changed his name because his father was dismissive and unsupportive of his poetry. The tattered biography given to him by Mother Superior Maria Victoria in the orphanage changed his life and he identified with Neruda who lost his mother after two months of giving birth, having grown up with a distant father and illegitimate stepsister. He had lived most of his young life in abject poverty barely eking out a living from his poetry and experiencing loneliness and hunger in his salad days.

Sister Maria Victoria had seen the creative spark in G and one Christmas presented him the well-worn volume of Neruda poetry as well as his early book *20 Love Poems and a Song of Despair*, all of which gave him a window into another world entirely. The two books were the only positive link to his childhood besides his friendship with Sant. It was inspiring that the volume of poems were first published in 1924 when Neruda was only twenty and over his lifetime sold millions of copies. G kept his books in his one small suitcase under his bed in the orphanage and Sant just scratched his head but was glad that his best friend had something he felt as passionate about as his own rasquinball.

G often read his favorite two poems and pulled out the well-worn volume when he had trouble or hit a wall with his songwriting and creative output. The simplicity of Neruda's words and feelings in "Tonight I Can Write (The Saddest Lines)" were all the more beautiful in Spanish and prompted creative outbursts that defined his songs and lyrics and the rawness of his words and feelings never failed to move him to tears.

He couldn't get over the intense feelings and the simplicity Neruda was able to feel, communicate and put onto paper. Often considered the national poet of Chile and eventually a diplomat, G felt that perhaps he could one day conquer the world as well through the arts the way his

Latin hero had done also from humble beginnings. There was also a sense of longing, love, and passion that certain Latin men responded to, and G felt that like Neruda perhaps his insecurities and sensitivities could turn out to be a strength and not a failure. The more biographies he read; Picasso, Josephine Baker who triumphed over early poverty and racism and even Churchill who he had been surprised to learn was an amateur painter, gave him the confidence as an artist but also a man.

G was working hard and coming to a place of authenticity with his new weekly sessions with Dr. Klinkov who was enabling him to pave new ground. The older doctor helped him to no longer feel unworthy but proud of his journey and that honesty was a new muscle he needed to develop the way most people went to the gym and worked out with weights. He longed to feel comfortable in his own skin and not avoid or mask his feelings and this became more apparent and important to him as Liz was one of the most honest people he had ever met as well as her mother. He often found himself laughing at the things that came out of her mouth not only because she was innately funny but because her and Linda's bluntness made him nervous, and he was always smiling and laughing around them which he felt he needed to control. Joseph also gave him confidence each week and told G how proud he was that he had started off his relationship with Liz with honesty about his past and that they were taking things slowly, which he felt was important as friendship in a healthy relationship was often overlooked at first.

His history with women was complicated and his abuse had him withdrawn in more ways than one could think of. In one particular wrenching session he had talked about the series of prostitutes that Arturo had hired for the boys on the road and that his bandmates high fived or jeered at them without thinking they were people. G talked to a few of the girls and saw the pain and the bruises from their pimps; they were simple country girls who had no choice and no future like his mother Josefina. It pained him even more that he knew his own mother had suffered the way these young girls did, and he couldn't bring himself to partake which put distance between him and his bandmates who then created disparaging rumors about his masculinity behind his back.

This changed when he turned seventeen and he met Adella.

Adella was Arturo's youngest daughter and was home from the prestigious private all-girls school Colegio Marymount in Bogota. She was sixteen years old with a wide smile, soft shoulder length brown hair and still had lovely dimples. Now that La Sistema was a worldwide success, she had brought her school friends to a charity concert and took them backstage. Each of the girls had a favorite in the band but G was Adella's choice, and she seemed to linger and talk with him the most. Adella had a shy, lovely smile and an easy manner and they had an instant connection, and when she and her adoring friends took photos he felt her hand linger on his waist when her girlfriends yelled for him to kiss her, which he did on her cheek. Adella went back to school, but she had asked for his number, and they started to text constantly.

It was in Buenos Aires that Arturo ordered G to his room and forced him to do things he would always be ashamed of. As the older man was zipping up his pants, he said in an offhand way that "everyone in the family thinks you are the cutest one." G sobbed at the pain that evening in his room and felt particularly bad as Adella was sending him selfies and their texting had become a constant, friendly banter. Strangely and with great relief Arturo seemed to suddenly ignore G over the next few weeks, giving him neither encouragement nor criticism, and then seemed to overlook him completely. He seemed particularly hard on Paco who had developed a bad case of adolescent acne and saw the hollow pain in his eyes as Arturo screamed at him during rehearsals and made him do his dance moves over and over again sending the rest of the boys home. Everyone left the dance studio in silence during these times, grateful it wasn't them.

In June, Adella returned home from school and one day Arturo cornered G backstage and told him that should take out Adella, handed him a wad of bills, and patted him on the back in an awkward fashion. From that moment on Arturo left G alone and turned his sights to the other boys. G was confused but sensed that Adella had confided to her father that she really liked him. The summer had the band traveling but in August they were back in Colombia and G and Adella started dating with dinners and innocent holding of hands and kissing. G was too scared and traumatized to ever reveal what her father had done and tried to push it all from his mind, and his new hit song and time with Adella turned out to be his happiest, most tranquil summer.

The boys had all moved to two apartments in a new building in Rosales with G sharing a two bedroom with his best friend in the group Paco, and G insisted on getting Sant a small ground floor apartment in the building and paying for it. There was a sense of normalcy as G was starting to enjoy his popularity and summer activities and days swimming and boating on Gorgona Island.

Once a month, he would also visit the kindly Mother Superior and go over his savings account and was pleased to see that monies were being put into the account as promised. Arturo had always made sure every aspect of his business life was handled correctly, had the right optics so that he could continue his nefarious ways without creating any other controversy. Therefore, the monies were handled by a proper accounting firm, and within 3 years, G Alvarez was moderately wealthy once Arturo cleverly subtracted his large producing fees and all his living expenses. The band was such a big success that unlike his other acts where the artists basically broke even, G was becoming a wealthy man by Colombia standards. Because of his healthy bank account G was thankful and generous to the orphanage, and donated enough money for a new gym, better food, and new equipment for the kitchen to the sister's delight.

It was late August and Adella tearfully went back to school. They had taken the dating to a new level and while they didn't sleep together, G explored Adella's young, nubile body and she pleasured G, and each told the other they were falling for one another.

Once September arrived and Adella went back to school the real work on the new album began in earnest and Arturo ordered the boys to do a six day grueling practice schedule with new songs and choreography for the upcoming tour. La Sistema, he barked, needed a new look and new sound. G was given more lead vocals, prompting the other boys to snicker that he was only getting better treatment because he was fucking Arturo's daughter. In Arturo's twisted mind he had dangled Adella but later that month in a hotel room in Buenos Aires he once again forced himself on G. It was a classic case of control.

One evening after a particularly grueling performance Arturo made up his mind that G and Adella would never see each other again. It was a decision Arturo made right after he raped G again, who was so traumatized and hurt by the act that he couldn't move for two days and stayed in bed, lying that he had a bad cold. Sant brought him food and sensed something was terribly wrong when he saw blood on the sheets. They never discussed it out loud, but Sant hung his head, gave G a hug, and went out and bought him his favorite street empanadas.

Since there were five members of the band, G later surmised that once he had his way with one boy Arturo went on to the others as the abuse seemed to occur every other month.

It was on a stormy night in San Paulo after a grueling concert that Arturo had ordered G to come to his suite and a terrible surprise was waiting. He had an investor from Europe in town and they all had dinner together and ordered in room service. The man was heavyset and a balding Swiss German and had a bit of trouble conversing at first but noticed the man was staring at him and sweating. G was shy and wondered why he had been invited to what appeared like a business meeting. After dinner was over and they sat on the couch, Arturo ordered G to sleep with the man. The investor he said was a super fan and while G begged and cried, Arturo slapped him in the face and ordered him to do it or he would show the press the compromising photos he had taken. G was too naive and scared to say no, yet after he was forced that evening he was so distraught that night that G knew he had to finally break free of Arturo's abuses and The System.

The next day happened to be his nineteenth birthday, and he went to church and sobbing, confessed to the kindly priest and later broke down with Mother Superior Maria Victoria in her office at the orphanage. He revealed to the kindly nun that Arturo was a very bad man who had hurt him and forced him to do terrible things. The sister innately understood all and held and comforted G and immediately arranged that he should stay with her sister and her husband at their farm in the country and insisted that he now had more than enough money and fame than to stay with the band and that she would handle it all.

Mother Superior Maria Victoria had a kindly, lined face and clear blue eyes but she also had a tough side having had to run and handle orphanage with all boys. The very next day she called and invited Arturo for a confidential meeting, poured him a black tea and told him G was leaving The System. Arturo threatened legal action and that he would ruin G.

"I wouldn't advise doing anything like that, Signor Nerada," the Sister said. "Or I will be happy to call the authorities, which I am sure you know would not be good for your reputation or your marriage," she said. "And I would delete any photos if you know what's good for you. And lastly, if I were you, I would go to church and pray for your forgiveness and do your penance for abusing a child." Arturo paled, looked down and quickly left with his hat in his hand. He was a G-d-fearing Catholic who was very superstitious and being dressed down by a Mother Superior for sexual abuse was not in his world view. He deleted the photos that night and knew it was time for him to wash his hands of G Alvarez forever.

Maria Victoria's brother Jose and sister-in-law Zaida had a working dairy farm in Monteria and their children had grown, and they were thrilled to have two young men stay for a few weeks to help do chores and also thankful for the company as it could be a lonely existence. It also was an added benefit that G Alvarez was now a household name in Colombia and one evening he did a small acapella performance for fifty in the small country town to great applause and appreciation. In their minds G was one of them who had beaten the system. Little did they know what he had to endure, but three weeks on the farm with Sant had done wonders and the fresh air and sunshine and swimming in the lake brought a sense of peace and serenity. G even started songwriting, and one sunny day he picked up his simple guitar and composed one of his favorite songs he would ever write, "Campos Dorados: Golden Fields," about a poor country boy who finds his golden-haired love in fields.

He was so happy and content in the country that he would eventually buy a five hundred acre farm he had seen from the side of the road when he and Sant were bicycling one day. Over the next few years, it would always be a place for him to come and recover from a tour or find his center and he would aptly name the old place "Alma Tranquila," quiet soul.

Back in Bogota, the press swirled about G's departure from the famous boy band La Sistema and Arturo cleverly did a country wide search for a new boy, eventually settling on a young man, Andres Aguillo, who was slim and boyish and started a huge press machine to create a new star. While he didn't have G's vocal chops, he would have short-lived popularity until he was in his twenties when he would drink to excess, gain a great deal of weight, and lose his hair, rendering him a has-been teen idol.

One sunny June afternoon at the farm, Jose picked up the old black phone receiver in the kitchen, handed it to G, and told him Mother Maria Victoria was on the phone. She told him that a producer from Sony Music Latin America, who headed the Latin division, had made inquiries about him and wanted to discuss a solo album. She said it seemed like a wonderful and different opportunity and that her name was Lara Vargas. G had heard of Lara's reputation as she was often featured in the trades and at charity events which appealed to him, and he happily agreed to take the meeting.

G and Sant soon headed back to Bogata feeling tan and stronger, and he brought Sant to the meeting. The Sony offices were modern and sparkling and the moment Lara and her team walked into the conference room G immediately felt safe and comfortable with her. Lara was in her late fifties and possessed a strong yet older sister personality; her long unruly gray hair, lined tan face and kindly auburn eyes put G and Sant at ease. After doing his due diligence and spending time with her at dinner, he signed with Sony. Lara recommended new management, including LA based Ryan Palermo, a well-known talent manager who handled other Latin and cross over stars. With Lara's advice, he hired a new top entertainment lawyer in LA and had them read over the new contracts. Although now suspicious of everyone who he met, he managed to put Arturo out of his mind and would never see him or Adella again although a few years later he had heard that she had married his replacement, Andres Aquillo. He could only imagine what the poor young man had to endure. While that part of his life was officially over, he carried the scars with him.

The Sony deal and new album were a dream come true and Lara and her team treated him as an up-and-coming star with great respect, arranging for him to work with the best producers, musicians and backup singers. Lara, while going through colon cancer treatments was devoted and sisterly and acted as his guide to this new world. She became his protector and surrogate family, having him and Sant for holidays and was a great cook. She also had great taste when it came to choosing the right material.

The album and video was released the following summer to great reviews and yielded one top ten hit "Amor Picante," Hot Spice Love, which became a huge club hit in Latin America and Spain. G was now a bona fide star.

Even though he was becoming more famous and successful, his anxiety and depression also reached new levels and there were days where G could not get out of bed. On his twentieth birthday "Amor Picante" had reached the number three spot on the charts, and G celebrated by drinking himself into a stupor with Sant who then had to put him to bed. Having to tend to him, Sant knew his hangover was so bad he almost had to call the hospital but called Lara who sent over her personal doctor. The next year of alcohol and drug abuse caused G to act in many ways like a typical pop star, with a number of drug-fueled affairs with groupies and personality mood swings. He entered into a year-long affair with a Norwegian model named Greta, his first real relationship, until she overdosed on oxycontin after knee surgery, having also combined alcohol with her meds after her dog died.

When Lara passed away the following spring after losing her battle with colon cancer, G fell into a deep depression and despair. Lara had been his angel, only giving and never taking, and he had always felt supported and protected by her. Lara had divorced and was a career woman who never wanted or had the time for children. Her clients were her family and deep down, Lara had sensed that G needed maternal and sisterly love and given his sweet nature and demeanor; his neediness meant they filled a void for each other. She always ended their phone calls with "I love you G," and he told her he loved her as well. Her greatest gift had been not only to advance G's career with the right material and best resources but to give him that extra dose of loving and personal attention. After the funeral in LA, G spiraled downward and Ryan intervened when G came close to overdosing from a combination of Xanax and vodka and had to have his stomach pumped. Ryan visited him in Cedars-Sinai and insisted he get further help. He arranged for him to speak to Dr. Joseph Klinkov in Manhattan, who was a trained Freudian therapist and had been his own therapist when he lived in New York City. Ryan put Sant on staff to look after him, and also hired G an assistant, an efficient and talented young woman Karolina he had met in the CAA training program who he knew would help keep tabs on him and help organize him and his affairs.

Two days later when Ryan showed up at his bedside, he was tough with G and insisted he meet Dr. Klinkov in person in New York after his recording sessions. After he was released from the hospital Ryan arranged a G4 to fly G and Sant to New York and personally made the appointment for G to visit the doctor at his small office. G was reluctant at first, but in so much emotional pain that he went to the appointment and sat with the kindly older man with a V-shaped goatee and a German tinged accent. G wore his dark sunglasses the first half of the meeting until Joseph encouraged him to remove them. It started with "being able to look at people and not cover things up and to connect," he said. G spoke about the loss he felt for Lara and let the doctor know he always felt deep anxiety at being creative and sensitive and never thought of himself as being particularly masculine. The sexual abuse he had endured also cemented and exacerbated his insecurities, and while he celebrated and supported his gay fans, it pained him deeply that people labeled him.

G was not used to talking about himself and the first session was painful and somewhat traumatic and after two sessions he pushed away wanting to continue. Now, a few years later he decided he wanted and needed the therapy, and when he reached out again to Dr. Klinkov the older man kindly made time for him. While Covid had restricted in-person meetings, the silver lining was they could do it on Zoom, and the sessions quickly became part of his weekly regimen, like his yoga, and he worked hard to get in touch with his emotions and become better. He knew he was on the right path after reading a quote by his hero Neruda one night before turning in.

> *"Someday, somewhere, anywhere, unfailingly, you'll find yourself, and that, and only that, can be the happiest or bitterest hour of your life."*

He would do it and find if it was happy or bitter or both.

And G knew the truth would set him free.

Chapter 39

Liz and Linda sat wide eyed as they flipped open the latest entry from the faded diary. Now it all made sense, but how and why did it all occur? If Elsa was indeed Liz's great-grandmother, then Linda was her granddaughter as well. Why had she never known? What family secret prevented Elsa from contacting her family and what were the issues at hand? And how could they have not known about it?

Linda lay propped up in bed contemplating the unfolding complex family saga as she looked at the boats in the distance cutting through the bay. She shook her head in disbelief that she herself had been in the dark her whole life, and voiced that perhaps Elsa was clever and making it all up; a crazed lonely woman. At that moment Liz's eyes lit up as she suddenly remembered something, and told her mother to wait as she ran to the library. She returned moments later with a black and white, gold framed photo of Elsa that had been on a high, dusty book shelf next to leather bound volumes of Shakespeare where she has placed the will. She had glanced at it from afar but never really studied it, until now. She turned the gold framed photo around and showed it to her mother. It was a classic 1930s portrait of Elsa in her prime and they both looked at her with new eyes; she was statuesque, blonde, and beautiful, dressed in fur and pearls, seemingly having gone to a fancy dress ball or event. They both stared at her and Elsa stared back. It was more than apparent she resembled Linda, who had always been told she had more of a waspy look, but the face staring back at them was eerily and decidedly Liz's. She remembered something else, took the photo, ran towards the elevator, and opened the door. As she flipped on the light, she compared Elsa's photo to the princess on the parapet. It was clearly painted as an homage to Elsa, and she remembered the first visit to the villa when Ira said the likeness could have been her. Of course! She looked exactly like Elsa and vice versa, with Ben's eyes! She took an iPhone photo of the elevator to show Linda who lay back in bed sipping her green tea and eating a handful of Goldfish. As Liz returned, she picked up the faded diary and read the next entry aloud to her mother and within moments they were transfixed.

July 6th, 2021,

Dearest Liz,

This process has been like peeling back layers of an onion and I hope it has not been too off-putting for you and perhaps your mother. Looking back, after my own father and mother had passed, I was unable to even write in this journal and became something of a recluse in Miami and felt anchored to the villa and the property.

Over the intervening years, I had kept tabs on Ben and the family from a distance. It was the day after Christmas in 1950 when I received word that Ben had passed due to cancer. Today, they would have called it an advanced case of melanoma—most likely from all the years of exposure to the sun. Everything they say you shouldn't do today we all did back then: the sun, smoking, red meat, and butter! Of course, I was devastated and fell into a deep depression knowing I would never see Ben again. Deep down, perhaps as long as he was alive, I felt a glimmer of hope and then there was the finality of knowing I would never look into those eyes of his again. Given my heavy heart and the burden I was carrying, the only solution seemed to me to go far away, and my Priest arranged for me to reside at a tranquil convent in Arles in France as he thought a change of scenery would do me good. One thing for sure, I certainly won't bore you with the convent years as they passed in a forced type of quiet, false serenity and borrowed inner peace that occurs when one is truly desperate. I had need of solitude and for many years it was the best I could do.

I made the decision to rent Villa Pompeii in my absence to an Argentine diplomat and the villa was cleaned and painted for their arrival. I do believe that it was the best thing for me at the time and didn't look back; a change of scenery, deep prayer, and a humble existence. When I arrived in France, I achieved a spartan and austere pose at the convent and tried my very best to forget, submerged in prayer. I eventually became in charge of the herb garden which gave me a purpose and to this day I adore lavender and rosemary and the perfume and healing effects they both produce. However, forgetting isn't easy when one has vivid dreams as one cannot banish the subconscious. I often would awake after a technicolor dream of the events that occurred, heart pounding in terror and cold sweat. I only remember pieces, no, rather fragments, as if I was in a movie theater watching a movie, from the outside looking in at my terrible secret.

Late August.

I recall the humidity that summer day, even though it was years earlier. It wasn't as hot as pea soup, but it was something of a cauldron and staying cool was barely possible. I had a fan and lemonade before Ben was due and notably out of ice. I powdered my face again but even my powder puff seemed damp and wilted. Ben was to motorboat over in the afternoon as he usually did, given the system we had worked out. It was always the same and on Sundays when Leland was out of town, I called the club to ask if Mr. Ben Brody would be able to make an appointment at 3:00 in the afternoon at Mrs. DeJonge's home on La Gorce Island. He was rarely unavailable, and the message was benign and only traceable to Flora's home, where she promised to cover should there ever be an issue. She always smiled and patted my hand but didn't ask and I didn't tell. Actually, she did ask once, slyly over tea, if my strokes were improving. I giggled and said I was becoming nearly professional in the act.

I always had a burning pit in my stomach in anticipation awaiting the sight of the gleaming Riva in the distance on the bay; the Dutch flag flapping and then the sight of his broad smile and hand wave, I knew it was him that led the way. It was a familiar sight but always thrilling and gave me butterflies knowing I would soon be in his arms and experiencing his tender caresses and I had a spring in my step as I gaily walked over to the dock as the boat pulled in with so much to tell him. I looked behind me to see if any of the staff were there, knowing that it was Sunday and that they had been given the day off, but I was always a bit cautious and slightly paranoid.

I remember how gracefully he threw and tied the rope around the mooring and jumped off onto the boat slip in his casual and athletic way, but not before kissing me. Yes, graceful is the way I would describe his body language and it was a sight for sore eyes I can assure you. He always looked so handsome, but that particular afternoon even more so; a mocha tan that set off his cobalt eyes and white teeth and was wearing a boat neck blue and white striped shirt that gave him the air of college crew or a gondolier against the red and white striped poles implanted in the bay.

"Hey beauty," he said as he hopped off the boat, tying it to the dock. Then he scooped me up in his taut arms and kissed me. I felt the electricity in my body from my sternum to my toes. Kissing Ben was like eating a potato chip, I always wanted another as it was sensual and refreshing. Yet, best of all, it was his easy-going manner and quiet sense of humor which always had me laughing. Leland had always dismissed me as silly, and I knew and accepted this as fact and at some point, had come to accept it as reality, but Ben always told me how smart and funny I was. It was surprising because I never thought I had a particular sense of humor, but I had him constantly in stitches and maybe, just maybe, in those early days I could have been. We spoke rarely about our spouses, but Ben did let me know his wife Sarah, while sweet, dedicated and a lovely woman, was somewhat of a sourpuss and a bit of a nag and they didn't laugh very much. He always said being with me was so easy and fun. It wasn't work for either of us and the time passed so quickly. I am not sure how we both ended up with such unsuitable spouses, but we were trying to make the best of it.

Ben then helped me onto the boat and lifted me like I was a feather. He took me in his strong arms and twirled me a bit. He had a habit of softly kissing and nibbling on my neck which always drove me into a frenzy as I kicked off my shoes and walked barefoot onto the small boat and into the cabin where there was a small murphy bed. He unlatched it and pulled it down and we sat on the bed talking about the week; he had lessons and a tournament coming up. Sarah was nagging him to get what she called "a real job" but he just wanted to finish out the season and see if he could go professional. He had promised her that if he didn't win any tournaments he would go back to school and get an accounting degree or go into something everyone needed, like the insurance business. It all sounded so terribly middle class at the time, but I didn't say a word. I felt incensed for him but then again, I was a spoiled young thing who hadn't had to worry about paying the bills. All I knew was that I loved him and would have gone to the ends of the earth to support his dreams.

He then reached over and artfully removed my blouse and under it, the foundation garments and kissed each part of my body with a loving reverence. He then stripped off his shirt down to his boxer shorts and I marveled at his body as I always did. He always looked like Michelangelo's David to me; sheer perfection in a man, his chest and stomach chiseled and his loins beautiful, never pornographic. We sat for a while and kissed and then we lay on the small bed, the ripple of the bay taking us both as we made passionate love. It always made us so sleepy afterwards, the rocking and his caressing my hair.

The next moment was awakening to a nightmare.

It is the terror I can never shake to this very day. I hear a bear's roar and look up and Leland and his red face and beard are above pummeling Ben. He takes him and throws him against the boat cabin headfirst and I hear a crack and a moan. Ben is naked and injured.

"You jew bastard," he screamed in a low, terrifying voice and he kicked him and beat him as Ben tried to cover his head from the blows of his heavy shoes. He looked at me with rage. "You're next, whore!" he screamed.

"Please don't kill her, she's with child!" Ben begged and pleaded. "My wife is pregnant. Have mercy!"

"Mercy!" It only served to make Leland angrier. He took out a glistening and terrifying serrated knife.

"You should have thought of that before you fucked my wife," he bellowed.

I got up from the bed and in slow motion I ran and reached for anything I could find; Arno had a small desk in the cabin, and I saw the glint of metal. It was a brass anchor paperweight that was on the desk. I didn't have much of a choice as protecting someone you love is instinctive and I don't know what came over me but as he raised his knife, I lifted the small anchor and with all my strength bludgeoned Leland in the head. If I hadn't, I had no doubt we would have both been killed and chopped up thrown in the bay for fish food. I heard a crack and a groan and then Leland collapsed but not before falling to the ground and pointing at me.

"You…" he uttered, his eyes leaking blood.

"You…" He pointed again before he died. The one simple word was terrifying. It will always be. Nothing more needed to be said. "You." I met Ben, I bewitched him, and it was I who betrayed my husband. The word and the way he accused me with that shall stay with me forever and no matter that I saved the love of my life, I was now simply a murderer.

What happened next was a fluid jumble. We sat for a while and then saw the blood and there was so much of it pooling out on the wooden planked floor. I was hysterical and Ben took me in his arms. It was now dusk, and Ben said we were lucky and that he would get rid of the body and insisted I go back to the house. I desperately wanted to go with him, but he ordered me back and promised he would take care of it. He pleaded It was his fault not mine and he would kill or go to prison for me if need be. After cleaning up with buckets of water, the last thing I saw was the boat, like a funeral pyre putting out into the sea and it would be the second to last time I would ever see Ben.

The next day, we met at our rendezvous post overlooking North Bay and he tearfully told me he had dumped the body near Stiltsville and spent the evening cleaning the boat over and over and then had taken the paperweight to another location and threw it into the sea never to be seen again as it dropped to the ocean floor. I often wonder how and why I soldiered on and the only reason I can give is that while my life as I knew it was over, our baby's was just beginning. I was the murderer not he and also a soon to be mother. I never tried to cover the tracks as I was resigned to my fate and I realized that I was guilty already living in the prison of my mind and whether it was a cell or palace on North Bay Road I was the judge and the jury. It was after all a crime of passion and self-defense but I knew better I was at fault for love.

Fragments. Pieces. They aren't stitched together like one whole garment or appear in a logical sequence of events. Four days later, Leland's barely recognizable body was found floating in the bay near his bar in Stiltsville and the resulting press was agonizing and scurrilous. Leland was too important a man in Miami to be brushed under the carpet like that...girl.

After I received the news they had found Leland, Mother and Father came to stay. I knew the police would also come round to see me and ask about his whereabouts and when they did arrive on Friday morning, I sat stoically with Mother in the drawing room and told them calmly that Leland had been on one of his business trips and that he never told me the details of his goings or comings. Mother corroborated and the Police Commissioner, a squat man with a rubbery face named Reilly, knew Leland quite well and sympathized with my plight as Leland often joked in public, he answered to no one let alone his lowly wife. I must have been very pitiful and convincing as I told them he was usually gone a month at a time and if he was in Miami he had only left three days earlier. I looked shocked at his whereabouts as did Mother. We pleaded ignorance on this Stiltsville bar and that he had a bedroom there. It was all too shocking for good society and a girl my age and Mother covered my ears when they spoke of the Stiltsville bar and the low business that occurred there. Luckily for me, Leland had wanted to surprise me at the house and hadn't left a car at the villa. Even more damning was our chauffeur Gerard's police deposition that he had dropped Mr. Barrett off at the boat slip in Stiltsville where a tender had been waiting and told not to talk about his whereabouts. Some of his luggage was also found in his room in the Stiltsville bar confirming he had in fact been staying there.

Two months later, I found out another clue. Three of Leland's empty suitcases and trunks were still in the elevator. He obviously wanted to trick me into thinking he was leaving for a lengthy trip with his stack of luggage but had only taken his overnight things to the bar. After the houseman discovered the cases, I called the police to let them know of my find. They motored over and shook their heads.

Leland had created his own alibi as the trunks were indeed empty and they confirmed his fingerprints. Once they took notes and a photo of the empty cases, I had them thrown out. Perhaps he had taken a taxi or had walked from Alton Road to surprise us, I shall never know but I was indeed shaken but happy that it did provide Ben with an unshakable alibi. Fights over money, women and turf I later found out were fairly common in Stiltsville and the fact that Leland was a hardened, yes, I shall say the word, bastard and found with a head injury came as no surprise to anyone. He wasn't liked but feared and there were too many suspects to include yours truly, especially with the poor girl found floating in the bay who was his known mistress. Within weeks the case was officially closed, and the press subsided, however, despite my pregnancy, I was now officially scandalous and shunned in public; a source of pity and scorn. Yet, after Leland's death I fell into a deep depression, and I also knew what I had to do and that was to tell mother the truth about the baby's paternity. At first when I revealed the father was not Leland, she did not appear shocked at all, as I think she suspected as much since he was so distant and also so appalling to me. There was talk about me raising the baby, but my guilt and mental state made me unfit to care for any child and I wanted it to have a proper home. When in a moment of grief and despair I confided to my mother Ben Brody was actually Ben Bromberg, she surprised me with her terse response and I knew better than to argue with her.

"Yes, I think it best we give away the Jew baby to the father." I heard the words as they were intended and was shocked but not surprised, and the only solution was to ask Ben if he would take his son or daughter and raise it when the time came. As I look back the months passed, and I had fallen into a deeper abyss as if the baby were draining my

life force and I thought I might even die in labor and that would have been preferable.

My water broke the evening of January 17th. I am a Capricorn, practical and grounded, and I thought perhaps it had something to do with my birthday being the next day. We decided to use a doula mother had found from her cousin in Charleston as she had attended many births and was skilled as it was clear we could not use a doctor in town and mother had thought of everything. Delilah was an ancient black woman with kindly eyes and her hair in a simple cotton kerchief. I think she instinctively knew the reason for her attending me as all she said was "G-d bless the baby. I am sure he will be well taken care of." "He!" There, she had said it. I had no idea how she knew it was a boy, but afterwards she told Mother she knew by the certain rise in my stomach. Mother was smarter and stronger than I ever thought possible, and she sent father away during the birth to his sister's in Sarasota and Beaulah more time off at her aunt's funeral in Alabama. Father thought the baby was Leland's all along and when he returned, he was only told I had another unfortunate stillbirth and most likely couldn't become pregnant again. It devastated him but he accepted his fate with courage and drank a bit more than he should have. Yet with Leland gone he would settle in and enjoy his role as master of Villa Pompeii.

The birth was grueling, and I was in such pain. I bled more than I should have, however, the many hours passed, and I actually welcomed the pain as part of my punishment for all the pleasure Ben had given me and my actions that day with Leland. I was delusional and not in my right mind as Delilah swaddled the baby. She showed him to me once but knew better that he was taken away quickly lest I change my mind. Of course, I cried as it looked exactly like Ben and all mother said was that she had him come to the house to collect his son. Ben had begged to see me, but mother wouldn't let him in. I saw him one last time from the courtyard window, imprisoned in my palace and my mind.

I also knew it was best if I left Ben alone and his family as I couldn't face him or the truth and I am never quite sure what he said to his wife, but I do know after giving birth, Sidney, our son, was taken in and raised as their own, her own. And for this I will always love Sarah Brody and know she was a good woman.

Dear Liz,

Years later I found out that Sarah had lost her daughter to an early childhood disease, and she had come to accept your grandfather Sidney as her own son. I never did know what he told her, but in the end, I knew it had all been the right decision.

I also came to understand my youthful naivete about money had most likely given Leland his clue. I had forgotten that the Bath Club was not only billing the DeJonges for the tennis lessons, but they had split the ongoing bills. I didn't know that Arno was also blackballed from the Bath Club by Leland and his cronies and the bills for all the remaining lessons were therefore sent to Leland. How fitting, in a way, that I found the stack of bills in Leland's desk drawer in the library and how truly little I had known about money and business affairs. The irony was that Leland had damned himself with his own prejudice and I with my own naivete.

The very next day, when Father arrived back home and heard the news, he bundled me up and drove me to a sanitarium in Virginia. I was less than a person; however, I knew that by killing one and giving birth to another now gone, I wasn't able to live in the real world.

That, however, is also part of my story and our family history.

Chapter 40

Despite the shocking, incredible discovery and attending questions, implications and intense discussions between mother and daughter, Linda's health seemed to deteriorate rapidly at the same time. There was an epiphany over the discovery, but a new solemnity and heaviness hovered once they had both found out that Elsa had committed a crime of passion which seemed to weigh on them both. Liz empathized with Elsa's plight and felt terribly for her, and all her mother said, in typical Linda fashion was "Well, I'm sure I would have done the same if it was Joe but I'm just glad it all didn't happen inside the house!"

They both shook their heads at the awful revelation, but it did have them understanding Elsa's reticence to contact her family. Now, regardless of the byzantine nature, it seemed to make sense.

The heaviness also extended to Linda's illness once again in full bloom. Liz had pushed the thought of her mother's apparent decline away into active denial but knew how bad it was when one late afternoon as the dusk set in, Linda called her to her bedside and drew out a faded velvet pouch and insisted she take possession of her prized charm bracelet. Liz protested and immediately started weeping as the transfer of such a prized possession could only signify one thing; that Linda knew she didn't have much longer to live. The bracelet had always represented everything that was important in Linda's life; the charms Joe had carefully chosen for her over the years for every special occasion and the love and adoration in which he did it. It had been his work of art to continually find special one-of-a-kind charms with meaning and had built the most extravagant, ornate, and original bracelet even the top jewelers had not been able to assemble or duplicate. There were the little fourteen carat gold baby shoes dotted with tiny rubies he had given her when they brought Liz home from the hospital, the miniature champagne bottle with the emerald cork for their twenty-fifth anniversary and of course the tennis racquet with the center pearl that Liz particularly loved after she won her first college tournament. Linda had coveted her bracelet even more when Joe died and now, she was passing it on to her daughter.

Liz protested loudly as she felt she could help restore Linda to good health if they both willed it and not to give in to negative thoughts. Yet for all her so-called optimism she was also in the dark as within days of the surgery, the surgeon had called Linda on the phone to tell her from her routine blood work that the cancer had returned with a vengeance. Linda didn't have the heart to break it to Liz or to undergo any more chemo or experimental treatments; she was still in pain from the surgery and the drugs had already taken its toll with nausea and dizzying headaches. She decided that she would let nature take its course and enjoy the time she had left at the villa at home with her daughter and friends, not in a sterile hospital room.

Elsa's diary did offer a diversion to Linda's imminent decline and there was much to take her mind off her unfortunate condition. Both were shocked at the news about Elsa, Ben, and Sidney and they were intrigued by Elsa's recent entries in the diary. While much of it made sense so much of it didn't and there was still so much to learn and so many questions that needed answering. When they apprised Ira of all they had uncovered, he said little, only that he was intrigued but not shocked as Elsa had been incredibly smart, informed and he expected there was more to the story than just picking out Liz's name from a phone book.

"Family histories are complicated and messy to boot." He added, "It is more the norm that there is some form of family secret," he sagely offered as he knew one day Liz would uncover the reason for her bequest. The diary and the family news offered a fitting diversion for Linda and finding out she was a quarter WASP gave way to a hearty laugh. "Now I know where I got my blonde hair and my passion for penny loafers and pearls in High School!"

The daily visits from friends also made things a bit more bearable; Marion came twice a week and ordered everyone around, Roy and Garvey stopped by daily to play old maid with her and to watch a few reality shows; the Beverly Hills Housewives reunion was particularly entertaining, and she loved seeing old black and white reruns of classic movies and musicals like *Singing in the Rain* on TCN. Ira stopped by weekly, and Sheila brought her babka and the occasional fruit salad. Liz had been right about Sheila and her mother; they were much too similar to have become close friends and butted heads on most topics but as mothers and women of the same generation and background there was a deep respect at hand. Ira absolutely adored Linda and he would sit with her when he was checking on the ongoing renovation work and they would chat and reminisce about life in Brooklyn and Queens back in the day. Linda really perked up when Ira had a Junior's cheesecake delivered, and she indulged in a small slice each day with her morning coffee. The creamy sweet taste brought back old memories and simpler times.

However, no one loved Linda's company more than G. He spent time with her each night before he took Liz out for dinner and brought her occasional trinkets, from magazines to small boxes of Godiva and seemed to savor her homespun intelligence and bawdy sense of humor. Any mother would have been a tad suspicious about any potential suitor however, as Linda got to know G, she would wave Liz away and tell her she wanted to spend time with "her boyfriend." She rolled her eyes, cackled in her deep throaty voice and Liz could hear them laughing together behind the closed door which made her so happy. Often, she walked in and was so touched that Linda had fallen asleep holding G's hand with G singing old fashioned lullabies in Spanish with his angelic, comforting voice. He craved the attention of a mother figure and once Linda saw that he was serious about Liz, she embraced him with all her heart and tried to cram in years of stories and family history knowing her time was limited. Liz fingered the velvet pouch; the gift of the bracelet was not only a transfer of a prized possession but a transfer of love and romance, from mother to daughter.

"Mom, I cannot take your charm bracelet!" Liz teared as she looked down and held the heavy, gold link in her hands "This is yours!"

"It makes me happy to know you have it and will treasure it, and I have an even better present for you." She smiled faintly.

"What could be better than this?" Liz looked at her mother with her wide blue eyes.

"He loves you," Linda said softly.

'Yes…"

"Just a little bit more." Linda's eyes teared up as she said it.

"You think so?" Liz knew but at hearing it was a bit shocked.

"I know so. I won't say anything more, but he is the one, Liz. He is crazy about you, needs you, loves you and respects you and that is the best gift I could ever have, especially now."

Liz smiled outwardly and wept inwardly for Linda's sake. What was her mother saying? And why had G come the day before and insisted on bringing flowers and closed the door for a half hour and insisted she go away? She didn't want to ask or know the answer.

"I did tell him though one thing that was important to me," Linda revealed.

"I can only imagine." Liz rolled an eye.

'I told him if you ended up together that I wanted to make sure that if you had children, they would have a bar or bat mitzvah," Linda revealed.

"Mom, you didn't!"

"Why not? I didn't ask him to convert or get circumcised," Linda said with naked honesty.

"Mother, this is really TMI." Liz rolled an eye.

"Well, I can only assume there was no snip-snip in Colombia." Linda raised an arched eyebrow.

"You are really too much, do you know that?" Liz shook her head in disbelief.

Linda added for good measure, "Make sure he washes down there, okay?"

"I'm leaving, I seriously cannot take part in this conversation." Liz laughed as did Linda.

"I dated a Greek boy once. We fooled around a little bit, and when he took it out of his pants I was horrified, I told my girlfriend it looked like a pig in a blanket." Linda confided.

"'I'm seriously going." Liz stood. "You are insane."

"No, I'm real, and you are too."

"Mom, thank you so much for this." Linda helped fasten the gold bracelet on her wrist. "It's the most beautiful and thoughtful gift I could ever receive."

"Wear it tonight on your date." Linda winked." It's good luck."

"You don't think it's too fancy?" Liz held it up to the light.

"I gave it to you so you could wear it. Promise me you'll wear it tonight, please!" Linda pleaded.

"Okay, okay." Liz shrugged, "I'll wear it tonight."

"Have fun! Pop in and show me how you look before you leave," Linda said with a wry smile and then went back to watching her favorite Laura Ingraham on Fox news who according to Linda "tells it like it is" and "is pretty to boot!" Linda fastened the clasp of the bracelet and they both admired it on her slender wrist as Liz reached over, kissed, and hugged her mother and then walked out of the room and upstairs to get ready for her date with G. Opening her bedroom closet she flipped through the rack, trying to find something that would live up to the glamor of the bracelet. She didn't want to go overly formal as Miami was more "casual chic and sexy" vs. the more "conservative formality" of Palm Beach. She chose a vintage Halston turquoise halter and white jeans. Once she did her hair and makeup and looked at herself in the large mirror, she knew she had achieved the perfect look with the bracelet making a real statement. When she stopped in to show Linda, her mother paid her the ultimate compliment with tears in her eyes "I think I was a pretty hot number when I was your age, but you just outdid me baby!" She smiled with pride.

G stopped in when he picked up Liz, gave Linda a kiss and wink and whistled at his date before he whisked her off to dinner and as they walked out into the courtyard. Liz was surprised that G had Carlos, Maria's husband, take them in his more formal Bentley for the evening but all he said was "he wanted to drink and not worry about driving afterwards." When they arrived at the Lido restaurant at Four Seasons restaurant in Surfside, they had a few people taking photos and when the maître d' sat them in the grand main dining room all eyes were on the beautiful couple as the waiter brought out a pre-arranged bottle of Dom Perignon. The pop of the cork signified it was a special evening and Liz marveled at how beautiful and flawless the dinner and service was. Everything was so crisp and fresh from the pressed white linens, aqua Italian Murano glasses to the sparkling cutlery reflecting the graceful palms and stunning '20s architecture giving it an old-world Palm Beach in Miami. Afterwards they had drinks in the chic champagne bar where G kept kissing her hand and neck and telling her how beautiful, smart, and funny she was and how lucky he was to have her. They had a lovely dessert of tea and biscotti before he paid the bill, and they made their way to the car to return to North Bay. With Eliad gone, Liz had been spending more time at G's home but had never stayed over as she always wanted to get back and tend to Linda. G understood and was patient but tonight would be different.

Carlos tipped his ebony Kangol hat and opened the door for Liz and she felt like a Princess as he wished them a lovely evening as he returned to his apartment over the garage. Liz noticed G tip him on the side and that unlike Cary, he was always very generous with waiters and drivers and those in service and it was one of her favorite qualities about him that reminded her of her late father Joe, who was famed for his over-the-top generosity. As they both entered the silent mansion, Liz noticed G had given the staff off and even Sant had gone to stay with a friend below Fifth so they could have the house to themselves. She looked around and noticed that even the security was gone except for hulking Rocky in the gatehouse.

They walked into the open kitchen and Liz heard the Sonos playing over the state-of-the-art sound system. G had thoughtfully put together a custom playlist of love songs and ballads of his favorite music as a gift to her, a mix of new and old classics. She smiled as she heard the latest demo of *"She's fierce"* the English version, which he had recorded in his basement studio over the state-of-the-art sound system.

"I thought you hate hearing yourself?" Liz elbowed him in jest.

"I do, but this song is dedicated to you so I'm breaking my rule." He took her in his arms, and they danced to the sensual beat suspending them both in time and place as she lay her head on his shoulder.

"That was beautiful, G," Liz said as he sang the final stanza as he led her up the modern infinity staircase. As Liz entered G's bedroom, she stopped, smiled, and started to sing along when she heard the distinctive voice of Gloria Estefan, the Queen of Miami Sound. The classic music now followed them into the stark white master.

"Oh, G it's so beautiful and you thought of everything. Even Gloria Estefan!" Liz was amazed as she saw the pink rose petal strewn bed and the tall sparkling champagne flutes and roses bedside it: a beautiful fantasy all for her. G turned and slowly took her in his arms and kissed her slowly and passionately starting with her lips, then her neck and then downwards. They had spent time together and explored each other but each had wanted to take it slowly and they had not yet consummated their love. G kissed her swan-like neck tenderly as he removed her halter. When she was naked, he kissed her beautiful, upturned breasts and coral-colored nipples and he bent down and carried her to his bed. He removed his white silk shirt and clothes in anticipation, and they lay next to each other taking in the beauty of each other's young and supple bodies. He nibbled on her neck again as his tongue traveled down her body and they seemed in perfect rhythm and harmony as she heard Gloria's lovely voice singing.

As she and G became one, the electricity and passion mounted to great heights they both had never achieved nor thought possible. It was sexy yet beautiful and enduring and as Liz reached a climax and she arched her body under his, he cried out himself in ecstasy as the music crashed over them like a subtle wave.

As they both lay next to each other in the afterglow, he smiled. Only this time, Liz loved and truly appreciated his dimples and his beautiful white teeth. He was after all the man of her dreams, and she had come to treasure the sincerity and playfulness of his smile. He rose from the bed, and he looked like the statue of David and Liz smiled to herself thinking of Ben and Elsa. As he returned, he suddenly dropped to one knee. Liz looked wide eyed at the moment.

"Liz, I love you." He presented her with a small velvet box hidden under the bed. "And I want to spend the rest of my life with you. Will you…marry me?" Liz could not get over the emotion and the love he had put into everything and she trembled and gasped as she slowly took and looked in awe at the small navy velvet box.

"Really?" She gasped a bit. "Me?" She teared. He nodded as she opened the box and saw a perfect round ten carat diamond. It looked so large and pure white and sparkled like one of the lights in the distance on the bay that it literally took her breath away.

"Are you sure? You want to marry me?" She gasped.

"Yes you, who do you think?" He laughed.

"G," she cried, "Yes, yes of course, yes! I would be honored to be your wife. I love you."

"I asked your mother's permission yesterday," he said proudly.

"I can only imagine." Liz laughed.

"And I promised her that I will always love you…just a little bit more!" He shook his head in agreement. Linda had always said she would find a great love and she knew it was something even Elsa had wanted for her.

"G, I'm the happiest girl in the world." She looked into his beautiful khaki eyes. "I have a gift for you too!" Liz smiled and looked at him intently.

"What's that?" He looked at her.

Liz kissed and hugged him firmly thinking she had finally understood Elsa's note. "When we get married, let's rip down that damn wall!" She snuggled into him for a second round of lovemaking.

Indeed, it was undeniable Liz's view had completely changed and then changed even more since she had moved to North Bay Road.

And met her Miami neighbors.

Chapter 41

The funeral was somber and well attended and the mourners masked and socially distanced at the service and at the cemetery. Liz had tearfully decided to have Linda's remains flown back to New York as the family plot resided in Elmont. Roy and Garvey kindly took care of the transportation and burial details which seemed a bit too gruesome for Liz to handle. Linda had passed peacefully in her sleep after getting a simple cold. While still in shock, Liz knew she needed to power through. She and G left Florida as soon as they could, taking a Wheels Up Citation to Teterboro which had been organized quickly by the ever-efficient Karolina. In the Jewish tradition the burial needed to happen within days and Liz went into overdrive to give her mother a fitting sendoff despite the complications of covid.

There were other complications as well; Liz getting used to the fact that while G was the most loving and normal man she had ever been with, nothing about his life was. The press was increasingly omnipresent, especially the Latin press following them everywhere and they seemed to know where they were before they got there, and a group of paparazzi was already gathered at the private airport when they arrived. They were also intrigued by G having a real love interest and when word of his engagement became public, they seemed to go into overdrive, but also were aware of the death in the family and kept a respectful distance at the airport. Liz had been only used to seeing her clients in the press but now that she was engaged to G, she quickly realized she was becoming public property as well. The gathered press clicked away but they seemed to notice the palpable difference in G as he and Liz were somber and forlorn before boarding and exiting the jet. G had also taken Linda's death particularly hard and was moved and tearful on the flight home. He had a few telephone sessions with Dr. Klinkov as Linda's passing also brought up lingering feelings of Lara's death and his mother's and he often felt deserted by older women figures in his life. It all made him even more supportive and loving towards his fiancée.

Once they arrived in New York, they stayed at Liz's childhood home in Russell Gardens on Wensley Drive. Photographers roamed the suburban street of respectable, '20s, tudor-style homes, hiding behind hedges to their dismay, and that of the neighbors. While an affluent area, they were still not used to having a celebrity in their midst. Over the next few days, G got to know another side to Liz as he roamed the lovely but modest rooms in the traditional style house and took in her vintage bedroom and framed family photos which showed Liz at camp, wearing braces to her graduation photo with winged and feathered hair. He laughed at the pink cordless phone, matching wallpaper and was impressed by her tennis trophies crammed together on her plain wooden bookshelves.

Linda and Joe had been socially active in Great Neck, especially the gregarious Joe, and close friends and family from both sides came to pay their respects. Due to covid, Liz decided to forgo the custom of greeting people in a receiving line in the Rabbi's study, and to also broadcast the funeral on Zoom for those far and wide or not comfortable to attend.

"I never thought I'd be Zooming a funeral," Liz remarked tearfully as she sat the day before with the Temple's technical people who provided the secure link. She was so grateful her best friend Lucy flew in from California, her husband staying home with the baby, and she stayed in the guest room and also supported Liz by talking well into the night, stroking her hair, and providing her with a cache of Kleenex at the ready. Lucy and G bonded and instantly became best friends, and she whispered to Liz how much she loved him through the tears.

The morning of the funeral was slate gray, her least favorite color in fashion and in life and it all seemed incredibly surreal and even the smaller tasks like getting dressed for the service seemed out of place and jarring. She had her morning coffee as she usually did and then suddenly felt like she had been hit over the head when she looked out the kitchen window and saw the somber black Limousine and uniformed driver pull into the driveway which would take them to the Synagogue. She was still in her Japanese robe as the black dress and shawl were laid out on her bed upstairs.

"It's really real." She sobbed internally. "Mom's never coming back!" She instantly thought as she downed the coffee in a bitter gulp and climbed the small, carpeted back stairs to her bedroom to get dressed, hearing G in the shower, the sound of the water feeling like endless tears.

Temple Isaiah in Great Neck is a reform synagogue that has a unique history and was equally appealing to Linda and Joe when they moved to Russell Gardens years earlier and chose to make it their spiritual home. For many years, the liberal reform house of worship was housed in a Korean church before the congregation pooled their funds and acquired their own building on Chelsea Place. They had gotten to know and deeply respected Rabbi Ted Tsuroka, whose Japanese American parents had met in an internment camp during the Second World War which paved the way for his own journey to seek out and convert to Judaism. Joe had felt instantly at home in this shul given his own mixed background and the liberal and inclusive sensibility also appealed to Linda's down-to-earth side. Like her father, Liz had fond memories of her own Hebrew school and bat mitzvah and always felt at home in the warm and welcoming community and was proud that in addition to the new rabbi they had a female cantor Leslie Friedlander as they were continuing to evolve their own inclusive roots.

The crisp, white, modern synagogue offered a sense of calm and serenity as the new Rabbi Jerome Blum started the service as Liz sat next to G in the first pew. They were both moved at the cantor's beautiful voice and haunting melodies and their hands were intertwined for support. While G had never attended a Jewish memorial, he respectfully donned the traditional white satin yarmulke as did Roy and Garvey who sat in the pew directly behind Liz and G. They all looked so handsome, groomed, and sweet and Liz was deeply touched as she looked at the diverse group who all respected her customs and culture. Ryan, G's manager, Sant, and Karolina had all flown in to not only pay their respects but to meet his intended. After a series of hugs and kisses, Ryan had taken G aside and said he had found the perfect girl and that he would have fallen for her himself!

Liz was especially touched when she saw that Ira and Sheila arrived and stood quietly in the back of the sanctuary with their N95 masks on. She knew they had traveled far and were fearful at their age of the new Delta variant, but nothing would keep them away and she was moved by their insistence to attend. When the mourners arrived, they had all noticed the omnipresent ring of photographers from the international press who used long lens cameras to snap G and his new fiancée as they walked into the Synagogue past the ominous hearse. Despite the intrusion, it was so heartwarming of everyone to turn out and Liz gave her mother's friend Marion an extra hug as she cried into her handkerchief. Despite how annoying she was, Liz knew she had ultimately loved Linda. All she said was "It's the end of an era" which it was.

The rabbi's eloquent eulogy in Hebrew and then in English had Liz sobbing as he highlighted her mother and father's love for each other and how much she had lived for and adored their only daughter.

"Linda was a woman of Valor." he intoned the traditional Old Testament prayer, Proverbs 31.

"A woman of valor who can find? Her worth is far above rubies." The Rabbi read the ancient prayer so apt at describing Linda and her relationship with Joe. "The heart of her husband safely trusts in her and he has no lack of gain…"

Liz, her head in hand convulsed her body shaking as the waves of tears overwhelmed her. G also started tearing at the intense beauty and poignancy of the ancient words, so relevant yet so modern and thought of his own mother and Lara. Once the Rabbi finished the prayer, Liz tried to compose herself as he motioned to her that it was time for her to deliver the eulogy. She quietly rose in a shaky fashion as G reached over and supported her and then lovingly squeezed her hand. He whispered to her he loved her and that she could do it and she looked at him with a faint smile, nodded and adjusted her shawl as she rose. She had chosen the same simple black, silk dress she had worn for Joe's funeral with a black cashmere pashmina and her mother's charm bracelet shone under the lights and looked down at the bracelet.

A price above rubies, she thought. *…Of course.* She saw the miniature baby shoes dotted with tiny rubies sparkling in the overhead light and the little manual treasure chest which opened to reveal it was filled with an array of rubies and emeralds and it all seemed to make sense now. She had never been a public speaker, and this was going to be her hardest moment besides the actual graveside part of the funeral, which she was dreading. She walked slowly up to the bima and held her handwritten speech which she carefully laid on the wooden pulpit before reading. She took a deep breath and made sure she had her simple, small white lace handkerchief in her left hand as she looked into the socially distanced but packed Temple as she read aloud.

"Today is a day of tears and humor. As many of you know, I often joked about my mother." Liz started slowly and smiled through tears. "My dear friend Marisa and I called our mothers 'smothers,' which she coined in one of her books." Liz smiled at her dear friend the cartoonist Marisa Acocella Marchetto and her dear mother Violetta who were sitting in a nearby row. "She could be an overpowering and overwhelming presence, but the truth is, my mother smothered me with her love, and I loved it, and I will miss it. I will miss her daily phone calls every five minutes and her advice on everything from men to movies. I will miss her fixed opinions and her prodding me to be the best I could be. I will miss her stuffed cabbage and her restaurant reviews. My mother had a habit, as some of you may know. If she didn't like a restaurant, she took a card so she could remember not to go back. When I asked her how dinner was, she would say she liked it or 'take a card.' Most people would take a card if they liked a restaurant, only my mother took one if she didn't like it, that was classic Mom. I loved her gutsy sense of humor and her innate beauty. And I loved her love of me, because it was beautiful and pure. When I got the call that I inherited the home in Miami, my mother went into overdrive. She wanted to first make sure at first it wasn't a scam and when she found out that it was real, she was the one who insisted I embrace life and go for it. She wasn't afraid, ever. The only thing she was afraid of was that I would miss out on things, on life and love, because she had it with my father.

"When she was young, she was a dead ringer for Lauren Bacall, and she started getting parts and roles and even modeled for a Cadillac Commercial where she opened the doors and did the hand wave over the interior leather. But the moment she met my father that was it; it was all about him and he was all about her. There was no one like them, their love was truly unique, and they gave to and for each other and that was beautiful to see and set a high bar when it came to dating." She paused as members of the audience laughed nervously.

"I thought I would never ever find that love, because it was too tall an order, but my mother always thought I should have it and would find it. I can't say I agree with all her choices, like when she suggested I join J date and would pretend to be me as she trolled the site for men she thought I should go out with, but in the end, she insisted I never settle. She urged me to fight for it the way she fought so bravely through her chemo and the solitary pain of Covid and she never once complained; her motto was 'never explain and never complain.' That was Linda. If it wasn't for her, I probably would have settled for a lesser love and state of mind. When she came home from the hospital after breaking her hip, one of the great positives was that G, my fiancé, got to meet and spend quality time with her and he loved her, and she loved him. It is and will be one of my greatest gifts and at the very end. G made my mother the happiest woman in the world when he asked her for permission to marry," she gulped, "me."

"Well, I think you can all see I'm wearing my mother's treasured charm bracelet." She held it up and it jangled it in the light for all to see. "I used to play with it when I was a little girl and dreamed of the day when it would be mine but now that it is, I wish it weren't. I was young and foolish and thought things were important but they're not. I didn't realize that by getting it I would be losing the person I loved, a woman who is valued above rubies! It's a wonderful token, of course, but what I would do to have Mom back! My mother, my 'smother...'" Her voice broke, and she sobbed. "I will love you every day of my life forever, just a little bit more." She dabbed her eyes, and everyone had tears as she walked back to seat and collapsed a little into G's arms.

In the tradition, the cars all followed in a cortege with the lights on as they drove to the cemetery in Elmont, a middle-class area in Queens adjacent to New York city known for sporting the Belmont track for horse racing, and a variety of cemeteries from Roman Catholic to Jewish which are carved out side by side. They all made their way through the cemetery gates in singular formation to the plot as they followed the ancient tradition of a rough and plain wood casket returning to its maker. Liz broke down when she saw that the existing headstone of Joe Galin, was waiting for his beloved and that Linda would be buried next to him for eternity the small stones atop sitting sentry. As the casket was lowered, the rain drops started slowly, then to a flood of tears and Liz noticed only little things; the mud on her shoes and the handle of the shovel; it was all too much to process.

After the somber graveside service where the Rabbi and mourners congregated under the sea of black umbrellas Liz and G walked through the line of friends and family that filed on either side of the mourners in deep respect and walked from the cemetery plot back to the onyx black limousine. Suddenly Liz saw a familiar sight standing in the rain with no hat or umbrella and his wet auburn hair had turned a dark mahogany brown plastered at his sides. At that moment Liz had already forgiven him and she walked over to see Cary as he looked down at his shoes and nodded. He gave a slight wave and a forlorn smile as he looked at her sheepishly.

"I heard the news and wanted to come and offer my condolences." Cary said, his eyes soft and brown with sadness. "I thought Linda was one special lady. She was truly one of a kind."

"Thank you, Cary."

"I'm so sorry, Liz." He stood there. "She made a mean brisket too!"

"That means a lot. I think it's really nice of you that you came, and I am sure Mom would have really appreciated it. She always liked you and rooted for you."

"Of course." He stammered. "I...I also wanted to apologize for the way I handled things in Miami, I was totally wrong. Please also tell G I am sorry and regret my words and actions."

"That's big of you." She stiffened.

"I heard you got engaged, and I'm really happy for you both," he said. "When I heard the news I kicked myself, of course, but then I realized that you two are really meant for each other and of course, there was Miami!" he explained.

"Location should not dictate love, Cary, but I appreciate your good wishes. I hope you find what you are looking for as well." Liz summoned her inner "big person" gene.

"Well, I hope you don't mind my telling you, but I'm also dating a nurse named Carla in my unit." he stammered a bit uncomfortably.

Liz looked a bit stunned, then realized it was all turned out as it should have. "Well, I wish you both the best, I really do. I think we both ended up exactly where we should have." Liz reached in to give Cary a hug.

"Thank you." Cary looked down sheepishly.

"Thank you for coming, it really does mean a lot; Mom was crazy about you. You knew that."

"I do."

"We're sitting shiva at the house in Great Neck if you want?" Liz offered awkwardly.

"I think it's best..." He shook his head no.

"Of course."

Liz turned and a gust of wind took the umbrella which she battled for and then turned.

"Cary, I know Mom would want me to tell you this, so I will." Liz looked at him with new eyes.

"Yes?" Cary looked open to her comments.

"I hope you and Carla are very happy together. Just make sure that you love her just a little bit more, okay? If you do, then you'll be fine. Linda always thought that way; un-P.C.-Jewish-mother-logic, but it works. The man always needs to love the woman just a little bit more if it's going to work. You're a good man, Cary, you really do deserve everything you wished for too."

"Thank you, Liz. I will." He turned and walked with his plain, solid, frumpy figure towards his plain, solid car. In that moment, Liz knew she would never have been truly happy.

She walked slowly back to the limousine and the driver held the door open and she slid in as he took the umbrella. G sat in the back seat and smiled at her looking so cute in his Kippah, like a little Bar Mitzvah boy she used to see at Saturday morning services in Great Neck. He held his hand out to her and kissed her on her forehead with his soft lips and his kindly eyes. She slid in next to her fiancé, snuggled in and felt a healing calm. She was sitting next to the man she was going to marry, knowing he was also the man she was supposed to marry. And through the tears and the pain of that day, Liz understood the sorrow and the sweetness of life.

Chapter 42

The screaming fans swarmed and swayed. Masked and unmasked, they waited patiently shoulder to shoulder in the sweltering July heat outside Rome's famed Hotel de Russie to catch a rare glimpse of international superstar G Alvarez. After an hour, agitated by the hundred-degree weather in their sea of chic Persols, masks, cream linen trousers, halter tops and summer espadrilles they became even more unruly and distempered. Located on the storied Via Del Babuino at the base of the grand Piazza del Popolo, the exterior salmon stucco walls and pale aqua shuttered palazzo hotel belies a modern sensibility and aesthetic on the interior. For those waiting to catch a glimpse of their favorite pop star, many of the locals had never been inside the old palazzo but knew it was where many of the top celebrities stayed when they were visiting the eternal city. Beyond the five-star hotel's regal edifice lies a classic yet stunning hidden garden in the inner, center courtyard replete with double rows of eggshell color umbrellas, and the modern Stravinskij Bar's elegant bartenders and waiters sport white, starched shirts and bow ties even on the hottest summer days.

Liz smiled gaily in the morning heat as she sat taking her continental breakfast alone listening to the symphony of cicadas as G was finishing a conference call in their suite. She sipped her luxurious cappuccino in the cooler elevated garden area where the elegant breakfast buffet was served each morning and looked around at the array of well-heeled guests paying over a thousand euros a night for a room during the height of the season; the large American family with tow headed kids most likely from the South given the father's crew cut and golf attire and an older New York couple notable for their matching accents, gold Rolexes and ever present shopping bags who most likely lived in Great Neck or Old Westbury. There was the chic Middle Eastern couple and virile Russian businessmen attended by menacing bodyguards and stunning blondes with requisite bling. Everyone was cordial and polite, and voices were kept at a discreet low octave enjoying the glorious idyllic garden which had been designed in the eighteenth century by the famed Valadier. Liz appreciated the lush, voluptuous statutory, white climbing roses and palm trees as she basked in the scent of tuberose, vanilla and orange slightly overpowering the early summer sun and the distinct sharp smell of pine needles burnt by the sun. The distant clang of church bells were heard wafting over the nearby piazza's offering an authentic Roman soundtrack. As Sant was taking care of the bill at the front desk, Liz reached into her new buttery Bottega leather bag she had gotten on the Via dei Condotti for her oversized Chanel sunglasses to avoid the glare and glanced at the Italian and international newspapers strewn about. She quickly flipped over the large format, salmon colored *Financial Times* for world news, but the typography was too small and dense for her that early in the morning as she scanned the weather.

"Grazie, Signorina." The seasoned waiter Mario smiled as she finished her perfect, frothy cappuccino and signed the bill. She never understood how espressos and cappuccinos just tasted better in Italy; was it truly the taste or was it enhanced by the surroundings? Either way it was far superior to American barista fare no matter the size of their confident, millennial man buns. The Italian career waiter then took notice of her sizable diamond ring and wedding band, blinked, and rephrased his salutation. "Ah Signora!" He nodded, making her more conscious of her new status as a wife and her impending honeymoon. She smiled to herself, excited about Capri and then the yacht to Sicily and the Aeolian Islands. She and G were also looking forward to an important stop beforehand that they had given a great deal of time, thought, and planning to. She opened her new wallet and left some small euros in cash for the waiter on the cafe table under the coffee cup, glancing at her pave diamond Cartier watch, a wedding gift from G, to check the time. She knew to gather her things and leave if they were going to make their important appointment on time, so she texted G that the hotel bill was being settled and to meet her and their driver outside. She knew he would be down soon, but it may have gone longer given his publicist Stephanie was briefing him on the day's events and bullet points for the press. She rose, thanked the waiter, and walked down the outdoor double sided stone staircase and then walked into the opulent lobby and took a peek at the ever-swelling crowds outside the hotel as an older American couple, who were waiting for their taxi, looked out at the sea of fans with dismay.

"Who is staying here? Must be Sting." A portly, balding guest shrugged to his painfully thin and bejewelled wife.

Liz smiled and stated proudly, "It's not Sting. It's G Alvarez."

"Who?" The American couple looked at each other like she had three heads.

"He's a huge Latin American star; he performed at the Super Bowl!" Liz laughed to herself internally at their reaction.

"Well, if it was Sting, I could understand it. It looks like half of Rome turned out for…what's his name?" The man rolled his eyes and shrugged. "All I know is they're blocking my taxi!"

Liz nodded and walked into the chic main salon off the lobby as G finally emerged from the elevator with his new head of security, Garvey. He gave her a slight wave and a kiss as she tousled his new platinum crew cut. She loved this new look on G. It highlighted his tan skin glowing against his crisp white shirt and Jay Kos Japanese silk pants. His sleeves were rolled up, showing a peek of his famous sleeve of tattoos, and the tiny diamond stud sparkled in his nose offsetting his platinum wedding band. The hotel manager Signore Ottazzi and the fabulous concierge Alessandra walked over to enquire about their stay and told them they were honored to have had them as guests. Warm handshakes and kisses bid the newlyweds adieu as they were presented with a beautifully wrapped and boxed mille feuille wedding cake the chef had personally prepared as a parting gift for the road. It was tied with beautiful paper and satin ribbon, as only in Italy and France were the small details as important as the larger ones.

"Ready?" Liz breathed in deeply and took G's hand as they both braced for the crowds as they ventured outside the hotel. A unified roar and cheer went up and G stopped and waved as he let the fans and some paparazzi snap some photos. G beamed as he held Liz tight and through his body language indicated he wanted Liz to stand with him so the fans could take pictures of the newlywed couple. Cries of *"Ti voglio bene!"* "G here G!" and *"Bello!"* filled the air. Garvey ushered G into the waiting black Mercedes minibus even though Roy lingered and waved to the crowd as part of the entourage, famous by association. The hotel had wisely put up metal barricades, and it had become apparent to Liz once they got to Rome that they needed to stay in hotels that catered to celebrities, given the security and protocols and G's active international fanbase. The de Russie had been a wonderful choice in this regard. The placed the myriad luggage in the back of the bus. Roy was last in and plugged into his EarPods.

"How long is the drive?" Liz looked up as she settled into the front row and asked Antonio, their dapper driver.

"About three and a half hours if we hit beach traffic, Signora," he answered, his hand on the wheel looking ahead at the Byzantine-Roman streets. "Saturday is always a bit terrible, Signora Alvarez," he said with deep respect.

"Signora." Liz smiled as she heard the word again. Everywhere she went now, she was a signora, not a signorina, and it felt so good. G nuzzled into her as they discussed the day's events and the plans for their honeymoon in Capri. They would be staying in the grandest terraced suite at the Grand Hotel Quisisana and then off on the yacht, just the two of them! Liz sat back in her seat and snuggled next to G as he looked at the iPhone photos and video of them slow dancing at their wedding only a few days earlier.

It had been a gorgeous and intimate affair which had been lovingly hosted by Ira and Sheila at their beautiful home overlooking the water on Hibiscus Island. Sheila had taken care of all the details and had created a beautiful traditional chuppah, a wedding canopy which she erected with wooden vines and masses of climbing roses in soft shades of coral pink and seashell white. What was even more important was the presence of family and friends, especially with Linda's passing. Besides Sant, G was an orphan with no distant relatives. They did know they were truly lucky as they had an array of close friends they considered family, and given Covid restrictions the ceremony was kept to fifty of their most important friends and relatives, all who had a PCR test beforehand. It made it even more poignant, and G and Liz were overcome with emotion when their surprise guest, Mother Superior Maria Victoria, arrived to bless the couple with her presence and her prayers. Sant had arranged it all as his wedding gift and the ninety-two-year-old nun was the highlight of the wedding and had G weeping with gratitude at the sight of his mentor and savior. She seemed only slightly diminished by a few more wrinkles and a small cane, and she and Ira and the Rabbi hit it off at the head table as he was able to converse with her in Spanish. The day had been filled with memories large and small and it was joyous, transcendent, spiritual, and healing on all levels.

Before he escorted her down the aisle, Ira had knocked on the door before peeking his head in as Roy was putting the finishing touches on her makeup and Sheila and Lucy were helping her with her veil and headpiece. Ira mouthed "wow" and told her how beautiful she looked in her gown and that he was honored to walk her down the aisle. He air kissed Liz so as not to smudge Roy's handiwork and dug into his jacket pocket, producing a familiar looking letter.

"From Elsa." Ira smiled and winked as Liz looked slightly perplexed. She wasn't nervous anymore about opening Elsa's letters, only intrigued as she scanned the familiar note paper and handwriting, not to mention the distinctive lavender perfume.

"On my wedding day? Wow, she was good!" Liz beamed.

"What did you expect?" Ira stated as she opened and read the contents. She handed him back the letter, and he smiled, his crinkly eyes twinkling.

"No, read it out loud so everyone can hear!" Sheila said as Roy touched up her hair for the photos. Liz looked closely at the sheet of paper and then handed it to Sheila.

"Shelia, you do the honors?" Liz asked. They were all intrigued.

"Of course, hon!" She smiled and started reading.

> *"Dearest Liz,*
>
> *By now you know the truth, my dear great-granddaughter. I have been hoping and praying for you. You see, I married the man I shouldn't have and didn't marry the man I should have, but love is love, and yes, despite all, love is eternal.*
>
> *For you, I pray that you enjoy your birthright and that you are not imprisoned by Villa Pompeii but liberated by it. I truly hope you fall in love and find the right person, the person you should be with even if at first you think they are too different. It is the differences in life and love that balance and create that certain frisson.*
>
> *So, my dear Liz, you should be reading this with my instruction to dear Ira before you are to be wed. If this makes sense to you, then run to the altar. And if not, run away dear. It's not worth it.*
>
> *You will find love in the end. I promise.*
>
> *And that makes me so very happy.*
>
> *All my love,*
>
> *Great-Grandmother Elsa.*

Liz fingered the letter which she now kept in her handbag for good luck. She would be bringing it with her on this special day. Given the Reznick's generosity, Liz and G had also insisted on paying for their first-class flight to Italy and were thrilled that they were able to join them.

As the bus headed down south towards the Amalfi Coast on the Autostrada, Liz looked out the large window at the rolling fields and the occasional ruin of a farmhouse or hilltop castle town. Italy was still very much an agrarian society and driving in the country wasn't like going to the Catskills or New Hampshire, she thought, taking in the thousands of years of history dotted with castles, ruined stone walls, and dizzying hill towns. Once they were driving out of the environs of city limits of Rome, the landscape became even more languid and beautiful, and Liz snuggled next to G on his shoulder. An hour later, they had a bathroom stop at the Autogrill and shopped for an array of snacks; potato chips and chocolate covered biscuits. G and Sant high-fived when they saw a small coffee bar offering toasted sandwiches, pizzas, and coffee, and also an older woman in a starched apron behind the bar making steaming bowls of homemade pasta with fresh marinara sauce. Only in Italy could one get fresh, delicious pasta at a truck stop served by a real Italian mama! Once they paid the bill and waited for the fresh food, they dug in, twirling and scarfing down their pasta and crunchy fresh bread before returning to the bus for the last leg of the trip. Finally after another forty-five minutes on the road they finally saw the signs to the ancient city. Liz and G looked at each other and smiled, as they knew the international press would be waiting as they arrived in Pompeii.

Throngs of press and government officials from southern Italy were on hand to greet them and a loud cheer went up through the group as the black, gleaming Mercedes bus pulled into the parking area. Italians, like Latinos, are a boisterous bunch and show their emotions more freely and differently than their American and English counterparts, and officials were all on hand to welcome them and offer buoyant pleasantries and despite Covid and masks, they all double hugged and a few kissed Liz's hands in the European fashion.

The Antiquarium, a museum located on the ruins of Pompeii and below what was originally the Temple of Venus, which Liz found quite fitting, had been heavily damaged during World War Two but recently reopened after renovation. The official delegation included the museum director, who greeted them and walked them through the impressive classical portico past the gleaming, classical white columns and gave some history in clipped English. After the newly renovated entrance, Liz stopped in her tracks as she was immediately confronted by the two ancient casts of victims of the eruptions. As she saw the two body casts lying together, intertwined, she imagined what Ira had once said: that it was an eternal love affair.

In fact, that is why they were there.

The photographers snapped and film crews recorded the newlyweds both hand in hand as they approached the Museum's new gift they had donated before their wedding. Liz teared up as she saw it finally installed. There was their famous ancient mosaic from Villa Pompeii back in its rightful place after almost a century. They had donated it as a wedding gift, and they had re-installed it in a place of honor on the entry floor with a lengthy written history in Italian and English about the villa it came from and its journey from Italy to Miami and back to Pompeii through the generosity of Mr. and Mrs. Gabi and Elizabeth Galin-Alvarez.

The dedication ceremony took a bit longer than expected, but G whispered it was Italy, with all the elaborate and beautiful flourishes in their language and speeches. Finally, Liz took G's hand as they walked over to the plaque she had commissioned. They looked down at their plaque as the photographers snapped away. "Gift of Gabi Alvarez and Elizabeth Galin-Alvarez in memory of Elsa Sloan Barrett and Benjamin Bromberg Brody. 2022. Everlasting, eternal love."

A museum photographer and videographer were on hand as Liz and G bent down and ran their hands over the mosaic. Liz joined G as he gave an interview to Italian newspaper *Corriere Della Sera* on the donation. The reporters fought for attention and peppered them with questions.

"Why did you and your new wife Liz decide to donate such an important and valuable mosaic to the museum?" The lead reporter from

Corriere asked in his accent-tinged English. G took his time answering. Being with Liz and his sessions with Dr. Klinkov had given him a more thoughtful and deliberate confidence, and he was now genuine and authentic in his answers. As a result, the press and the fans were increasingly impressed and loved him more for it, not less.

"I grew up in an orphanage, and despite my poverty and abuse I have achieved success and love I never thought I would have." G teared openly. "I hope this gift inspires all those who want to break free of the past and embrace the future." He smiled widely as the press clapped enthusiastically, and intertwined his hand with Liz's.

"The past does not dictate the future." He bent down, caressing the newly installed mosaic, "and a house is not a home unless it's filled with love. Welcome home, eternal love," he said, the mosaic now newly christened and for all the world to see. Liz saw Ira and Sheila beyond the crush of the reporters and waved them over. They waited until the press subsided and then walked over, hugged, and congratulated the happy newlyweds.

"Uncle Ira, we couldn't have done this without you and Sheila. We are so happy and thrilled you were able to make it!" She kissed them both, noticing that Sheila looked surprisingly elegant in a white linen dress, pearls, and Chanel cap toe shoes, all of which reminded her a bit of Linda.

"It's a marvelous gesture and I can only imagine how much the museum must appreciate the gift." Sheila nodded, and she hugged and kissed G.

"Well, it was something you said, and also in Elsa's first note. The view might change everything." Liz nodded as more press converged on G.

"And has it?" Ira asked.

"Yes. At first, I thought I was supposed to end up with Cary. And yet, G is the man I should be marrying, I understand that all now." Liz smiled.

"I'm so happy for you, Liz." Ira's bright blue eyes twinkled in the Italian sun. "The gift to the museum is a beautiful gesture; to think you took my statement about eternal love seriously!" Ira's blue eyes sparkled kindly. "Elsa would have been quite pleased."

"Yes." Liz nodded her head in agreement. "It was the deciding factor in our decision. Also, the museum is in the process of creating an exact replica of the mosaic for the Villa, which will be done next fall," she explained.

"I think if you make the right choices, things end up as they should." He nodded.

"When do you arrive in Capri?" Liz looked at her watch.

"We are at the Sirenuse in Positano and Saturday we'll be in Capri for two nights for a third honeymoon!" He laughed.

"Dinner on the boat on Tuesday as planned!" Liz hugged them both.

"Liz, Linda would have been kvelling and so very proud of you!" His eyes misted over.

"Thank you, Uncle Ira." Liz smiled and took in his kindly gaze. Ira Reznick was the perfect father figure, and she was lucky to have him.

"I really do consider you my uncle, and Sheila my aunt."

"I know, and we feel the same way about you and G," Ira said and intertwined his own hands with Sheila's.

One thing for sure, Liz thought.

Linda had been right about calling Ira back promptly, and she now realized that the Villa Pompeii had not been her only gift.

Chapter 43

Fifty years after the founding of Miami, in 1945 an emotional protest by the city's vibrant African American community helped to create Virginia Key Beach, the one and only beach that welcomed Blacks. Today the beach has a civil rights museum and markers that detail the painful segregation that extended even surfside. The "colored only" beach, which was visited by Muhammad Ali and Martin Luther King, doesn't want anyone to forget its history but also promotes that, at its best, Miami is a cultural melting pot.

Only a few miles away the array and piercing sound of drills and hammers on North Bay Road would have been considered ordinarily obnoxious and annoying, ruining the sunny and tranquil afternoon only today it signified a certain sense of future excitement and optimism. The myriad workers were removing a lengthy piece of the coral stone wall that separated Liz and G's estates and it was the sound of love in the air.

Any top real estate broker in Miami could agree that despite the extra generous bay frontage there was no way to make sense of the two properties from an architectural point of view. One could not marry either style of the neighboring estates; one so modern and one so classically Mediterranean, however when the wall came down and the vegetation pruned back to create a new coral stone pathway to the two properties, all would agree that the combination was the *primest* of prime and the double lot could go as high as $50 million dollars for the dirt alone. While the Cuban sugar magnate to the left of G's property backed out of selling his home, the combination of his and Liz's estate would create one of the largest parcels on North Bay Road. However, real estate wasn't the only thing joining together.

Liz's eyes opened as a kaleidoscope of sunlight streamed in through the large glass window. She smiled at the view. G was naked, sitting on an ottoman at the foot of the bed, tanned from their honeymoon and looking at her intently while strumming his guitar softly.

"What?" she asked as her eyelids fluttered.

"I love looking at you." He had a tear in his eye and was joyful and content. G was happier and lighter with his demons at bay, and his recent creative output was startling. Liz had helped to free him of the past and the recent sessions with the therapist and some couples therapy had comforted him, helping him deal with his childhood trauma and the lasting, yet fading, scars.

She smiled softly. "What a beautiful way to wake up, a private concert! I know people pay a lot for front row." She stretched in a languid, feline movement.

"It makes me happy to see you asleep so content." He beamed.

"Yes. Here. Now." She yawned lightly and felt the softness of the down pillow. It was hard to comprehend all that had occurred within the past few weeks and months. Only now she truly felt at home. Love had made her feel more comfortable in her own skin, and she had a sense of ease and calm she had never experienced. Their honeymoon had been more romantic and memorable than one could possibly imagine and the last day on their yacht off the volcanic island of Stromboli they had made passionate love on the upper deck as the sky turned golden purple and peregrine falcons flew and communicated through their ancient calls. It was a moment that Liz hoped she could hold in her hand forever, but it slipped like sand through their fingers until they discovered a lasting gift.

"I love you more than anything," he said.

"You still love me a bit more than I love you?" she teased.

"Why are you asking?" G looked perplexed.

"Just checking," she joked.

"Well, I do." G strummed and smiled.

"As you should," she teased. "Your abs look good, you know," she offered.

"Finally, a compliment." He had his old guitar in front of him and started singing the lyrics, but this time as a slow ballad.

"*Ella es Feroz, ella es feroz,*" he sang. His eyes sparkled. "When I wrote that about you, you hated me."

"I never hated you, I was mad at you—there's a difference. I always liked you, I have to admit." She patted the bed. He approached her and started to nuzzle against her swan-like neck, but she gently pushed him away and excused herself to brush her teeth. He protested but she wouldn't listen. He heard the sound of the running water stop and Liz walked back in the room looking like a dream, naked under her beautiful antique silk robe.

"You look stunning in the morning." G surveyed his statuesque wife.

"Yes, Elsa bought this on her honeymoon. She bought two, and this was the companion piece."

"She was a clever one, that Elsa." He marveled.

Liz walked over to him. She touched his soft lips with her hand, and motioned over to the window. His platinum crew cut and diamond nose stud sparkled in the streaming Miami sun. They both walked out onto the modern terrace overlooking the bay, the azure blue popping against his vivid green eyes.

"Trust me?" she asked.

"Always."

She removed her robe and handed it to him, totally naked except for her thong.

"Out here?" He raised an eyebrow at the thought of lovemaking.

"No, silly." She had a flash of an idea.

"What?' He looked at her like she was a bit crazy.

"Put it on." She motioned.

"Why?"

"Just put it on." She insisted as he shrugged and put on the antique silk robe which seemed like a sensual second skin. It was a few sizes too small for his frame, the silk pouring like liquid over his hard, tan muscles and rippled in the humid air. The skimpy size emphasized his lean, wide torso and muscles. She walked up to him and like the stylist she was, she gently had him face towards the bay, and then she pivoted his head backwards and motioned for him to stand still. She framed a bold and incredible image and then she picked up her iPhone and started snapping away. G's apple green eyes popped against the bay, and the pattern of the antique silk bird of paradise and dragon front and center offering a hint of tattooed arm. She smiled to herself. They had been struggling over a creative concept and rejected a few of the studio cover concepts and suddenly there it was.

"There's your album cover." She said confidently as she handed him the phone.

He took it in his hands and could not believe his eyes as he saw the image; bold, fresh, and undoubtedly Miami.

When the title track was released a few months later, the graphic of the dragon and the birds of paradise would grace the cover of his new album *Fierce* and be used as the main graphic on merchandise; hats, tee shirts for his international tour. Fans around the world would love this image and their replica silk robes would be a sellout. It was such an iconic shot that it would eventually be compared to Clapton's *461 Ocean Boulevard* cover art. In New York, Cary would later see the album cover on iTunes and shake his head sadly. *Leave it to Liz*, he thought, knowing he had not been ready for greatness.

"You're the only man I know that looks better in a silk kimono than me." Liz looked at G and laughed. "But I don't care since you're all mine." Then they returned to bed, and he played her like his guitar with soft yet confident strokes. Afterwards, they lay in bed after a long, languorous session of lovemaking. Liz ran her hands over her distended belly as he also walked his fingers across her skin. The baby had been made in the shadow of the volcano on their honeymoon, and it was more special that it marked their forever love.

One thing was for certain; if it was a girl, they would name her Elsa Linda Josefina, and she would be raised on North Bay Road.

It was the most fitting gift they could think of.

Epilogue

Ira's pristine Cadillac turned left through the newly installed electronic gate, past the security checkpoint. He pulled into a designated spot near the bubbling fountain and exited, opening Sheila's door first and helping her out by the elbow. He then walked around back, popped the trunk, and was attended by Garvey as they both pried the enormous stuffed white and pink teddy bear with a polka dot bow out of the trunk's firm grip. After Eliad's hasty departure, Liz had the idea to hire Garvey when he and Roy started dating seriously, and now he and Roy occupied the guest quarters where Zosia once lived on the weekends, as she had officially retired. She had wanted to return to Warsaw to live with her one remaining sister and the day she left, Liz and Ira gave her an envelope containing $10,000 in cash; it was the only time either detected a misty eye from the older woman. This freed up her staff quarters as a place for Roy and Garvey, however, when G was touring with Sant, they would both move into the main house with Liz and baby Elsa. Having Garvey and Roy made it one big happy family, not to mention that Roy was officially baby Elsa's g-dfather.

After the international success of *Fierce* and Elsa's birth, Liz decided to move everyone into G's modern home as their main living quarters, as it was clean and bright and Elsa's nursery overlooked the bay and featured existing electronic draperies convenient for her nap times. It also felt a bit smaller and more manageable for a young family, and the grand Barrett mansion was now used mostly for large parties and holidays like Christmas, Chanukah, and Thanksgiving, as well press events attended by the popular and dynamic Mayor Suarez, and charity fundraisers, which were a big part of Miami's social life. As Mrs. G Alvarez, Liz now had the funds to start a formidable contemporary art collection featuring Latin American artists like Marina Perez Simao from Pace, and threw a celebrity-studded cocktail event for Miami Art Basel each year which had immediately become a coveted invitation. G performed with many of his musical idols on a stage they constructed over the pool. Liz also took her weekly tennis lessons in the pavilion which had been fully renovated, including refurbishing the iconic bar to bring it back to full luster. She had the portrait of her grandfather Ben reframed and proudly hung in the center of the bar for inspiration on her game. While she also loved the Mediterranean classic pool, she preferred the infinity pool at G' s house as it had a shallow end which was perfect for Elsa's swim time. The combined estates offered a unique variety of options both socially and professionally and they were grateful for all.

"These damn heels!" Sheila remarked as she navigated the uneven paving stones holding onto Ira's elbow from Villa Pompeii to G's mansion in her Chanel slingbacks. Sheila was the type of woman that preferred an escalator to stairs and did not see the charm in ancient paving stones, and while she understood and appreciated the aesthetic, she had half her property on Hibiscus Island blacktopped over for convenience.

Liz looked up and waved happily from the modern kitchen as she saw the Reznicks enter the property. She was delighted to see them for Sunday brunch, especially since G had just started his new South American tour. After Elsa's birth, they had become surrogate grandparents, in more than name only. Ira also had developed a deep and meaningful relationship with G, who had asked him to handle the estate planning and create new legal documents for Liz and baby Elsa and a set of wills and trusts for their growing family. Ira was happy to do so but even more enjoyed spending time with G, who relished having a trusted older male friend and mentor and a sounding board who could help guide him on his burgeoning business affairs and constant stream of lucrative endorsements.

They all walked into the airy, open kitchen where Maria had put out the requisite platters of sliced bagels and smoked salmon on the white

Caesarstone waterfall island. A native Colombian with a kindly face punctuated by a singular gold tooth, she had been initially perplexed at the addition of another cultural cuisine and the smelly platters of Nova, tuna, whitefish salad, and onion bagels baffled her and took some getting used to. However, in slight defiance and proud of her own country's cuisine, she always also added a platter of her famous Colombian empanadas, which Ira always savored and indulged despite his growing waistline. Ira put on his wire framed aviators which made him look like an older graduate of *Top Gun*, and Sheila walked outside and settled into a lounge under an umbrella. She immediately lit up a cigarette as Liz brought over an ashtray and some fresh fluffy white towels. Ira happily twirled baby Elsa in his burly arms in the pool slowly telling her he was giving her a "baby ride" as Sheila and Liz happily watched from the shade of the lounge chair. Liz wished that Sheila wouldn't smoke so much for her own health but every time she brought up the subject Sheila waved her beringed hand and shooed the subject away. She had smoked since she was a teen and that was that! In those moments she so reminded her of Linda; once she had a fixed opinion you couldn't tell her anything.

Afterwards, Kelly, their new bright and cheery nanny, collected Elsa and took up to her room for her much-needed nap as Ira toweled off, put on his Lacoste shirt and joined the two at the stone table under the umbrella before they all rose for the Sunday buffet. Liz craved a bagel but decided to forgo the carbs and layered lox, spreading a dollop of scallion cream cheese on GG crackers, as she was almost down the ten pounds she needed to get back to her pre-baby weight. Sheila told her she looked great and was impressed at her discipline but felt she was going overboard by not enjoying a toasted scooped out bagel. "So, there will be more of you to love!" She blew a smoke ring and waved her manicured hands in defiance. Ira placed his heaping plate of Nova and empanadas on the table as he sat down, then reached into Sheila's oversized translucent Chanel beach bag and retrieved a familiar sight. It was the final letter.

"I was looking for the proper time to give this to you." Ira smiled like the cat that swallowed the canary.

"Don't tell me it's another letter! I thought the one you gave me on my wedding day was the last one?" Liz marveled.

"Elsa always had another trick up her sleeve, and she planned things meticulously." He handed it to her as Liz looked at the envelope, which had been clearly opened.

"What, you read it?" She laughed.

"Elsa wanted me to know the contents of this one, and I promise you this is the last one," he added.

"I can only imagine what's in this one!" Liz shook her head.

"I think you'll be pleased. Do the honors!" His kindly eyes twinkled as he prompted her to read it out loud. She started slowly appreciating Elsa's distinctive cursive script.

> *Dear Liz,*
>
> *If you are reading this, you will have found the man of your dreams and are enjoying life together. I did tell my co-conspirator Ira that I wanted you to have this last letter and a special gift for you once you were wed. You are after all my family.*
>
> *Many years ago, in the early 1960s when I first returned from the convent in France, I was eager to find out what had happened to our son Sidney. I was curious and I hired a private eye and a photographer to take his photo. I wanted to see if he had Ben's looks and those gorgeous eyes of his. Unfortunately, I was too late, as news came back to me that Sidney had died in a car accident in the mountains in New York and I, of course, was once again devastated. I would never get to see him and felt great guilt over my timing. It was wonderful, though, to hear that he and his wife Gloria had given birth to a girl, Linda, your mother. I immediately dispatched the photographer and was pleased to see she was a beautiful, healthy baby. Each year I would receive*

some information and photos, but I must say if you are wondering, Linda looked so much like my mother Lorene it brought up complicated feelings and emotions in me. As the years passed when Linda married your father Joe, I sent him many accounts and made sure a few businesspeople I knew paid him well for their policies as I wanted to ensure everyone was well taken care of. Then, my dear, you came along and when you were about three years old my curiosity got the best of me, and I decided to pay a visit in a park where she strolled with you each morning. All your mother Linda ever knew was a kindly older woman praising the beauty of her child. As I looked into the carriage, I saw Ben's eyes staring back at me. Finally! At that moment I felt a bit healed.

As you grew each year, the photographers I hired sent me photos and I was thrilled to see you turn into a great beauty. I was proud that you followed your Grandfather Ben, attending college and joining the tennis team, and I kept up with your press articles. I read with pride when you won your matches, however, it seems that wasn't your passion. It was only after you finished college and went into the fashion business that I decided to see if you were up to my test and if you were, I would enact my plan for your legacy. I wanted to see if you and I were at all alike, and once I was diagnosed with this awful cancer, I put my plan into action. The first test took place in New York. I checked into the Plaza Hotel, and I conspired to see what you were made of. You might remember an incident…

It was a warm summer Sunday, and you might recall there was an older woman who you found sitting on the stoop of your apartment tending to a sprained ankle. I told you I had fallen, and a young boy ran away with my purse. You were kind enough to lift me up by the elbow and insisted you give me some money. I asked you not to call the police and once again you insisted on walking me to a taxi as I told you I was meeting my son. You held my arm, hailed a taxi, and gave me what remaining money you must have had. I was so happy that you had generosity and kindness of spirit. I was also so thrilled to see your beautiful blue eyes tinged with gold, it gave me a lift. And even more thrilling was you passed my first test. Liz, you were indeed a kind and generous soul with good character.

Liz sat back in disbelief. "I can't believe this. I do remember that old woman. That was Elsa. Ira, Sheila, I met her!" She laughed and shook her head and continued reading.

My second test; I wanted a sign that you would appreciate the old-fashioned grandeur of Villa Pompeii. I devised a fairly ingenious plan, if I say so myself. I hate to tell you that I hired a private eye, but I did. He followed you in LA and In New York to see where you went and what you did. His report stated that you enjoyed certain shops on Melrose Avenue for your styling jobs and that you frequented one specific thrift store. My contact's brought the other silk robe I had bought on my honeymoon in Paris and put it on consignment in your favorite shop. We put it front and center on the mannequin and created a narrative that said it had belonged to the silent film actress, Gloria Swanson. The store owner was paid handsomely to only sell it to you if you saw it and wanted it and to no one else. He put it on display on a mannequin near the front door in the store and held to this story, although more than a few people tried to buy it. The day you visited the store, I paced many times before I called the store owner. She said in fact you had made a beeline for it and that you had been lucky enough to find some remaining cash in the bottom of your purse which, unbeknownst to you, had cleverly been put there by the photographer who bumped into you. I saw it as a sign that you, my dear, had passed my test possessing beauty, brains, compassion, and style. You are and were a Miss Harris's girl through and through!

Liz, if you haven't figured it out already, the portrait in the tennis pavilion is your great-grandfather Ben. It was taken from a photo of him that was published years ago in the Miami Herald. *Wasn't he handsome and dashing? Look at the eyes, my dear, your eyes. The eyes I only had eyes for.*

If you had been a different kind of young woman, I would have donated the villa to the church and the effects to the Miami Historical society. But you were you.

Now for one last surprise which I hope you will enjoy. Ira can present you with my jewel case, which has been all this time in the safety deposit box. While I don't have many jewels, what I have is very good. Feel free to keep it, sell it, or give it to a daughter or daughter-in-law, one day.

I hope you have enjoyed the journey and wish you a lifetime of love and happiness.

With love and affection, your great-grandmother,

Elsa Sloan Barrett

Sheila smiled, reached into her oversized beach bag, brought out a small jewel case in faded scarlet velvet, and presented it to Liz. She was stunned at the gift and looked at the case with anticipation before slowly opening it, not quite prepared for what was inside. Once she unsnapped the top of the old-fashioned case, she unzipped the body of it with the tarnished bronze zipper and then peered inside. No one was prepared for the sparkling bounty glowing in the afternoon light. They oohed and ahhed as Liz first drew out a long rope of opera length golden pearls. They marveled at the luster and satin sheen of the perfectly matched strand. She had always coveted perfect south sea pearls and each were at least ten millimeters; their beauty was otherworldly. As she slipped them around her neck, she felt like a jazz-age flapper. Then she withdrew the platinum and diamond parure Elsa had written about; a magnificent set of deco geometric diamonds and baguettes artfully crafted by Cartier, and a huge round diamond ring, an old mine diamond one didn't see in modern shops. Then her eye discovered a large fifteen carat emerald set in platinum and surrounded by two simple baguettes. She tried it on her left finger and it held it up to the sun. Shelia admired a delicate, bow shaped diamond brooch set in platinum with ribbons of small rubies, and as Liz saw the older woman hold the sparkling jewel in the light she insisted Sheila keep it as a gift. There was much going back and forth as Sheila and Ira protested, but Liz insisted and pinned the brooch on Sheila's blouse to great applause and kisses. After everything the Reznick's had done for her and G, she thought this gift was particularly fitting. Sheila delighted in her new, extravagant brooch, her spine rising ramrod straight like a Queen. Liz looked down at all the treasures and was particularly attracted to the emerald ring. She had always had a thing for emeralds but could never afford them, and now she had a masterpiece on her index finger. It fit perfectly; a sign. There was much to celebrate as they all toasted, and Liz asked Maria to bring out champagne to make mimosas. After brunch, she motioned for them to walk up the modern stairs to the nursery. Liz put her finger to her lips as they walked softly so as not to awaken the baby and when she reached her room she quietly opened the door, and they all silently walked over to the bassinet. Elsa had been napping but opened her blue and gold-tinged eyes and cooed as Liz opened the electronic curtains. The light streamed in and Liz saw her baby looking directly back at them; loving and fearless. Liz leaned in and Elsa immediately smiled as she reached up to grasp the golden pearls around Liz's neck as they all laughed.

"She already has good taste!" Liz nodded as she let Elsa caress the lustrous strand.

Then Liz took off the large emerald ring and offered it to Elsa to play with, the light refracting through the jardin of the stone and casting a glow around the room. Elsa held the ring in her tiny fingers and tried to put it into her mouth as she cooed, and they all laughed as they removed it for safekeeping.

As they all looked down at the baby, it wasn't lost on Liz, Ira and Sheila that the newest princess residing on North Bay Road was now the embodiment of Miami itself. Elsa Linda Josefina Galin Alvarez was the ultimate mix; Afro Latino, Jewish, Catholic, WASP, and Italian, and it all reflected in her unique beauty.

"Elsa, meet Elsa," Liz said as she smiled, letting her reach for and play with the line of golden pearls which she put in her mouth as they walked to the commanding seaside terrace. Liz held Elsa and kissed her forehead as they looked out onto the glittering emerald and turquoise waters of North Bay and the sparkling, vibrant city beyond. Ira looked on and whistled the famous Ray Charles tune "Moon Over Miami" and then sang a raspy rendition as Elsa cooed at the lyrics.

The End

Acknowledgments

In the winter of 2020 when Covid was raging, I made the decision to move our family to Miami to weather the Covid storm. I was lucky enough to find a wonderful Mediterranean villa on coveted North Bay Road and surprise my wife, Dana, and the kids. Life imitates art—or vice versa. The moment we walked into the outdoor courtyard, past the reflecting pool and over the mosaics, we were all thrilled to see the Bay of Miami in the distance and felt we were home. It was a dream come true having all our kids and their friends with us. Next to the grand staircase, I discovered a door and when I opened it and turned on the light, there was a manual elevator from the 1920s painted in chinoiserie...and *North Bay Road* was born.

To my brilliant and beautiful wife Dana, thank you for being my muse and to my wonderful and interesting children Georgia, Talia, and Lucas, thank you always for being the best there is and adhering to the Kirshenbaum motto: "One great sin is being **BORING**."

Special thanks to my incredible literary agent, the Princess of Publishing Laura Yorke, who has guided me on my literary journey and my wonderful editor Debra Englander and Heather King at Post Hill Press for your belief in and expert guidance with the novel. Thank you to my entertainment lawyer Eric Rayman. Thanks to Ernest Lupinacci, co-producer of *The Offer* and his eye! As always, special thanks to the legendary Wendy Finerman for all of your advice. To the stars in my firmament, the fabulous and super talented Adriana Trigiani, Tim

Stephenson, Marisa Acocella Marchetto, and the epic Sally Richardson for your ongoing support.

To my partners at SWATbyKirshenbaum: Joseph Mazzaferro, Kiri Wolfe, Melissa Witkin, and Jonah Kaner, Carol O' Connell. Thank you.

To my partners in SWATEquity: Mark Hauser and Sarah Foley. Thank you. To my partners in Loyl: John Noe, Tim Rich, and James Blackwelder. Thank you.

To everyone at the Princess Grace Foundation, I am honored to be on the board.

To my sister Susan and my brother-in-law Rob Perry, Marcia and Fred Geier, Aunt Paulette, and the Joachims. Family first! To my incredible assistant, Carol O'Connell and her husband Ran, I could never do it without you. Thank you Mary Garcia for all you do!

To my chosen family, Jordan Schur, Patty and Danny Stegman, Susie and Kevin Davis, Marc Glimcher and Fairfax Dorn, Jamie Mitchell, David Mitchell, Ali and Jason Rosenfeld, Lauran and Charlie Walk, Jay and Amy Kos, Karen and Mark Hauser, Susan Krakower, Mark E. Pollack, Lois Robbins and Andrew Zaro, Chris Blackwell and Marika Kessler, Chip and Susie Fisher, Alexis and Erik Ekstein, Muffie Potter Aston and Sherell Aston, Robert and Serena Perlman, Meg Blakey and Glenn Pagan, Tim and Saffron Case, David and Lauren Bush Lauren, Ali Cayne and Franklin Isacson, Harlan Peltz, Barry and Lizanne Rosenstein, Ana Rosenstein, Sting and Trudie Styler, Doug Robinson, Lew and Bobbie Frankfort, Rosanna Scotto and Louis Ruggerio, Penn and Cornelia Kavanagh, Jennifer Miller and Mark Ehret, Steven and Ilene Sands, David Liebman, Michelle and Howard Swarzman, Carolyn and Marc Rowan, Rena and Marc Gardner, Helene and Ziel Feldman, Stacey and Jimmy Garson, Gunter and Katerina Frangenberg, Dustin Cohen, Joseph Klinkov, Rabbi Adam and Sharon Mintz, Jordan and Debra Teramo, Anton Katz and Sharon Cardel. Shoshana and Kenny Dichter, Jarrod Moses, Julie Collins, LIz Nickels. Bill Koenigsberg, Bruce and Maura Brickman, Billy Gerber, Kim Heirston, Brisa and Mark Carleton, Kevin Thompson, Dr. Bernard Kruger, David and Sheila Wiener, Michael Ostin, and the dynamic Nikki Field at Sothebys.

To the late Joyce Ostin…your star is always shining,

In Miami, thank you to Jason Zarco, Esther Percal, and Keston Superville at the Bath Club. To the Fisher Islanders: Pam and David Berkman, Craig, Lauren and Cynthia Nossel, Archie Drury, and Karolina Kurkova. Thank you for welcoming us!

Thank you to everyone at my favorite places: the Beverly Hills Hotel pool, Goldeneye, The Grand Hotel Quisisana, The Hotel de Russie, The Hotel de Paris in Monaco, The Edition Hotel in Miami, Ashford Castle, The St. Regis in Aspen, the beach club bar on Fisher Island, La Mamounia, and my favorite watering holes in NYC: Nerai, Nobu 57, Fresco by Scotto, Sen in Sag Harbor, Avra 48, Avena, Nicola's, Thep, Wa Jeal, the Lotos Club, Casa Cipriani, The Whitby, Emilio Ballato, and The University Club in NYC. In Miami: The Bath Club, Call Me Gabby, Sushi Garage, and Blue Ribbon Sushi. In Capri; Villa Verde, Da Giorgio, and Fontelina where I wrote most of this book over long lunches, drinks, and dinners.

And to my late grandparents, Elsie and Harry Goldberg, for starting my Miami journey when I was six years old, I will always remember the coconut patties, the tram on Lincoln Road, spotting Meyer Lansky walking his dog in front of the Fontainebleau, the amazing pool and cabanas at the Raleigh Hotel and the rolls everyone took home from the Wolfie's bread basket, and when Collins Avenue still had burlesque houses! And to my late parents, Marilyn and Stanley, who honeymooned in Miami Beach in the 1950s, you were all ahead of the curve.